ABDUL & RAJ

BUCHI RAMARAO VELURY

CONTENTS

Contents

ACKNOWLEDGEMENTS

I dedicate this book to my mother, who, with her limited resources and adverse circumstances, nurtured my other six siblings and me to stand on our feet and excel in life.

I am grateful to my wife, who is my weakness and strength and who supported me in all my endeavours with her critique that guided me whenever I lost my way.

I am indebted to my editor Ravi Yellayi, who refined this book to make it readable.

Further, I am thankful to Covai Care management and its scholarly residents, who provided the infrastructure and encouragement to pursue my passion.

Above all, I want to thank my Guru Bharatbhai Gosalia, who always found something worthy in me.

Countless others remain unnamed who provided valuable inputs on various topics: police procedures, judicial case histories, Pharmacy related processes of drug delivery, validation and approvals and the like. I had no access to one-to-one interactions with the leaders and employees of these organisations because of the pandemic, having been confined to one apartment complex. Google came to my rescue.

May 2022

PREFACE

"The Things that matter in life always come unexpectedly."

– Berlin, a character from Money Heist.

"God does not seek your gratitude for having done good to you, nor does HE want censure for the grief HE has caused you."

– Anon.

A fiction writer has the liberty to twist, tinker and abuse facts to suit his narrative. Writing is an arduous task: style needs to be lofty; prose subtle; the story and its suspense complex. If I failed in any or all of the above, I seek your indulgence.

Much of the information in this book is taken from personal experience, Google, Wikipedia and Judicial pronouncements. Yet, there are numerous instances where they have been reconstructed to evolve a compelling storyline. Certain scenes have been dramatically recreated to effectively portray the personalities involved in the story and the atmosphere surrounding the events upon which this story is based. Some peripheral characterisations and actors, with no direct connectivity to the story's development, were created to enlighten the readers about few organisations and people who run them. Unbeknownst to most readers, these people's behaviour affects our lives.

An author has the freedom to create ideal role models and exemplary organisations he would want to flourish in society.

For instance, the anti-racist liberals would be pleased to have characters like Atticus Finch populate the World. I have created two such personae (Altaf Mallik and Adarsh Naik) and one firm (Shafique Travels and Tours).

The book exemplifies the lives of two sons who had different upbringings. One had a loving father and the other an abusive one. One grew with love and the other with fear. Both had expectations thrust upon them by circumstances. One believed in GOD with a commitment to a cause, and the other was a disquieted person with a constant trepidation of the unbearable prospect that all pleasures in life will cease one day. The Profound & The Superficial.

The Profound had constantly reworked his identity to suit the changing situations. He realised that you must win in the deadly survival game called life, but you must allow others to live too. He did that without any conscious effort.

The Superficial was fragile and wobbly, succumbing to the quirks of Fate that destiny threw at him. The price he paid for leading such a false life was enormous. The avaricious he became to seek the abject pleasures of life, the worse labyrinths of misery he was led to.

The Profound was an example of inner happiness that ensured moral behaviour. An odd indiscretion was redeemed as his wont. The utter inhumanity of the incarceration of his innocent wife by the corrupt police did not obliterate his faith in LOVE and GOD.

The Superficial could not come out of terrible parenting; add a loveless marital life. He yielded to every temptation – some he was offered; some he sought; few he snatched. Yet, in some rare inspirations in his life, he could spurn immoral advances too. He could shrewdly mask his mediocrity to achieve corporate success.

This book is a narrative about many women too. Women generally are relegated to postscripts in life. In this book, I had given them central but subtle roles. Women have their destinies scrawled across their foreheads. Many silently follow the path laid for them. Some try to change the course; when they fail, they succumb. Few defy and make their calling. I had depicted a restrained character with minimal dialogue as an example of the last category. This book is the story of her extraordinary courage, who never lost hope in her GOD and in her LOVE despite the misery that Fate played on her. Both the Profound and the Superficial had played their assigned parts in this character's life.

The book contains information on the Construction Industry, the Pharmaceutical Industry, the Indian Police, and the Judiciary, which were central to the storyline's development and shaped the characters in the book. Most of what was depicted in the book regarding the Indian Pharmaceuticals Industry is based on media reports. References to these reports are given at the end of the book to aid the discerning reader. However, I stretched my imagination in the conception of Goud Pharmaceuticals as a contract manufacturing firm that has agreements with a few well-known Indian Pharma companies to help weave my story.

Similarly, the statements attributed to some characters regarding Police governance are sourced from real-life case histories whose judgements are in the public domain. The Indian Police is an organisation that has the least accountability. The Indian Police have the authority, wherewithal, and greed to detain or arrest any innocent citizen simply taking a walk in the park on trumped-up charges for which she would have no recourse. The Judiciary's role comes much later and too infrequently, by which time irreparable damage would have been done.

The above does not happen as frequently as I had depicted in this book, because of the fear of the law of Karma. This philosophy is embedded indelibly in the psyche of the Hindus – constituting 80% of the Indian population – thanks to their Scriptures, Sages, Saints and well-intentioned Swamis since aeons. A Hindu subscribes to the notion that life events visiting him during this lifetime result from the twain Karmas: Prarabdha (outcomes of the actions accumulated from a past life) and Kriyamāna (consequences of the actions performed during this life affecting the present and the subsequent lives also). The family culture of Hindus ensures this doctrine of the visitations of Karma into one's life from time to time is carried forward for generations.

This philosophy of Karma is as ingrained in the cultural ethos of the Indian populace as the indoctrination of the twisted Islamic faith with Jihadist extremism that brain-washes innocent Muslim youth to radicalisation. Both these canons have their after-effects – good and evil. One community ensures the continuity of their philosophy, delivering it across generations by word of mouth and literature; the other is a mute spectator to the debasement of their magnificent culture, lyrical language and insightful holy values.

This book exemplifies the consequence on society's well-being if the religious leaders propagate truthfully the tenets enshrined in their sacred texts without twisting them to suit their evil agendas.

PROLOGUE

Abdul was not comfortable with flying. While travelling from Mumbai to Riyadh, he was too excited about the future lay before him to worry about the fear of flying. Today, on the return journey, Abdul had different anxiety. He did not notice the aircraft had been airborne. The task at hand mentally consumed him. To camouflage the nervousness, he tried to recall the pleasant times he had with his wife. Meanwhile, a smiling `stewardess offered his choice for a drink. Wine? No madam. Orange juice? Okay.

He fiddled with the in-flight magazine and flipped a few pages. Nothing registered. He managed to doze off after counting sheep. Another stewardess came and woke him politely and offered him his meal choice as registered against his seat no. He gulped it with another glass of orange juice. The screen in front of him displayed the flight path; distance covered, distance to destination, expected arrival at Mumbai - still five hours away. The Bulk on the next seat was snoring and did not respond to the stewardess's prodding for a snack or a meal. Abdul wondered how one could sleep so peacefully.

Abdul smugly fitted himself in a foetus position and tried to sleep again.

After what seemed an eternal wait, some brisk activity suggested the flight was about to land. Plastic trays removed, seat upright. The lights were up, and in-flight entertainment terminated. Aircraft landed with a thud, waking up the Bulk with a frown. Slowly the passengers started piling up before him to alight. Abdul picked up the mini suitcase he bought at Dammam mall from the overhead bin and landed in the night sky just turning to dawn. After immigration and customs, Abdul waited in the lounge for his connecting flight to Vadodara. He could have gone directly to Hyderabad, which was his desired destination. There were direct flights to Hyderabad from Riyadh too.

But he did not want to give an impression to his ammijaan that he valued his wife more than her. To maintain domestic peace and tranquillity, you need to be politically correct. In Vadodara, he spent an entire day with family, exchanged the incidents of his work life in Saudi, and distributed the gifts he bought for ammijaan, Nusrat and Munaaf. Though he was physically present through these small talks, he was not in peace. His anxiety was boundless. He could not share his predicament with anyone. Nazma wanted him to meet Quadri Pasha to pay respects to him; after all, he was the elderly person of the colony whom they depended upon during Abdul's absence. Abdul gave the excuse of official work and rushed to the airport to book a ticket to Hyderabad. There was only one direct flight to Hyderabad from Vadodara, which had left already. He had to wait for another day.

Before embarking on this unscheduled journey, Abdul had contacted his friend Baroodwala in Mumbai and confided in him about his need to go to Hyderabad. Baroodwala was familiar with Hyderabad as his wife spent her childhood there before marrying him. He often went to Hyderabad, accompanying his wife to visit her relatives.

He also had some contacts in that town, which Abdul wanted to utilise. Mohd Ghouse and Baroodwala were colleagues when they worked in a company in Mumbai as young salesmen in a Shoe shop thirty years back. Both had since parted ways and settled elsewhere quite securely. Their friendship revived one day when Baroodwala accidentally met Ghouse in Mumbai, and they exchanged pleasantries and relived their old days at the stores. Since then, they have remained in touch – thanks to mobile technology. When Ghouse's daughter married a boy in Mumbai, Baroodwala helped them find a koli[1] for a reasonable rent.

Ghouse was more than willing to help Abdul when he knew that Abdul worked in Saudi, where he wanted to send his son. He wanted as much information as possible from him. He was not otherwise aware of the real purpose of Abdul's visit to Hyderabad. Baroodwala never shared this detail. Ghouse never asked.

Abdul quickly disembarked from the plane and rushed to find a taxi to take him to his destination.

He pulled a yellow slip-paper from his pocket, which had the address of the friend of Baroodwala who had promised to accommodate him at his shop-cum-residence for a couple of days and help him out with his problem. Abdul had no choice. Most importantly, he wanted a safe house to store the cash he carried with a known person in an unfamiliar city. He was carrying cash because Ameer insisted on it.

Ameer said you don't know when you would need some money for the challenging task.

"His shop is very near to Hyderabad Railway station," Baroodwala had told him and gave him the telephone number and address of Mohd Ghouse. Abdul called Ghouse before he landed at his shop.

"Salaam alaikum. Is this Ghouse sahib? "

---

1 Koli is a Mumbai word for a small room with a shared bathroom with other tenements. Most immigrants in Mumbai start their married life with such a meagre accommodation.

"Alaikum as-salaam, are you Abdul Wahab?"

"Yes, I am on my way in a taxi. The driver said it would take another 30mins to reach."

"Okay, Fine. Please come straight to my shop, it is on the main road itself."

The taxi arrived at a shop when Google Maps announced it as his destination. Abdul saw a giant signboard over a three-storeyed structure. Greenland Shoes. The Urdu matter under the title, which Abdul could not decipher. The shop had adjoining walls painted with a caricature of a boy with a skullcap holding a sports shoe about to slip onto a lady in a burqa. Abdul arrived at Ghouse's shop and exchanged adaabs. The conversation mainly centred on the journey itself. Fortunately for Abdul, all the talk was in Hindustani. He felt comfortable. In Vadodara, most Muslims speak Gujarati and less Urdu.

While taking him inside the shop, Ghouse asked how he knew Yousef Bhai.

"He worked with my abbu when he was young. Being the same age, we kept in touch." Baroodwala's first name was Yousef.

Ghouse called out, "Chandru, Darwaza khol beta[2]." A small door opened next to the shop's main entrance, through which Ghouse let Abdul through.

The back exit of the shop led to an open area where the quarters of the staff were arranged with a makeshift tin roof. At the end of the quarters, one room had a proper roof and appeared to be well maintained. Chandru took Abdul's luggage inside. On his way inside, Abdul found boxes of leather and polyurethane foam sole shoes of all kinds stacked in a disorderly manner, resembling a busy executive's desk. Abdul did not notice any well-known

---

2   Open the door, son

brands. He found shoes marked as Aadidaz, Nuki and Police. All locally made with mutilated foreign brand names. But the display shop and customer chairs were well arranged for comfort. There was a section in purdah for burqa-clad ladies to try the shoes sans the gaze of male customers. They walked through the dark alley to an open-to-sky area. At the left, Abdul could see some rooms, and the opposite end had the bathrooms and toilets. Next to the toilets, a door led to a spiral staircase that was an entry to the rooms upstairs, where Ghouse's family lived. Later Abdul found the staircase had access from outside too. The zenana of the Ghouse family were thus secluded from the shop' personnel with personalised entry and exit through this outside access.

Pointing at the rooms, Ghouse said, "These are three rooms my workers share. The last one is for guests like you. Other rooms are for my workers. I do not normally employ local boys as they are not sincere and take leave for no rhyme or reason, so with my contacts in Nizamabad, I hire my workers from outside of Hyderabad, for whom I have to provide accommodation. I also have two day-workers."

Chandru brought a fresh duvet; white bedsheet; arranged the bed neatly. Chandru was staring at Abdul as though the visitor had taken away his home.

"Chandru! You are still here only. Go to the shop," Ghouse shouted at the boy, who appeared hardly 16.

"Jaa *raha hoon*," Chandru replied with the same tone without adding any salutation.

Their relationship is not above board.

Ghouse ignored him and explained his abode to Abdul, "Opposite these rooms are two other rooms, one of which has a paikhana and the other has hamaam and paikhana together."

Ghouse opened the room and let Abdul in. It was empty save a single unmade bed with a mattress rolled. It smelled leather and had no window with only the entry door.

What a change from the Saudi flat given by my employer! I should not have taken Baroodwala's suggestion. Baroodwala said as I was going to an unfamiliar town, he may as well take the help of his friend as he was well connected in Hyderabad, especially as I was embarking on a difficult mission. I reluctantly agreed. I am determined to shift to a hotel as soon as I can.

He thanked Ghouse and went into the room allocated to him. Ghouse retreated into the door that opened into the lane which had the staircase to his home. Abdul freshened up and waited for Ghouse to interact with him.

RAGHUNATH SASTRY

The year was 1953.

The clamour for separate Telugu-speaking Andhra was at its peak. Before independence, Coastal Andhra and Rayalaseema belonged to Madras Presidency as a province of British India. A youthful 25year old Raghunath Sastry participated in the movement to separate Andhra State away from Madras state, though he was a government clerk in Madras. Finally, the area of Andhra State was carved out of Madras State in November 1953, with Kurnool as its capital city.

Raghunath was first employed as a steno-typist in the administration of Madras Presidency and later shifted to Kurnool as per the agreements between governments towards Andhra born and Telugu speaking employees, as per their choice. After three years at Kurnool and post the seizure of Hyderabad from the Nizams, Raghunath moved to Hyderabad as the new state organisation committee ruled that the Andhra region and Telangana region should merge to become the Andhra Pradesh State in 1956.

Raghunath transferred to the Directorate of Medical Sciences, the department administering all the government hospitals in the State, as a senior clerk. DMS dealt with the recruitment, posting and transfer matters of all staff of the hospitals, purchase of capital and consumable requirements, and many other issues related to the State's public health.

During Raghunath's vacation trips from Madras and Kurnool to Palakollu, where his wife was nestled in her in-law's place, he sired three children – a son and two daughters. The eldest was Raj Krishna.

Raj Krishna was not the name given to him at his birth. He was Kanchibotla Varaha Venkata Gopala Krishna Sastry – KVVGK Sastry.

Raghunath's friend, who had accompanied them to the school while admitting the boy, suggested that the name was too traditional, long and dull and suggested him to register the boy as Raj Krishna Sastry, ensuring the Krishna part of his grandfather's name remained. This change of name annoyed his grandmother. She emphasised that the names of second-generation children should appease the Gods the family revered and contain a part of the name of departed elderly souls, in this case, her husband, Gopala Krishna. Overtly they claimed this naming ensured the memory of the departed soul.

But the covert narrative was that a lady could not utter her husband's name during his lifetime lest his lifespan may shrink, as the religious leaders decreed. Therefore, the grandmothers insisted on naming their grandsons with a part of her husband's name so she could address the child in the first person singular. Also, she could use an expletive or two playfully with her grandson.

That was the female gender's revenge against the societal norms.

His Grandma continued to refer to Raj as Gopala only. Raj Krishna hardly remembered his childhood until he became a teenager. His dad, Raghunath Sastry, continually put pressure on Raj Krishna to do well in school, which Raj could not manage. His dad was rarely home, so Raj and his two sisters had never had the privilege of their dad's love and care.

Raj always wondered why his dad behaved the way he had, as he noted the neighbours' dads' took their children on vacations and outings to cinemas and shopping, while his dad was hardly present at home even during festivals.

After the AP formation, Raghunath shifted his family to Hyderabad, managed a decent roof over their head using his official position, and got a government accommodation allotted to him at Jambagh. Jambagh in those days was the fruit and flower market busy 24/7, dominated by Muslim traders from the old city.

After a quickest of quickies, Raghunath Sastry confided in his wife in a rare candid moment.

"I want Krishna to be a doctor. I have seen doctors earn a lot and do not have any retirement age unless they are physically incapacitated. They continue to earn as long as they can," said Raj's dad.

"But it costs a lot of money to continue to educate for over five years!"

"Also, I don't think he has that kind of strong interest in studies. You know, with great difficulty, he passed his matric exam," added Raj's mom.

"I can manage that, but I want him to be a doctor." Sastry announced with such finality that could rival the decrees of a military dictator of a banana republic in Africa.

Raghunath Sastry pushed Raj Krishna to appear for matriculation when he was hardly thirteen. He employed three tutors to help Raj learn by rote, recall and transcribe by memory.

Raghunath's ambitions made him greedy and consumed him all the time. He got frustrated when not receiving the gratification he sought, and as a result, his family suffered mentally, physically and financially. Raj's mother often had to beg him for cash to run the house.

Raghunath Sastry was a quintessence of what a husband, a father, or a public servant should not be.

He ceaselessly terrorised his wife and told her how worthless she was. If she gave an opinion or a suggestion on any matter, he raged, "You are a worthless village girl. Don't tell me what I should do."

Raj did not remember the sequence of events that led to such altercations between his parents; the beatings were too frequent and left a lasting impression on his psyche. He was scared and pissed in his pants a few times. He made a vow that he would treat his wife with respect and consider her views in all family matters.

Raghunath wanted his dress to be ironed and laid out in a particular manner, food to be hot and steaming even when he came home late: sometimes close to midnight. One night when he found the sambar had fewer onions than he desired, he threw the hot sambar on his wife's face; fortunately, she did not burn herself as she quickly moved away. His wife did not have the cash to buy onions, but she dared not tell that as a reason.

Even a simple request for money to buy baby milk powder for her children made him lunge forward to grab her hair and hit her all over. He even kicked her 7month bulge when she was pregnant.

He was bigger and stronger, and she had nowhere to go for redress. Also, the idea of anyone else, even if it was her brother, getting involved in her problems embarrassed her. In those days, this patriarchal behaviour was typical, and society accepted these fights as part of family life of adjustment and compromise to ensure family lineage.

Her whole world contracted into her bedroom and kitchen. Her children were her only solace. She had to give in to her husband's sexual attentions at all times, and her pregnancies were an embarrassment to him. She had to abort two foetuses in a matter of three years. In marital life, the consent of the weaker gender was always taken for granted.

He was absent from home for days on end and suddenly appeared one fine morning to show extreme emotions of joy or anger, mostly the later. Raj's mamas[3] were aware of his obnoxious behaviour but could do nothing but sympathise with their sister. They told Raj and his mom that he was moonlighting with a 35yr old spinster at Shahabad, about 100Kms from Hyderabad.

Raj had accidentally come to know of his dad's other vices. One day, he was rummaging for a misplaced stapler in the front room table, which had three drawers and an HMV radio. The radio in those days had a vertical pointer moved with the help of a knob to locate the station needed. But this radio's knob was broken, so it can't move the pointer to change stations, so the transmission was stuck at one station only, All India Radio. Raj, in his ingenuity, found he could move the cursor by tapping on the top of the radio several times – three times to listen to Radio Ceylon and seven hard taps to get back to AIR. He ensured the indicator was back at AIR lest his dad would find another reason to give him a smack or two.

In the bottom-most drawer, he found a small printed book of 4" x 3" size, the details of which were not clear to him. It

---

3 Mother's brothers – maternal uncle

had COLE printed in bold in a circle with a pic of a man racing on a horse. When he inquired about it with his mamas, who often transited via Hyderabad on the way to Mumbai from their hometowns, they educated him about the horse racing club book.

It is a handy pocket guide for the racing community. Without this guide, the racegoers would be helpless. It contains the details of horses with their lineage, weight, previous racing history, and jockeys' details, including the winning probabilities of various combinations. The country's six racing centres are connected to the Cole race book –Pune, Bengaluru, Mysore, Hyderabad and Kolkata, apart from Mumbai, where the book originated in 1920.

They guessed Raghunath Sastry must have been an addict to racing, which he might have picked while working in Madras, which after Bombay and Kolkata, was famous for punters and racehorse owners – small, big and the extravagant.

Horse racing is concerned with both horses and gambling, and it is more than mere sweepstakes. The central role betting plays in horse racing is obvious. For most race-goers, placing bets and then being proved right or wrong is fun. The excitement of the sport lies in its immediate and competitive nature. The probability of winning is so low the winner is rewarded handsomely.

Conversely, the loser can be devastated, if he bets on a considerable sum based on some unsolicited advice, which in the racing course one gets many. Thus one becomes an addict as with any other vice such as smoking, club-card games, lottery and alcohol.

It was now clear to Raj why his dad could not spare money for their daily necessities, which made his mom a nervous wreck and a cause of fights and loud verbal altercations. She had to beg funds to run the house with three children growing up.

Raghunath was often under stress. His losses in races and his skirmishes with his bosses because of his unexplained absenteeism and suspicious behaviour in his job contributed to the tension at home.

They were rumours he had a chain of staff working in the department to help him arrange and fix transfers of doctors, nurses and ward boys as he was working in the Director's office. But no one could nail him, as it would expose many others in the chain of the command structure. He was a convenient front man for every corrupt officer or clerk in the Directorate. He cleverly managed the transfers by finding some loopholes in the rule book. It was whispered that the Director also had more than a passing interest in the workings of Raghunath though no proof was forthcoming. The Director's driver had once seen Raghunath at the Director's house one morning of a festival day. The rumour then got some more air but was hushed up soon as the Director was a darling of his staff.

One day a nurse, Kutti Chettiyan, came to Raghunath's table.

"Sir, I want a transfer to Vijayawada," she announced.

Any person who wants a transfer, a posting, or a grievance is always directed to Raghunath as he was well-read in the department's rules, regulations, and processes. He also knew how to circumvent the rules or interpret them favourably when needed.

"Which is your home town?" asked Raghunath

"Alleppey."

"Then why Vijayawada? And Alleppey is in Kerala, a different state where we don't have any say."

"No, Sir, I want to be relocated to Vijayawada only. Dr Siddhartha got transferred there recently, and I want to work under him to learn more and be useful to society," pleaded Kutti.

Raghunath guessed the matter was more complicated than what she reported. He would be the last person to miss such an opportunity to gain some material gratification.

"Please meet me tomorrow morning at Sea Rose café outside," he said and got immersed in his transfer application files.

At the appointed time, Kutti came to the Irani cafe in a lavender chiffon saree with mogra flowers strung in her loose hair with clips and slippers, which made flapping noise when she walked. She had a slim body with small breasts in a matching semi-transparent purple blouse with a black bra strap peeping through her loose blouse.

Raghunath was sipping chai with another person who was animatedly explaining something and appeared in distress. Raghu waved at Kutti to sit at the table while conversing in Telugu with the man in ragged clothes and seemed to be on the verge of crying. Kutti had no idea of what was going on. She picked up a few Telugu words but couldn't understand complicated sentences. She ordered tea for herself, and the bearer delivered with an assortment of Osmania Biscuits as was the practice with Irani restaurants in those times. One paid only for what one ate.

Once the troubled man had left, Raghunath turned to Kutti.

"You have to be frank with me on the reason for the transfer to help you."

Kutti then confided. She said she was in love with Dr Siddhartha, who promised to marry her. She wanted to be near him at Vijayawada to persuade him to marry her soon.

This information surprised Raghunath. Dr Siddhartha was a sought-after anaesthetist in all four government hospitals under the Directorate. His transfer was a mystery to Raghunath. His assignment papers did not pass through his table. It could have happened when he was in Shahabad, He told Kutti he needed more time to know how to help her as hers was a case where she could not put forth any credible reasoning for the transfer. She was also due to be promoted to matron next year, as was apparent in the folder she presented him containing her employment matters. Both agreed to meet after a week.

Raghunath's investigation revealed that Dr Siddhartha had a roving eye, and his wife, the daughter of a local MP, had a hand in his transfer. He found a petition by many surgeons requesting the Director to stop his transfer as he was a very skilful person, especially in complicated surgery cases.

But the appeal was of no avail.

A committee of four made transfers in the department – two deputy directors, one Finance manager and the Director himself duly assisted by a couple of staff members, invariably including Raghunath. These assemblies were conducted with a little more seriousness than a friendly house party. The committee passed through most of the recommendations presented by the Director and his staff except for any particular case presented by a member who may have a personal interest for undisclosed gain. In such cases, after discussions and debates, a consensus would be arrived at for a future quid-pro-quo. Though vetted by the Director, the list prepared by the staff members would leave some room for his close staff – including Raghunath – to push their files for generating cash. It was rumoured that the Director used such monies for staff welfare, as the state budgets always fell short. That was how the Director came to be revered by his staff, as compassionate person. The accounting of such cash was always a point of discord as some rouge staff members do not report all that was collected. Raghunath was one of them.

After a week, when Kutti called on Raghunath, he was ready with his proposal.

"I can push your case, but it is risky as some big people are involved in Dr Siddhartha's transfer," said Raghunath.

"Please do whatever you can; I need to be posted to Vijayawada as soon as possible," Kutti pleaded.

"I cannot do anything out of turn. It has to look as routine for which I have to work with many people, including your admin staff at the hospital you are presently working. Unfortunately, Vijayawada is not a hill station; otherwise, it was easy to create records of health needs to push your case. I hope you understand."

"Yes, I do. Tell me what it costs." *Come to the point.*

She is desperate, thought Raghunath Sastry

"It will cost you ten thousand, and the next meeting for transfers is due only in the next quarter," said Raghunath.

Kutti immediately agreed and promised to bring the money in a couple of days. Raghunath gave instructions on what convincing reasoning had to be shown in the request letter for transfer. Kutti's transfer was an easy one for Raghunath, as the next meeting had no quorum with only one deputy director and the Director present. He could quietly push the case along with many other pressing matters, one of which was the disciplinary action on a drunk doctor who botched up a surgery, which took the most time. By the time Raghunath's file came up, the team was exhausted from discussing the Surgeon's matter and the process of the recommended action. Kutti's case went through with precision like Arjun's arrow.

With Kutti's cash in hand, Raghunath bet on Morning Star, Gold Finger and Thunder Storm, which came last in the Sunday treble.

On the same day, Raj's competitive entrance exam results for MBBS were announced, and his rank was such that he would not be eligible for admission to any medical institution in the State. It did not occur to Raghunath that Raj was not exactly a child prodigy to get a suitable rank at the age of sixteen. Raghunath's aspiration of relying on Raj Krishna as an ATM post his retirement disappeared annoyed him. Raj's house that day reminded one of London during the 1942 blitzkrieg. Raghunath was so upset he refused to admit Raj in any other stream in any college.

"Let him wander like a vagabond," thundered Raghunath when his wife pushed his case.

Admissions to colleges were getting closed, and Raghunath was not even seen at home to plead to reverse his decision. It took a few more years and exposure to college life for Raj to understand how his life was evolving.

Raj Krishna

You have to have grown to full sixteen to understand how your parents influence your later life and your psyche with their financial and emotional power. When things do not go the way your parents had envisioned for you in all their wisdom, you can be either bold and revolt or succumb to their revised plans. I was fearful and timid, so I did what I was told to do.

My father guessed I was masturbating, the leading cause of my failures of the mind and its focus, as per him. He constantly admonished me: "What were you doing so long in the lavatory? If I ever catch you doing wrong things, I shall not spare you."

Wrong things, were never spelt out.

But I found forbidden places to masturbate. It had become an addiction. First time I sensed the pleasurable sensation was when my penis accidentally rubbed while I glided on a staircase arms instead of walking down the steps. My father might have had his reasons for censuring me as I had a weak frame, which he attributed to his perception of my addiction. But no substantial evidence was available for him to pin me down. Whenever he was home, he found some reason to reprimand me. During summers, he was fond of devouring tarbooz[4], and I was given the task of buying it. I could never satisfy him by purchasing the right one.

He admonished me: "What, you cannot even buy a fruit correctly?" Then he would explain how to select one which, according to him,

---

4   Water Melon

should be sweet and pulpy at the same time. Brown in colour, correct weight, no transport damage, and not pricey. I failed time and again in any or all the parameters. It did not happen only with tarbooz, add banana and mango to this list of my failure to select a good fruit. I was ridiculed all the time for not paying attention to his instructions. The more I was chided the more errors I made. My inability to get admission into medical college was the main reason for his outbursts.

His tirades about his perception of my incompetence continued unabated from the moment he was home till he left for office. Little did I know then this kind of behaviour towards me would manifest a few decades later when my wife would deride me for such tiny error as swapping the slots of the spoons and forks in the kitchen drawer. I hated my dad for this mental abuse. I had to swallow my pride for the sake of my future.

One morning I found my eldest mama arriving at my house unannounced. My mother had written to him about the reluctance of my father to admit me into college. As usual, my father was not home. So I took my mama to his office. They both went to have coffee in the Tajmahal hotel. I was not privy to their discussions. The next day my father and mama admitted me into the science stream of graduation. I was determined to do well for my family's sake and get a good job to make my mother's life happy. I had no trouble working hard and passed every test, topped the class, and was awarded a rank in the final year of my graduation. I went through humiliations of all kinds during all these years, and my mother had a miserable existence, thanks to my father's moods. I had to often go to my father's office to collect monies for our daily needs. When asked for a hundred, he would give a twenty. So we lived literally from hand to mouth, as the cliché went.

My mother somehow managed with this measly house allowance, supplementing through tailoring. We lived on the cheapest vegetable found in the market for days on end. Vegetables like potatoes, lady's fingers, and eggplants were prohibitively expensive. My mother could only feed us with cluster beans fried with coconut gratings seasoned with mustard seeds and red peppers. Half a coconut from the nearby temple would cost us 25 paise. Once, we ate this vegetable prep for almost 8days, as my dad did not come home to give us the money. I had never forgiven my dad for what he made us suffer. I survived this tyrannical abuse, its effect hanging over me like an evil shadow even today. I always felt inadequate and scared, wondering why I let myself in for so much grief. I could only rebel against this abuse much later in my life. It did cost me my peace, though.

Years later, I realised that this particular period of my life had made me very timid and subservient. I never possessed the courage to defy authority or give a convincing argument to do anything that was not to my liking. I reluctantly followed instructions even when they were not to my convenience or interest. I hated myself for being used by people who had power – real and supposed, over me.

ALTAF MALLIK

Altaf Mallik was the sixth child of seven of his parents. His parents were not well to do; they were barely surviving. Altaf grew without much intervention from his father. He was his mother's favourite child as he was the most obedient of all her children. She always depended upon him for all household errands. Altaf was always helping his mother in her household chores and sat next to her while she was offering namaaz.

Like his brothers, he, too, never went to college. After completing secondary school certification, he dropped out but attended the local madrasa as insisted by his mother. In the evenings, he spent time with his close friend, whose father had a motorcycle repair shop. He mastered the rudiments of the trade from this association. Later when he became an adult, he joined as a workman in an MRF Tyre Dealer shop which also had a wheel alignment and balancing service. Because of his diligence in the job and being the only one with some education, his employer trusted him to interact with customers.

He married Nazma, the daughter of his Khala[5]. Nazma's family were well-to-do. Her dad had a famous pharmacy shop in the khanapur area of Ahmedabad. After his marriage, Altaf got promoted as salesman handling customers, as the owner found him to be well-mannered and obedient. He believed that Nazma brought luck into his life. While working as a salesman, he had

---

5   Paternal aunt

time on his hand, which he cleverly used to study and understand the Islamic Law of Sharia.

MRF trained him in Chennai as part of their sales training targeted at their marketing channel workers to enable them to detail their product to prospective customers. While in Chennai, he learnt about the manufacturing process, which would help him later in his work.

Altaf Mallik grew into a stocky, tall with an untrimmed beard, a clean-shaven upper lip, and a devout Muslim. He performed Salah precisely as told by the maulvi: pray first standing and later kneeling on the ground, reciting from the Quran and glorifying and praising Allah. He followed all the rituals of fasting. When free, he would listen to old Hindi film songs on Bhule Bisre Geet or watch Chitrahaar with his wife at home. He rarely called his friends home but kept excellent social contact with most neighbours. Unlike other Indian husbands, he worked deftly with his hands, oiled creaky hinges, drilled holes for fixing domestic devices, changed fused bulbs, and fitted lights during IDD. Any woman would love to have such a handyman as a husband.

Altaf was a fatalist; he believed his life – and his death – were in Allah's hands.

Altaf thought if Prophet Mohammed, peace be upon him, had shown little more compassion, probably he could have given better living conditions to his wife. Or so, he believed. Allah seemed to have heard his demands. He granted him some of his wishes. After a couple of years of his marriage, after the birth of Abdul, Altaf resigned from his job. He opened a workshop for tyre re-treading and recycling with generous help from his father-in-law. The workshop contained a tin roof propped by metal frames. It consisted of open space for the manufacturing process, and a small cubicle held the record books of orders received. Altaf mainly catered to owner-driven truckers.

He developed and sustained a loyal and regular clientele.

In re-treading, a new lease of rubber is put on the casing of a worn-out tyre without changing the Nylon cords. Hence, the quality of the re-treaded tyres always stays a lot down than that of the new tyres. No matter how well it works after re-treading, there has to be some issue with a re-treaded tyre. But many small-time truckers use re-treaded tyres to save on the capital cost of buying a new tyre.

The business was mostly on credit, and the turnover was enough to manage a couple of bad debts.

"Nazma, I might take more time to return the loan to your abbu. How can I tell him? I am confused," said Altaf while having dinner.

"You told me the business is good. Why this sudden U-turn?" wondered Nazma.

"Business is indeed okay, but the customers who give the tyres for re-treading do not come back in time to take their repaired tyres, even though I keep reminding them. They are always on the move, and it is becoming impossible to contact them."

"So?" Nazma was unable to comprehend his problem.

"Firstly, they occupy space, which makes it almost impossible to take on new tyres, and also have a cash turnover problem. Unless they take their material back, I do not get paid. Can't you understand?" showing frustration as Nazma could not understand his predicament.

"Oh!" exclaimed Nazma.

"Can't you auction them off if they don't come to pick them up?"

"It is not that easy. I have loyal clientele with whom I cannot be discourteous."

"Also, I have this problem of taking them out to stack exposed at opening time to allow space for work and later putting them back before closing. It's unnecessary labour. Once I kept the tyres unattended inside the workshop during last IDD, and when I tried to move them, I found a snake coiled inside," added Altaf.

"Ya Allah!" shrieked Nazma.

"Consequently, this is blocking my working capital. I am short of cash. I have to find a solution," rued Altaf.

They mutually decided to go to Ahmedabad as soon as convenient to plead with Nazma's abbu for more time to return the loan. Altaf managed his business well with all these teething problems, which made him dream of a larger house.

But presently, let me concentrate on improving the business by finding corporate customers like RK Roadways, Gujarat Transport Company, etc., and keep the bigger house dream a grand burial.

He worked diligently, which resulted in his growing reputation as a skilled tyre re-treader. He had won many transport company contracts, though on a smaller scale. Nazma never interfered with Altaf in his business, but they ruled the house with an iron fist. Nazma was the vociferous one as far as domestic matters go. Altaf had always been mild-mannered and respected in society. Though he could hard bargain with truck owners, at home his mildness degenerated into passivity necessary to maintain domestic peace.

Nazma sired more children. Two girls and two sons. She could have added more to her tally. Abdominal pain prevented her from conceiving which limited their conjugation to tender touches.

With his tyre business improving and Nazma's insistence, he shifted to relatively larger accommodation. She also convinced her abbu to give her more time to return the loan. This concession helped the family move from Mandvi to the Navrang Park Society, an up-market locality.

Raj Krishna

"Congratulations, Raghunath. I understand your son had passed with distinction in his graduate exam," said the Director Vishweshwaraiah.

Vishweshwaraiah was well-built with broad shoulders and rose through the ranks purely on his academic and research credentials. He brooked no interference in his administration. He had no political masters to please, though it cannot be said the same about his two deputies. They often used political pressures to influence decisions related to procurements and transfer placements, much to the chagrin of the Director, fondly referred to as Diro by his staff.

Yet wherever possible, he let merit and principles take precedence. In many cases he had to compromise. However, those who benefited from this generosity suppressed the rumours of under-the-table transactions. Presently, Diro's team of two LDCs, the finance manager, and his two deputies were sitting to finalise the department's following year's budget.

"Thank you, sir," said Raghunath.

"So what are his next plans?" asked the finance manager

"I had not thought much, though I was disappointed he did not get admission to medicine after his inter," grumbled Raghunath.

"It's okay. It all ended well now. Be happy," said one of the deputies.

"Masters may be one choice, though," said the Diro giving unsolicited advice.

"But sir, with masters, one can only end up as a lecturer at the most, and it is not lucrative as the growth is slow and unrewarding," said another deputy.

"Raghu, my sister, who is an assistant professor of pharmacology in the department of pharmacy at Bombay University, told me the other day that the university was trying to introduce a new curriculum wherein they can also admit science graduates directly into the second year of their four year degree course in pharmacy. I think you can probe this route of admitting your son to the pharmacy," said the finance manager.

The finance manager gave the contact of his sister, who lived in the Chembur, to pursue the matter further.

Raghunath appeared elated. At least the boy can be gainfully employed in a Government Hospital, which as per Raghunath is a cash-cow for its staff.

"Thank you, sir. I will ask my brother-in-law, who is in Bombay, to meet her and get more details," said Raghunath.

Later the meeting proceeded and ended with many debates of give-and-take. The political leaning deputies had managed most of the decisions in their favour, backed by the not-so-honest finance manager. With the help of his brother-in-law, Raghunath succeeded in getting more details on the course and pushed Raj to seek admission into Bombay College of Pharmacy.

Bombay, then as it is now, was an expensive place to pursue education.

But Raghunath was determined. Fortunately, Raj Krishna's top ranking was helpful, and he topped the entrance test too, which helped him with a scholarship and a tuition fee waiver. The course had a three-year duration for those who graduated in science with a direct entry into the second year of the regular four year course. The department conducted special classes for the second year's direct entrants separately to familiarise them with subjects such as biology or maths as the case be. They were also given extra coaching in anatomy, biochemistry, microbiology and physiology, which were part of the first year of the regular four-year course. These students merged with the four-year stream from the third year onwards.

Raj had come to know that another student from Andhra was also pursuing B Pharma, albeit in regular course. He tried to interact with him to familiarise himself with the college culture. Vikas Patil was a Maharashtrian whose mother was from Vijayawada. He mostly lived all his life in Hyderabad because of his dad's job. Raj met Vikas accidentally in the college canteen while Vikas was interacting with the cashier in Telugu.

"Hi, I am Raj Krishna from Hyderabad," said Raj in Telugu.

"Hi, I am Vikas Patil. Are you a fresher here?" replied Vikas.

After exchanging their introductions, they sat down with their respective coffee mugs. Then Raj saw a girl in light blue denim with half sleeves white top embroidered at the neck and the sleeves with some flower motif. She tied her hair in a bun and wore rimmed glasses. She walked straight towards their table and tapped Vikas from behind. Her breezy outgoing personality was strong and attractive.

"Hello, Vikas. Are you bunking the toxicology lecture?" asked the pleasant voice.

"Hey Push, meet this gentleman, Mr. ....sorry I missed your name," addressing the girl and turning towards Raj simultaneously.

"Raj Krishna Sastry from Hyderabad," replied Raj.

"Pushyami Joshi," she said and put her hand out, which Raj took while at the same time devouring her countenance.

"Can I get you some coffee?" Raj asked as a courtesy.

Ignoring and turning away from him, she said," Vikas, I need a coke."

Vikas got up to get her one.

The canteen was a shack with a small counter for a snack and hot beverage delivery. There was a kiosk from which one could get cool drinks. The tables and chairs were laid out under two giant trees giving shelter. During the rainy season of three months, the canteen management covered the place with tarpaulins. There were more chairs than tables, which gave an impression of only snack and beverage service.

"Which year are you in?" Raj asked her.

"I am in the second year. How about you?" she asked.

"Me too," Raj replied.

"How come I did not see you?" wondered Pushyami.

Meanwhile, Vikas came back from the counter announcing the non-availability of coke and offered her hot chocolate instead.

"No thanks," said Pushyami.

"You knew this gentleman before, Vikas?"

"No, I just got introduced. From the same city, you know," said Vikas.

"He is into the special course after graduation in science."

"Oh! During the second year, they have special classes and will merge with us in the third year," said Pushyami.

Pushyami then explained the background of the introduction of this bridge course.

Pushyami should know. Her father was partly responsible for introducing this lateral entry into the second year of the four year B Pharma course for science graduates.

Bhanuprakash Joshi was posted at Armed Forces Medical Corps hospital in Bhuj during the 1965 war. One night an Army Officer brought a soldier to the hospital with a bullet lodged into his right shoulder while patrolling the border. It was a minor case considering the numerous mutilated bodies in the hospital in various states of shrapnel wounds, spinal cord injuries, loss of sight and hearing, limb loss, etc.

Dr Joshi had removed the bullet from the shoulder and gave the nurse instructions to provide him with a Penicillin G, a broad-spectrum antibiotic, and paracetamol to relieve the pain. In her enthusiasm to ease the soldier's pain, the Nurse had added a variant of barbiturate to induce sleep. The next day morning, as the patient did not wake up even at 9 a.m., the duty sister had to call Dr Joshi to take a look. Dr Joshi was annoyed that the night-duty Nurse had gone beyond her brief and administered a sedative.

Dr Joshi noted that the prolonged sedative state could have resulted from an inter-drug reaction or an idiosyncratic reaction to the antibiotic, which he wished to investigate further. He summoned the hospital head. The Captain, along with the Head Nurse, came quickly. He asked them what regiment the soldier belonged to.

"Sir, he is from 16th BN from Bhopal," the Captain said.

"How long will it take to get the patients' medical records?" asked Dr Joshi. "Sir, it may take at least ten days, as this is wartime, and medical records are the lowest priority," said the Head Nurse.

"Okay, I understand. But do you have this soldier's knapsack from the bunker?" asked the Doctor.

"I have to check, but even if it is not here, we can get it within six hours," said the Nurse.

"Please get it for me," requested Dr Joshi.

The knapsack duly arrived and was handed over to Dr Joshi. Dr Joshi inspected the contents and found it had strips of Rimpazid. Dr Joshi was aware these tablets contained Isoniazid, a generic antibiotic for treating Tuberculosis. He then concluded that the prolonged drowsiness of the patient could be attributed to the interaction of the barbiturate and the TB drug. Fortunately, the effect did not last long, and the patient woke up by afternoon. It was a blessing in disguise as the soldier's sedative state helped him manage the surgery's pain.

Dr Joshi wished to investigate further the interaction between various drug molecules. He inquired about the availability of Pharmacy graduates to help him study drug chemistry. To his surprise, there were no pharmacists available in the entire Kutch region of Gujarat. He had to call on his contacts in a Pharma Company in Ahmedabad requesting their help on the issue.

When asked about the reason for scarcity of pharmacy professionals, Dr Joshi was told not many pharma graduates were available in Gujarat, and those available preferred to work in cities only. Also, female students had limitations in working in remote areas.

In the subsequent interaction at Indian Pharmaceutical Association's (IPA) annual meeting, Dr Joshi raised the topic of improving pharmacy graduates' availability across the country's length and breadth.

After further investigations and reports of similar nature appearing from other regions, the Association, in their subsequent governing council meeting, had decided to recommend a unique three-year course for science graduate students. However, the body that regulated medical education in India is the Medical Council of India. After considerable persuasion and documented data by IPA, MCI introduced the bridge course in Bombay College of Pharmacy as a first experiment, directly funded and managed by the Pharmaceutical Association of India.

"So, I am indebted to your dad for allowing me to pursue this pharma course," remarked Raj

"It was not my father alone. The medical profession raised this matter earlier too. But my father had relentlessly followed his findings with more verifiable data before the MCI and the Board of Governors at BCP. MCI is an independent organisation and does not simply go by one person's or Association's opinion. They may have studied other instances also in remote areas of the country before deciding on tweaking the course structure," opined Pushyami.

"What happened to the soldier? Did he recover?" asked Vikas.

"The soldier got discharged after fifteen days, but his shoulder was not strong enough to hold a gun or a rifle anymore. At least he could put his arms around his wife and kids," said Pushyami.

Raj wanted to extend the conversation to ensure Pushyami stayed longer with them.

"Which semester of our curriculum teaches us about drug interaction?" inquired Raj.

"I think it is in the fifth semester. My dad discussed this topic of drug-drug interactions with me recently. As per my dad, these reactions occur when a drug alters the effects of another drug in a combination regimen. The alteration can be so severe that not just the efficiency of the original drug is minimised, but the other drug may cause unknown effects, "said Pushyami.

Pushyami inquired about Raj's subjects in his graduation and was glad to know Raj had opted for mathematics as an elective.

"I was surprised to know the need for advanced mathematics knowledge to pursue a course, essentially concerning biology," wondered Pushyami.

"Mathematics is required to understand the rate of drug absorption with the help of first-order differential equations; ADME – drug absorption, distribution, metabolism, and excretion also require the use of mathematical equations, which many pure science students who had not studied higher mathematics find it difficult," said Vikas.

Vikas was inquisitive and often interacted with his seniors. "Similarly, the application of physics is found in all pharmaceutical science and physical pharmacy areas, including pre-formulation, formulation design, and drug substance and product characterisation."

When Raj was told he had topped in mathematics and physics but was weak in chemistry, an immediate bond got established for a quid-pro-quo arrangement to transfer knowledge amongst the three.

Raj had no problem with his finance during the first year at the college as the scholarship took care of it. But for the second year, he could not top the class, and the scholarship went to a studious Tamilian. Raj had to depend on money from his dad, who was not forthcoming as per his needs. He had to visit home every vacation and request his dad for money. Raghunath had tough times both at the office and at his second home in Shahabad. His behaviour towards his wife and Raj had not changed. Raj dreaded his way home during vacation as he had to go through the same routine of fights, abuses, and insults, which disturbed him no end.

Every time it was the same thing. I felt like crying. My throat goes all tight, and I do my best to control myself. But sometimes, it gets tricky. I hardly keep myself from sobbing.

Raghunath somehow managed to fund Raj. Raghunath was ensuring resources for his retirement life to continue his indulgences.

Raj looked forward to his time back in Bombay to quickly finish his graduation and look for a decent job and make his mother happy, at least financially. After finishing his graduation, he could succeed in campus placements and got a position as a management trainee in a US-based drug manufacturing company with six units across Western and Southern parts of India.

Pushyami had joined Masters as per her interest in pursuing a teaching career. Vikas had migrated to Australia.

The firm Raj joined had recruited three more pharma graduates from other institutes. All four of them were in a training ritual of the company. After which, they would be posted to the department of their choice and company's need, though the latter always took precedence. They were asked to overlook what they had learnt in college and learn pharmacy afresh from an industry viewpoint during the training period. At the end of the mandatory training period, Raj was called by the HR manager for a formal assessment and future departmental allocation.

"We are glad you have completed your training, and we have received good reports about your initiation into various sections of the company," said the HR manager.

"Thank you, sir."

"We have placements in Production, Marketing, Good Manufacturing Practices and Distribution departments. We wondered what would interest you and why?" asked the manager, assisted by a lady whom Raj came to know later was from MD's office.

"I prefer Marketing." Raj knew Marketing would give quick growth and some extra money, he could save during business travels.

"I hope you know Pharma Marketing is quite different than what they teach in management schools and marketing textbooks," said the Manager.

"Yes, sir, we had a fifteen-day interaction with Mr Ganeshan in the Marketing department. He told us about how to create brochure content, detailing processes and other promotional aspects of marketing."

"However, we are looking for MBAs in the Marketing department, not pure pharma grads," said the elderly matriarch who accompanied the HR Manager.

Then why did you give me a choice in the first place?

"We urgently need someone to look after implementing good manufacturing practices in all the six units. HR has recommended your name," added the Lady.

It was a fait accompli.

"I may need further initiation into this aspect as we were not exposed to GMPs in our study, though a passing reference is made during the course," Raj added. "Can I be a part of the distribution department? I had a good interaction with Mr Brar, the department VP, and I quite like the job profile."

"That would be a good choice, though. But our GMP section requires young and enthusiastic people like you. We have big plans for your career growth in GMP. We may acquire new businesses or use outsourcing units in which the culture of the good manufacturing practices we have designed needs to be replicated," said the HR manager.

The company was looking to entice Raj into a domain area, where no other pharma grad would like to be employed.

Raj wanted the job desperately. So it was settled, and Raj was inducted into the GMP department. Raj's life would have been described as listless if one only considered his relatively slow progress in the corporate sector. Albeit, he was declared Top Performer for two consequent years. Raj's income had bought him the financial freedom he hadn't realised he'd been missing. The independence opened up his world, even thinking about something as ordinary as indulging in Juhu's Falooda with Rabadi.

I travelled in public transport over weekends and vacationed in Bombay like a vagabond. Theatres that screened English films at Eros, New Empire and Regal were my favourite haunts to adore the Bombay gentry all in their finery.

At times Ramesh – my roommate- accompanied me when he was not busy with his girlfriend cum cousin. Bombay had a lot to offer for a bachelor with some spare cash. You can also hear Usha Uthup croon in Talk of the Town. Or adore Zubin Mehta's jazz at Tata-manged National Centre for Performing Arts. But I had still a few responsibilities to my family back home, so I resisted these expensive temptations.

***

Raj achieved what he promised himself during his troubled teen years on the home front.

The family was a bit more comfortable with Raj's income, which gave them the extra comfort of ease of living, and he got both his sisters married. As luck would have it, Raghunath could not enjoy the monetary success of his son as he died during a simple operation for the removal of kidney stones. Doctors at the hospital could not fathom this peculiar and unfortunate turn of events. Some of the department officials in the DMS office where Raghunath worked attributed his death to brain hypoxia due to mismanaged anaesthesia. They wondered why general anaesthesia was required when a local one would have been equally effective.

Usually, brain damage during anaesthesia is rare but can occur with even a minor error of putting in the breathing tube.

Living in Mumbai as a bachelor had its problems in the form of decent accommodation. Most immigrants like Raj survived by sharing a room in a lodge or a hostel-type boarding house. Raj found one near Dadar - a nice place with basic amenities for a small charge. They provided morning tea but no lunch or dinner. However, lunch was never a problem for those who had day-shift. Either their workplace provided canteen facilities at their premises or outsourced as a part of their welfare activities. Being within the factory premises, Raj had his afternoon meals at the office cafeteria.

It was dinner which was a pain. He spent time in the office in evenings long past his scheduled closing hours so he could directly go for dinner while travelling back from the office and then retire to bed. Mumbai offered a variety of cuisines for the connoisseur. A budget-conscious person can comfortably satiate his hunger by just eating pav-bhaji from roadside vendors or going to a formal restaurant for a thali. Once in a way, Raj would indulge in an expensive thali at Samrat or Purohit on the salary day.

However, like Raj, the middle-class vegetarian Andhra Brahmin genus was not exposed to diverse foods other than those cooked by their mothers or grandmothers. An obsession with a particular type of food was not limited to Andhras. Still, this clan was not experimental in their eating habits. They were not exposed to varieties of foods, partly because their limited financial resources and also their upbringing did not allow them to indulge in fancy restaurant offerings, which was considered blasphemy.

Even with her limited resources, his mom's cuisine left an indelible mark on his palate. He was unable to enjoy the culinary variety Mumbai offered. When time and opportunity provided, Raj gorged on his Mumbai-based aunt's meals, which though not a complete substitute for his mom's fare, gratified him somewhat, as it was of Andhra origin.

After four years of such bachelor days, Raj decided to find a bride for himself.

Raj had already become a hot property in the marriage market in Andhra. His maternal uncle was inundated with proposals, many of which did not find favour with Raj. Many of his classmates in Mumbai found their life companions themselves. Raj had no such luck.

Most of my friends and colleagues married without the intervention of their parents. They euphemistically termed their alliance: Love Marriage. In actual practice, Love has nothing to do with it. It is just a marriage of convenience. School, college friends, office colleagues or a familiar neighbourhood acquaintances decide mutually that a known devil is better than an unknown angel and tie the knot, after many sessions of tête-à-tête. In western countries they call it a date prior to final exchange of vows. Only difference is: in India one dates only after plenty of dialogues over coffee in public – that too with no sleep-overs. I derogatively labelled such marriages as self-arranged – leaving the Love part - to conceal the lack of such opportunity in my case.

Raj had to settle for an arranged marriage: arranged by his mama. Vaidehi was the second child of a Bank Branch Manager, with his office at Cuff parade. They had a four-bedroom apartment just above the branch of the same building. Vaidehi's dad was a classmate of Raj's mama who had proposed the alliance with Raj. The adolescent Vaidehi was pretty was an understatement. She could stop traffic. No wonder Raj accepted the proposal without batting an eyelid.

VAIDEHI

Generally, a woman's interactions with men are limited to three members – her father, brother, and husband/live-in partner. If she hailed from an extended family, add a cousin, a chacha[6], a mama etc. Working women would have a couple more of such interactions. A promiscuous – nay, adventurous- woman would have few more. Yet, this sample size would be too small to conclude the characteristics of little more than one half of the world's population. But I am entitled to my opinion based on my personal experiences.

Men cannot be trusted. Some of them behave like leeches. Many cheat on their sleeping partners. They create more work than help women at home. My mom's brother, my mama, who was almost 15 years younger than her, was a vagabond. But they got him married, and he sired two girls – both always looked malnourished. On consistent nudging by mom, my Dad, with the help of his friend and neighbour, got mama a job as a clerk in the local electricity office. Later they transferred him about 200 km away from our place. I thought my Dad had a hand in it.

My Dad was the only son of well-accomplished parents. My granny was a professor of History in the local college, and my grandpa worked as a warehouse manager with Food Corporation of India. My Dad, never got beyond graduation.

In one of his rare candid moments, he confessed his failings. His father wanted him to become a Chartered Accountant. After

---

6 Father's younger brother

three attempts, he finally gave up, taking up a job at a bank as a probationary officer through a competitive examination and an interview.

"Your granny and grandpa never questioned me on my sloppiness in academics," he said. "They gave unbridled freedom to me and never interfered with my decision making."

Dad started his career in a small town – Sonepat – near Delhi. He was in Sonepat for most of his bachelor days; he married while he was there; the first three years of their married life, mom spent in Sonepat. She learned the local Haryanvi dialect, much different from the Sanskritised Hindi she learned in school. My brother was born there towards the end of their posting in Haryana.

My Dad was a diligent worker. He rose through the ranks in the Bank by sheer will and passed the mandatory departmental examinations and training schedules. Mom told me he was well respected. Many of his peers and co-workers spoke highly of him whenever she attended the bank parties, picnics and other events the office organised.

Being the only sibling and living member of my maternal grandparent's family, my mom's brother was her major weakness.

My mama would often come to our house with his wife and their two children, whose favourite pastime was crying. The family stayed for days together on some pretext or the other. It was surprising to note the electricity department granted him so many leaves. Dad always complained he could not get time off to take us on vacation because of some inspection, training or audit.

At the end of my mama's family stay, my mom supplied them with goodies – many pairs of dresses, pickles to last one year, some cash too – the last one clandestinely. I was then studying 11th standard in a local missionary school. My brother was off to do his engineering. He rarely visited us, except between semesters. During his visit, either he feasted on mom's recipes as though he had just come from a famine country or slept that rivalled legendary Khumbhkarna[7]. He visited his school friends in the evenings or went to a movie. Sometimes I accompanied him.

When my mama visited us, he used to be about the house as though he owned it. He always wore a smelly vest – baniyan, it is termed – with nothing over it. That was his permanent upper garment when at home. He sweated so profusely that the baniyan itself morphed from white to yellow. I wondered whether he had only one of those, washing it at night and wearing it in the morning. When I pestered mom about this a couple of times, she reprimanded me for being impertinent.

One day when I was sitting at my desk, preparing for the next day's botany slip test, he walked in and said: "Chinnu, what are you doing?" I almost wanted to tell him, "can't you see?" instead, I politely replied, "I am preparing for my Botany test tomorrow." He put his hand on my head and caressed my hair, and said, "You need any help? I am good at botany." That was news to me. I did not reply.

He took out a candy and put it on my book. It was orange in colour, wrapped in a transparent cellophane wrapper twisted at the ends anticlockwise. When you wish to open it, you have to twist it clockwise. These candies of Ravalgaon-make were very popular – children loved this candy that came in various colours and fruit flavours. Orange was, of course, my favourite. Every kirana store put these candies in glass containers right in front of the counter for display, luring the children who came along with their parents.

I put the candy away from the book and continued to concentrate, ignoring his presence.

---

7   Legendary character in Hindu Mythology – sleeps for six months at a stretch

Then something unexpected happened. My mama bent down, shoved his head between my face and the book, and kissed my forehead, blocking my reading. I looked at him confusingly. "Study well and get good marks," he said.

While he took his head away, he grazed his palm against my right breast. When at home in summer I don't wear any inner liners in the blouse. At 16, we are not done growing yet. My breasts had not developed three-dimensionally enough to warrant a proper bra. Such small cup sizes were also not available in the market. Like my friends, I wore the body-fit camisoles and other strapped inners when out of the house. We also tuck the slip into the trouser or legging, so it does not ride up. Otherwise, it was always a plain cotton gown or a blouse or a comfortable t-shirt, ensuring it was opaque enough to forego wearing undergarments. Thus we were a bit vulnerable at home if any guest or a visitor appeared unannounced.

The swiping touch of his palm did give me a pleasurable sensation. It must have been an accident, I thought. I stood up and walked away on the pretext of wanting to drink some water.

My mama and his family's frequent visits to our house never surprised me.

My Dad frequently got transferred from Sonepat to Delhi to Guwahati, Aligarh to Mumbai, and to Vishakhapatnam, where he retired. Each time we were getting used to a place we had moved to, got to know the neighbours and made a few friends, we had to move somewhere else to meet people we did not know. Sometimes we joined him if the posting was to last longer and other times, we would stay put to continue our education. He would visit us during his earned leave, or we joined him during our vacation. Luckily Dad had a 7-year continuous stint in Mumbai, during which time I graduated and got married to a pharmacist.

My mama's family visited us at all these places on the pretext of exploring a new city, staying at least for a fortnight and often more. Especially during the festivals, he was our permanent guest. Mom indulged him and his family at the risk of my Dad's annoyance. But he never said a word. On an early morning in June, sitting on the parapet wall of our veranda in Delhi, I was working on the periodic table. I was learning it by rote, group-wise, just like my teacher said. She often said we should memorise the periodic table the way we do our multiplication tables. Her opinion was it would make us understand the characteristics of the elements better and how they relate to each other.

I was recreating the table in my mind with my eyes closed; when I got to the seventh group of halogens, I felt a hand on my waist. I was wearing a legging and a loose white semi-transparent blouse with a considerable gap between the blouse and the legging as it was hot in Delhi at the time of year. I felt his hands touch the void rubbing it as one would knead the wheat flour dough to make Rotis. I opened my eyes to see my mama standing behind me, standing uncomfortably between the veranda and the garden. I was taken aback by this touch.

Mama smiled and said," I got you!" His hand was still on my bare skin. I noticed his fingers were also trying to find their way through the blouse. I forcefully removed his hand, not before letting a mildly intoxicating sensation consume me. He then smiled and walked away.

It took me some time to come out of the experience. Whenever mama visited us, I made sure I dressed appropriately and maintained as much distance away from him as possible. I dare not confide in mom on this matter. She would be upset.

Yet, he always found a way to touch me inappropriately. And all the time, I found the touch pleasurable, as much as I detested it. My brother, who was learning German for his proposed master's in Karlsruhe, told me about a German phrase - Schaden Freude, an expression to represent a person enjoying the misfortune of others. I wish the English language also finds a word or a phrase for my emotion. An emotion, instantaneously pleasurable yet loathsome immediately after. That would explain the reaction I felt whenever he touched me. I felt sad I couldn't take out the pleasure part though I was disgusted.

After a couple of years, my Dad was transferred to Mumbai, the Cuff Parade branch. Dad had risen in rank, and so did the standards of the accommodation given to us. It was a 4BHK apartment with one balcony overlooking the sea. I got admitted to Sydenham College of Commerce to pursue graduation in Economics, thanks to Dad's contacts. During Diwali vacation, my mama's family dropped in on the pretext of touring this new city, Mumbai. He had developed a paunch and looked like a grocery store merchant surrounded by dals, condiments and rice in gunny bags. He wore loose trousers and a striped shirt with one middle button missing, with his trademark yellow-stained baniyan missing too. I thought the baniyan was finally liberated. One could often see his hairy chest whenever he heaved and hoed himself.

A day before Diwali, which northerners call Choti Diwali, I was in my allocated room drying my hair under the fan after shampooing it vigorously. I was wearing a long loose blue-faded kurta top without any undergarment with shorts underneath. My legs were exposed. My head propped on my bed, and my hair hung over the cot's wooden head plank, allowing the breeze from the fan to extract the moisture from my hair. I was to dress later after the hair dried as the damp hair would wet the new dress I had planned to wear. To pass the time, I was reading the Diwali edition of a Telugu weekly, which Dad bought from a magazine kiosk outside Matunga station. This edition contained stories and serialised novels that won awards in *competitions conducted by the publications. New authors were getting discovered by this. Enthusiastic readers would rush to get hold of the copy before the stocks were exhausted.*

Immersed in the mag, I did not notice my mama entering my room quietly and bolting it. He came and sat next to me on the bed. It startled me. I quickly sat up ramrod straight. "What are you reading? Can I see?" he asked.

I did not answer but thrust the periodical into his hands. He flipped around and placed it on the table nearby.

"Where are Mami[8] and the kids?" I asked.

"They went shopping with your mom," he said.

"So early in the morning?" I said. Shops in Mumbai don't open till 11 unless they sell groceries. He did not answer. Later I learned that my mom took them to meet another Telugu family on the fourth floor for a social visit.

He then did the most unexpected. He laid his hand on my thigh and started caressing. My shorts were well, short – above my knees. I pushed his hand away. He slipped onto his knees on the floor with the upper part of the body over the bed and thrust his hands under my loose kurta; he started feeling my breasts. I tried to take his hands away forcibly, but he shoved me onto the bed, forcing me to fall on the slanting pillow propped up onto the cot head, which saved my skull from hitting the wooden mast. He lifted my legs over in a flash and made me flat on my back on the bed. He then lifted my shirt. He then started licking my nipples. I felt a strange sensation. I tried to push his head away forcibly with both hands, but I stopped struggling as an unknown weakness overtook me. Suddenly he pushed my shorts down and moved his hand between my legs, and his hand went all the way to my vagina, which was dripping wet. Instead of tightening

---

8 Mama's wife

my legs to prevent him from touching my privates, I spread my legs apart. His finger was now inside my damp vagina, working its way into the innards of ecstasy. I felt drowsy. I could not even see the swirling fan overhead.

Quickly better sense prevailed, and I twisted his ear hard with one hand and with the other I tried to pull and tear his hair, trying to push his head away from my breast. He lifted his head, rubbed his bruised ear, pulled his hand away from under my kurta, and walked out of the room. I went into the bathroom and cried. I washed my face and looked in the mirror to find a messy face staring back at me. I put my head under the shower, fully clothed. I undressed and showered again. I could not find any liquid soap to clean my vagina, so I used Listerine, which gave me a sharp tinge at first and a lot of soreness later.

The horrifying experience left a bad taste in me. I could not even tell my mom. How could I explain this to her? Your brother almost raped me!

I realised I was equally responsible for this embarrassment. Some external force guided me to accept the pleasure and the mental stress that followed. I became a malleable dough for him to mould me to suit his dirty designs as he saw fit. I hated him for making me enjoy a forbidden sin. But his acts were inexcusable. The only way I could go on with my everyday life was to bury them deep inside myself.

Nevertheless, they still troubled me, destroyed me emotionally, and turned me into an angry misandrist. I became suspicious of all men who would never let go of any occasion to lay their hands on a woman. They might even design an opportunity to find either a willing woman or a woman like me who doesn't have the will to say no. I promised myself I would never share this experience with anyone. Not even with my future husband.

ABDUL

Altaf Mallik was a man of measly desires. He managed to buy a three hundred square foot house from the funds he saved from his business.

Navrang Park Society was initially multi-ethnic, though Muslims were in the majority. A popular mosque and a madrasa nearby were the reason. Peace was shattered by a minor incident between the two ethnic communities. This episode led to more skirmishes that made the minority Hindus uncomfortable and insecure. Hindus from the Society left in droves, some even selling their abodes for paltry sums. Two Hindu families doggedly stayed put, displaying courage or defiance or helplessness.

The place Altaf bought has initially been a grocery shop with the main door leading to the Society entry lane, with a small opening on the sidewall jetted out towards the main road. This opening would allow outsiders who don't live in the Navrang Park Society to draw their daily necessities. The grocery owner, who was a Hindu Marwari, could not sustain his business with the strict rules of the Society and sold the premises to Altaf for a good bargain. The place had a mezzanine for storage of stocks of the shop, which was converted into two bedrooms by Altaf with a clever design. He kept one for him and Nazma; his daughters shared the other.

The house did not have a toilet facility, as the shop never needed one. Altaf had to illegally convert the space between the boundary wall and his home into a makeshift bathroom, draining the waste into an open gutter outside the society border limits. This necessary innovation resulted in regular visits of the local municipal sanitary engineers to his house to collect their monthly hafta[9]. It suited both parties.

The colony consisted of 46 houses, primarily single-storied, but a few had built a room or two above, ignoring municipal laws. The Society had many such deviations, and no authority dared to question the members or even send a formal notice, let alone penalize them. Vote-seeking politicians of all hues duly protected them.

The Society had two main streets with entry and exit manned by semi-professional security. Four cross streets presented the image of a well-laid colony, and it also had an open space initially reserved for a municipal park that never materialized. After convincing the local corporator[10] not to pursue a park, the residents used this available land for their Friday namaaz. On other days the space is liberally used for cricket and other sports by the colony's youth; Sunday evenings is for guftagu[11] time for the elders.

The entry into the gated Society was regulated for visitors not connected or related to the residents. However, some salesmen do sneak in from time to time. The society members would keep a tab on these intruders.

Mostly the Society was made secure for all the residents by the Elders.

Altaf made the colony members into one unified group and managed the colony's affairs with an iron hand. The society

---

9   Illegal weekly collections by local goons
10   Municipal elected representative
11   Informal meetings between friends

members well respected him for his efforts to keep the flock together in thick and thin. When the colony members had any doubts about the interpretation of Sharia, they would prefer to reach Altaf instead of a maulvi.

Altaf had raised Abdul from a very young age with much care and love. He wanted Abdul to be well educated and be a good Mussalman. Altaf admitted him to a nearby madrasa-e-Ahmad Mustafa.

Abdul had a curious mind and had questions that inspired Altaf to spend more time with him. Altaf insisted Abdul spend his vacation time with him in his workshop. He supplemented the education he was receiving from the Madrasa with his knowledge of the Quran, though he could not add much to his regular subjects like language, science, math, etc. Post dinner at night was usually when the father and son spent quality time with each other.

"Abbujaan, what is the difference between Ramadan and Ramzan? Why do some people call Ramzan as Ramadan?" asked Abdul.

"Both are the same. It is the end of fasting and time to celebrate," said Altaf, "Originally, we were influenced by Persians as the Islamic rulers had come from Persia and its neighbourhood. In Persian, it is Ramzan. But nowadays there is the influence of Arabs as many of our people go to Saudi and other Arab countries for jobs and use Ramadan instead of Ramzan."

"My teachers always correct us to use Ramadan instead of Ramzan."

"Most of these madrasas are funded by Saudi Arabia and other prosperous Islamic countries. These teachers are just being loyal to them. That's all. Similarly, you may have noticed the greeting "Khuda Hafiz" has changed to "Allah Hafiz", that is because lately,

Mussalmans want to be more demonstrative of their religious roots."

"My friend Hasmukh tells me that they have many castes in their religion, and one caste does not socialize with the other. Do Mussalmans also have such a caste system?"

"We don't have castes as such. But we have sects like the Hussain's, also called Shias. The battle at Karbala was to determine who represents the Prophet; may his grace bestow on us. One of the grandsons of the Prophet, peace be upon him, died in the battle, and some Mussalmans who have supported the grandson formed Shia sect to represent their lineage," said Altaf.

"Also, unlike the Hindus, when we pray, we don't segregate people based on their caste. The great warrior king Mohd Ghazni always prayed with his slave together, their knees touching," said Altaf. "Also, there are Sufi Muslims – who originated from Kashmir. Unlike us, they venerate shrines. We don't. Non-Muslims consider these Sufis as the secular version of Islam. This claim is debatable, though. Sufis are part of us, the Sunni Muslims. Sufis emphasize universal love, peace, acceptance of various spiritual paths and a mystical union with the divine. Their dance is a traditional form of Sufi worship, a continuous twirling with one hand pointed upward, reaching for the divine and the other hand pointed toward the ground."

"What is secular?"

"The dictionary definition of secularism is recognizing a multi-cultural and multi-religious society and respecting all religious orders are valid forms of worship", said Altaf.

"Then Sufis are more secular than we Sunnis?"

"Well, that is the belief the Sufis have propagated. But every good Muslim, whether Sunni, Shia or Sufi are, secular as per our holy Quran, and we in our household follow this path as enshrined in the Quran," said Altaf. "That is not all. We have Mussalmans across the country – in the south, in the north, and the east. Each has its own culture, language and food habits. But all follow the tenets of Islam as enshrined in Quran. Especially in south India. During my training at Chennai, I found that Mussalmans blended well across the Tamil Nadu Society, accepting their culinary tastes and culture than those in our own Gujarat or other northern states. Mussalmans in other parts of south too have mixed well with other religious sects of the Society by being a part of the local culture, with the sole exception of Hyderabad."

"Why not in Hyderabad?" asked Abdul.

"It is partly political and partly because of the preachers who are too aggressive in misinterpreting Quran for their benefit," said Altaf "It is regrettable these chasms have developed for which the devout and ordinary Muslim is paying a huge price".

"The other day, some new preacher had come and talked about Kafirs. And he referred to all Hindus as Kafirs!" said Abdul.

"Kafir is a derogatory term, and we should not use it. Kafir means who does not believe in Allah. But this is misused by some Mussalmans. They propagate that all those who don't worship Allah are Kafirs; they must be treated as infidels. But there are many other religions like Hinduism, Christianity, Judaism, Jainism and Buddhism that don't worship Allah, which does not mean they are Kafirs. Some very uddamwaadi[12] Muslims use it to refer to the idol-worshipping Hindus as Kafirs," said Altaf.

"What is uddamwaadi?"

---

12   Person with radical views. Word in Gujarati

"Uddamwaadi in Gujarati means one with rigid ideas and who is not open to reason that other forms of ideas, religions and beliefs exist."

"Whatever else happens in your life, Abdul, you must not forget the five pillars of Islam," said Altaf. He hadn't, and unlike so many children who might have grown up hearing the weary tales their parents told them, Abdul hung to his abbujaan's words.

Altaf had enough of this and asked him to go to bed, and he contemplated what his son was inquiring.

He realized the Madrasa he chose for Abdul may not have well-read and honest mullahs to give his boy secular education but driven him to learn a narrow view of Islam's holy book of surahs and ayats with an agenda-driven interpretation. He knew the Madrasa teachers had poor backgrounds and enrolled in free boarding schools during their training. They know only some rudimentary verses of the Quran and interpret what their masters told them. Such madrasas don't have enough resources to attract talent. The result is that the teachers are not well-versed in modern subjects his son had to learn to find jobs apart from the fact that their explanation of Islam is not entirely above board.

Although Altaf was attracted to the safe environment of these schools, he became aware that purely religious education would not help Abdul earn a decent living. Because of Madrasas' outdated, traditional methods and techniques of teaching and learning, with a peripheral approach towards current topics, job-oriented subjects such as science and mathematics are not taught with the required importance.

Altaf decided to shift Abdul from the Madrasa to a Christian missionary school that followed government-specified learning. Altaf was confident he could teach Quran and its practices better than any mullah.

Abdul joined the Convent of Jesus and Mary school in Fatehgunj.

Abdul was a bit uncomfortable singing hymns in praise of Jesus and mentioned the same to his Abbujaan.

"Even these Christian Missionary schools get funds from catholic organizations across the world just like our madrasas get from seminaries in the Middle East," explained Altaf, "so they too have to propagate their religion. But unlike the majority of madrasas, they give due importance to formal education and limit their religious interaction towards singing Bible hymns during morning prayers and celebrating Christmas with enthusiasm as we do during Ramadan. They don't thrust their religion on their pupils, as far as I know. That is one of the reasons you find many Hindu children get enrolled in these schools. Our Madrasas should learn from these schools and modernize their educational training! You will never find a Hindu, Jain, or Buddhist pursuing schooling in a Madrasa."

"But let me be clear. Some Madrasas led by Ulemas have played an important role in protecting Islamic social values. These institutions have also played an important role in the survival of Islamic practices, publication & dissemination of Islamic literature, protection of Islamic faith, development of its culture alongside contributing to the country's development."

Abdul continued his education in the missionary school and became one of the best outgoing students to complete his School Leaving Certificate Course. Abdul approached his abbu for advice on furthering his education.

"You better get admission into a polytechnic and get a diploma in civil engineering which would have good job opportunities in construction," advised Altaf, as some of his friends suggested.

"But Abbujaan, I want to go for inter and then graduation as suggested by Ameer's abbu," pleaded Abdul.

"You see, dear, it is tough to get jobs nowadays for non-professionals. And I don't think I can fund you for higher education, as my business income is insufficient for such extravagance. Also, we recently bought this house too. I can assure you that higher education does not guarantee jobs, as you would have noticed by now. Rahim *Chacha's* son graduated in science and could not get any job," Altaf said "he had to settle as a lab assistant in a diagnostic centre for a pittance of income."

So, Abdul became a civil engineer. He temporarily worked in an Architectural firm on a daily worker basis for a year before he managed to land a job with Patel and Patel Constructions.

Raj Krishna

Like all women, men also have expectations, desires, and hopes regarding their life partners. Most men relate their knowledge of women to their mothers or sisters, who would be the only women he would have interacted with intimately. Raj did not have the privilege of networking with the opposite gender in school or during graduation in Hyderabad. He believed that exhausted, tired and menstruating women behave differently, which was impossible to observe in female classmates. In his time, there was no live-in concept.

Raj had to list acceptable behaviour of his life partner based on his home data on how his mother was treated and his idea of a good companion. He mentally prepared the bullet points and stored them for eventual recall. Raj also promised himself not to insult, belittle and scorn women, which his dad often did to his mother. His dad never cared for his mom's interests, and he was selfish in marriage. Raj disapproved of what his mom had to go through in her life and promised himself he would be a good husband.

He also wished he would have a wife who took sides with him in his decisions and respected anyone he respected. And she would help in getting her younger sister married by sacrificing or postponing her wants.

***

In Indian arranged marriages, the first night of sleeping together is a ritual. It is discussed threadbare with friends before the event. Everyone would have an opinion on how to go about it – based on hearsay or their own experiences. Women would be warned it would be painful. Men would be cautioned if one was a virgin (which Raj was, a botched attempt in a whorehouse, notwithstanding); the premature ejaculation could be the point of derisive laughter by the bride.

Thus both participants would be nervous.

Vaidehi was bolder. If she had any jitters, she did not show. Raj learnt the techniques of extending his orgasm thanks to plentiful reading and friends' advice. He was confident. He hoped his frequent masturbation did not affect his performance. What surprised Raj was when his mother-in-law, while gently showing the way to the bedroom, said, "Go, enjoy".

That was audacious. Some of her mother's traits were evident in Vaidehi. He was to learn later. Vaidehi wore a simple mango-shaped image printed in green on a white cotton saree with an orange border and had some scented flowers tucked in her hair. She appeared high-spirited. She could sting with her energy. While they discussed the topic of protection, they mutually decided Raj would use a condom until a final call on their family extensions is debated later. Raj was anxious to touch and feel her breasts. The shape and enormity of her breasts were a reason for accepting her as his bride. They quickly undressed and allowed nature to take its course.

Raj and Vaidehi had terrific sex life for many years. They tried all positions in the house – on the bed, on the sofa, on the dining hall, on a chair - with Vaidehi being the dominant and willing partner. On this count, Raj could never complain. Raj always felt he was lucky to have a partner like Vaidehi to fulfil his carnal pleasures. From his side, also, he practised all he had learnt on holding orgasms until the partner had her fill. She had fully rounded buttocks which made missionary positions extremely pleasurable to both. Understandably Vaidehi also enjoyed those moments and was willingly available whenever the opportunity arose.

At other times Raj found a different Vaidehi who wanted to dominate.

I sat down to lunch on the first day of her cooking session in our married life. A rectangular steel plate came up with a yellow dal and rice. At the far right corner, placed a morsel of a pickle. At my home, we ate on round steel plates. Rectangular ones were new to me. Every house had its own culture. I had better get used to this change. Marriage was, after all, a compromise.

"What dal is this?" I asked.

"Why are you asking without tasting? Taste and let me know," she said.

'Answering a question by a question is typical of all wives,' my much-married friends told me. As those were the early days of my marriage, I had ignored the outburst.

As I finished what was on the plate, she asked," Could you identify the dal?"

"Mango?" I hesitatingly suggested.

"No Madras cucumber," she said.

"But it was very sour, so I thought it was mango," I explained.

"I added a bit of tamarind."

My mother never uses tamarind for preparing dal. She leaves the ingredients' original flavour untouched. So she picks only those veg additives to dal that are intrinsically sour. For instance, she always told me to pick only round tomatoes and not oval-shaped ones.

"Oval shaped ones will not be sour, Krishna. Get these exchanged if you can."

I had to forget my mom's culinary method and learn to appreciate my wife's. It was a part of growing up together, I think.

"You want some more?"

"No, that's enough," I said.

"Why, you don't like my cooking? I may not be as good as your mother. As per my mother's recipes, I cook," said Vaidehi, "I prepared a large quantity thinking you would like dals, as your mother told me recently."

She large-spooned some more from the main vessel and pushed it onto my plate. I ate with deceptive relish just not to hurt her sentiments.

Raj was exposed to such unpredictable behaviour of his wife from time to time.

"I always wanted to marry a doctor," said Vaidehi, while adjusting her saree post a Sunday afternoon quickie.

"Then why didn't you?"

"I informed my parents of my wish, and they had tried their best. This guy completed MBBS from Kurnool medical college and was employed as a duty doctor at Kakinada," said Vaidehi, "he tried to complete Post-graduation too. Yet, he failed the three times in the entrance test. He came to see me from Kakinada accompanied by his mother. He was not exactly Devanand but was good looking. He was his farmer-parents only son. He promised he would try harder and get an MD qualification within the next two years in a person-to-person talk. I rejected him," said Vaidehi.

"Why?" asked Raj.

"A doctor was, of course, my first preference, but my husband should have an outlook that comes from living across cultures in the country. This guy lived all his life in Andhra Pradesh only. Such people would have a narrow view of dealing with educated women from bigger cities. Therefore, I told my dad my husband would have to have exposure to all cultural hues."

"Then my dad's colleague arranged for another alliance, also a doctor. His academic achievements were extraordinary – he graduated from AIIMS and PG from Chandigarh. However, he looked sissy, short and dark in complexion. Also, his MD was in gynaecology. Creepy. He would look at my vagina not as a sex object but as an organ of his study. I did not think twice about rejecting him too," said Vaidehi.

"All doctors are the same," said Raj.

"True. But Postgraduates in ophthalmology, clinical biochemistry, radiology, pathology, microbiology are not so much organ fixated," countered Vaidehi.

"So that was how I got trapped!" said Raj mockingly.

"Pharmacy was closest to the medical line. Therefore, I compromised. I was also impressed by your work across the country, which would have exposed you to other cultures and cuisines, and above all, you graduated in Mumbai as I did. That was the clincher," said Vaidehi.

She got up from the sofa and walked out into the kitchen to make coffee for herself while Raj took the mandatory Sunday siesta.

***

Later years that bond had changed so much that anyone who would have been privy to earlier bedroom exploits would wonder what had caused the chasm. Sometimes when other issues took precedence, she was a different person altogether. During such times, the real Vaidehi took over.

The first two years of our married life in Mumbai were a breeze. Vaidehi's parents were still in Mumbai, and we spent our weekends with them. Our most memorable routine was on Sunday. We caught the 123 from Colaba bus station, sat on the top deck, went past the marine drive and alighted at Taraporewala, walked to Chowpatty, had typical Mumbai snacks for dinner, and walked back to Nariman Point. She proudly pointed to me her alma mater, Sydenham College of Commerce, near Churchgate station. That was our routine on Sundays. Saturdays, we spent time with my in-laws gossiping or watching a matinee. My mother-in-law was a good cook, and I immensely enjoyed her recipes. Some Sundays, we walked from their home near President Hotel to Nariman point and watched the sunset, munching fried peanuts. We always got back to our home at seven bungalows the same night, as I had to attend office the next day.

This pattern was changed when her father persuaded his Bank Management to post him back to his hometown in Vishakhapatnam to complete his last days in service, pending retirement. In addition, Vaidehi was pregnant with her first child. She had some complications and was advised bed rest. That ended our little honeymoon. However, even during our in-frequent bedroom rendezvous, she conceived again within two years, and we were bestowed with another pretty daughter. Later I got busy with my career, she with the children. I had wisely resisted the temptation to guide, help and monitor Vaidehi in child-rearing, which anyway was being remotely controlled by her mother. I let her be.

As a child, my elder daughter, Sagarika, shared my enthusiasms for life's indulgences but later, when she was fifteen, she shifted her allegiance to her mother. When she had grown enough to be of marriage age, my father-in-law took control and managed to find her a groom from our own Brahmin sect. The marriage was performed in Vishakhapatnam as, coincidentally, the parents of my soon to be son-in-law too lived. I attended the wedding as a guest.

My second daughter, Spandana, was more rebellious and insisted her education was a top priority. Thus she firmly resisted her granny's attempt to find a boy for her.

After a couple of years, she succumbed to the temptations of Cupid and announced she would marry a boy from Patna, Bihar, who was her classmate. It created quite a stir in the house. Vaidehi blamed me for giving in to her indulgences. Spoilt child, she lamented. Vaidehi had always imagined things from hearsay; she presumed all northerners were misogynists, women beaters, treated women as doormats, and her daughter would later regret her decision. Spandana was adamant. She explained that both of them had been placed by HSBC bank in Singapore, and they would not be staying with his parents, even presuming his parents were the authoritarian type, while she objected to the reference. Spandana did not inform my wife that she spent a week in Patna at would-be in-law's home while dating her future husband, as he insisted on the same. Finally, everything went off well. It helped that both of our families were vegetarians.

We had performed the marriage in Mumbai, Shivajipark hall, with some rituals of their traditions and few as per our Vaidiki Brahmin norms. Within a month, they left for Singapore, where they are living now. Vaidehi's parents could not attend the marriage of Spandana, as they were ill. Vaidehi's parents died a few months later, within two months of each other.

Raj's married life had always been a life of turmoil and unhappiness. The signs he recognised from his childhood life were there – the insults, the affronts, the ridicules. Vaidehi had a habit of announcing her decisions in all matters and would only ask for opinions to endorse her decision. She continued to refer to his not so upscale life in Hyderabad by pointing to his silly misdemeanours– such as slurping tea, choice of clothes, greeting style with her relatives and the like. He wondered where he erred in relationship management. He had given her more freedom than his mother had received from his father, as he promised himself — respect for a woman's right to individuality. But did he let the door not ajar but fully open!

Raj imagined that most people live in denial that a man starts to lose his freedom after marriage. Raj did not understand household chores and couldn't be trusted to pour coffee into a cup from the kettle without spilling a drop or two on the kitchen platform. Any wife would be annoyed, let alone Vaidehi – not for spilling but leaving it spilt. She would look at Raj with one of those stern looks all teachers use when the child is doodling without paying attention to them. Eric Berne would categorise these transactions as Parent-Child. Treating an adult as a child is insulting.

Raj wanted a woman who could satiate his sexual wants, gratify his palate peculiarities, and be a good mother and housekeeper. After years of life with Vaidehi, Raj realised that those were not the only characteristics one's wife should have. She should trust her husband, ignore his quirks, and don't question his every action. She had failed on those fronts.

Raj had to find an outlet for his frustrations at home.

As long as you don't boast about your sexual exploits to all and sundry, you would have many opportunities to find willing women. The pleasure-seeking women are scared of the bragging nature of men as it would expose them. I realised soon enough that discretion is the better part of valour. It worked to my advantage. There is a vast difference between men who abuse vulnerable women and men who respond to or spot a woman looking for gratification. With my childhood experience of my mother's travails, I was not interested in taking advantage of weak women.

Raj had an uncanny ability to spot a woman who needed sexual gratification. He shifted his allegiance from his office-mate widow to sixth-floor spinster to one of Vaidehi's friends. He found it was advantageous to have a pretty wife. Other plain Janes would try to cultivate you to prove they are better in bed, companionship and intellect. He moved from one affair to another while Vaidehi was busy with her household activities of raising children and other society indulgences Mumbai life offered.

Based on her reading of other men's perceived behavioural patterns, Vaidehi interrogates, doubts, and is perennially suspicious of potentially adulterous activities. But she could not pin down Raj. His frequent travels helped him to cover up his casual affairs. But she knew something was amiss. Sixth Sense of a woman. She is the last person to give up on any such doubtful behaviour. She decided to confront him.

***

Men had never bothered what a woman wore, as long as she helped him remove her clothing part by part; pin by pin; hook by hook. Vaidehi knew it. Her gestures and body language could arouse and consume him. Raj's eyes moved around like a bee buzzing and waiting to sting. She need not utter a word. When they had violent sex in their youthful years, she would be spent and sometimes seemed to lose consciousness. Such was her involvement in their lovemaking. Especially when she was on top of him, she would violently do sit-ups, rub her clitoris viciously against his penis, and suddenly fall on him, totally exhausted. She did not want that to happen today.

So, she took her time by playing coy seductively. Vaidehi had other pressing matters on her mind. Raj needed to be tamed, not aroused. She needed him to be composed enough to understand her inquisitive interrogations. Vaidehi knew a man would be most vulnerable post-coitus and would be willing to bid to her whims and fancies. She ought to have a perfect setting; she needed that moment to get an unrehearsed reaction before he returned to his usual self. But she could be spent too. After all, she enjoyed it as much as he does. He was a consummate and sensitive lover. She had to fake an orgasm so that she was not totally out of breath for the impending questions.

They were on their backs, covering their nakedness with a duvet. Raj closed his eyes while enjoying the fan's swirling breeze. She turned towards him, with her naked breasts touching his hairy chest and murmured, "Did you enjoy it?"

The standard question every woman asks her man. A trap into which every man inevitably falls.

"Yes, of course, and you?"

"I too," said Vaidehi, "can I ask you a question?"

"Yes, anything," answered Raj sheepishly.

"Am I the only woman in your life?" asked Vaidehi

"What kind of questions is that you silly? Of course, yes, "replied Raj, surprised by the sudden change in her mood. He immediately realised that he was being trapped in admitting his clandestine getaways.

Fortunately for Raj, the discussion ended then and there itself. A doubt indeed lingered in Vaidehi's mind, significantly affecting their subsequent bedroom sessions.

When a woman doubts the fidelity of her partner, she would never be at peace to seek pleasures from him. Women can abandon the conjugal relationship under the slightest doubt of their partner's unfaithfulness. More so, a strong-willed woman like Vaidehi.

ABDUL

Abdul decided to try his luck with construction companies in Gujarat. His part-time employment with the Architecture firm did not assure him growth – either in learning or in emoluments. He sent applications and resumes to all and sundry. No luck.

Altaf requested Quadri Pasha to help Abdul to find a suitable job.

Quadri Pasha's acquaintance with Venkateshwar Rao of Patel and Patel Constructions (PPC) facilitated Abdul to get an interview call. Venkateshwar Rao was one of the partners of the construction company involved mainly in building apartment complexes in Vadodara, Ahmedabad and Surat. Venkateshwar was originally from Nellore in Andhra Pradesh and migrated to Gujarat to pursue an engineering course in Surat. On completing his graduation in civil engineering, his Gujarati classmate suggested he join him in his family business. Venkateshwar could convince his dad to invest in the Company, which proved to be a masterstroke as the business grew in leaps and bounds. Soon Venkateshwar had taken responsibility for all construction activities of the firm in the Vadodara area as a separate profit centre, leaving the other partners to concentrate on other cities.

Abdul had just walked into the office of Patel and Patel Constructions in the Padra area at the appointed hour. The office appeared to be of modest means, with around ten tables, only five occupied. He found four cabins on the right side of his entrance. A man with a pandharpur-devotee cap, betel-chewed red-stained lips and a tray with teacups accosted him.

"*Kisko milne ka hai?*[13]" the man inquired. Abdul answered him.

"*Jamni baaju ma chella cabin*[14]," he said in Gujarati.

Abdul walked past the corridor and saw the first cabin was unoccupied, which had a walnut coloured table with chairs. The second one had a round table, five chairs, and a whiteboard with something scribbled. The third one had a stout man talking to an elderly lady.

All cabins had doors with the top half fitted with a semi-transparent glass except the fourth one, which had an opaque designer glass. The fourth was a large one, the size of a bedroom in modest flats, which Abdul presently knocked hesitatingly. A voice said," Come in."

Abdul entered silently and closed the door behind him.

The voice belonged to a man in his late forty's, thin but not bony, dark-complexioned with a jet-black crop of hair, neatly parted and combed, with round spectacles slid onto his nose end, browsing through a legal document in front of him. An oversized swivel chair held him in the sitting position. Venkateshwar Rao lifted his head pushed his spectacles up, and noticed a clean-shaven young man in dark brown pants with an embroidered white shirt tucked, holding a plastic folder to his chest. Obedience personified. He signalled the entrant to sit.

"Would you like a cup of tea, young man?" asked Venkateshwar.

"No, thank you, sir."

---

13 Who do you want to meet?
14 Last cabin from the left

Without any formal introduction, the man with a timbre voice spoke. It appeared Quadri Pasha had briefed him.

"We are not presently hiring engineers, and I would never allow my friendship to influence me in a matter that would involve this firm. But in your case, I am willing to make an exception provided you shall agree to work as a coordination engineer and customer interface," said Venkateshwar Rao.

"Sure, sir, does it involve sales, sir?" said Abdul.

As if I have a choice!

"No sales. You will surely be at the site to coordinate with various contractors apart from interacting with customers who come to the site to check the progress of their flat. Your work won't be direct with me, but you will find I am easily accessible. I am pleased that you will be with us, and I trust you will never give us any cause for regret. Our Company is one of the finest establishments in Vadodara's building industry sphere, and we mean to keep it that way."

"Presently, you will report to Admin manager Mr Ghosh."

Venkateshwar Rao led Abdul to the next cabin and introduced him to Sambit Ghosh.

"Ghoshbabu, please train and initiate Abdul into our Company. He is the same person I discussed with you yesterday when you asked for a technical person to assist you in coordinating the contractors' activities."

Venkateshwar Rao left the cabin leaving the two to interact. Ghosh was a stout man with a round face and bald head. The chair he sat on could not contain his bulk, yet he did not appear to be in any discomfort. He motioned the elderly lady to leave his room so he could spend time with Abdul. Sambit Ghosh had been with the Company for over ten years. He was considered loyal by all partners of the Company. All the mandatory paperwork required for the smooth functioning of the business was his responsibility, which he performed with élan. No one in the Company knew his qualifications, but he was a Man-Friday for the Company, and all the partners trusted him with bank-loan related works of buyers. He was the first customer interface to solve disputes or disagreements. For legal documentation, the firm hired professional lawyers. His voice betrayed his size. It was low key and friendly. Ghosh explained to Abdul the woes of the construction industry and how he had to work within given constraints.

The apartment construction industry in India is most maligned amongst all business establishments. Construction delays have plagued the sector for quite some time now. Many developers are also at fault for using the funds of one project for another. It is estimated that from the initial advance amounts the buyer pays, at least 30% is diverted to fund the next project. The reasons are mainly greed to grow big quickly and partly to spread the risk amongst many projects. For a housing project in a metro city, a developer needs innumerable regulatory approvals to start construction. It takes anywhere from several months to a year or even more. It not only delays a project but also increases the cost of the property by 10-20% for both buyers and developers. The industry cannot acquire any institutional funding to operate even though they employ many people – last estimated to be 40 million. They depend on buyers' home loan schemes to fund their projects. This industry is the most symbiotic in commerce: dependence on the buyer /vendor/seller interface. The industry hired researchers had analysed to conclude that medium-scale construction establishments such as Patel and Patel Constructions faced many problems. These are related to clients' delayed payments (clients also don't help with proper documentation for the banks to disburse quickly), fluctuation in material costs, worker absenteeism, and others. PPC also did not believe in recruiting the staff for their roles – white and blue-collar – to avoid compliance with cumbersome labour laws and the labour department staff's interpretation of these rules. Venkateshwar had to make an exception by recruiting Abdul.

"Most of our design work is outsourced to an Architect firm in Ahmedabad. After, the plot is selected, and its viability concerning the income levels of the people hoping to live is checked, the partners give the contract to this firm, which does the survey, design, and makes all project drawings. Except for one partner, all are civil engineers, ensuring the project does not exceed the budget and ensures aesthetics and utility. To that extent, we consider ourselves the best in the state, if not the country," said Ghosh proudly.

"So I will have no desk role?" asked Abdul.

"Not completely. Most of the design and drawing work is frozen before laying the foundation stone. But sometimes, some buyers would request changes based on their versions of Vaastu compatibility or some other family quirks, which may require the tweaking of the construction drawings. We presently have to request a consultant to help us out in such cases. Though they will not object to such modifications, they delay the delivery of drawings as it is given the lowest priority amongst their other urgencies. So we decided to fix these modifications in-house. So that is also one of the many reasons we have recruited you."

"Whatever you have learned in your course will be helpful, and Sir will give guidance and train you," he added.

"Sir also referred to coordination jobs I am to handle? What could those be?" asked Abdul.

"We face synchronisation problems with various contractors working at the site, delaying our works, annoying the buyers, and affecting our cash flow. You might know sanitary, electrical, carpentry and tiling works are typically taken up at the end of the civil works after the base structure is completed. We hire different contractors to perform these functions. We find the management of these diverse contracting companies needs improvement. And we needed a single person to coordinate all the activities. If any contractor's personnel is absent, all the other works get held up. Some contractors do not inform their absenteeism to circumvent the censure by the site engineer for delays. So they employ unskilled labours to fulfil the duties that otherwise need to be attended to by skilled workers. It affects the quality."

"Also, there is significant attrition of our site engineers. Site work is tough, and one is exposed to the elements of nature all the time. Only a tough engineer can survive these conditions. These days because of IT employment opportunities for engineers – irrespective of their domain area – there is a mass exodus to the IT sector. Many civil engineers we employ take up our job only as a stop-gap with no long term commitment. Also, the large construction companies such as L&T, Mittals, Lodha's, Rahejas etc., pouch our trained engineers," said Ghosh.

Ghosh instructed the lady with whom he was interacting when Abdul walked in to introduce him to other company members and show him where the construction drawings were stored. Abdul studied the structural drawings and other layout drawings of the projects under construction, the details of which were far beyond his comprehension. He decided to improve and upgrade his knowledge of AutoCAD to contribute better to his work.

Venkateshwar Rao was busy with board meetings with his partners and could not find time to spend with Abdul. However, he introduced Abdul to his other partners during one such meeting.

"We have many expectations from you. Technical knowledge alone will not do in our kind of business. Man management, scheduling and cost control are important. I am sure Venkat will explain these in detail later," said Hasmukh Patel, one of the partners.

Abdul nodded and assured them he would do his best.

***

After a couple of weeks of initiation, Venkateshwar requested Abdul to study their upcoming prestigious project.

"We shall be going to our Project in Sama Area – we are developing a 15-storied building with three blocks each block of 150 flats. This project is huge and prestigious for our Company. For the next two years, I want you to take care of this project as a coordinator. We have two site engineers – both civil and senior members of our Company. But your job will be independent and shall report to Ghoshbabu and me directly," said Venkateshwar. They were presently going to the site in a Hyundai car driven by Venkateshwar.

"What kind of coordination work do I have to do, sir?"

"I think Ghoshbabu would have already explained the interfacing problems between various contractors. We had many snags in our previous project, which delayed the project beyond the schedule, annoyed our customers, and affected our cash flow. However, this project has not come to that stage yet. We just completed the slab work till the final floor. We shall be starting the brick masonry for the walls next week. But we are yet to finalise the sanitary, electrical and flooring contractors," said Venkateshwar.

"Sir, you already have approved contractors at the other sites for these jobs. Can't you use them?" wondered Abdul.

"You are right. But we want a different approach to this project by bringing fresh talent from outside of Vadodara. We don't mind some higher costs because of this. But we want to approach this project with a focused approach to this contractor coordination. Since core activities of construction companies revolve around contracting engagements, we want a systematic approach to these issues of interfacing," explained Venkateshwar.

They reached the site while discussing the various instances where the coordination with sub-contractors could have been better. "That's not all. Another important aspect is customer interaction, which I want you to help me handle," said Venkateshwar while locking the car in the parking area. Venkateshwar introduced Abdul to Raman and Desai – the civil engineers who came to the car to greet him. "Please go around the site and see the progress and come back. I will be with these boys to take stock of the situation," said Venkateshwar.

Abdul was overwhelmed by the responsibility entrusted to him with no experience in such works. He wondered what Quadri Pasha had told Venkateshwar about him. Abdul felt a chilling feeling he might not measure up. The redeeming part of these discussions was Venkateshwar had promised Abdul to hand-hold him during his work, take him under his tutelage, and train him. The salary wasn't huge, but he had engineered enough out of it to help abbujaan run the house.

It took four more months for the civil works to be completed on the project, now named Tirupathi Towers A, B and C. Meanwhile, Abdul acquired more knowledge of construction methods and also practised AutoCAD. There was hardly any interaction with the Boss during this time. However, Ghosh guided him when he had any queries on the admin aspect of the project, and at the site, Raman helped him. Raman was middle-aged with over 15 years of experience in civil construction.

Abdul visited the other Patel and Patel Constructions completed projects to learn about the project's glitches during the contractor interface. He found two significant problems, which he discussed with Raman.

"Sir, I visited the Padra Road building and interacted with the flat members. They had too many complaints on the construction quality," said Abdul.

"It was one of the earliest projects of PPC before I joined PPC, but I knew that the construction and other infra works required much better supervision," Raman clarified.

"The contractor did not maintain slopes in bathrooms to enable draining, which resulted in a stagnant pool of wastewater leaking to the floor below through the gaps of the tiles. He did not also lay the tiles as per standards. The repair work was a pain in such cases," explained Raman.

"The bathroom belonged to an upper floor resident who had no problem, but the floor below had to face the leaks, which was annoying. The upper floor member had to permit repair, and not many residents cooperated. The members of the building thus often clashed amongst themselves because of this. Many such problems existed in the electrical works also. For instance, they fixed the control switches for fans seven feet above the floor, which an average female cannot reach. An old lady showed me how she used a ruler to get to the switch to operate the fan."

"Thanks for the information, sir. I shall work under your guidance to ensure these things don't recur in Tirupathi Towers," said Abdul.

"Please don't call me sir; I am Raman for you," said Raman.

"Okay, Raman," said Abdul smilingly.

During further interactions with Raman and Desai, Abdul noted he needed to certify the contractors' personnel only after approving and validating their work at other sites. He ensured the replacement workers to counter absenteeism of regular staff should also be approved by him. The Tower B superstructure was completed, and brick masonry for walls and fixing the window grills were fast-paced and ahead of schedule. The material lift has been dismantled and carried to Tower A. The lift ducts inside the building were awaiting the equipment and the service staff to install the elevators.

"When are we installing the lifts?" asked Abdul while having lunch with Raman, Desai and a centring contractor inside their container site office.

"We have the ducts and wiring ready, but the passenger lift body shall be placed after all the workers leave the site," said Raman.

"Do you expect our supervisors to climb the stairs for quality control?" asked Abdul.

"In this building, we are fixing a hoist lift at the end of the corridors for materials, tools, and other equipment to be taken to floors. The same shall also be used for workers and supervising engineers," said Desai.

During further analysis, Abdul had learnt that the passenger lifts were the last item to be installed in apartment complexes, with no provision for work lifts – except in large projects. He surmised this could be one of the reasons for the supervisors not being willing to climb stairs to check the workers' performance. Sometimes he noticed the shoddy work happens for many other reasons – not just lack of supervision alone. The sub-contractor would replace absentee workers with unskilled or semi-skilled workers, especially plumbing and electrical jobs. He made a list of such errors, which he shared with his Boss:

The sanitary-ware suppliers did not conduct any formal training on the fitment of their   state-of-the-art wares as part of their supply contract. An expensive Jaguar tap would have a GI elbow brought from the local market with poor threading, thus degrading the functioning of a fancy brand.

Lack of records of pressure testing of pipelines.

No supervision on the bathroom floor-tile sloping.

Lack of electrical-wiring drawings; no quality check of peripherals used in the works such as glues, pipefittings, threading tools, electrical goods and the like.

Abdul promised himself he would ensure these snags were adequately attended to in his job.

ALTAF MALLIK

As years passed, Navrang Park Society showed glimpses of prosperity. One could find SUVs and Sedans parked on the road. Quadri Pasha, who had a hosiery outlet in a mall in the Alkapuri area, who could even build a double-storeyed structure. Illegal, of course.

Altaf's expanding family obligations did not allow him to pursue his house expansion. Also, his house was adjacent to the gate adjoining the Society compound wall. Any structure on the home will attract the attention of random municipal officials travelling on that road which can invite avoidable hassles. He already faced enough problems with the toilet he had erected.

Their second son, Munaaf was a polio-affected child with a muscular disorder; he walked with great difficulty and a limp. For longer walks, he needed support. Nusrat was stocky like her abbu but petite, unlike him. Her nikah was a constant worry and an element for endless debates between the parents. Nazma often tried to persuade both the father and son to find Nusrat a suitor, even if it was a second or third marriage. Nusrat had not been taking care of her physique as an unmarried woman should. She was too indulgent in red meat; eventually, it showed up on her figure. Yet Nazma recommended her cousin's much-married son Nazir as a would-be suitor.

"Nazir had no children from either of his two wives and has promised to take care of Nusrat. My cousin's family is known to be liberal and respect women," pleaded Nazma.

"I will not want my daughter to be a tawaif or a child-bearing machine. The age difference is over fifteen years!" thundered Altaf. "This we discussed many times. Please do not raise this matter again."

And he retired to bed. A few months later, bad luck struck Altaf Mallik.

***

Altaf had just shut off DD-Gujarati on a fateful night and was about to retire to bed when the phone rang.

He rushed to his workshop on his second hand Honda mobike. He shouted at his wife to close the door after him, which woke up all his children. Altaf's household members were awake the whole night, not knowing what to do. Nazma tried to push Abdul to go and find out where Altaf was. But lack of transport in the middle of the night prevented any such search. They decided to wait till morning.

Just as azan rang out from the nearby mosque, Altaf rode his bike into the front of the house and snuffed out the engine and dismounted without looking at anyone. He appeared devastated. He was never like that. He usually kept his emotions to himself. Today it was clear something had gone wrong. Nazma did not dare ask him lest he might shout at her. Meanwhile, Altaf suddenly broke down.

"We have lost everything Nazma," Altaf said, sobbing. Children had never seen their abbujaan like this. And then explained the tragedy that would change his family's lifestyle. Last night, the car painting and denting shop adjoining Altaf's unit caught fire seemingly because of an electrical short circuit. The highly combustible oil-based paints and the rags used to clean up added the necessary fuel to the fire. It was spontaneous combustion.

The tin roof of Altaf's business caved in. Piles of burnt tyres, sorted and stacked by type, told the story of a successful business reduced to rubble. A nearby mattress maker also suffered huge losses. The next day the rumours were rife on how the fire started. Some locals tried to give the fire communal overtones by suggesting all the three gutted shops belonged to Muslims and local Hindus must have had a hand in it. Already one local tabloid picked up the story and planted doubt in the mind of its readers, attributing the account to a local maulvi. But Altaf doused the rumours by showing the evidence of an electrical fire. This made-up story died its natural death, fortunately.

Altaf recollected his conversation with a salesman who strolled into their Society when he was having his Sunday afternoon tea on his front doorstep. A short man with a sharp nose and a scar on his temple had approached him with a proposal for fire insurance for his house. The scar-face told him it would be a veritable disaster if something happened to the house. Altaf realised he should have listened to him, though not for his home, at least for his workshop, making him feel rather stupid now.

Altaf was aware it would take months, if not a year, to bring the business back to its original glory. His father-in-law again helped him to recover by lending some cash. He rebuilt the shed and cleared the debris. But the problem of customer property lost in the fire was an issue to be tackled. Altaf hoped with a bank loan; he could even manage that. The local bank branch was helpful with an immediate cash loan secured by his house in Navrang Park Society.

"I want to pull out Munaaf from school and use him in the workshop," declared Altaf a month after the tragedy. The family sat for dinner around a mound of Gosht[15] Biryani and mirchi-ka-

---

15   Urdu for mutton

salan[16]. The discussion came around the plans for the future of the workshop.

"But abbu, how can he be helpful with his limp?" quizzed Munni, their young daughter, the only person who could dare question her dad.

"I can manage," countered Munaaf. Munaaf was sounded earlier by Altaf on his plan. Altaf was eager to have Munaaf handle the customer interaction. Many customers do not pick up readied tyres even though Altaf shared the information about the readiness of the work entrusted. Munaaf could persuade them to pick their merchandise, citing the fire event.

Abdul interjected," Abbujaan, I can quit my job and join you so I can take care of customers, and you can manage the fabrication and repair part of the workshop."

"No, that is not recommended. At least one person in the house should have a regular income," Altaf declared with the finality of a boss.

For unfortunate eventualities, Altaf wanted to add but did not.

"Abdul beta, you are well aware we have fixed your nikah to be performed in a couple of months. If you resign your job now, the nikah could be cancelled, which will be a great setback for our family izzat[17]," Nazma objected.

"Also, bhaijaan, you got promoted to Supervisor recently," proudly added Munni. Munni was very fond of her brother and respected him for his contribution to the family's wellbeing.

Abdul had been with Patel and Patel Constructions for over 8 yrs. as the business grew, the proprietors had reposed faith in Abdul's sincerity and craft. They made him a supervisor

---

16   A Mughlai culinary dish

17   dignity

responsible for upcoming buildings in Surat, Valsad apart from new sites in Vadodara. He was the last snag -detector cum facilitator for the houses before being handed over to customers. He had found half a dozen things at the construction sites that could do with some improvement. His commitment, more than his skill, had helped the efficiency of all the contractors, and the flats delivery increased a great deal, for which he was duly rewarded.

"Nothing doing; you are not quitting the job. That's final," reaffirmed Altaf.

"But abbu, how shall Munaaf travel to the workshop? "

"It is taken care of. Rahim Chacha promised to give his second hand Maruti Omni for hire. We can adapt the entry door to suit wheelchair entry for Munaaf," said Altaf.

Rahim Chacha owned a car workshop next to Altaf's unit from where the fire emanated. He had incurred similar losses. Actually, much more. He usually did not keep vehicles in his workshop for the night, but one SUV came for a denting job which got delayed because one of his staff did not report to duty. The SUV was completely gutted in the fire. Rahim was at his wit's end on how to assuage his customer.

Even though the car was insured, the insurance company does not give full money as it just disburses as per their rules, which often are at least thirty per cent less than the actual repair cost.

The issue flared up, and Altaf, along with another member of the shopkeepers association, solved the matter – by sharing the extra cost the customer had to incur over and above the insurance money. Rahim had to forego his labour charges also. Rahim had decided he needed more working capital and therefore decided to lease his second-hand car to Altaf.

"But we don't have a wheelchair for Munaaf to travel and move around!" said Nusrat. To complement her size, Nusrat also had a high decibel larynx.

"I think I can manage that matter. Ameer's wife works for a hospital; they regularly auction their condemned wheelchairs, one of which we can pick up and refurbish the same," suggested Abdul.

"What will Munaaf do as he cannot move around?" asked Nusrat.

"As I told your ammijaan, I have a massive problem of a stock pile-up of finished material which the customers are not picking up despite repeated requests. I want Munaaf to regularly follow up and threaten them with an auction if they don't pick up within a stipulated time and manage the accounting end of the business. I cannot afford to employ anyone now. I need him now," said Altaf.

"This will only be for two years max, after which Munaaf will go back to school," reassured Altaf to all family members. "I wouldn't want Asif to join me in the business, as we are now running with much lower capacity because of the fire that destroyed most of our stores. I already have Munaaf with me, and we can manage". Abdul continued his job, and Munaaf managed the customer end of the business at the workshop.

***

"Altaf Bhai, you have pulled out Munaaf from school?" asked Narendra Solanki.

Narendra Solanki was a PT teacher in the school where most boys from the Society studied. His wife, Jayshree, was also a botany teacher in the same school. Theirs was one of the two Hindu houses in an otherwise predominantly Muslim locality.

Presently the members of the community were gossiping, sitting on a semi-circular bench in the open land of the Society. It was their regular Sunday meeting. The meeting was called mainly to discuss the ruckus the youth of the colony were creating while playing caroms[18] in one of the lanes abutting the compound wall. All the residents of the street complained to Altaf on the matter. Narendra's inquisitive question had digressed the main subject. Altaf was not comfortable discussing his family matters in public. But he had no alternative.

"Yes, I did. Because I need Munaaf for my business, I cannot employ more people after the fire, so a family hand is useful. Anyway, you told me many times that Munaaf is not concentrating in the school, and we decided Munaaf should learn the tricks of my business for his future." answered Altaf.

"Hope you are not pulling out Asif, too," asked another member. Asif was the youngest son of Altaf.

Altaf shot him a look of venom. *Keep cool.*

Before Altaf could answer, Narendra interjected, "Asif is a brilliant boy. He is the pride of our school. I don't think it is wise to discontinue him."

"I am not doing anything of that sort. I shall fund Asif to become an engineer at any cost," announced Altaf.

"Yes, we have to whip our children to be more academic-focused than they are now. Unlike Hindu castes, we don't come under a reservation system. So only by merit can we progress and claim the jobs and opportunities commensurate with our population of 11% of the country," opined a clean-shaven with a Fez cap.

---

18   Indian board game, similar to snooker but on a smaller board

"Altaf has been expressing this prerequisite of education for the future of our Muslim youth. He led by example by insisting on sending his two daughters to school and ensuring they are given a good education," interjected Narendra.

"Our leaders have failed us. They have not been able to encourage Muslims to educate their children. As a result, most of our youth become motor mechanics, drivers, fruit vendors, and petty labour in factories. In fact, in IT sector, which works purely on merit, also does not have enough Mussalmans as professionals. Even Azimbhai's[19] unit does not employ enough of our biradri because our boys and girls cannot compete with meritorious Hindus," lamented Altaf.

"Yes, even the minority education institutes cannot attract Muslim talent; instead, they became business units of the select few Muslim leaders who pocket the capitation fee from the Hindus. The majority of Hindus usurp the seats. Of course, there are not enough competent Muslim youth for these institutes to fill their places, too," said the Fez.

"True. Because the very definition of minority institute is the crux of the problem, it says minorities shall administer minority education institutes. The rules do not insist the minority institute has to employ or educate minorities exclusively," said Altaf.

"Article 30 of our Constitution provides for such establishment to ensure the minority religion, culture, heritage, language, and script are protected. But these institutes do nothing of that sort. Muslims constitute around 12% of the population, but their literacy is abysmal 59%. But look at Christians, whose number is 2.3%, but their literacy rate is an astounding 80%," opined Narendra

---

19   A rich Muslim businessman: Promoter-Investor in many conglomerates

"Unfortunately so. Kerala is the only state with the maximum number of minority institutes, and in that State, Muslim minorities compete equally with others," added Fez.

"Also, Kerala is the only state in India that included Muslims as part of their OBC quota. They get government jobs and other perquisites the selected Hindu castes get," said Quadri Pasha, the businessman.

"Then why cannot all the governments follow this?" asked the Fez.

"Hoping that the Muslim parties or leagues or their leaders to give any attention to our plight except lip sympathy is foolishness. We have to raise above all this and start a campaign amongst us Muslims to send children to schools and colleges. There are too many drop-outs from post-secondary schools amongst Muslims. We have to stop this. I am guilty of this, too, as I pulled out Munaaf from school as I needed a helping hand free of cost. But I promise as soon as my business comes back to normalcy, I shall provide as much learning opportunity to Munaaf as his wont," said Altaf.

"If you have noticed, the very purpose of allowing minorities to have institutions to increase their culture, language etc., is all hogwash. How can a minority engineering college or a medical college advance the knowledge of Urdu? Do they teach engineering or medicine in Urdu? These institutes are allowed to flourish to quieten the voices of the influential Muslims by bribing them legally. They auction the seats of their colleges to earn money as wealthy Hindus garner most of these seats," said Quadri Pasha.

"I hope someone does a statistical analysis of how many minority Muslim higher secondary schools operate compared to minority funded professional engineering, pharmacy, medicine etc.," Fez added.

"We have to persuade all our Muslim brethren to inculcate the importance of education, the way Hindu Brahmins do," opined Narendra.

"Education is not enough. They should have job opportunities – preferably government jobs. The Indian Constitution does not allow reservation based on religion, only on the Indian Caste system. I am surprised to know that even though when Gandhi was alive during the drafting of the Constitution, he never fought for the Muslims to be included in article 46 of the Constitution. His professed love for minorities and secularity of the country was only a lip sympathy," complained the agitated Fez.

The discussion then died down and shifted to the original agenda of the meeting: the racket the boys of the community generate during their playtimes – that too at odd hours. The members decided the families of the youth had to be summoned for further action on the matter. With that decision, the members dispersed.

While walking back home, Quadri Pasha cornered Altaf and broached the topic of Abdul's marriage.

"Presently, we are too busy reconstructing my business. Nazma did raise the topic a couple of times with Abdul. But, he refused to be drawn into any conversation relating to his marriage."

"He is almost 30!" exclaimed Quadri Pasha.

"29 to be exact. Nazma has found a bride too. Her cousin, Bira has a pretty granddaughter who is a Commerce graduate and recently passed the Intermediate examination of Chartered Accountancy. But Abdul had not reacted to this suggestion too," said Altaf

Quadri Pasha too had more than passing interest in Abdul's marriage as his sister's daughter had come of age.

Raj Krishna

"Am I the first person to arrive?" wondered Ramesh Gandi as he entered the apartment of Raj and Vaidehi.

Ramesh Gandi and Raj shared a flat while studying in Mumbai and never lost touch even though they graduated in different domains. A couple of other office colleagues too were expected for the day's lunch meeting hosted by Raj. Every third Sunday of a month, these buddies meet at a place hosted in turns. Today was Raj's turn. With all their children either in hostels studying or working outside the state and country, this assembly was always an exclusive parents club.

"Yes, but the others are on the way. Mansukhani's car broke down, and Chacko is picking him up," answered Raj. Robin Chacko, the Malayali, was married to Pushyami, Raj's classmate in Pharmacy College.

When Ramesh was attending a Master's in Business Management course from Narseemonji used his free time to hang around the pharmacy college. He got introduced to Pushyami through Raj. As Pushyami's parents were in Assam, she lived in an apartment shared by three other girls. So the company of Ramesh and Raj was a welcome change for her. Raj and Ramesh had a crush on her without confiding in each other.

Their hope for Pushyami never receded, though they never dared to express it.

But fate had a different idea when Robin Chacko appeared on the scene. Chacko was employed as a Production Manager with an Andhra Entrepreneur-owned large Pharma unit in Mumbai. Pushyami pursued post-graduation and joined her alma mater as a faculty member, where Chacko was a part-time visiting professor. The Pharmacy College had a program inviting drug manufacturing personnel to give guest lectures and also had them in the role of visiting faculty. The companies do not object to this arrangement as it helped in campus recruitment. Their staff could quickly identify the bright student for eventual employment. It was a win-win situation for both. That was how Chacko and Pushyami met frequently. Chacko proposed, and she accepted. He later opted to become a full-time faculty when offered. Pushyami, of course, had a role in the change of his job profile.

"Good Morning Ramesh Garu. Where is Sunita?" asked Vaidehi while coming from the kitchen, wiping her hands with a napkin hanging on her shoulder.

"Her mother fell ill last night; she had to go to attend to her," explained Ramesh.

"How is she now?" asked Raj

"Last heard, she shifted to Leelavati for observation, but I am not sure what the matter is. But Sunita appeared calm enough. May not be that serious," informed Ramesh.

"After our lunch, let us all go and see her. Leelavati Hospital is not far from here," opined Vaidehi.

"Yes, that's a good idea," concurred Raj.

Meanwhile, Mansukhani, Sadhana, Chacko, and Pushyami walked in. Pushyami was smartly dressed. She was wearing loose shiny imported blue jeans with a white lace top and a cotton-silk hand-printed stole around her neck. Neither Raj nor Ramesh could take their eyes off her. Fortunately, no one noticed, and Vaidehi was in the kitchen when they walked in.

One could see how Chacko got attracted to Pushyami. She was gorgeous, round-faced with sharp facial features and long hair up to her buttocks. Her clothes represent the society she belongs to because of her Dad's Army background. The Chackos have a daughter who married a software engineer employed by CISCO in Boston.

After the initial pleasantries, they all sat down with a glass of RoohAfza[20] served by Vaidehi's maid as a starter drink. Vaidehi always wanted to be remembered as a good host. Having been in Mumbai, where her Manager dad worked for a long time, she learned a few modern manners of presenting her home and culinary skills from her mom. She worked to impress all her guests. She worked extra hard while adding her signature touches to let her guests know she was the best. She forced the other house members to help her. Raj would often have to lend his hand to ensure his desk was neat and arranged; the sofa covers were well laid, the chairs strategically placed, supervised the maid while she was dusting. She had this tremendous urge to show she was different and went out of the way to seek appreciation.

"That was a very sumptuous spread," "This table cloth is nice; where did you buy it from?"; "This gaajar ka halwa[21] looks as though made by Sanjeev Kapoor,"; "Can I carry the tomato chutney? My mother would love it." Such encomiums would make her day. It did not matter to Vaidehi that her OCD inconvenienced other family members. She would ignore her family's needs if they came in the way of treating her guests. Vaidehi felt she never received compliments for her culinary skills from her family members.

---

20   Indian soft drink

21   Indian Sweet made with carrots

When friends were invited, Vaidehi would prepare meals that appeared to have taken a day to prepare. She would take extra care to select the vegetables and grind special masalas procured from branded companies that she would get ready the previous day. She picked up the habit of singing to herself when she was doing something extraordinary to impress her guests, which could invite appreciation she longed.

She would freeze a few special curries she had prepared the previous day to save time. She prided herself in making traditional south Indian chutneys, especially with boiled and marinated tomatoes and various salads she would have learned from FOOD channels she often watched.

***

"You are reading Chetan Bhagat[22]? What a comedown from Neville Shute and Alistair Maclean," wondered Pushyami, picking up the book - "Two States" by Chetan Bhagat from the bookshelf.

Pushyami knew his reading habits right from their college days, during which time they shared their books and views about the writers often. Raj was responsible for shifting her allegiance from Sydney Sheldon to Irving Wallace and Arthur Hailey. She was forever grateful to Raj for introducing those well-researched authors.

"Check again; he may have a Shobha De too," added Vaidehi walking in after giving instructions to her maid on how to lay the table.

"It is only to know how clever marketing can sell average products," defended Raj.

The suave and dapper Chacko said, "Raj, It is unfair to criticise Chetan like that. He writes about contemporary middle-class

22   A popular Indian author – writes in English

India, and he has his clientele. The one who reads PG Wodehouse may not read Somerset Maugham. They cater to different markets and genres. Last week when I flew to Kolkata for a conference, I had over 4 hours of free time – airport to airport and taxi time included - which I used to read up on Chetan. It's light reading and does not require the excess attention you need to read, say a John Grisham or a Robin Cook, though I read all three."

"I agree. But when you want to have a lasting impression of a book, Chetan and Shobha may not fit the bill," said Raj, "I was reading this latest book of Chetan. I was shocked to notice some ubiquitous phrases and sentences as though a tenth class student, authored the book. He often uses the word "said" while closing a dialogue – such as "I said,"; Bindu said,"; Saurabh said,"; "Anjali said,"; etc., never used any synonym for "said." A good author would say "inquired," "wondered," "questioned," "admonished" and so on to give more punch to the dialogue."

"You cannot blame Chetan for that. It is the job of the proof-readers", said Mansukhani.

"No publishing house can afford to employ such skilled proof-readers. Also, it is his brand that is at stake. He should have been more careful," added Raj.

"I was reading Jhumpa Lahiri[23] the other day. Let me read a passage from her book which will give you an adequate reason for the need for professional proof-readers," said Mansukhani.

He then read the passage from "The Interpreter of Maladies" from the Kindle he always carried.

"*In this manner, the next half-hour passed, and when they stopped for lunch at a roadside restaurant that sold fritters, and omelette sandwiches, usually something Mr Kapasi looked forward*

---

23   Indian Author based in US

to on his tours so that he could sit in peace and enjoy some hot tea, he was disappointed".

"What does the author want to say?" asked Sadhana.

"Read the above passage with 'usually which' replacing 'usually something' you will understand," Mansukhani said, handing over the Kindle.

"Maybe that's the American way of saying. After all, she is an NRI."

"Raj are you writing anything lately?" asked Sadhana, changing the subject.

Raj, in his youth did indulge in writing stories for Caravan. Many were rejected, and only one or two got published.

In those days, Caravan was not what it is today, the liberal critic of the establishment; it was primarily targeted at bored homemakers. It was equivalent to today's TV soaps.

"That was long back; I have neither time nor inspiration now," said Raj

"I recollect you had written a story in a Telugu periodical, a verbatim translation from Readers Digest," said Ramesh. Ramesh dared not utter such embarrassing statements had Sunita been around. She would never approve of his insulting references, which he often indulged in. Ramesh had always been like that. He appeared to suffer from an inferiority complex. Unlike many Raj's friends, Ramesh's academic pursuits were nothing to write home about.

"I never knew that!" exclaimed Vaidehi.

"When did men confide their dark secrets to their wives?" joked Pushyami.

"I was too young then, maybe 18 or so, and Ramesh exposed me with a letter to that magazine's editor, "said Raj. Ramesh approvingly winked.

"And plagiarism is not limited to me alone. IITs and IIMs have also been exposed. One IIT physics professor lost his HOD post as he had copied the research work of his student without acknowledging the source. It is difficult to distinguish plagiarism from inspiration," defended Raj.

"Inspiration is fine, but one must credit the original. There are many such cases in Bollywood of such downright reproduction of the originals, without credits," informed the well-read Chacko.

"Even Lancet and Nature, the famous publications of medicine and science, have not been spared of the ignominy of apologising to the public for their inadequate peer-review processes when their published research papers were exposed to plagiarism."

"It is not inspiration alone. For instance, I read a book, and some powerful words and sentences have an indelible impact on me, I may store the same in my memory, and I may subconsciously use them somewhere. Is it plagiarism? For instance, "She fell in love with him, hopelessly and desperately" is a typical sentence that I may use in a different context with a changed sequence of words; She fell hopeless and desperately in love with him. That's disguised plagiarism. But I have not deliberately copy-pasted the sentence; it just came out involuntarily when I was writing, as it left an impression in my mind when I read. I'll give you another famous example; wait, let me get my laptop," said Raj.

He went to his desk, picked up his laptop, and opened a" Power Words and Sentences file."

"Let me read a passage from "The Prophet" by Khalil Gibran. Khalil Gibran is a Lebanese writer of the early 19th Century who wrote in English," said Raj and went about reading the passage from the book, which sold millions of copies.

"You pray in your distress and in your need, would that you might pray also in the fullness of your joy and in your days of abundance. – That's a passage by Khalil Gibran."

We all know about Kabir, a mystic poet of the 15th Century. He wrote two-line couplets known as Dohas– one of them is strikingly similar to the passage I have just read. Let me read out this Doha for you, which most of us are familiar with:

दुःख में सुमिरन सब करे सुख में करै न कोय।

जो सुख में सुमिरन करे दुःख काहे को होय ॥

Is the passage of Khalil Gibran not verbatim of this Kabir Doha?

So what do we say to that? Is it inspiration, subconscious reproduction, plagiarism, or a coincidence of thoughts?" questioned Raj.

"I have some interesting paragraphs from a book by Arundhati Roy. One such is: "he thought two thoughts and the two thoughts he thought were these", and she goes on listing those humdrum thoughts. Because it is Arundhati she could get away with such routine stuff. If any of us write such a para, no publisher will touch you," said Mansukhani.

The party continued for another couple of hours, and they parted company with confirmation of the following date and venue.

"I noticed you and Ramesh were ogling at Pushyami. It's embarrassing," said Vaidehi

Raj and Vaidehi were relaxing after the guests had left for the day.

"Ogling is not the word. We just glanced at her, as we had not met for a long time. We were exchanging notes that is all. "

"Anyway, I made my point," and left in a huff to watch telly.

***

After a few weeks, Pushyami invited all of them to her apartment nestled between Breach Candy Hospital and the Mahalaxmi Temple. As per Mumbai standards, the place was huge, with a balcony facing the sea. Chacko served beer and other alcoholic drinks as per the guests' requirements. The girls, except Sadhana, had soft drinks. Raj and Vaidehi had not arrived yet.

"You have deliberately delayed our departure for the party," complained Raj.

They were driving on the way to Pushyami's house, stuck in traffic at Haji Ali.

"What could I have done? Spandana called for some recipe details."

"But it was only for about ten mins. You were discussing mundane matters that could have waited for our trip back, "protested Raj.

"What are you trying to say? That I don't like your parties? Yes, especially I don't want to go to Pushyami's place. They serve alcohol, and you guys leave us girls to fend for ourselves, and you guys drink and indulge in banter that is not to my liking. And Pushyami shows off too much."

"That's not fair. We hardly meet my friends these days, except those you are comfortable with. That's driving me nuts."

"I have come now with you to the party; please don't argue. Drive properly. You could have almost sliced the side mirror off going very close to that van," said Vaidehi.

Raj did not want to create a scene as they were approaching the apartment complex. The apartment gate entry board said, "No outside vehicles." He requested Vaidehi to alight at the gate and wait for him. He had to park his car inside the Breach Candy hospital. He had a hospital membership card given by his employer, which came in handy. After parking, he crossed the road to where Vaidehi was waiting for him near the apartment gate.

"What took you so long? People were staring at me," complained Vaidehi.

"I had to go inside the hospital to hoodwink the security to make them believe I had indeed come for a visit to the hospital and not just to park my vehicle," explained Raj, and they walked towards the lifts in the building. The lift emerged into a long corridor on the seventh floor with rows of flats on both sides of the passage.

They knocked on the door marked "The Chackos." Pushyami opened the door and welcomed them.

"The boys are waiting for you, already one round of drinks done," said Pushyami coyly.

"Traffic," said Vaidehi and walked inside. Vaidehi would never be late for parties hosted by those whom she liked. She felt these meetings between friends of Raj were somewhat plastic.

The couple entered the front room, which looked simple with a large sofa, three single-seater sofas, and a large centre table with a glass top. Some pharma literature and the day's newspaper, a dated National Geographic, were seen under the table. Direct to the front of the entry door was a bas-relief of a bleeding Jesus Christ on the cross. Dark brown wooden cupboards, with handles designed with old-fashioned brass keys in ornate locks, contained numerous gifts and medals and quite a few books - academic, fictional, and spiritual. Ostensibly this room was designed to entertain official guests such as researchers and students who frequent the Chackos. Some typical family snaps hung across the room - poorly filmed, some out of focus, some overexposed, many red eyes from the flash. Raj recognised a young Chacko.

The opulence became striking once Raj and Vaidehi passed into the main room. It was a living-cum-kitchen room. The hall was huge, at the far end of which was an open kitchen. The kitchen had a long granite top table in the middle, the one you see in Food Channels, with three bar stools at one end. The table had three full-sized gas burners and an infrared heater. Clean ceramic and glass vessels adorn the table on one side.

An L-shaped cupboard surrounded the table with a gleaming stainless steel sink at a corner and double-stacked cabinets, which displayed understated luxury. One wall had an oven and a microwave smug-fitted into the cabinets. The cabinets were fitted with transparent glass packed with containers of all shapes and sizes – mostly either steel or ceramic, or glass. No plastic. The kitchen design would have the approval of Sanjeev Kapoor.

The other end of the hall, where all had assembled, was a well-decorated sitting room that was instantly engaging and impressive and functionally designed for comfort and ease of use. The arrangement of sitting accommodation gave a showroom feel with sofas and chairs. The room had a mix of new and vintage elements, which created an interesting, eclectic, and individualised place with low lighting instead of overhead lights. A designer low-noise fan was another originality Vaidehi noticed. Strategically walled gallery art gave an aesthetic and luxurious look to the room. The surrounding wall-to-wall cabinets spruced with artefacts show the grandeur and taste of the lady of the house. One cabinet was full of souvenirs from their frequent travels to Europe: Pissing boy statue, Brandenburg gate, Eifel tower, Guard at Buckingham Palace, Hagia Sofia miniature, Trevi fountain, and many such attention-grabbing keepsakes.

"There is no dining table," whispered Vaidehi.

Raj strained to answer without being heard. He signalled at the side tables, stacked one over the other placed at one corner of the sofa set. "Perhaps they believe in buffet type serving," he murmured in Telugu.

Raj settled with gin and tonic from the bar served by Chacko and joined the group. The nibbles placed on the table to accompany the drinks were proof of the house's wealth—a broad choice of snacks including cashew nuts, almonds, and Pringles, to name a few.

Had it been at Raj or Ramesh's house, you will be served with salted peanuts, Haldiram's sev, and potato wafers packed in cheap plastic wrappers sourced from Aggarwal superstores and served with RoohAfza or Orange Squash. No Alcohol. The Andhra Brahmin ladies are not culturally trained in understanding the concept of social drinking. For them, alcohol consumption led to addiction. There is no concept of moderate drinking.

"Any news on your daughters' graduation ceremony date?" inquired Raj.

"Not yet. It better be delayed, as Robin has an assignment in Berlin which he can't avoid", said Pushyami.

"Will you also join him in Berlin?" asked Mansukhani

"Not decided; I also have some urgent work at the university. However, I want to go. I am told Berlin is a lovely city with WWII and cold-war related interests of historical significance", said Pushyami.

Ramesh's wife Sunita and Vaidehi had gone into another room for a private chat in their vernacular. Before going in, Vaidehi noticed the kitchen platform did not appear to have been used for some time.

Food was probably being outsourced.

After a while, all assembled in the hall with their respective drinks. Mansukhani proposed a toast to Chacko for having been selected as the visiting professor at John Hopkins.

"Congratulations." There was a ripple of applause.

"What was that?" asked Sunita, coming out of another room, having missed the event. Mansukhani explained the reason for the toast. They all relaxed while the mobile of Pushyami rang. She gave directions to the house and flat number into the speaker and sat down.

"I ordered Indian-Chinese and Italian food for us. Hope its ok?" said Pushyami.

"Perfect," said Raj.

"To take forward our previous discussions on writer's stimuli, I dug deeper into the subject of inspirations from others published works," said Raj," 'A Passage to India' by E.M Forster was prescribed as non-detailed text in our graduation in Osmania University. This novel was published in 1942. Most of you indeed would have read 'To Kill a Mocking Bird' too, as it was one of the best 100 books of the Century. TKMB was published in 1960."

"Yes, I read TKMB, but not aware of the other one," said Pushyami.

"Anyway, what are you hinting at?" asked Mansukhani.

"Ok, let me briefly explain the subject of API for us to analyse further, "said Raj," An Indian Muslim doctor, Dr Aziz, is falsely implicated for the sexual assault on an English woman in a cave they had gone for a picnic. He is arrested, and the trial goes on. What happens afterwards in the trial is irrelevant to our discussions", said Raj.

Sadhana butted in. "And in TKMB, Tom, a black man, is charged with the rape of an American white woman and is detained. Is that what you had in mind when you said inspirations not acknowledged?"

"Yes, exactly, these novels are twenty years apart. Harper Lee, the writer of TKMB, might have read Forster because the underlying theme is strangely the same. Is it a coincidence?" wondered Raj.

"Did you guys watch Gregory Peck in TKMB, a very unusual portrayal of an upright lawyer Atticus? He was mostly given the role of a romantic hero because of his looks, as in 'Roman Holiday'; combat man with guns fighting for a just cause as in 'Guns of Navarone.' But this role in TKMB had changed his image", said Vaidehi changing the topic from books to movies in which she was more comfortable participating.

The topic then deviated to movies, actors, and their respective artistic qualities. Raj had contributed his bit by comparing Audrey Hepburn with Indian Actor Madhubala. As per him, both have a comedy element in them apart from beauty with acting brains.

"He is obsessed with both the actors. He bores me with repeats of both films," complained Vaidehi.

The discussions continued for a couple of hours more with dialogue rendering by the versatile Chacko. He had one of those retentive memories most people would kill for. A memory that rivalled a spell-bee champion. Post dinner, everyone left almost at the same time. The journey back for Raj was challenging. Not only because of the rain-battered, blocked drainage-induced traffic jams. Vaidehi demanded to know why Raj always ignored her when he was with his friends.

"Sometimes it's awkward, and sometimes it is downright insulting."

Her rant quoted old transactions between the two, which were never registered in his neurons to counter her. He let them pass.

I had never been asked how I lived before I wed Vaidehi, but if anyone had asked me, I would have answered that the tyranny had not died out from my life, only the gender of the tyrant changed.

ALTAF MALLIK

The pressure from the family made Abdul relent. His nikah with Nafisa was performed in a solemn ceremony.

There are certain things which are fundamental to all Muslim marriages. Marriages have to be declared publicly. They should never be undertaken in secret. The publicity is usually achieved by having an enormous feast, or walimah - a party specifically for announcing the couple is married and entitled to each other. Considering the financial condition of Altaf's family, Bira did not insist on a grand ceremony. It was limited to close relatives from both sides and a few selected members of Navrang society.

If Nafisa felt cheated by coming to Abdul's dungeon from a reasonably well ventilated and modern house with running bath water, she did not overtly complain. Several times she thought she might throw up. She cleaned her hands every hour with soap until they reddened. She endured all this for a future she had been waiting to happen. However, whenever frustration claimed her, she went over to her room, collapsed on the bed, and burst out crying. She was aloof and snobbish with all the other members of Abdul's household.

Within a few days of the marriage, Nafisa confessed to Abdul that she was against their marriage for various reasons. One was she wanted to complete her CA course, and she wanted to pursue her career in finance sector and not simply be a housewife. Secondly, she was in love with her childhood friend, pursuing an MD course in Ophthalmology at Nair Hospital. They decided to get married only after accomplishing both of their academic pursuits. But she was forced into this marriage by her dad, whom she loved greatly.

Though Abdul was shocked by this revelation, she respected her wishes and did not attempt to consummate the marriage.

Nafisa also felt remorseful for denying Abdul his earthly pleasures. She became fond of him for caring for her even though she was uncooperative. She did feel like running her fingers over Abdul's hair when he was fast asleep to compensate for her obnoxious behaviour. However, the atrocious attitude of his sister, Nusrat, was a pain. Because of her obstinate behaviour and a few unfortunate coincidences, Nusrat remained a spinster. Nafisa had to deal with Nusrat and a handicapped Munaaf which she never anticipated while accepting Abdul's alliance.

In Islam, an unmarried woman is a source of psychological distress compared to men who do not have a negative outlook of a delayed marriage. Usually, a girl's fears start when she realizes that the age of marriage is passed. The obsessive idea of spinsterhood is increasing, and the concern of social isolation is growing; spinsterhood becomes a source of threat to her future dreams of emotional stability, childbearing, motherhood, and fellowship with a male partner. Her frustrations will be an embarrassment to other members of the family.

Nusrat's behaviour towards Nafisa was a source of awkwardness for Abdul. His mother never interfered with their silly altercations, which continued for hours. A tiny infraction by Nafisa would invite the ire and sarcasm from Nusrat, mocking her upbringing without a mother.

Altaf realized the awkwardness of Nafisa and indicated to Abdul that the house they were presently living was not convenient for the newly wedded couple. Altaf persuaded Abdul to find a one-bedroom apartment in the Alkapuri area by seeking a loan from his company and some from banks. Nafisa was happy with this arrangement, which suited her plans. Every Sunday, a holiday or during Ramadan, Abdul and Nafisa would shift to the home of Abdul's parents in Navrang Society and spend the day there to ensure family togetherness. That was Abdul's understanding with Altaf for consenting to shift to Alkapuri.

Six months passed when an unexpected tragedy struck Altaf family. Altaf had a stroke while in his workshop and had to be admitted to the hospital. Within 48hrs of his admittance, the doctors pronounced him dead.

Abdul had become the only earning member of the family as Munaaf had informed him of his inability to run the business with his handicap. On the advice of Quadri Pasha, who now assumed the role of the eldest well-wisher of the family, they sold off the workshop. In the condolence assembly conducted on the 40th day of his death, many members of the Navrang Society had only good words for Altaf.

"We miss Altaf a lot, not only as my friend, but his talks on Sharia and Muslim Personal Law, especially regarding marriages and divorces, are unforgettable. You may recollect how he amicably solved the triple Talaaq matter of the family of Ansari brothers," said Quadri Pasha while presiding over the assembly. Many members remembered his illuminating talks on Muslim Personal Law.

Altaf's talks also related to marriage and its dissolution so that there was no discord in the families. He successfully prevented spontaneous, thoughtless, regretful and rash Talaaqs that threatened to disrupt the lives of women and children in society. He specially educated Muslim women in the community on their rights. These talks sometimes riled the traditional elders of the Navrang Society. Still, they had to keep mum as Altaf had the backing of many progressive members, such as Quadri Pasha, who knew Altaf had adequate knowledge of Muslim Personal law.

On seeking divorce by Muslim women without any specific reason but incompatibility Altaf quoted:

Kitab – Al – Talaq - Volume 7, Book 63, Number 197.

The wife of Thabit bin Qais came to the Prophet and said," O Allah's Apostle! I don't blame Thabit for defects in his character or his religion. Still, I being a Muslim, dislike to behave in an un-Islamic manner (if I remain with him)," On that, Allah's Apostle said to her, "Will you give back the garden which your husband has given you (as Mahr)"? She said, "Yes". The Prophet said to Thabit, "O Thabit, accept your garden and divorce her at once."

Altaf explained the methods available for divorce for Muslim women, which he listed as Talak-e-Tafweez, Khula, Talak-e-Mubarrah and Fask. He said that the contractual nature of Muslim marriage led Muslim women to impose such conditions on their marriage which safeguard their interests in the face of uncertainties of marital life. He informed that some of the rights available to Muslim women under the Muslim Personal law were not available under other religions' marital laws. This fact was a revelation to many women who thought Muslim men had an unrestrained hold on marriage and divorce.

The attendees of the ziyarat[24] recalled all the information he had shared to benefit the society and prayed for peace, finally acknowledging that he belonged to Allah and to Allah he returned. When Altaf was alive as Abdul and Nafisa lived separately at their

---

24   Pious visitation to a grave or a tomb

Alkapuri home, the differences with Nusrat had never surfaced. As the family's economic status changed, Abdul had to rent the Alkapuri house and shift back to the Navrang Society. Nafisa did not object, despite Nusrat's dislike towards her, as she had some other plans.

NAFISA

It was Ramadan - the end of Fasting. Feasting and festivities began. Everyone in the society was busy celebrating Idd. Altaf's family celebration was low key, as the family had not recovered from Altaf's intaqal[25]. They had just finished their dinner and were out onto the road enjoying the cool breeze. Nusrat and Munni were walking with Nazma and chatting with other society ladies on the steps of a locked house a few blocks away. In the lanes, children screamed and laughed. The balloon seller was busy filling flexible plastic pouches with air pressure from a pump. Children swamped around him with cash in hand. The crowd blocked the vision of the gossiping ladies away from the gate, which was a godsend for Nafisa.

Nafisa brushed her hair quickly, picked up her already packed stroller, put on her Hawaii flip-flops and rushed out like a breeze.

Dehradun Express, a train from Dehradun to Mumbai via Vadodara was on time. Western Railways at Vadodara had a couple of bogeys parked at a less used platform to be coupled to the incoming train. They could get into these compartments and sleep peacefully. When the train finally arrived, they would shunt these cubicles along the tracks and attach them to the main train. Thus the late arrival of the incoming train thus would not inconvenience these Vadodara-boarding passengers. Nafisa

---

25   Death in Urdu

found her berth and relaxed as much as her complex state of mind allowed.

She found the air-conditioning soothing and wanted to sleep. However, her co-passengers had not arrived yet. She opened the India Today magazine she bought at the Railway book shop and started reading, hoping all the remaining three passengers occupy their allotted berths quickly enough. Fortunately, these berths belonged to one single family, and they came with colossal noise and settled into their assigned seats.

Parents and a boy of twelve or so. She opened a few pages of the mag read an interesting article on a lady who defied all odds and climbed Kilimanjaro.

Before long, Nafisa closed her eyelids with the magazine spread over her chest.

I sincerely apologise for making a mess of your life, dear Abdul. I could not contribute to our marital happiness. As I informed you, my interests lie elsewhere. I know you tried your best to make me happy. You even moved from your parental home for my sake, to ensure my privacy. I am particularly sorry for abbujaan, who showered so much love on me as though I was his child. We had been married for a little less than two years now. I respect you for your calmness in distress and for never uttering a disrespectful or hurtful word. Even though I denied you the marital pleasures, you did not show your displeasure in our interactions either by sarcasm or direct reference. You heard with attention all the anecdotes of my college life and the troubles I faced after my mom's demise.

My dad was adamant I marry as soon as I graduated. He had already suspected my relationship with Irfan. I am not sure why dad was against Irfan. I suspected it had something to do with Irfan's abbu. Business rivalry, I guess.

He overheard the conversation I was having with Irfan. Irfan needed at least two more years to complete his MD, after which he would marry me. I should not have agreed, but he also has his dreams, which I should help him attain as a devoted, loving would-be wife. So reluctantly, I decided to wait for two years. I wish my mom were alive; I could have confided in her. I decided to follow my instincts.

Ever since my mom died, my dad never remarried with the sole purpose of making me comfortable. I owe a lot to him for this sacrifice. Nevertheless, I cannot give up on my love and longing for Irfan. We were childhood friends. Neither could I disregard dad's wishes. Therefore, you became the guinea pig. It was an understanding with Irfan I should respect my dad and marry. We decided to tread on a difficult path of waiting with absolute purity of thought and action. It was a massive risk for me, but I decided to take the chance.

Fortunately for me, my dad found you a thorough gentleman. You overlooked all my nakre[26]. In the beginning, you thought I was not in the mood for a marital relationship because of some mental block. You never forced yourself on me, which was a blessing. I don't know what I would have done had that not been the case. Allah, the omnipotent, was merciful.

I enjoyed a warm welcome to your house. One of the vivid memories of your family was the Sunday lunch, which we never missed. Your ammijaan used to make the best of pakwaan[27], which I relished immensely. In addition, the small talk during the lunch and after about everything under the sun on as varied a subject as films, politics, and Urdu couplets recited by Munaaf, were a great source of entertainment. Except Abbujaan was a silent spectator but never interfered with our silly subjects of discussions. He occasionally added a line or two of an old filmy song just for nostalgia.

---

26   Tantrums
27   dinner

"Unko a shikayat hai ki hum kutch nahin kahete, kahane ko toh bahut kutch hai gar hum kahane pe aate" was his popular filmy stanza whenever ammijaan coaxed him to say something.

I did not have time to form an opinion on abbujaan, as he went about his business and was not much of a conversationalist. Whatever I learnt about him was through you. You often said he always kept his family above everything else and went out of the way to keep his folk happy, if not prosperous. His popularity in society was an eye-opener to me. He rushed out to help people even in the middle of the night whenever called upon.

Abbujaan was liberal to a fault. During iftar – evening meals during Ramadan to break the day's fast – he allowed Nazma to hold iftar separately for ladies. This unusual concession was resented by many old generation residents of the society as they opined that women should be home preparing iftar for their husbands. As years went by, the community had accepted this ritual but only for the last Friday of the fasting month.

When I heard this from you, I was amazed at how forward-looking this Navrang society had become, thanks to abbujaan. He constantly reiterated the importance of all the five principles of Islam – shahada, Salaat, zakat, sawm and hajj. He extended the tenet of zakat of giving alms to the needy and sharing knowledge and education to the poor - both formal and informal, academic and religious. He professed the need for girl education by goading all the members to follow his example of sending his daughters to regular schools. He practised what he preached by pushing Nusrat and Munni to concentrate on education and went out of the way to provide them with necessary infra.

It was difficult for me to overcome his sudden death. I miss him as much as your family did. This death changed all the peace in the house. After the death of Abbu, ammijaan became dependent on Nusrat for all her needs and whatever Nusrat said was the law.

One person in your household with whom I could not see eye-to-eye was Nusrat. She always found an excuse to insult me. She was on the sofa spread-eagled and watching the telly munching a katori[28] full of Gujarati savouries. While helping ammijaan with meat preparations, she squatted with her sari hitched up like a Koli woman with her fish basket. She appeared strong enough to squat like that forever. She expanded visibly, enlarging day by day. I sometimes wondered how she evacuated her waste in the lavatory. I have told you many times to persuade her to reduce weight so we can perform her nikah. Somehow she had her way with ammijaan supporting her indulgences.

On ammijaan's persistence, we visited many doctors, including a shrink, to ensure I could bear children. For them, two years is a long time in marriage to start expanding the family. I followed your directions and put up with pretences. We did not disclose the actual reason why I did not agree to have a life of an average married couple. Your friend Ameer's Hindu wife – Kaamini – who was a nurse, also suggested to me in private, ways to make love and conceive – much to my merriment.

On her insistence, I agreed to visit SSG hospital, where Kaamini worked for a 'thorough examination' – Kaamini's words. The doctors – one lady and one gentleman – asked me routine questions about my periods and their regularity. They even wondered whether I was abused as a child. I understood that some women, when physically molested in childhood, could have a traumatic association with their private parts. In addition, in some rare instances, they may hate any sexual contact, even within a legitimate bond.

---

28   A small stainless steel container

They asked whether I get abdominal pains during menses. That was silly, which woman does not. I nodded. The gentleman Doctor gave some instructions to the lady gynec and left the room. She then asked me to lie down on the bed and undress, bend my knees and spread my legs for further examination. It was embarrassing.

Nevertheless, I did what was asked. Then the lady doc and Kaamini covered my exposed nakedness with a white sheet – which reminded me of a kafan[29]. The gynec peeped inside the sheet with a hand-held torch.

She started examining my vagina by parting the labia. She tried to insert her fingers, and a metallic object, may be a probe. I cringed. Involuntarily I closed my legs and squeezed the head of the Doc. My private parts are reserved for my love, Irfan. No one is allowed to touch it. The Doctor's head soon came out of the covering, and she looked annoyed. I apologised and said I was uncomfortable, got up from the table and began to dress.

That terminated the visit. I am not aware of what the Doc confided to Kaamini and through her to you, but you did not broach this topic again. It was the last of our visits to Doctors on our marital association – rather disassociation.

The train stopped at Dadar; the daylight had not revealed itself yet. The conductor made a wake-up knock. The other passengers had quickly readied themselves and disembarked with their luggage. The young boy had come back to the cabin to recheck for leftovers if any. Nafisa had to wait until the train reached Bombay Central. As soon as she saw Irfan, she waved agitatedly. She descended with her stroller and went straight into his arms.

---

29   Shroud over a dead body

BHIKU MANE

Bhiku Mane's marriage to Nandini was a tame affair. Both families living on subsistence did not spend on extravagances— just bare necessities for the marriage. After marriage, Nandini accompanied Bhiku to Pune, where he was then working. Bhiku had a mechanical bent of mind though not formally trained. He learnt everything on the job. Rahul Construction Company's (RCC) material handling equipment like excavator, backhoes, and forklifts maintenance was his job.

Suddenly there was a slump in the construction industry in the country, which had not spared RCC too. Bhiku was worried they might retrench him, as they did several workers on temporary and permanent muster. Fortunately, Bhiku was not retrenched but retained with a lower salary.

On top of that, Nandini conceived and delivered a baby girl. During delivery, there were complications, but both the baby and mother were saved with good medical care. However, the girl appeared a bit malnourished. This experience sapped Nandini; she had difficulty doing her regular homely duties.

Meanwhile, to overcome the slump, RCC was trying to diversify. They learned that Vadodara Municipal Corporation is tendering for a gas pipeline job in Vadodara for household gas connections. Rahul Construction Company was not new to pipeline laying but had to collaborate with a German company proficient in gas pipe laying and maintenance practices, which helped them clinch the contract with Vadodara Municipal Corporation. Rahul Construction Company offered Bhiku to move to Vadodara as they closed their office in Pune. As many of his colleagues got layoff notices, Bhiku had no alternative but to accept. Also, as there was a slump in the construction industry, and no other company would seek his services, however much he tried.

***

Vadodara Municipal Corporation had a very dynamic Mayor, Ranchoddas. He was educated in the US and came to India to become a full-time politician. His experience in the US came in handy when he learnt that the Oil and Natural Gas Commission (ONGC) was flaring the excess gas from their oil fields. He approached them to supply the gas for the city's domestic gas distribution network. In those days, the LPG cylinder supply was erratic, and households had inconsistent supplies, resulting in many inconveniences. ONGC readily agreed but was unwilling to ensure long term supply as they were not confident. The part of ONGC's reluctance for a long term supply guarantee was kept secret by Ranchoddas from his colleagues and political bosses. His own experience in the US had shown that as long as oil is extracted, the associated natural gas would be ensured. However, ONGC bosses were unsure partly because of the lack of knowledge and mainly because of their penchant for avoiding risks.

Yet, Ranchoddas had to push this scheme through the council committees for budget sanctions, but he found tough resistance from the opposition parties. The opposition was confident of securing a majority in the imminent elections scheduled within six months. The members wanted to stall the proposal to get credit for the project when they hoped to hold the reins of the Corporation after the next polls. Thus opposition had managed to create false narratives to prevent the present party from getting the credit, which could sway the mandate away from them once again. They said: ONGC is not giving assurance for contiguous supply; the gas pipelines laid would be death traps in dense societies; the cooking time would increase because the calorific value of natural gas was far lower than LPG. Even some Ranchod's party members showed reluctance to back the budget demands.

Ranchoddas was not a man to be cowed down. He had the chief minister's support, who also wanted the credit for the middle-class convenience that could come in handy as a poll issue. Ranchoddas then did some politicking and managed to wean away some members from the opposition with an assurance of sub-committee chairmanships. He started a campaign to educate the public with seminars and roadshows. Finally, the opposition had to bow down, as the public opinion built by Ranchoddas made them look anti-progressive.

Finally, the tenders were issued. And Rahul Construction had bagged the first ten thousand connection tender. It was a bold move by Ranchoddas. Any other bureaucrat of IAS pedigree would never risk such a proposal with no assurance from a supply source. ONGC refused to sign the contract for regular and continuous supply, whatever political pressure was brought on them. However, they assured a viable price for the gas and deferred payments. Ranchoddas managed to find a Bengali from Dhanbad who had worked in a coal gasification plant to be the Project Manager. Ranchoddas ensured he had the mandate from the Standing Committee members to select a contractor for pipeline laying not solely based on price but with good weightage for gas pipe erection experience and having qualified welding teams. The project took off well, and many attributed its success to the Mayor and his dogged pursuit. Ranchoddas retained his

Mayor ship for four terms- one term with an opposition majority. That was his popularity with the public.

***

Bhiku's salary was lower than he received when maintaining the heavy construction equipment as he shifted to Vadodara for the new job offered by RCC. Like all cities in India, Vadodara too was crowded. It is difficult for a low-income family to find a good roof over the head at an affordable price. He managed to find a one-room tenement with low rent in an otherwise predominantly Muslim locality, though it did not bother him as long as he had a roof. Saarika grew to be a fine young lady. All of twelve years, she was able to manage her school and helped her *aayee*[30] in her household chores.

Much to her annoyance Nandini conceived again. Bhiku and Nandini decided to keep the baby and not abort it. However, this time during the delivery, many complications arose. The Doctors could save neither the mother nor the child.

In medical terminology, they called it postpartum preeclampsia.

Saarika could not overcome the profound reality that *aayee* wasn't alive anymore. When she saw the dead body of her *aayee*, all the pent up tears came pouring down, but she decided baba needed to be looked after. She took the responsibility as a mature woman would.

Bhiku had a desk job regulating the labour of the gas pipe works but with a much lower salary.

Saarika was forced to quit school to work as a housemaid. It annoyed Bhiku, but he had no alternative, as he had spent all his savings on Nandini's hospital bills.

---

30   Mother in Marathi

While Bhiku was in Pune, he had joined an organisation that propagated Hindu religious practices. He continued that association by opening a branch in Vadodara. After his wife's death, he spent much time with the organisation to keep himself busy.

After working for a few years in Rahul Construction, with generous help from a Puneite Engineer in Vadodara Municipal Corporation, with whom Bhiku was associated in the same Hindu organisation, Bhiku managed to find employment in the Municipal Corporation. His previous experience of pipeline work while working with Rahul Construction came in handy for the Corporation as the domestic gas demand has grown beyond the original proposals. He was given the task of pipeline maintenance and ensuring last-mile connectivity to consumers. Bhiku became a popular member of the Corporation, and his team controlled the gas connection allocation in the city. Bhiku forced Saarika to quit her maid job, as his income was enough for present and future necessities. As she was age barred, she could not pursue her schooling further.

Meanwhile, Saarika had come of age; when her Mausi[31] from Parbhani came to see them, she reprimanded Bhiku for ignoring such an essential filial responsibility as Saarika's marriage.

---

31   Mother's sister

Abdul

Quadri Pasha came to Altaf's house to exchange IDD pleasantries and sat on the cot, hoping to feast on the kheer Nazma would serve him. He found Abdul distraught. Before Quadri Pasha could ask, Nazma explained the entire episode and the note Nafisa wrote to Abdul before leaving home, though she wasn't privy to its contents. Abdul was reluctant to share the same. Quadri Pasha was about to corner Abdul for not noticing the patterns in his married life but decided otherwise.

"Let us talk to her abbu, "Quadri said, addressing Nazma

"I already spoke to him, and he was equally appalled at the turn of events," Nazma said.

"Nevertheless, I would like to talk to him," Quadri said

"It is of no use," Abdul pleaded.

Abdul could understand the reluctance of Nafisa to consummate their marriage as he was briefed on the matter. But the manner of her desertion was a bit jarring. He did not disclose the entire contents of the note she wrote to Abdul to either Quadri or Nazma. Nazma was upset that his cousin forced the marriage without taking the bride's consent. She felt cheated and apologized to Abdul.

"We have to find a way out of this embarrassment and forget Nafisa ever existed," added Abdul. Having succumbed to the circumstances, Nazma requested Quadri Pasha to help Abdul by getting a formal divorce.

***

It was almost three years since Nafisa left Abdul. During this period, the family performed Munni's nikah, and she went to Dubai with her husband, the floor manager in Lulu Stores. Asif had just entered Engineering. Abdul could fund both the events, thanks to the generosity of his employers. In addition, he rented out the flat he had purchased on his parents' insistence to ensure privacy for Nafisa for a considerable sum as it was in the Alkapuri area – the central business district of Vadodara. However, the family's lack of income from the tire re-treading business was telling. The entire burden of running the house fell on Abdul. Abdul declined many requests by Nazma to re-marry and start a family. Nazma wanted to quickly correct her error of fixing Abdul's nikah with Nafisa.

He was particularly concerned about Nusrat and Munaaf. His family had accepted that Nusrat would have to live as a spinster, but she needed to be taken care of monetarily and emotionally to live her life in the future. Fortunately, Altaf had provided a roof over their heads. Abdul's Employer tried to help Munaaf find a job in a sanitary shop, but his disability came in the way. Hence, all the three family members with no income were necessarily dependent on Abdul. Abdul was confident Asif would help lend him a hand running the house in the next four years. Yet, the current income from his job wouldn't be able to meet the mounting expenses.

That was when Ameer suggested to Abdul the job opportunities in the Kingdom of Saudi Arabia (KSA). He knew an Agency in Mumbai, Shafique Travels and Tours, who could arrange employment and work visas to work in Dammam or Riyadh.

This proposal enthused Abdul; he started working towards it by collating the required documentation as instructed by the Agency. The Agency also indicated each person would have to possess rupees one lakh for further process. Though it was a tough ask, they decided to pool their savings and take loans from friends; they would settle the same with Provident Fund and gratuity contributions after their resignations. They enrolled in Arabic classes conducted by a maulvi in one of the Jama Masjids near Mandvi gate.

They both had decided to continue working diligently in their present positions until they completed the formalities and received the job confirmation in Saudi.

It was not until March that Abdul and Ameer received notification from the Agency. They were to produce their passports, copies of birth certificates, testimonials from their past and present employers, photographs and evidence showing they had enough money to buy the tickets and visa charges. They promptly provided what was asked. However, the extra cash part troubled them. Fortunately, Abdul's nana[32] helped them. They were already smarting from the bribe money they gave the local sub-inspector to get a no-objection certificate.

After the 2002 riots, all the Mussalmans travelling abroad from Gujarat had to obtain an NOC, confirming no FIR or charge sheet against them was pending in any PS in Gujarat. Fortunately, the state was digitally well connected, yet it took them just over a month to get the required certificate in the acceptable format to Saudi Consulate. Twice, the Agency staff rejected the NOC for the lack of conformity to the requirements of the Saudi authorities. Every correction required visits to the PS with more cash.

---

32   Grand Father from Mother's side

A fortnight later, the Agency initiated a conference call with Ameer and Abdul at about ten in the night.

"Hello, this is Syed Lateef from Shafique Travels and Tours. Am I speaking to Mr Ameer and Mr Abdul?" said a voice in a soft tone.

"Yes," said both in unison.

"Sorry to have bothered this late in the night. This is the only time I am free to talk to my customers," said Syed.

"It is all right, sir," said Abdul.

"I have examined all the documents you have sent. Some of them are not in the format we want. I will send you a detailed message on the missing data. Please fulfil the requirements, as we need. From what I have observed from your experience and qualifications, we can probably find a Sponsor in a short time, subject to all the amendments as suggested in my next mail are fulfilled."

"Thank you, sir," said Ameer

"Also, plan to come to Mumbai as soon as you hear from me, which would be after I receive the corrected papers," said Syed

"Sure, sir. We have no problem with that," said Abdul.

"Ok, Good night," said Syed and cut the phone without waiting for a reply.

As assured by Syed, they received a message from Shafique Travels and Tours to visit their Mumbai office for further process. The news did not elaborate on what the process would be.

***

Abdul and Ameer were visiting Mumbai for the first time. The big city enamoured them. They found a three-storied 2-star lodging in the fort area and parked themselves into a double-bedded room with a shared bathroom catering to 6 such rooms. The room was surprisingly neat and clean. Later, they checked the directions to the Agency they were required to attend with the receptionist. Fortunately, the Agency office near Mahatma Phule market next to Haj House was within walking distance from the lodge. A rickety lift with a flexible grill door took them to the fourth floor of the Office of Shafique Travels and Tours.

As they entered the office, they found five staff members seated behind a long table; each had a chair in front of them occupied. Few more people were waiting their turn in a steel 3-seater silver bench you often find in hospital or station waiting rooms. A man in a blue uniform approached them and thrust a coupon that contained a number, 18. After what seemed to be a terminal wait, they saw their number displayed on a LED display board, leading them to counter number 2.

A lady in hijab operated the counter. The material covering her head and neck – a light blue satin – indicated she came from a well-to-do family. She smiled at her customers, which made them comfortable. She called for an extra chair to seat them both.

"Good afternoon, gentlemen. Sorry for having kept you waiting." The nametag on her lapel displayed Sharmila.

"We are to meet Latif here," said Ameer.

"Which Latif? We have two –Mohd and Syed," she said.

They looked at each other and said, "Syed."

"He is on leave today. But you can tell me your business; I can help," said Sharmila.

"We had registered for jobs in Saudi," said Ameer and showed her the letter received from their office.

"Let me get your folders." She got up and went out inside the office. The guy in blue uniform, who gave them the coupon, directed them to a conference room inside their office.

"Madam said she will meet you here."

After they were seated, they were served tea and biscuits. Sharmila walked in with two brown coloured folders and opened them both.

"I see from these folders that you have different skills, yet you would want a placement in the same city," said Sharmila. They nodded.

"I am not aware how much Syed had briefed you on our company working, but you may want to reconsider this requirement," said Sharmila. She checked all the forms and information the two applicants gave her and nodded her satisfaction.

She explained the process of finding sponsors in detail. In response to Sharmila's question about finding employment in different cities, they said, "We can waive the requirement if that comes in the way of finding a good employer for us."

"And, if the interested Sponsor accepts only one of you, the other has to wait till we find another Employer", added Sharmila. "For every Sponsor, we fix a video consultation, and there will be an additional cost of Rs five thousand, apart from what you have paid."

"We have already paid Rs fifty thousand as the first instalment so far. Another five thousand for the video interview?" wondered Ameer.

"Out of the fifty thousand paid, twenty thousand is a deposit which shall be returned once you accept the employment offer and reach the Saudi shores. As requested, we shall arrange for its return here in Indian Rs or Saudi Riyals. For the first video interview, no payment is sought from you apart from what's already paid. However, if the first selected Sponsor rejects you, we have to find another Employer for which this extra amount is sought. Further, a maximum of three interviews shall be arranged, and if you don't find employment within these three video meetings, we shall take you off our list as a prospective candidate," said Sharmila.

Ameer and Abdul looked at each other in surprise at this new development.

Disregarding the shock, Ameer said, "Have you selected any Sponsor for us now?"

"I am recording this conversation, and I need a firm yes from both to proceed further," said Sharmila

"Yes," both of them said in one voice.

"From the folder, I see Syed had been in touch with a prospective Sponsor in Dammam. Tomorrow Syed is expected to come to the office. He will discuss the further process with you," said Sharmila.

Sharmila stood up to convey that the meeting was over. She gave them a one-pager brief on their prospective Employer collected by their Riyadh office. Abdul and Ameer left the office; their minds were overwhelmed with the new information.

***

A fortnight earlier, Syed Lateef had detailed discussions with them at around ten in the night during a conference call; apologizing for the late call, he explained the functioning of their placement processes and the background of their Agency.

Shafique Travels and Tours was an established firm with over twenty years of service to Indians who wished to migrate to Saudi for jobs and, in rare cases, for permanent immigration. "Unlike our competitors, we deal directly with Sponsors and Employers in Saudi. We do not have any local agent to mediate in the employment. However, we do have a branch in Riyadh, which helps the migrants in their distress, if any. This branch, though owned by an Indian, is staffed by locals. They also help us validate the information given by Sponsors to ensure our customers are placed in a good environment as per agreed rules of engagement," said Lateef, "I have scanned through your resumes and other documents sent by you. They are in order."

"Ok, how long do you think the further process will take?" asked Abdul.

"We are to match your skills with the requirements given by the Sponsor, and we shall have to ensure a best-fit so that both the parties are satisfied. It may take a week more. Meanwhile, please hurry with the police verification."

"After we match the prospective Employer, the Employer shall have a video conference with you in our office. The status of your employment prospects can be firmed up if the Employer selects you for further salary and perk negations," said Syed.

Syed explained to them the work environment in Saudi and their obligatory conduct in that country as per the prevailing rules and customs. He would contact them as soon as any Sponsor showed interest in their resumes.

***

Shafique Travels and Tours Office has a long term contract for technical man-power recruitment with HG group of KSA.

Hasan Gosaibi is not related to the famous and affluent Al Gosaibi family, nevertheless owns a large business establishment in Dammam, the port city of Saudi Arabia. Gosaibi has a Bachelor of Business Administration degree from England; the HG group has wide-ranging investments in trading and shipping. The Group is the authorised distributor for Mercedes Benz and BMW cars. Additionally, the Group has recently entered into real estate – Rakeem Real Estate - with a contract to build a multi-storeyed building for Port Authority, Dammam. He appointed Shafique Travels and Tours as his contact to source all his workers for his businesses. Shafique Travels arranges the labour and staff for the Group's car sales and service department. Shafique's employee recommendations are given due consideration because of their experience with Gosaibi Group. However, they would never bypass the video interview. Most of the time, Mr. Gosaibi would personally select his staff during the discussion. He believes that the well-planned recruitment process he follows is the foundation for his success so far. From the employee's point of view, Shafique never had any complaints from his customers, including the HG. Presently Shafique was given the contract for sourcing staff and skilled labour for his new real estate venture, starting with the Port Authority contract.

***

The call from Syed did not materialize, which worried Abdul and Ameer. They had already invested their life savings in this gamble.

They decided to visit and stay put in Mumbai to pursue the matter. They spent time roaming around the city. Movie-going was expensive compared to what it was in Vadodara. So, they travelled in buses like vagabonds. With the help of the hotel concierge, they got the trip details of bus numbers that would take them to places of interest. Sometimes they walked too. Chowpatty,

Gateway of India, Marine Drive etc., were within walking distance of their lodge. Food was cheap in Mumbai. They could manage night dinners with vada-pav with lasoon-ki-chutney or pav-bhaji with dollops of AMUL butter at an affordable cost from the street vendors near VT. In the afternoons, as suggested by the counter receptionist, they preferred Udupi thali which would be within their budget. These restaurants were quickly locatable in every nook and corner of Mumbai. As suggested by Kaamini, they shunned non-veg food. Upon the cashier's recommendation at the counter, they ventured to visit Haji Ali, a tomb of a Sufi saint.

"It is obligatory for all visitors of Mumbai to pay obeisance to the Saint irrespective of their faiths. It is constructed in the sea about 200 meters from the shore. There is a causeway leading to the tomb. Walking on that is exhilarating. Also, don't forget to taste the fruit juice at the causeway entrance. It is heavenly," informed the cashier.

They spent considerable time on the parapet wall along the pavement abetting the road, watching the people who sat in their cars waiting for the vendor to bring fresh juice topped with cherry to their car windows. They saw modest Marutis to expensive BMWs waiting patiently for their turn, sitting in their air-conditioned comfort. The breeze with considerable humidity that came from the west cooled them. They promised to thank the cashier for his suggestion, especially about the fruit juice. It was a beautiful place to enjoy the tasty concoction.

Three days passed by. They decided they would not wait for the call from Syed. Instead, they wanted to visit the Agency office, uninformed to check the status of their applications. Meanwhile, Syed telephoned them and he was surprised to know they were already in Mumbai and called them to visit the office.

They met the same blue-uniformed person at the office who was about to thrust a slip with a number on it. Meanwhile, Sharmila recognized them and pointed them to Syed, sitting next to her. Syed waved away the security guy and signalled them to follow him into a room inside the office. Syed was brownish like the trunk of a teak tree, nevertheless with a pleasant demeanour. He was dressed in western clothes and wore his beard long. The man was tall, nearly six feet. He led them to a room; made them feel comfortable. The room was not the same as the one they had been to earlier with Sharmila. This room was larger with a giant LED screen with external speakers attached to both sides and a large table with many chairs around it.

"It took longer than I thought for me to contact your would-be employer as he was busy," said Syed. "I talked with him yesterday, and he showed interest in a video meeting with Abdul. Who is Abdul, between you two?"

Abdul raised his hand. Syed turned towards Ameer and said, "The HG group to whom I had sent your application regrets informing you that your experience does not match his requirements. He deals in state-of-the-art car brands such as Mercedes, BMW, Audi, etc., which are of German make. They are mostly electronically operated. Your experience does not show that you have such exposure. However, you need not feel dejected. I will send your resume to another Car dealer who operates from Riyadh."

"Does that mean I have to pay Rs 5,000 again to find another Sponsor?" asked Ameer, remembering what Sharmila told them the other day.

"No, we are waiving this requirement this time," said Syed. "However, I need another couple of days to find another interested

Sponsor for your application." Ameer appeared sad but could do nothing other than wait.

"Abdul, I shall fix the meeting tomorrow, i.e. 4 p.m. IST, subject to the Sponsor's availability. Please come to the office at about two in the afternoon. We have to train you to manage the meeting. There are some protocols we need to follow," said Syed.

"Surely, we shall be here by two tomorrow."

"Ameer can come too, but he will not be allowed to be present in the meeting with the Sponsor. The meeting is confidential between the Employer and the candidate. Even we are not allowed in the meeting," said Syed. "However, Ameer can come to the office and be present for the training session. In the actual meeting, he has to wait outside."

After bidding "Allah Hafiz', both walked out of the office. It was now clear to both of them they might have to live in different cities in Saudi. The next day, at the appointed time, they went to the Office of Shafique Travels and Tours and were ushered to the same room they had met Syed the day before. Instead of Syed, another person entered the room and greeted them.

"Hi, I am Ambrish Chavan. I am the trainer. Who is Abdul?" Ambrish was in his jeans with a neatly tucked striped shirt and was clean-shaven. His English diction showed he was well educated.

Abdul raised his hand and said, "Is the appointment for the video meeting been fixed?"

"Yes, maybe so, I don't have much idea. My job is to train you for the meeting, whenever it may happen".

Ambrish then updated them right from greeting the Employer to courtesies shown during the conversation. "No interruption while the Employer is speaking. Never ask questions about salary and benefits. That will be negotiated by the Agency later after acceptance of your candidacy. If you are not fluent in Arabic, say so and speak English. Answer to the point. If the Employer asks your opinion on any matter he may have made, be polite and don't give any controversial answers," cautioned Ambrish.

The training went on with mock questions and answers for an hour and a half. When Ambrish found Abdul was ready to face the prospective Employer, he intimated on inter-com to Syed and proceeded to leave the room.

"Sir, I have a question for you," said Ameer," you need not respond if it is inconvenient to you or confidential".

"Ok. Go ahead. To answer or not is my prerogative."

"Your Agency's experience is exemplary, as is evident from our meetings with you and other staff members. Did you find that the candidate you have provided employment had faced difficulties in his workplace – contract violations or ill-treatment etc.?"

"I am not obliged to answer it. But off the record, I can describe one situation you may not refer to in any conversation with any other staff of our Agency," said Ambrish.

"You have our assurance," said Abdul.

"A few years back, when I was new to this organization, I had come across a case wherein we had to bring the candidate back to India at our cost because of contract violation by the Sponsor," said Ambrish

"Could you elaborate?"

Ambrish looked at his watch and said," we have little time. However, I will be brief on the matter. We had engaged a lady from Azamgarh, UP. We employed her in the house of a well-to-do businessman in Jeddah as a home nurse for his mother, who needed 24/7 attention. The other house members harassed her by asking her to do domestic chores like washing clothes, ironing, cooking food etc., which was not a part of the contract. In addition, they were not giving care by providing timely meals and a comfortable place to stay; she was denied medical help when she fell sick. After a few months, she managed to contact our office in Riyadh and explained her predicament. Our local office could not do much as the businessman was very influential; we were afraid we might land into trouble if we interfered. Fortunately, the lady sneaked out of the house one night and came away to our Office in Riyadh. Please appreciate her guts travelling from Jeddah to Riyadh alone. Our manager had then contacted the Indian Embassy and explained the matter. When we offered her another suitable job in Saudi, she refused as she was traumatized by this experience. Hence, we flew her back to India at our cost."

"Do such events happen now also?' asked Ameer.

"No. It never happened again. Maybe with other agencies. We have incorporated a validation of the Sponsors' system in our Riyadh office. We strengthened our Riyadh office, wherein we thoroughly check the antecedents of the Sponsors before we accept their contract. That is one of the reasons we have staffed our Riyadh office with locals with good educational backgrounds and local knowledge by paying high salaries. This adds to our infra cost," said Ambrish, defending his Employer. They thanked Ambrish and waited for Syed to start further proceedings. Syed requested Ameer to leave the room.

The interview was a smooth sail. Surprisingly, contrary to what Sharmila told us, the interviewer was not the owner. The evaluator was one of the managers, who appeared to be of Asian descent —a Bangladeshi maybe. It was indeed a one-to-one meeting. The interviewer had introduced himself as Mehdy Hassan. None from the Agency was present, except for a brief period Ambrish fixed the technicalities of the video transmission and left the room to us. As per the protocol suggested by the trainer, I followed all the courtesies, including the greetings of Assalaam Alaikum and Shukran. I came out with the pleasant feeling that my varied experience with Patel and Patel had impressed the assessor. In the end, Hassan told me to wait for a week to hear from them, as the Agency and his boss had to agree on the contractual clauses. After a couple of days, Ameer also had his interview with his Sponsor from Riyadh. He said that he also hoped for a good result. After both of our interviews concluded, we decided to return to our family and jobs at Vadodara.

Abdul and Ameer locked their room, came down, and handed over the keys, asked the cashier to settle their account, paid the amount, and waited for the change.

"How are you guys going back? The Vadodara train leaves at night at 10:30 from Central. It's only 5 p.m. now," asked the concierge.

"We don't have reservations for the train. We are planning to catch a bus", informed Ameer.

"Have you bought the tickets for the bus?"

"No, we are told they are easily available at Borivili highway where the buses stop to pick passengers."

"No doubt, but you may not get a seat you would want, not side-by-side. An agent near New Empire theatre who has the authority to book on any bus to anywhere can help in booking your passage," said the cashier, who just handed them the balance cash after adjusting their rent.

"Are his charges too high?"

"Just nominal. However, it gives comfort feeling you are sure to board the bus," added the cashier.

They gave the clerk at the counter the required amount to buy the Bus tickets and waited.

A man squatting down on the floor with knees bent next to their sofa asked them," How are you planning to go to Borivili?"

He was the hotel porter lugging customers' baggage up and down the stairs. They told him they would catch a suburban train.

"We are told all the trains from Churchgate go through Borivili!" said Abdul. "Yes, but be careful with your wallets and other belongings while on the train, especially while alighting," said the porter.

They gathered further information on the ways of reaching the Inter-city Bus-stops from Borivili railway station and left for the terminus much in advance, eager to go home.

***

Frequent absence from work by Abdul had inconvenienced Venkateshwar Rao. He called Abdul to his room and reprimanded him. Abdul could not afford to annoy him, as he was unsure of his Saudi job prospect. He walked into his boss' cabin and apologized while giving some silly reasoning about his mother's illness.

"We need to get the final handing over formalities completed immediately. Festival season is coming. Many clients want to take over possession, register the property and perform gruhapravesham[33]. Please concentrate on all pending snag points and get things going. Raman has the list of flats that are required to be handed over. We also need finances to do the finishing work, which can only be paid after the handing of the flats. Would you

---

33   House warming

please ensure the jobs are done and registrations completed? Please seek guidance from Ghosh on registration formalities. Please see that no further complaints arise of your absence. Have a good day", said Venkateshwar and dismissed Abdul with a wave of a hand.

Abdul felt sorry for his behaviour and swore to himself to be more diligent in discharging his work priorities. He could not annoy the present boss till the final formalities of Visa and Work Permit arrive from the Agency.

SAARIKA

Abdul had seen Bhikubhau's door ajar and entered without knocking. He saw Saarika covered to the neck with a makeshift quilt, watching the telly. She was watching a Marathi film immersed deeply. She felt a cold breeze, gazed at the door, and noticed Abdul at the door. Abdul had a specific purpose for wanting to meet Bhiku. Bhiku was known for helping people in speeding up their piped-gas connection approvals. Abdul wanted Bhiku's help fixing gas connections to all the apartments of the new building of P&P Constructions before the flats were handed over to the owners. His boss wanted a unique selling opportunity for his company that no other builder could offer.

Saarika knew Abdul as the brother of Munni, who was her friend in the neighbourhood. As Munni was her confidant, she knew Abdul's family and their internal problems and disputes. She stealthily used to watch Abdul whenever she visited their house when he was around. She learned about him from Munni: he was kind, soft-spoken, and the family's darling. She had fallen for Abdul- hopelessly and passionately.

With Munni, our pet topic of discussion was love. What is love? Where shall we find it? Who will give us eternal bliss of love and togetherness? Munni has a practical vision of love, whereas I am romantic. She thinks love is the fruit of planned choice, whereas I believe it sprouts from pleasurable impulses in strange settings. Ganesha decides the place and person of my love. Munni was a transformed person; whenever she came to our home, we danced, sang, and made merry, whereas she behaved like a docile girl in her home. After Munni had gone to Dubai after her nikah, I had none to share my thoughts. I miss her.

"Baba, not at home?" inquired Abdul. She turned sideways, fixing a friendly gaze, the likes of which he hadn't seen before.

The kind of gaze that, when aimed at you, makes you feel like the most important person on earth.

When she stood up, the quilt fell sideways, and he could see the shape of a mature young girl. He never noticed Saarika so closely, even though she was a frequent visitor to his home. She had long hair tied firmly as a bun secured with bobby pins. He was taken aback by her looks. An understated form of beauty masked by rustic simplicity. Her garment gaped open. Abdul could see one perfectly formed breast sans bra.

"Baba had a call from the office, and he had to rush as there was a gas pipe explosion near Sayaji hospital," informed Saarika. She muted the TV that was blaring when he entered.

"It is ok. I will be back," Abdul replied while he traced his steps back.

"Come in and have some tea, *aap hamare ghar kabhi bhi aaye nahin!*[34], "she said in a coyly complaining tone. Saarika had that intimacy with Abdul, her friend's brother.

While visiting Munni's home, Saarika participated in songfests that Munaaf frequently organized to pass the time. Sometimes Abdul too attended these events during holidays and Sundays, and the entire household of Abdul became close and friendly with Saarika, as though she was a member of the house.

---

34   You never came to our home

Before Abdul could reply, the mobile rang, and she picked up and spoke. Abdul realized it could be from Bhiku, evidenced by the respect in her voice. He overheard some dialogues, which were later confirmed by Saarika: the explosion was a big one; though no one was injured, it required immediate repair; otherwise, it would deprive the entire locality of gas. Her baba needed to be present to supervise and facilitate the work. So he said he would take at least two more hours to come home, and she should finish her dinner and sleep. "Please sit down; I will make some tea for you."

How relationships develop and ripen is all a matter of a series of coincidences.

He sat down while Saarika unmuted the TV. Captivating romantic music from the film soon engulfed the room. Bhiku's house was small compared to the Navrang Park Society norms. The house consisted of a single big room, more like a hall, with an open kitchen and a small adjoining room. It had one small single bed, which gave some privacy to Saarika. A toilet opened into the hall facing her room in the narrow passage. Daylight into the narrow path came via the bathroom from the glass slits of a vent, which opened into the lane outside. The main room had a large bed facing the TV.

Apart from the single bed, Saarika's room was filled will all the family's belongings tucked up in the attic and an old wooden cupboard propped by a brick as a fourth leg. The room had walls on three sides with no door. It opened directly into the main kitchen-cum-hall via a narrow passage. She used *hessian* as a curtain on a string to hide her bed and belongings from the main hall. The large bed on which Saarika was presently sitting while watching the telly was flush to the wall in the main hall. The bed was large enough for the big-sized Bhiku to sleep with heavy snoring. The light in the room was very dim, with no ventilation. They kept the main door partly ajar to ensure sunlight to save on electricity. The rest of the room was almost empty except for one plastic chair presently on which Abdul sat as directed by Saarika.

Bhiku was the other Hindu family, apart from Jayshree teacher in the society, most of which were Deobandi Muslims. Since 2002, Hindus and Muslims hardly had any bonding, let alone brotherhood, even though there were never riots. However, the tension between the communities was palpable. Bhiku's income did not allow him to find more suitable accommodation and he stayed put in the predominately Muslim locality. He found the locality safe for his daughter, when he had to work at odd hours, as it is walled and secure colony.

Abdul saw a photo of a woman in a saree worn in Maharashtrian style draped like a dhoti hung above the TV. Abdul watched Saarika making tea. He noted her sensuously round body as her thin housecoat could not conceal her shape. He experienced an unexplained tickle in his groin.

Women have this uncanny ability to understand the stare of men even without having to look at them.

Saarika quickly fetched a cotton towel and proceeded to cover herself while at one hand stirring the teapot. She ground some masala and added it to the boiling tea mix. Milk was already in the mix. She found two ceramic cups and poured the brew into them after straining. The strainer had seen better times; presently, some tiny tealeaf shreds came through the sieve into the cup. While she was serving the tea, her bun was undone, and she let her hair fall loosely on her back.

She placed both the cups on the stool, "Please take your tea," she requested. Abdul picked up the cup and proceeded to sip. She poured her tea into a ridged steel plate and drank with a slurping sound.

"I understand Munni has left for Dubai already," Saarika asked more as a conversation starter than any need for information, as she already knew.

Without lifting his look from the cup, Abdul answered," Yes, it was sudden. Her husband managed a visa for her, and she had to leave urgently."

The towel was slung on her arm to facilitate ease of relishing the tea. Being nearer than she was when she was in the kitchen, her unique aroma filled Abdul's nostrils. He took his eyes off her chest lest she felt offended.

Abdul was uncomfortable. He wondered if what he thought was happening could be true. Meanwhile, the front door creaked slightly, and a violent gust of cold winter air pierced the room.

Saarika asked, "Cold breeze is coming. Shall I close the door tight?"

He nodded. Saarika took the cue and bolted the door with a horizontal bar that old houses had.

While lifting the empty cups, Saarika's hair brushed lightly against his face, and it bought with it a body odour he felt he was destined to own. He wondered whether it was deliberate. She put the cups in the kitchen sink and sat on the bed, now nearer to his chair than when she watched telly. The movie was still on. Some very gory scenes were being depicted, which disturbed Saarika, and she changed the channel to ETV, which was telecasting the Christmas celebrations from some western countries. He got up from the chair to go.

"Do you have to go? Do you have any urgent work?" she asked while she gently pulled his arm to make him sit on the bed next to her.

Abdul did as directed as an obedient student would.

"Nafisa Bhabhi respected you, as I learnt from Munni. Why did she leave you and run away to Mumbai?"

Saarika was excessively inquisitive. She immediately regretted what she said. Abdul was not particularly interested in discussing this forgotten episode of his life. He shrugged his shoulders.

"*Maaf karna*[35], I should not have raised this topic," said Saarika apologetically.

"It's ok", he said sheepishly.

Sitting next to her was becoming torture now. Abdul again got up to go. She got up with him to lead him to the door. Then an unexpected thing happened. A shriek from outside suddenly pierced the air. She immediately clung to him out of fear. The scream was an ecstasy from a group of youth playing caroms – a local version of a board game similar to billiards though on a smaller table - in the neighbourhood.

"Sorry," she said, and he saw a blush bloom on her cheeks in the dim light. He pulled her gently to him. She did not resist. He hugged her, and he lost control. Reluctantly he let her go. However, she would not. She drew him to her. He involuntarily moved his hands over her breasts and found erect nipples touching his palm. She moaned and pushed his hand into her housecoat, and she let him feel the softness of her skin. It aroused him further.

Before they knew what was happening to them, they were in bed naked and caressing each other. Abdul moved his hands, slowly with skilful sensuality, as he knew by now what she wanted. When she was responding to him, doubts and anxiety still plagued him. However, soft murmurings made her pleasure

---

35   Excuse me

clear. She wanted more of him. She could feel his back lifting and fall on her, and she could feel his body heat, his smell.

The ethical issues were now in a maze of an inexplicable quest for love and sex. She now lost her virginity to a man she all the time silently loved and admired. No wonder she was more self-assured in the act of lovemaking. She wanted him, and she got him. She was triumphant as though she had won a lottery—no guilt for her.

There was no dialogue between them during or after the act, except she moaned a lot. She guided him to spots that gave her pleasure as though he was a teenager on his first date. He obliged as directed. Later, he dressed and limped out of the door. He did not look back. He had no courage to face her. Saarika relaxed and was in a trance on the bed, looking at the ceiling. She vaguely remembered her baba knocking on the door late in the night, and she involuntarily led him inside, gave water to him and walked past him to her bed. She also remembered baba telling her he would be late to work the next day and need not wake him for tea in the morning.

All night lying in bed, Saarika pictured Abdul kissing her belly, the feel of his hand on her chest, her neck and back and below the navel. She was reliving the roughness of his skin and the tickles his chest hair gave her when she lay on him spent. Saarika had this peculiar warm sensation spread upwards and felt a spontaneous smile come to her. She was sleeping with this smile still on her face when dawn creaked through the gap in the bathroom shutters.

The belief that it's worth taking a chance on love transcends all rational thinking, and the gambler instinct in us takes over. It is intoxicating.

Saarika woke up with some difficulty and beamed to herself about what she had experienced the night before. Soon there was spring in her step. She quickly said her prayers to her favourite God, Ganesha.[36]

"Vakra-Tunndda Maha-Kaaya Suurya-Kotti Samaprabha

Nirvighnam Kuru Me Deva Sarva-Kaaryeshu Sarvadaa"[37]

She began arranging the utensils in the kitchen as though she had bought them the day before. She cleaned the house with a broom and later with a wet cloth. She went to the bathroom, washed all her clothes, and dried them on the string above her bed. All the time, while humming the lilting tune she watched the previous night. She ensured there was as little noise as possible not to disturb her sound-asleep baba. With unbridled energy, she set about cooking a meal for her baba. Whenever her baba went late to work, he preferred hot meals at home; otherwise, she had to pack a lunchbox for him. She made her baba's preferred *aamti*[38], which she learnt from her *aayee* and some aloo *palak subji*[39] which she observed Munni's *ammijaan* preparing it.

I shall make rotis when he is awake, and he can have them hot.

Any girl who spent an unscheduled conjugation with a man 15years older with unprotected sex would be worried about the dangerous repercussions. Not Saarika. It did not matter to her he was a Muslim, and she was a Hindu. She was confident her Ganesha would protect her. After all, her periods were due within the next ten days, and she would be free of any untoward effects. She remembered Shah Rukh Khan's dialogue in a recently watched film.

---

36   Hindu God

37   A prayer to Lord Ganesha – the Hindu God

38   Maharashtrian preparation of lentils

39   A curry of north Indian origin

When you desire anything sincerely, the whole universe will conspire to help you achieve your wish.

Instead, she imagined the would-be times when she and Abdul would sit in a theatre and watch films about love, longing and some melodramatic tales of separation and final reunion. Later come back home and make more passionate love. She would sew for him and shampoo him like her mother used to do. She would cook his favourite dishes, those she learnt from his ammijaan.

Abdul

It was a different scene with Abdul. Guilt troubled him.

What have I done? If she conceives, there would be riots. Imagine the headline in the papers: MUSLIM MAN RAPES A YOUNG INNOCENT HINDU GIRL. Moreover, it might affect my Saudi job prospects. My family would be devastated. What should I do?

"Abdul *beta*, come down for dinner." That was *ammijaan*.

"I am not hungry," curtly replied Abdul shouting from the room upstairs.

Abdul tried to sleep off his guilt. Nevertheless, he could hardly catch a wink. He was tossing on the bed the whole night, and his brother on the other side of the bed was complaining of the continuous movement that disturbed his sleep.

No, I must do something to prevent any complications. Abdul resolved.

The next day he quickly dressed and left home without breakfast, his *ammijaan* shouting after him to have *nashta*[40]. His motorcycle did not fire as it usually would. He tried several times and finally gave up. He felt it was a bad omen and waved a rickshaw instead.

Mandvi, a locality in the city where his family lived before shifting to the Tandalja area, was Rs60 away by auto rickshaw. Ameer lived there with his Hindu wife. Ameer, being a car

___
40   breakfast

mechanic, had been working with a private Maruti[41] approved workshop. They confide in each other over all matters of family and life in general. They have been friends for over ten years now. They had been improving their respective skills to be eligible for jobs in Saudi for immigrant labour. However, presently Saudi job was not uppermost in Abdul's mind.

Abdul paid off his fare and walked into the workshop. He had already informed his employer he would be late for work, having given an excuse of taking his ammijaan to hospital. Abdul saw Ameer walk towards him dressed in his work overalls. He took Abdul to a corner of the reception room where the drivers of the vehicles would come to either hand over their cars for repair or servicing or take them back. As there was not much privacy; on Abdul's suggestion, they walked into a nearby Irani Restaurant.

"I did not understand much from your call; there was too much disturbance," said Ameer

Abdul explained the situation without the intimate part of his misadventure.

Abdul said," Ameer, I don't know what I have done; it was a moment of passion. I am worried; please tell me what to do now?"

"What's to be done? Just chill. Forget the episode, "Ameer stated matter-of-factly.

"What nonsense! What if she conceives? It will be hell to pay. The whole Vadodara city will be up in flames. Have you forgotten March 2002?" asked Abdul irritably.

"Meet her and ask her to take morning-after pills ", advised Ameer. Ameer was aware of these nuances of a woman's biology, coached by his spouse, a nurse.

---

41   Popular Indian Car brand

You need to take the emergency contraceptive pill within 3 days to 5 days of unprotected sex for it to be effective – the sooner you take it, the more effective it'll be.

"And it is available over the counter," added Ameer.

"Have you gone mad? You want me to knock on her door again, give her pills, and request her to gulp them. How can you think of such a ridiculous suggestion? I am not a frequent visitor to her house. I cannot simply meet her alone at any time. I had been there just once, only because my company wanted some help from her dad. That's all. No, this won't work. "

"You are indeed in a shit load of trouble," declared Ameer.

"Now tell me what I should do. There isn't time to guess. We need some concrete plan."

"We have to know when her periods are due", said Ameer

He had come out of a statement that defied credulity.

"How can we know that? Even if an *Aladdin-ka-Chirag*[42] tells us, how does it help?" wondered Abdul

"At least it will tell us when our uncertainty will end," replied Ameer.

"You are not being serious."

Just then, Ameer's mobile rang. He picked and answered, "Yes, Shilpa, what is it?"

Meanwhile, Abdul was sipping tea with total disinterest, blankly looking into oblivion. His mind was not functioning. Ameer cut the phone after a five-minute conversation and returned to sipping tea. He did not know from where to resume the conversation.

---

42   An Arabic folk tale reference

I was very indifferent. I must be more proactive.

Ameer broke the eerie silence between them, "I think we have three possible options. One is to confide in my wife Kaamini, with her help to reach Saarika and convince her about the morning after pill. Moreover, this has to bed done within two days. The second one is to wait and pray to Allah for forgiveness by performing *Salaat*[43]. The third option is to meet Bhiku Mane and sincerely apologize and ask him to take his daughter to a doctor if she misses her periods with a promise to compensate." Abdul looked through him without uttering a word. He was at a loss for words.

Finally, he spoke," All the three options are not feasible. Firstly, I cannot confide in Kaamini. She thinks I am the epitome of all Islam teaches about giving respect to women. I dare not tell her that I fucked a Hindu girl fifteen years younger without protection, and I need her help covering the culpability. That's embarrassing. I am not also comfortable facing Saarika's baba." They sat for a few more minutes, and when Ameer's phone rang again, he abruptly cut the same and apologetically ran back to his workshop with a promise to meet again in the evening to discuss the matter further.

Of all the hardships a man has to face, none would be more exhausting than waiting for your girlfriend's menstrual cycle after you had passionate and unprotected sex.

Abdul found his way to his workplace. After convincing Abdul, Ameer took Kaamini into confidence and requested her help in the matter. This indecisiveness cost four precious days, as the original proposal of the morning-after pill would not work. Kaamini could convince Saarika to meet Abdul at a park to come to a solution to the matter. The park, which was on the backside

---

43   One of the five pillars of Islam – a prayer

of the dome of a planetarium nestled between the station and Sayaji hospital, had a wooden bench on which the threesome sat with Abdul standing staring into space. He felt as if his mouth was full of quick-setting cement.

Ameer had seated himself on the edge of the park bench to give space to both the ladies. No one talked for a few minutes. All the three of them were looking around to see whether they were indeed alone on an odd afternoon.

Only vagabonds and lovers come to the park in the afternoon!

The men did not know what to say. Both men now fell silent, engrossed in their thoughts.

"It is difficult to explain," Abdul broke the silence. "Kaamini, please help."

Kaamini wondered whether to tell Saarika how precarious her position was, worse than she could have imagined. Nevertheless, Saarika appeared nonchalant. So she decided against it.

For her part, Kaamini's thoughts were on the future. Her main priority was how to help Saarika get through this. In the discussions before this meeting, when Kaamini met Saarika, she had requested her to come to the park meet, Saarika stubbornly hoped that Abdul would marry her. She had complete trust in her lover.

Finally, Kaamini broke the silence when she murmured," Obviously, Abdul had not discussed the enormity of this matter with you yet. Can I do a D&C quietly?"

"What is D&C?" asked Saarika. Abdul and Ameer were mute spectators to this conversation.

"It is a brief surgical procedure that clears the uterus walls of semen so you will not be pregnant because of this incident, or we can do a manual vacuum aspiration to remove the remnants of the semen on the uterus walls, as per my doc recommendation."

"It is safe and requires half an hour of work in the clinic. You can go home almost immediately", added Kaamini.

Saarika looked at Abdul, which made him feel guilty. Looks said it all.

Finally, Saarika opened up," My periods are due in another week max. I am sure Lord Ganesha is with me, and I shall not be pregnant. If it is GOD's will that I become a mother to Abdul's child, so be it. I don't want to do this procedure. My decision is final."

"But if you become pregnant without marriage, your baba would be furious", said Kaamini

"I am leaving this matter to Lord Ganesha and Abdul to sort it out as I don't want to go through any medical procedure against God's will", said Saarika. She started to walk away without waiting for anyone to react to her bombshell.

For a moment, Abdul sensed something he could not fathom. It exasperated him.

There were many tangents to a woman's thinking. Their thinking crossed yours at a 180-degree angle. The younger they were, the less understandable.

Abdul ran after her, put her in a rickshaw and asked the driver to take her to Navrang Society. Abdul, shell shocked, returned to Kaamini and Ameer sitting on the bench.

They had no idea how to circumvent the potentially explosive situation that could consume their family peace and that of the city, state, and beyond. Saarika was unaware of these complications, as she had no clue of the ramifications of their impromptu conjugation, which appeared to her as natural between lovers.

"I shall marry Saarika," announced Abdul breaking the silence.

"Do you understand the repercussions of this?" shouted Ameer.

"Saarika had trusted me, and I shall not disappoint her. I think she loves me a lot, which I could feel on the night of our meeting. Anyway, my divorce papers have come thanks to Quadri Pasha."

"How will ammijaan react? Have you thought of that? Another important matter is both of you belong to different mazhab[44]. It further complicates the issue," said Ameer

"You and Kaamini are of the same complication," said Abdul, mockingly stressing the word 'complication'.

Ameer and Kaamini were neighbours, and their parents knew each other well, so there were not many objections to this alliance, though some elders from both sides tried to create doubts about the future of this marriage. Interfaith marriages were not rare in Muslim households, provided the bride converted to Islam. However, in the case of Ameer and Kaamini, neither parent insisted on the conversion. The wedding took place under the Special Marriages Act.

They spent some more time discussing all the pros and cons of the situation and yet could not arrive at any consensus. The sun began to set and sent coloured rays slanting under the trees. The threesome had decided to meet the next day again. They did not have the luxury of postponing any decision. Abdul requested Ameer to check with the sub-registrar office if there were any changes in the procedures for marriage under the Special Marriages Act since the time they got married. Ameer said proof of birthdate would be essential. Saarika's date of birth proof

---

44   Religion

would be difficult to obtain in this present scenario, as she had not completed her schooling. Kaamini decided to check about what kind of proof Saarika could provide.

***

Kaamini adjusted the patient's pillow in the ICU and topped the IV bottle. The bed was made upright as per the wish of the patient. She was about to move to the next patient when her mobile beeped inside her apron pocket. She wanted to ignore and carry on with the last patient and take up this call later. However, curiosity made her check the caller's name. It was Saarika. She immediately moved out of ICU, went to the nurse's corner, and dialled that number.

"Hello, Kaamini!"

"Hello, Saarika. What is the matter?"

"I got periods," informed Saarika

"Wow, that's good news," said Kaamini

"I shall call back in the evening again after my rounds."

"Okay," said Saarika and pressed the off button on the phone.

Kaamini could not wait to tell Ameer the news.

She sent a text message: *Saarika got her periods. Call when free.*

Ameer called in the afternoon. "Let us meet with Abdul in the evening at his home," suggested Kaamini

They met at the open ground in Navrang Society in the evening after work. The day was losing to the night.

The three were sitting on the parapet wall. On Abdul's suggestion, they avoided meeting Saarika within the compound of Navrang Society.

"So, now there is no need for you to marry Saarika," said Ameer.

"That's nonsense. I want to marry Saarika, not as an atonement for my action because I like her. She likes me too."

"The only advantage of her periods is that we don't have to hurry the matter. We can try to get consent from both parents," said Abdul.

"So what is the next course of action?" asked Kaamini

"You, please call up ammijaan and fix a time for all of us to meet her this week", pleaded Abdul

"How about Saarika's parents?" asked Ameer.

"Saarika's mother died. She has only her dad," said Abdul.

"But we shall talk to him after we inform ammijaan and take Saarika's opinion on how to go about it with her baba".

Accordingly, they met at Altaf's house the next day evening. They decided Saarika should walk in after receiving a missed call from Kaamini after ensuring a proper *mahol*[45].

The television was blaring when they entered. Nazma switched off the set. She offered them two plastic chairs and pulled a plastic stool from the bathroom to the middle for Abdul to sit. She sat next to Nusrat on the sofa. Nazma inquired whether they needed tea.

When they declined, she sat down and said," It is a long time since you and Ameer visited us. How is your work going on?"

"Good, some Malayali nurses are on strike. So there is more work for us these days", said Kaamini.

"Ammijaan, Abdul wants to marry Saarika," announced Ameer.

---

45   Atmosphere

"Saarika! That Hindu girl who is a friend of Munni?" asked Nazma.

"Yes, ammijaan, "volunteered Abdul.

"When I have been requesting and pleading with you to marry for the past two years, you had all the time rejected the idea on one pretext or the other. Now, this *behuda*[46] proposal?" angrily questioned Nazma.

"Do you understand the effect of this suggestion on our family?"

"There is no disgrace as such. Many Hindus and Muslims marry and live happily", said Kaamini

"Kaamini, *aap iss maamle mein dakhal nahin dena*[47]," intervened Nusrat.

Abdul got upset at the tone of Nusrat and said, "Kaamini is my friend's wife. She is here on my invitation. Please treat her with respect." Unlike the hostility of Nusrat, Abdul spoke softly.

"From your look, this appears to be a well-thought-out proposal. You all have become adults and can take your own decisions. Who am I to object?" said Nazma with apparent helplessness. There was nothing for Nazma but to go along.

"I am sorry, ammijaan; I should have told you before. But I did not have the courage," said Abdul and got up from his seat and hugged Nazma to soothe her. She loved him and loved him from childhood. In addition, economic considerations for family well-being were now utmost on her mind. She had better not annoy Abdul. She needed his support!

"Did you discuss this proposal with her abbu?" asked Nazma.

---

46   Ridiculous proposal

47   Don't interfere in our matters

"Not yet; we wanted to discuss it with you first. And also want you to meet Saarika under these new circumstances if you want to ask her anything," said Abdul.

"What do I have to discuss with her? Can we call Quadri Pasha to help us in the matter?" asked Nazma.

"This matter is within our family, ammijaan. We can surely update him of our decision later as we need his support within the community," said Abdul.

Abdul signalled Kaamini to make the call to Saarika. "We shall call Saarika so that you can discuss the required formalities," said Abdul. While they waited for Saarika to arrive, Nazma made chai and placed some naankhatai[48] biscuits on the plastic stool. The door opened, and the evening sunrays graced the house. Saarika in salwar-kameez walked in shyly; a dupatta covered her head. Her long hair gleamed brightly in the evening sun. Saarika noticed a portrait of Altaf hung eccentrically behind Nusrat's sofa. A bunch of dusty plastic flowers on a stool paid obeisance to him.

"Please come in and take your seat, Saarika," politely welcomed Nazma. Saarika looked around to sit but had no chair left for her; Nusrat had to make way for her on her sofa.

All the visitor's eyes were on Nazma. "*Ammijaan, this is, above all, terrible for you*" was the feeling all of them sensed.

"Abdul is a great son and has all the qualities of his abbu. He puts family welfare above everything. He will make a good husband. You have chosen the right one," said Nazma in a conciliatory tone.

Saarika nodded and looked at Kaamini for a cue to say anything. There was silence in the room as Nazma offered tea and

---

48   Surat, Gujarat savoury

biscuits to Saarika, which she politely declined but took a piece of naankhatai and chewed it slowly.

"As you may know, Muslim men are prohibited from interfaith marriages, for instance, Hindus, Jains, Buddhists, etc., unless the man/woman converts to Islam. That is the law for the nikah as per our faith," said Nazma, "So you have to convert to Islam before performing the nikah."

Tears welled up and spilt down Saarika's cheeks, glistening in the sunlight. Abdul hated to see her cry. It made him want to cross the room and hug her tight in his arms. However, he could not. The atmosphere was that of a session's courtroom – quiet and ominous.

"No." She was still sobbing; her voice was low, hardly audible. "I don't want to convert."

Her statement was precise. Her voice firm.

"Then what do you want? I need to know because I have to take the elders' opinion in the society. If Abdul's abbu was alive, I need not have to go through this embarrassment for my family," yelled Nazma. She turned to Ameer and said," She loves him and yet she can't abide by his religious devotion?" she complained.

"Stop making a spectacle of yourself. You have driven Abdul insane with lust." That high pitched voice directed at Saarika was that of Nusrat. Sarcasm was rich in her voice. "*Hawas ka shikar*" was the actual phrase she had used. Abdul wanted to control the caustic voice of Nusrat. However, he couldn't reprimand her in front of strangers. With a plate full of fafda on her knees on the sagging couch, Nusrat looked like the glutton she was. Next to her sat Saarika with her arms crossed obediently. Saarika, Munni's friend, used to frequent her house, and Nusrat was a familiar figure, though they did not interact much. After Munni left for

Dubai, Saarika reduced her visits to sharing her batata[49] vadas with Abdul and Asif whenever she made them for her baba.

"Enough, Nusrat," shouted Nazma.

"Abdul let us discuss this matter with Quadri Pasha, and then we shall see what we have to do," announced Nazma as she stood up from her seat as a cue to say that it was time to disperse. The gathering drifted *en masse* out of the house.

Abdul was at a loss for words. The involvement of Quadri Pasha in their family affairs was not a welcome sign.

I hope Quadri Pasha will not put any spoke into our plans.

Later, Nazma briefed Quadri Pasha on her predicament. Abdul was not privy to this conversation.

As Saarika was adamant that she would not convert to Islam, Abdul from his side also did not insist. However, his ammijaan needed to be convinced. Quadri Pasha, fortunately, helped arrive at a compromise. She would change her name to Shabnam from Saarika and wear a burqa when she was out and about. It was acceptable to Saarika as in some Hindu sects; the woman changed her first name too after marriage – not only the surname.

***

"Now what's left is to convince Saarika's baba," said Abdul.

Presently, Abdul and Ameer sat at a table in the corner of Sri Krishna Udupi, Vadodara's thriving South-Indian Restaurant. They ordered Coffee. Abdul added his usual amount of sugar to his beverage.

"Kaamini had a talk with Saarika in this matter to fix a time to meet her baba, but she said her baba would never accept this

---

49   Potato in Marathi

marriage, and there was no point in meeting him at all," said Ameer.

Saarika was wary of broaching this inter-faith marriage proposal with her baba. She was confident that he would bring the roof down on hearing this and even threaten to torch the house of Altaf. He would believe that the Muslim family made his innocent daughter a scapegoat for their despicable needs. Saarika informed Kaamini (without giving full details of her baba's activities) that her baba would never agree. Further, he would blame Abdul's family, which would lead to unthinkable repercussions. Saarika knew why her baba would react the way she had informed Kaamini.

Hindu Sanskriti Abhyuday Manch (HSAM) was an organization registered as a society to propagate Hindu Culture amongst all Indian citizens, headquartered in Pune. Bhiku, is a card-holding member of HSAM. There were unconfirmed rumours that HSAM had a hand in the 2002 Vadodara communal riots. Before Saarika was born, Bhiku was a regular attendee of their drills and pravachans[50] while he was in Pune. Vidur Saraswat Narayan founded HSAM in 1992 during the Mumbai riots as a rival to Shiv Sena, another Hindu organization taking firm roots in India. Originally the Manch was formed to counter the western ideas in economics, agriculture and daily cultural life, which were influencing policymakers in India, manipulated by the travelling Non-Resident Indians. In due course, some of its members shifted part of their focus to anti-Muslim propaganda as much as anti-western. All members of the Manch were advised to inform their womenfolk not to wear pants – but only salwar kameez or saree – the Indian dress codes.

This interference often created tension with college-going women, who were comfortable in western clothes. On the first day of a new

---

50   Religious gatherings

academic year at Fergusson College in Pune, the members of HSAM had forced the jean-clad girls to go home and told them that they would be allowed entry only in Indian clothes. This uncalled for directive has alienated the Manch from youth, who found this regressive. The Manch also opposed the music concert of Michael Jackson organized by Shiv Sena in Mumbai, with a massive demonstration in which many HSAM members have lost limbs. Few lives too in the stampede consequent to lathi[51] charge by Shiv Sena controlled police force. This protest gave the Manch much-needed fillip as the protector of Indian Culture. They also supported some Hindi Bollywood singers in their boycott of Muslim singers from Pakistan. Yet the Manch could not gain much ground vis-à-vis Shiv Sena and RSS, two forums of similar ideology.

That was when a new President who took office after fresh organizational elections declared that they should oppose all inter-faith marriages because they felt these alliances were meant to convert Hindus into Islam. They formed a particular cell to notify such marriages. They strongly and sometimes violently demonstrated against these weddings. Bhiku became the Chairman of this cell. The member's job was to visit each Sub Registrar Office in their jurisdiction, which mandatorily notified on its display-board in their office of all marriages that were being performed under the Special Marriages Act, to note the details of the bride and groom. If any member found that the couple belonged to different faiths, they were to be directed to the Chairman, who would give instructions on dealing with the situation. Some traditional Muslims who believed it was blasphemy to wed a converted Hindu also joined this particular cell of the Manch, renaming Faith Forum. Under Bhiku's leadership, this Forum spread its tentacles across Maharashtra, Gujarat, MP, Andhra Pradesh and West Bengal. Bhiku's involvement in the Manch activities required much travel, which was a source of attrition

---

51   Wooden round stick used by Police to control crowds

between him and his wife. In addition, his bosses at work did not take kindly to his frequent absence.

The death of his wife gave him more freedom to be militant in the Forum's activities. He often escaped being jailed helped by proxy members who took his place instead.

The Navrang Society members were unaware of this facet of Bhiku. He was seen only as a municipal employee in charge of piped gas connections to residences as he did not have any social interaction with the residents. He was cursing his financial status that he could not move out of this Muslim dominated Navrang Society. He always referred to Muslims as Aurangzeb-ke-aulad[52]. He never allowed any of his Manch colleagues to visit him at his house. He was afraid that if residents of Navrang Society came to know of his activities, they might force him to find another accommodation outside of Navrang Society.

"Does that mean we have to wed without Bhiku Mane's knowledge?" asked Abdul.

"Apparently."

"But we have to display the notice at the office of the Sub-Registrar about the impending marriage, "said Ameer," with photographs and proof of residence and date of birth."

"Yes, we have to find a way out of this. So that her baba does not object on some flimsy grounds," said Abdul.

"I will ask Kaamini to get details of her birth data and other details to be incorporated in the Notice as per the SMA act," said Ameer.

Consequent to Kaamini's talk with Saarika, they decided that the marriage would happen without the knowledge of Bhiku Mane. However, there was a problem with proof of date of birth,

---

52   Children of Aurangzeb – a derogatory term for Muslims

as she had not completed her school-final boards - discontinued after 8th standard. Though Saarika was past the minimum age of 18, the authorities would not accept the marriage notification unless the couple submitted authenticated date of birth proof in the required format.

With the help of a kind-hearted principal of Vasna Government School, where Saarika studied, Ameer managed to get a birth certificate, the date which suited the Act's requirement. Now the problem was how to disguise the notice in the board such that it did not appear as an inter-faith marriage to prevent it from coming to the attention of Bhiku's Manch members. On Raman's suggestion, Abdul hit upon the idea that some mock applications should also be filed along with their own so that the notice board becomes so full that space on the Notice Board would be cramped. This idea ensured that other notices on the board would camouflage Shabnam and Abdul's Notice. In addition, they decided to write Saarika's name as Shabnam, aka Saarika. Shabnam in larger font and Saarika in a much more challenging lower font in italics. They also took some staff members of the Sub-Registrar office into confidence. The address was an easy one, with ration card details, but cleverly Abdul had shown the house number as A.72, which was A.27.

In the north and some western Indian languages, which originated from Sanskrit, two-digit numbers are pronounced with the unit number first and tenth digit number next, unlike in English and some South-Indian languages. So this error could be ignored as accidental by an employee of the Registrar's office.

Saarika and Abdul's love for each other had not diminished in the face of all they had been through. If anything, it grew stronger. They could not meet in person without being too conspicuous as Bhiku's house was at the end of the lane, and the local boys play caroms most of the time near their house. Abdul longed to talk to her and spend more time with her. The intensity of his longing astonished him.

Kaamini helped their rendezvous at her home, where they planned their post-marriage life, including his approaching job trials in Saudi Arabia.

Some days when Kaamini was on night shift and Ameer would be late from his workshop; the lovers would have the whole house to themselves to be together. Sometimes they talked, sometimes they caressed each other, but it was enough that they joined their bodies together in a tight embrace. Then they drew away because they were both frightened of too much passion. She did not tell him she loved him and that he was her reason to breathe, to live. She wanted to say that the days for her would be endless without him. She didn't need to say these to him. He already knew. When he was not around, she would relive these moments and smile to herself.

The plan hatched by Ameer and Raman worked to perfection. The mandatory thirty day period passed without any hitch. However, they decided to wait for the day Bhiku would be out of Vadodara for one of his HSAM meetings before they registered their marriage. Finally, the ceremony took place at the sub-registrar office when Bhiku was out of Vadodara attending the annual three-day assembly of his Manch in Pune. The night before Saarika was to leave for the Sub-Registrar's office, she washed her hair, combed thrice in different styles, and felt sick with excitement.

Amir was one witness, and Abdul had requested his office colleague Raman to be his other witness. Quadri Pasha did not grace his presence as he disapproved of the matrimony that was not as per Islamic procedures, though he did help Abdul to get a divorce as per Muslim law. Kaamini could not attend as she had some pressing engagements at the hospital. Nevertheless, she accompanied the couple to their new house after the ritual.

Abdul's mother and siblings also did not attend the function.

However, they welcomed the groom and the bride to the house without any pomp or show. After all, Abdul was the eldest of the family, and they needed his income and emotional support for the family to survive after Altaf's death. The word spread within the society. They now attracted the piercing gaze of all neighbours. Quadri Pasha gave a mild Farman to all the society members to leave the family alone to sort out their matters.

***

Bhiku Mane found his house locked when he returned from Pune late evening with his backpack, tired of travelling by bus for 14 hours. He opened the house with his key, wondering where Saarika could have gone, and left the front door unfastened for Saarika to enter without knocking, as he would be in the toilet. Not finding her back from wherever she had gone, he gave a call on her mobile that went unanswered. That worried Bhiku. He came out of the house and found the local boys playing caroms under a light tapping the power illegally from a streetlight across the compound wall. He was about to ask them when he saw Saarika walking with a man he could not recognise from a distance. He went inside the house to change into nightclothes.

Abdul and Saarika walked into the house, and Saarika hugged Bhiku, said "maaf karna," and started crying. Abdul explained to Bhiku about his marriage with Saarika two days earlier in the Sub Registrar's Office.

"Hum ek doosare ko chahate hai. Isiliye shaadi kar liya hai," said Abdul in Hindi.

Bhiku turned to Saarika and said" तो काय म्हणाला [53]"

Saarika did not answer but started weeping again with her head bowed down without looking at him.

Abdul intervened, re-explained the events with more details and confirmed that his family welcomed Saarika as their *bahu*.[54] He would personally assure her well-being until death does them apart.

Bhiku's mind was swirling, his brain muddled, and he could not think clearly. He felt a splitting headache coming more so after the fatigue of extended travel. He walked away from the house and into the night.

"He is in shock. He will take time to understand the situation. Please give him space to come to terms with reality. Let us leave now and be back tomorrow with ammijaan and Ameer to assure him that you are in safe hands", said Abdul. A weeping Saarika trudged back to her new abode with Abdul holding her tight. The next day, the sweeper of the colony saw the door Bhiku wide open and found Bhiku's limp body hanging from the ceiling fan. He immediately alerted the security and Quadri Pasha, who informed the police that this was not a natural death. Later the police would describe the scene in their report.

An older man of around 60years was found hanging from a ceiling fan hook at his residence in Navrang Society. He was identified as Bhiku Mane, a municipal employee. The death appeared to be a case of suicide. Bhiku used a sari allegedly to hang himself. He left a suicide note addressed to no one in particular, which in summary, said that he did not wish to blame anyone for his death. A post mortem report from Sayaji hospital stated "asphyxia due to hanging; as the cause

---

53   What did he mean?
54   Daughter-in-law

of death. The victim was a widower living with his daughter, who married recently.

Saarika was devastated and felt that she was solely responsible for her baba's death. She never expected this extreme reaction from her baba, as he showered enormous love on her and gave no reason to complain. Though they conversed little, both knew each other's needs and functioned accordingly. Saarika was aware of his extracurricular activities but was unsure of the extent and significance of his involvement in the Manch until she read the suicide note.

माझ्या मृत्यु साठी कुणालाही जबाबदार धरू नये. मी माझ्याच घरात माझे विचार, ज्याचा मी सार्वजनिकरित्या प्रचार करतो, तेच विचार मी माझ्या घरात लागु करु शकत नाही. यासाठी मी माझ्या सर्व मित्रांची आणि सहकार्‍यांची, जे माझ्याच घरात येऊन आपलीच विचारधारणा लागु करण्याचा प्रयत्नही करतात,क्षमा मागतो. मला आशा आहे आणि मी देवाची प्रार्थना करतो की, माझी मुलगी तिने घेतलेल्या निर्णयाबाबत नेहमीच आनंदी असावी. मी अशी ही प्रार्थना करतो की तिच्या सासरचे लोक तिला माझ्या विचाराबद्दल त्रास देणार नाहीत.[55]

Abdul had tried his best to console her.

I noted that I greatly underestimated Shabnam's resilience. Poised between love and death, she appeared composed amongst both emotions. She took charge of her dad's mobile and dialled a couple of numbers. One was to her Mausi[56] in Parbhani. The other was to one Mangesh Gosavi, who had organized his staff Manch members from Vadodara to assemble at Navrang Society to take control of the situation and report to him for further instructions. Like in Islam, I learnt that Hindus, too, would not let their women folk attend

---

55   *No one is responsible for my death. I cannot enforce the rules in my own house that I have publicly promoted. With this note, I seek the pardon from my Manch colleagues for flouting the preamble of our Constitution. I hope and pray that my daughter will be happy with her decision. I urge that her parents-in-law shall not victimise her for my beliefs.*

56   Mother's sister

to the last rites of a dead person. I wanted to help, but ammijaan objected vociferously, which made me retreat and leave the ground to the Manch members. It was also the intention of Shabnam, I later learnt. The last rites went off without any controversy, and Shabnam cleaned the house and returned to our home.

It took a few months for Shabnam to be normal again.

***

Finally, the contracts from Agency arrived within a gap of a day, for both the applicants.

Syed called Ameer the next night at ten p.m. as he usually did.

"Your Sponsor wants you to accept the contract and report within the next two weeks. Please plan and let me know so I can make arrangements from my side," said Syed.

"Isn't it a bit too short a time to decide? I need to notify my employer, and I have not read the contractual clauses in detail, too," pleaded Ameer.

"You may have to manage that. Your Sponsor's workshop superintendent has resigned and had to go back to Pakistan as his mother is ill, and he has some property related issues to be settled there. Therefore, your employer wants you early to have an overlap period before the present employee leaves Saudi shores," said Syed.

Ameer was astonished by this sudden development, as he needed to give his present employer two months' notice.

"Okay. I shall get back to you in a couple of days." The conversation ended abruptly. Ameer thought Syed might have been annoyed by his prevarication. Ameer's request to continue employment by granting him a sabbatical during his absence was rejected by his Manager. He decided to take a chance and go ahead and informed Syed accordingly. A couple of days later, Abdul's contract too arrived by mail.

Not able to decipher the contract, both of them decided to go over to Mumbai and have a face-to-face interaction with Syed and his team to understand the import of the agreement. Fortunately for Abdul, the final check of finished flats at Tower B and C was completed and snags attended. Tower A had some problems with roof leaks which needed to be attended to by the civil contractor, which would take at least two weeks. So his employers would not notice his absence. However, he informed Ghosh about his upcoming visit to Mumbai with some made-up story of a distant relative's death formalities.

"Welcome and congratulations to both of you," said Syed. Presently they were sitting in the mini-conference room in Agency's office in Mumbai.

"Thank you," they said. A short while later, Ambrish, too, joined them.

"Do we did not go to any a lawyer to validate the contents of the contract? Hope it is okay," asked Ameer.

"We don't as a policy object to you to get any advice from anyone. Let me caution you that the contract's contents, clauses, and conditions will not change. You either accept or reject," said Syed, "I only suggest you see mainly two aspects of the contract: whether the job responsibilities described suit your qualifications and experience; reporting date is convenient to you."

"Rest of the clauses regarding working conditions etc. are our responsibility. We shall ensure they conform to the regulations, laws and labour hiring rules prevalent in KSA and as per Indian Government directives," concluded Syed.

Later they studied the contract again with the help of Ambrish, whom Syed deputed to help them. Ambrish briefed them about the living conditions in KSA, cost of living, public behavioural norms, rules to be followed during namaaz etc. He answered all their doubts and assured them the contract was the best he had seen in the past year. Despite the 2008 financial collapse, KSA increased oil production much against the wishes of Americans and OPEC countries; Brent Crude was over $100 per barrel[57], and the Saudis raked dollars by billions. Because of the relative prosperity of KSA over other countries, Ambrish said they had received a lucrative offer, and one would be naïve not to accept, as long as their job responsibilities were in order.

He reiterated his Agency's Sponsors insisted upon their would-be employee's acceptance of the written job description. That was not all. From their side, they would never be reneging on these accepted conditions. If the contract required any changes or amendments because of business environmental changes during their employees' tenure, they would re-draw the contract taking the Agency into confidence. Ameer and Abdul negotiated their arrival dates and mutually decided they would go together by the same flight. Abdul was pleasantly surprised that his salary and perks were generous enough for him to send money home to help his family have a comfortable life as good as his abbujaan provided, if not better. He also believed by prudent spending; he could save too.

They signed the contracts, handed them over to the Agency for further process and returned to Vadodara.

***

It was almost four months since Abdul and Saarika had been married.

---

57   Since changed havocking the Saudi Economy

After our marriage, ammijaan handed over her room on the mezzanine floor to us, with Nusrat sharing the space with ammijaan in the adjoining room. Munaaf shared the common hall-cum kitchen with Asif.

Shabnam hardly had the opportunity to hug Abdul and profess her love to him. The room they allotted was being used by Asif for his academic pursuits as the downstairs hall had the deafening T.V. sound tuned in by Nusrat, much against everyone's annoyance. Asif would come down only after 10 p.m. after both Nusrat and Nazma retired to leave the hall. Only then Asif could leave the room to Abdul and Shabnam. Yet, sometimes Nusrat kept the T.V. on even after ten p.m. Munaaf would also watch the T.V. with her from his wheelchair.

Shabnam rarely expressed her displeasure for the lack of privacy. Abdul sensed her discomfiture.

"We wanted to shift the T.V. to their room upstairs so Asif can continue his studies in the hall without disturbing our sleep routine. But, as you know, Munaaf would also want to watch the T.V., but he cannot climb the stairs. That was how we had to make this adjustment," explained Abdul. When Abdul came home tired, he would have a quick dinner and retire to his room while Asif was still studying there.

Shabnam would have to wait for the T.V. to be turned off and Asif vacate the room, allowing her to go upstairs and spend time with Abdul. Yet, the couple could not indulge in any aggressive and passionate love as the wall between their space and Nazma's room was not soundproof. Their union was limited to touching and feeling – braille style. On one of those days when Asif would go to his friends for a night's stay, they would have room for themselves. At that time, Shabnam hoped Abdul would come home early and be not tired.

By Ganesha's will, it did happen, though not often.

She would lay on the bed waiting for him. When he came to her and put his arms around her, all the worries and fears of his impending absence from her vicinity vanished. They would stroke each other bodies, exploring tenderly and then passionately. They would join in a conjugal embrace with wild stroking, and when there was an explosion within her, it made her scream loud, which merged with the claps from INDIAN IDOL that were blaring from the T.V. downstairs. He slumped there on the bed, spent. She lay beside him, dripping fluid inside her body, holding him tightly, never wanting to let him go. She would never let the remnants of this experience erase. Abdul knew she loved him passionately. That had not changed, despite the family inconveniences. When he went to Saudi, she would settle into the new routine, yearning for someone to talk to, the smell of a man, and a bearded face to feel. She would think of Abdul.

I will miss her too, he thought.

"I could never leave you here, like this, and yet I have to go, in the long-term interest of our family and us. You need not worry about your religious status. Our abbujaan taught us all to be secular in theory and practice. In our room upstairs, you can keep your Ganesha and pray. You don't have to join namaaz with ammijaan. However, you may sit next to her in a sadza position when she performs namaaz; she would like it. Note that the namaaz hardly lasts five or ten minutes – five times a day. She is a bit more orthodox than abbujaan, but she loves me a lot, and to that extent, she will surely treat you with respect," assured Abdul, hitting the bed, trying to sleep and hoping Shabnam would adjust.

"Was this how lovers are entangled with each other?"

Four months earlier, he could never have imagined having his life intertwined with a Hindu girl, but now the thought of separation from her was painful, however brief. Suddenly it wasn't easy to think of life without her. Right from the day of marriage, she demanded nothing from him. Though their privacy in the upstairs room was not appropriate for them to make passionate love, she made no demands and asked no questions. She just wanted Abdul to be with her, that was all. Now he was going away from her to a far off land, where she was forbidden to accompany him.

She had to live a routine life bound in domesticity, with no one to share her emotions and feelings.

Between the days we signed the contracts and today, about two and half weeks passed – long enough for the KSA's famed Royalty red tape to be taken care of – but it seemed to us that we might have to wait longer. We resigned to our fate when the mail from Syed came asking us to come over to Mumbai ASAP. We rushed by our usual means of the overnighter-sleeper bus. I had taken Venkateshwar Rao in confidence and informed him that my family position required me to find a lucrative job in Saudi. Raman also recommended my case. He agreed to relieve me and assured me I could come back anytime to his company.

Abdul and Ameer, walked to the office of Shafique Travels and Tours, deftly avoiding bumping into morning office-goers sprinting to their respective destinations. Sharmila waved them inside as soon as she saw them and led them to the mini-conference room. In the earlier visit, they saw her sitting, her body hidden behind the long desk; the woman appeared thin. As she stood up, the excellent colour in the cheeks, the light bones structure and the graceful way she moved led them to conclude that she was lean but otherwise healthy.

"Your appointment with Visa authorities is fixed at two p.m. the day after", she said, '"I have some good news for Abdul."

Abdul looked surprised.

"Your employer has agreed to pay for your airfare; here is your ticket, which you must carry when you go for the visa interview," she said, "The money you paid to us for the ticket shall be refunded within a few days directly to your account."

"Shukriya."

Then Sharmila explained the formalities of the visa interview and made them sign the forms, which were already sent online to the consulate and proceeded to do the ticketing as agreed.

He was back in Vadodara after completing all formalities of Visa, ticketing and final departure dates. He was relaxing with Shabnam in their room after dinner while everyone was down watching the telly. Abdul explained the import of the contract they had signed, which could give them the life's comforts they wanted.

As per my routine, I briefed Shabnam in the night when she was alone in our room on the day's happenings. As the upstairs room was not very convenient for a newly married couple, I promised Shabnam that the flat at Alkapuri would be ours once the loans we had taken were cleared off and Asif settled down. I had also explained the need to earn quick money, which was only possible if I found a lucrative job in Saudi.

Further, I promised her if I could impress my future boss by providing us proper accommodation, we could start our family in Saudi. I told her such platitudes, which I regretted a lot. Because it is unlikely I get married-accommodation right away as per what Syed already briefed us. After my interview with my future employers and the Agency, I was confident I would find a job with enough to save to clear loans and provide for the family.

"I brought so much pain to you. I am sorry. If it had not been for my obsession with you, you would have gone to pursue your career without much grief and worry," said Shabnam.

"Never say that. Our love is mutual and remains so under whatever circumstances. We are in it together. In a matter of two years, my present contract ends. If they renew it, I hope to convince them to give us married accommodation and take you to Saudi with me. We can start our family in Saudi," said Abdul reassuringly and went to pack. Before leaving, he opened a bank account with a local branch in the joint names of Munaaf and his ammijaan. He explained to Munaaf that he should personally manage the domestic financial needs while ensuring Shabnam's mobile top-up from time to time. She was to be given pocket money whenever she asked. This conversation happened in the absence of Nusrat. Asif would be busy with his education and connected tests, interviews and examinations, and hence he should not be burdened with domestic finance matters.

A few days later, on the appointed day in April, Ameer and Abdul left for Riyadh by Saudia and landed safely on the soil of their destiny, the Kingdom of Saudi Arabia (KSA). At the immigration counter, Abdul thrust his Passport, return tickets and work permit into the reading slot at the control booth and exposed his face and fingerprints to be verified by the reading equipment. The robed figure at the counter checked and rechecked the papers before him and validated them with the computer information displayed in front of him. He then stamped the Passport and pushed a button to open the wicket gate for Abdul to go through. At the other counter, Ameer had also passed through the same procedure, and their entry into KSA had been smooth.

At the airport concourse, they were met by a gentleman holding a placard with their names. The gentleman introduced himself as Jabbar and said he worked with Shafique Travels and Tours in Riyadh. He did not look particularly handsome, but he had a body of muscle, a broad chest, and a paunch.

He began with lavish salutations, which surprised them. He took them out of the terminal to a waiting Mercedes Benz car that was to be driven by him. He spoke in Urdu in a subcontinent dialect, which made Abdul and Ameer at ease. He opened the passenger-side car door for them, took the luggage from them, and shoved the four pieces of baggage into the car's boot. Within half an hour or so, they reached the Agency office in the city. He asked Ameer to alight and report to the office; Ameer identified his baggage, which the driver downloaded and delivered to the office. Abdul said Khuda Hafiz to Ameer and sat back in the car – now in the front seat duly belted. The driver said it was a further three-hour journey to Dammam and asked Abdul whether he would like to eat. Upon his insistence, Abdul also had a snack at Romance Hotel on the way, even though Abdul was anxious to reach the destination quickly. Jabbar was talkative. He explained life in Saudi and how the migrants were expected to behave. Jabbar filled the information gaps Ambrish of the Agency missed out on.

He explained the KAFALA policy—a sponsorship system that gives employers considerable power over migrants, including their right to leave and re-enter the country or move to another employer. Many Saudi firms were great beneficiaries of this policy, restricting workers' rights to choose their employers freely. This policy gave the Employers significant hold over the unsuspecting workers.

"There is a significant wage gap between Saudis and non-Saudis. Saudis get at least twice the amount migrants are paid," said Jabbar, jokingly adding, "Saudi has many Malayali Mussalmans at the worker level. These Malayalee workers in Saudi slog quietly under these oppressive work environment, whereas the same people, would raise in protest against what they perceived as oppression in their own Marxist Kerala State, prodded by their political masters."

Abdul found Jabbar very useful in giving information on the work environment, which he was shy to ask the Agency person before accepting the job offer. When asked for further information, Jabbar presented a cornucopia.

During the three hours of the journey, Abdul could learn much about working in Saudi and its lifestyle.

"You are a Mussalman, and you should be aware of prayer rules. Unlike in India, all the work stops during prayer times. All Mussalmans are expected to participate in the prayers during the times specified by the Sharia law," said Jabbar.

"Even during office hours?" asked Abdul.

"Yes. While coming to work, you should have already completed the first Morning Prayer – Fajr. There will be three breaks for prayers at the workplace, which you have to follow. Work stops for prayer. If you are Mussalman, you have to pray. There are religious police and volunteers who focus on enforcing strict rules of daily prayer attendance, "said Jabbar,

"Officers are authorised to pursue, detain, and interrogate suspected violators and issue a punishment that includes public flogging."

"If there is no mosque near the workplace, who will conduct the prayer?" asked Abdul.

"Often, one of the workers is trained in imam functions, and a special prayer room is mandatory in all workplaces, where you are expected to attend the prayer. In some cases, they may employ a professional imam," said Jabbar.

"What happens to the non-Muslim employees during prayer times?" asked Abdul

"They are exempt and wait for their staff to resume duty."

"Have you worked at any construction site?"

"No, but I used to drive a big van to take staff from their living accommodation to the construction site."

"What times does a typical day start at the construction worksite?"

"Labour is expected to attend site at 6 a.m. At the end of the previous day, the managers allot the work. Supervisors of your category, I think, can come in at 7. I am not sure. Rules vary from Manager to Manager and site to site," said Jabbar.

Meanwhile, the car came to a halt near a four-storied building, and Jabbar asked Abdul to alight.

"This is where you will be accommodated. Please go to the reception area and introduce yourself. Meanwhile, I will bring your luggage. The person at the counter will guide your further," said Jabbar.

Abdul entered the building and was impressed by the simplicity and functionality of the entrance hall. He submitted the letter of offer from the company as proof of identity at the counter as instructed by the Agency, and the man took him to his allotted room. The concierge also handed over a sealed envelope with his name printed. He noticed a prayer hall door next to the staircase and a lift. The Mitsubishi lift took him to his floor, accompanied by the man at the reception counter and Abdul's luggage.

This particular apartment was of four floors above the main dining hall and kitchen that provided dining facilities for the inmates. The floor he was accommodated had three other rooms and a shared bathroom at the end of the corridor. He presently saw a man in a towel coming out of the bath and rushing to his room opposite Abdul's own. His room had two beds; one appeared unkempt.

His roommate could be at work, he thought. He noticed this room had an attached toilet apart from the public bathroom he saw at the end of the corridor. He was pleased with the amenities provided – modern by Indian standards. After finishing the signing formalities, he took a tour around the building.

A small grocery shop was attached to the building, whose entrance was from outside to enable non-residents to shop. The only fresh items the small grocery appeared to contain were eggs, cheese, pre-packed meat and bread. Rest all were standard toiletry consumables. The concierge told Abdul to go to a mall a few blocks away to buy his other needs.

***

Abdul remembered about the envelope and read its contents. It was a welcome letter giving information on the timing of the pick-up vehicle and rules of the house regarding prayer, use of the dining hall, general civil behaviour etc. It also contained crisp notes of riyals in 50 and 100 denominations totalling four thousand. However, there was no mention of it in the covering letter. He presumed it to be an advance for the salary of the coming month. He was delighted to know his employer was kind enough to take care of his immediate needs.

He could not sleep properly at night as he was too anxious to get to work for the daybreak.

Also, he found his bedroom claustrophobic and the air-conditioning too strong; he was constantly moving around with a sweater. He was unable to find the controller to wind down the effect. He did not know who the housekeeper was. It was too early to start complaining. He had better adjust for some time before he listed the inconveniences.

When Abdul woke up, he found his roommate asleep.

It took almost 36 hours to meet his roommate in person. He introduced himself as Mathew George from Mumbai, originally from Cannanore, Kerala; he was employed with Siemens in Mumbai as Electrical Engineer and posted in Dammam. Siemens have power transmission contracts across KSA. He said his timings were odd, as the transmission tower works were going on in rural areas, and he usually came late at night as travelling took time. On Fridays, he preferred to sleep long hours.

Presently, Abdul quietly tiptoed to the toilet, finished all his morning ablutions, and quickly ran down the stairs without waiting for the lift. He entered the prayer hall and finished his namaaz. He had boiled eggs for breakfast with some hard-to-chew bread.

The apartment allotted to him was quite a distance from his site. As mentioned in the welcome letter, a vehicle came to pick him up to go to the workplace at the appointed hour. He checked and rechecked to ensure all the documentation he was told to carry for the first day at the office was in place in the backpack. A gleaming air-conditioned van took him to the site in about an hour. The van picked up three more persons to work – one Kerala Muslim and two from Bangladesh. The route took them away from posh residential areas of the city, past industrial areas and regions that weren't suited for human habitation but had nevertheless been colonized by the hordes of workers imported from the sub-continent and beyond.

The other inmates of the van welcomed him warmly, and pleasantries were exchanged. They were all employed at the same site: two with the main contractor like himself and one hired by a plumbing contractor from the U.K. They informed him of all the administrative-related formalities he had to go through before taking on the work assignment.

Abdul found Hadil, one of the co-passenger, to be boisterous, funny and quick-witted. Abdul and Hadil became good colleagues despite their language difficulties. When Abdul learnt that Hadil would be assisting him in his job as a supervisor for electrical and plumbing works, he was pleased.

I was led to the humongous, reasonably luxurious, air-conditioned site office. The floor was covered with red and green striped Persian carpets. Near the window was a large stuffed sofa, two chairs and a coffee table. At the far end of the room was an Asian man busy looking at the screen as he drummed viciously on the keyboard.

Edward Jenkins looked at the young man standing opposite him and addressed him," Welcome to our grand Project, Mr. Abdul."

Jenkins's handshake was firm. He looked like a plump and muscular version of Alec Guinness of The Bridge on the River Kwai. Typical British. He had a confident demeanour that seemed to permeate the room like a fog, engulfing all the staff.

"Thank you, sir," I said and introduced myself, showing him the appointment letter and the work permit.

"Our Admin manager, Mr. Grower, will take you through the initiation formalities today, and from tomorrow we shall start our work. Welcome again, Mr. Abdul. Is that how I shall call you?" asked Jenkins.

"Yes, sir, Abdul Wahab is my name. You can call me Abdul".

"Okay, see you tomorrow," and he got up and led him to an adjoining room to introduce him to Larry Grower.

Working for Edward Jenkins was Abdul's first fundamental instruction on managing a massive state-of-the-art multi-storeyed building construction. Until then, Abdul had been no more than an ordinary civil supervisor ensuring plumbers and electricians do their assigned jobs. Here he had a project with all electronic gadgets required to be wired with skill and care. Even the contractors who handled these jobs looked sophisticated. One could see German equipment or Japanese machinery at the site, with their well-trained workers in trim overalls, pockets bulging with tools of all kinds. As months went by, Abdul became a favourite staff member of his boss, Jenkins. Jenkins would offer to drop him back at his apartment when he worked late hours as the pick-up vehicle would have left.

Jenkins often cautioned Abdul about the need to follow engineering processes and the country's laws to complete a project.

"We have proprietary technology on the construction methods – not just civil, but state-of-art electronic gadgets and skill to perform as per the design. That is the reason the company had teamed with us. Many other players are very close in tech, performance, and reliability to ours. The Saudi government contracting system is not transparent, not on a level playing field, as it is elsewhere in the World. The big guys skirt rules and use their relationship advantage with the kingdom personnel and thus have the inside track of the management functioning and bend the rules to make some extra money. Which we cannot. Therefore, we must work with extra diligence to avoid unfortunate culpabilities, even those caused by uncontrollable events," explained Jenkins.

Abdul soon became comfortable working in the hot environs of Saudi Arabia. He found some of the customs interesting and some scary. Whenever Abdul spoke to Asif, Munaaf or Shabnam- at least two times a week - Abdul explained the different lifestyles and how he managed food, time, and work. The information he gave filled them with awe. Abdul went on to describe life in Saudi to his attentive audience.

Saudi Arabia is much hotter than even the Rajasthan desert. But if the temperature goes above 50C, the work has to stop. Legal mandate. From June to Sept – it may happen at least ten times in these four months. Friday is a holiday for all offices and sites across the country. Some shops are open till 10:00 a.m., when the major prayer for Friday is obligated. Till 4:00 p.m., everything would be closed – except mosques. Till recently, only religious channels were allowed. Highly censored news is broadcast. Lately, the authorities have permitted some Indian media, but with subscribers' dishes for transmission. You can have your DVDs and libraries.

We have a common hall in the building we are put up, where we usually watch the Hindi movies. All the money can be saved as there is hardly any opportunity to spend. Sometimes all seven days are workdays, depending on the Project's urgency.

Places of interest to see are Jeddah and Mecca – one half an hour plane journey. It is cheap. Daily necessities and transport are very economical compared to the salary levels. That gives much room to save. Also, there is zero-tolerance for labour mischief. Punishment is very severe. It could range from lashes by the whip to cutting parts of your body. Theft could lead to cutting off your hands. It depends on how the company projects the incident– jail term, lashes, cutting off limbs, or even death. It is all based on Sharia law. No grey area.

"In meetings and other gatherings, Kahwa, a traditional Arabic drink-thick pure Coffee, is served. Kahwa is made from green coffee beans flavoured with saffron and cardamom. It is often served with dates. It is poured from a unique coffee pot called dallah and into a small porcelain cup – 20ml – with no handle. You have to hold a dallah, cupping it with both hands. A man always stands around with the dallah – the jug. As soon as you finish, he will pour you another. If you are not interested in sipping anymore, you have to shake the cup, which is an indication you don't need any more," Abdul said.

"Kahwa in Kashmiri is sweetened tea," said Munaaf.

"Is that so? But here in Saudi, it is Coffee. I am told the Turkish word for Coffee is kahveh," said Abdul.

Such exchange of information kept the family conversation going, and they felt that Abdul was just next door. Nazma was happy his son would be helping her family to have a good standing in society. Nazma would talk highly of her son whenever the opportunity arose amongst her biradri and society ladies.

Asif asked many more questions about his work, which Abdul shared and also sent him some of the work catalogues which would be helpful for his studies in engineering.

SHABNAM

Shabnam was waiting for the call from Abdul, which as per routine, was two days late. It was the same all that week, with no message or call from him. Kaamini said a call from Ameer mentioned both were fine and working conditions were good; the pay and the accommodation were as per the promise given by the Agency. That relieved her a little. However, the message from Abdul was what she was waiting for. She had so much to talk about. She would take the lead and talk, she told herself.

She was disturbed by the last night's behaviour of Nusrat. The following day she woke up early, eased herself from the bed, put on her dupatta, came downstairs, put the tea vessel, and waited there at the gas stove. She found Asif deeply engrossed at his usual study table in the corner of the hall. Something churned in her stomach. She rushed to the toilet, leaned over the basin and vomited. "Are you all right, Bhabhi?" asked Asif. She leaned back against the nearby wall, hoping the sickness would ease, and signalled him with a reassuring hand gesture.

"Would you like some tea?" she asked. "Sure, with lots of sugar and milk," replied Asif. She shoved a few tea leaves in the boiling water, hoping the hot black tea would calm her. She opened the fridge and found no milk. "Maaf karna, Asif, no milk. We have to wait for the vendor to come; it is too early for him to deliver," she said. "It is okay, Bhabhi; I don't mind waiting."

***

Nusrat made a long-distance call to Munni on Shabnam's phone and spoke for almost twenty mins.

"You cannot do that on Shabnam's phone," Nazma reprimanded her. Nusrat was still only 33 years old, but her hair was partly white and matted haphazardly, and her cheeks were puffy. She glared at Shabnam from the sofa with a look of spiteful anger on her face, as though it was Shabnam who had objected. The chasm between Nusrat and Shabnam was growing exponentially. Nusrat's behaviour towards Shabnam has become violent lately; she throws things at her. She used vulgar language, especially when Nazma was not around at home. She would make Shabnam soap-wash her when she showered and made her clean her private parts; shave her pubic hair, and many other unmentionables. Her behaviour was insulting and disgusting to Shabnam. When Nazma found out about this behaviour, she often called Shabnam away from Nusrat on some pretext to spare her from the ignominy.

The next day was long and painful, and that afternoon a crazy frantic compulsion came over me. I stared out of our bedroom window facing the lane back of our house and saw an older woman cleaning the drain as though she was forced to do it because of circumstances beyond her control. At that point, I made up my mind. I would escape from this prison and contact Mangesh Gosavi.

Mangesh Gosavi was the one whose help Saarika sought when her baba died. Mangesh and Bhiku were working in the same construction company in Pune, and both had joined HSAM at the same time. They had become family friends, and Mangesh had become kaaka to Saarika. They often visited each other even after separating from the company they had initially been working for.

Mangesh picked up after the second ring "hello?"

"काका, मी सारिका बोलते[58]." It took a few seconds for Gosavi to realize who was on the other side.

"सांगा बाळा[59]," said Mangesh.

"I want to get out of this home in Vadodara."

"Why? What happened? Has anyone hurt you?" he said with concern.

"No, nothing of that sort. I want to get out of this house and stay elsewhere. I want your help."

"You are not being clear to me. I am worried. Would you please tell me if anyone in the house misbehaved with you, or are they forcing you to do things you don't want to? Please come clean on the matter."

Mangesh sounded disturbed.

"Kaaka, please don't worry. I am not comfortable here, that's all. Typical family problems occur between daughter-in-law and sister-in-law. This time it has become a bit unbearable. So, I want to leave the house and live elsewhere," said Shabnam.

"Have you informed Abdul?"

"Abdul is in Saudi. I don't want to trouble him on this matter. I want to solve it on my own."

"When did he go to Saudi?"

"It's over five months, now."

"You want to stay alone? Did I understand it correctly?"

"Yes, Kaaka, till Abdul comes back."

"Let me think about it and call you."

---

58   Kaka, Saarika speaking
59   Tell me, my child

"Please, don't call me. I will call you tonight at eleven after everyone is asleep."

Shabnam quickly swiped the red icon on the phone to put off the call, having heard the footsteps of someone climbing the stairs.

The situation was tailor-made for Mangesh. Suffering Hindu female in a Muslim home. Husband deserts her and leaves for Saudi, making her an unpaid housemaid. Female inmates of the house ill-treat her. The media will lap it up, and he will be a hero, saving a damsel in distress.

Mangesh picked up the phone at the first ring itself.

"Yes, Saarika. You sure don't want to stay in that house?" He was recording the conversation unbeknownst to her.

"Please find me a place where I can shift. As quickly as possible."

Mangesh did things, as any Good Samaritan should, except for his personal gain of instant fame. He found a home for Shabnam in Mumbai with a member of the Manch, Raju Bombatkar. Raju lived in a chawl in Worli with his wife and had no children. The one room-kitchen tenement he was now living in, was what his father had left him by paying two lakhs by pagadi[60] to a gang member who held sway in the area. His father died when he slipped from a crowded train on the Sion-Matunga section. His old mother died too of cancer a few months ago.

Raju was indebted to Mangesh Gosavi for finding a wife for him even though he had no regular pay. Presently, he managed the house by running a hired Auto service, with an income just enough to survive. His wife supplemented him by providing lunch to migrant bachelors who throng the maximum city to earn a living.

---

60   Initial deposit for house rent.

When Mangesh informed her of the arrangement, Shabnam was very excited and said," When can I shift?"

However, Mangesh was not ready to settle the matter hurriedly without waiting to rub in his agenda.

"One of our Forum members will come tomorrow to your house for an interview which we want to publicize so that other unfortunate victims of in-law torture can take such bold step you have taken." He did not add the dreaded words "inter-faith marital issues".

Shabnam was evident in her mind she would not do anything that would hurt her beloved Abdul and abbujaan's reputation as they were good men of culture and respecters of beliefs of all religions.

"Kaaka, I respect my husband and my abbu very much. I have known them for the last five years, as we stayed in the same society, and I am aware of my saasre[61] ‹s respect in this society and beyond. I am going out of the house not because of any religion-related issues. They have given me total freedom to practise my religion and never interfered with my beliefs and practices. It is just that the ladies of the house have been mistreating me, which happens in any household without any particular reference to religion."

"माझ्या आईलाही तशाच समस्येचा सामना करावा लागला[62]."

"So please kaaka, जातीचा विवाद नको[63]. Just help me out. Please, I beg of you." That put a dampener on Mangesh's agenda. He shifted to another gear.

---

61   My Father-in-law
62   My mother also had the same issues with her in-laws
63   Don't raise religious disparity issues.

"Saarika, I will not do anything that will hurt my dear daughter. You know me well enough. Let us forget what I said and plan for your departure."

"Please send one of your men from the Manch to pick up my luggage early in the morning at 6, before my household members wake up. In addition, I need the bus ticket for a late-night bus. Abdul always left by the 11 p.m. bus, which is convenient for me, so I could sneak out when everyone is asleep."

They agreed on the plan and assured Raju would pick her up from Borivili in the morning. Shabnam decided to inform Abdul only after she reached Mumbai, taking advantage of the time difference between India and KSA. She knew Nusrat would be the first to notice her absence as her morning tea would be missing from her bedtable. Yet Nusrat would not be able to contact Abdul, as it would be 4:30 a.m. in KSA. By the time Abdul woke up, he would have been briefed by Shabnam.

As per the plan, Raju picked up Shabnam in his Auto and drove to his Worli chawl. The U-shaped four-storeyed building she entered had 16 tenements on each level. A central staircase serviced the building along a passage that ran each floor's length. Worli chawl was built around a small courtyard filled with people filling their utensils with municipal drinking water from a common tap. Raju's wife Parvathi welcomed her, gave her tea and made her feel comfortable with small talk.

Shabnam could not make the call to Abdul as her phone did not work for unknown reasons. With the help of Raju, she went to a nearby phone booth and made the call to Abdul.

Abdul answered after a few rings absentmindedly.

"It's me, Shabnam," said Shabnam. "I am speaking from Mumbai."

"Shabnam? In Mumbai? Is everything okay at home? Why did you have to come to Mumbai," asked Abdul surprised and shocked.

"I have left Vadodara and came to Mumbai to stay with my friend, Parvathi." She did not want to expose Mangesh and his arrangements in Mumbai.

"Why, what happened suddenly? Has anyone abused you?"

"I have already informed you of the problems I have been facing with Nusrat. It has now become very humiliating for me to tolerate her behaviour concerning me. I can't even say those awkward events on the phone to you, though I have hinted. I understand your position, and I am not blaming you. Would you please let me stay here independently until you come back? I insist, in the larger interest of our future. I will inform Asif about my absence and request him to inform ammijaan that I am safe. Ammijaan has been kind to me in whichever way she can. However, she is also helpless when it comes to Nusrat."

How can I tell him that Nusrat's room was always a chaotic mess of discarded clothes, used tea mugs, and damp towels lying on the floor? I had to tidy up regularly, retrieving the used dinner plates from under the cot. Within no time, the scene would reappear as though it was a filmy set that required a re-take. How can I tell him about the disgraceful things she made me do?

"Are you sure you would be safe in Mumbai?" asked Abdul, having given up on the matter.

"This friend of mine is a childhood schoolmate from Pune, so I am safe. Let us not inform Nazma and others that I have gone to Mumbai. We need to inform them I had gone to Parbhani to see my Mausi, who was sick and needed my services. Therefore, I had to rush. Let us stick to this story. However, I will take Asif in confidence and update him that I am in Mumbai. He is the only other sensible person in the house now."

Abdul did not speak for a few seconds. He was lost in thoughts. Helpless. He felt a cry building in him. He could not help her, so he fell silent and hoped she would be happy in Mumbai.

"You there, Abdul?" asked Shabnam.

"Yes, sitting this far, I can do nothing to alleviate your suffering. I am sorry. Be assured, that I am with you in whatever decision you have taken. Please keep updating me regularly. Mumbai is a dangerous city for a single woman. Just be careful. I am worried about you. Now I have to rush to the shower to go to work. We will talk again in the night," said Abdul.

"Okay then, we will talk later after I settle down here," and she cut the phone.

***

He never knew how far Abdul walked away from his apartment from the moment the limousine dropped him back. He had to trudge back. But by the time Abdul got back to his apartment, the heat was still scorching. As he came in, the darwan said adaabs and asked whether he was all right, and Abdul said he was fine, just a little tired. He took the lift to his floor and fell on his bed. His roommate had not arrived, which gave him much-needed privacy. He did not draw the curtains but went directly to bed and lay down on his back, wrapped in his thoughts. Without blinking, Abdul stared at the ceiling, watching the fading sunlight struggling to come through the curtains. He saw a reflection of his sadness in the shadows. He vowed to give Shabnam the best life when he returned to India after his assignment.

Shabnam dialled Asif. No response. After a few rings, she pressed the phone off quickly for fear that someone else might pick up the phone. She called him again from the same kiosk and updated Asif on what she had told Abdul. In this conversation also, she did not mention Mangesh Gosavi. She had gone to live with her friend, her childhood schoolmate.

It took a couple of days for Shabnam to be acquainted with the house rules and Bombatkars' living system. The tenements were all of only one room, 10' x 16', with just a washbasin at a corner with a tap – which was mostly dry. Common toilets, poorly maintained, were at the end of the corridor. Like most other residents, Raju also partitioned the room by making a thick wooden floor-to-roof divider with shelves used as storage for utensils and other kitchen paraphernalia. They made a raised platform too to enable ease of cooking. Parvathi informed Shabnam her mom-in-law slept in the kitchen while the couple shared the bed in the other room, this ensuring some privacy. It is evident to Shabnam she would also need to adjust to sleeping on the floor in the made-up kitchen. The door that separated the kitchen and the front room was a slider with built-in cabinets. The slider did ensure a semblance of a screen against light but could not muffle the audio. Whenever one pushed the slider, the vessels inside the racks would rattle. Shabnam realized her room in Vadodara had the same privacy issues.

The poor should not indulge in boisterous lovemaking.

Shabnam helped Parvathi prepare lunch dabbas[64] to send to homes and offices. It appeared to her that it was a lucrative business. She pleaded with Parvathi to find a job in any pharma or cosmetic company as a packer or any other decent job. After sending the lunch boxes, both the women would travel around Mumbai to seek employment in factories. In many instances, they could not get past the security. In a few cases, which they

---

64   Lunch boxes – peculiar to Mumbai

did, the admin manager had offered a housekeeping job for a paltry sum of ten thousand rupees that too through a sub-contractor who takes ten per cent. It hardly met their needs when they calculated the take-home pay with all cuts and transport.

Parvathi had Raju under her thumb. I could understand why. Nightly sounds of muffled screams, moans, creaking cot, shrieks of Khoop chaan[65], and the sudden thump of a spent trunk- like-body on the bed are proof enough. The next day early morning, I heard them speaking in a lower tone:

"Please find a way to send her away?" a male voice.

"I will do something shortly, don't worry," a female voice.

Raju came home late one night while Parvathi was fast asleep with a painkiller tablet she took for severe 'body pains'. Raju had his separate key, walked into the flat, and slid the divider door apart. He peeped in and saw the figure of Shabnam on the made-up bed on the floor. With the sound of the door, Shabnam opened her eyes, and she recognized danger from his appearance and the shakiness in his voice as he said, "sorry." She looked at him with something akin to fear in her eyes. At least he read as fear. He walked past her, poured some water into a tumbler, and drank the same in one gulp. He almost fell over Shabnam while walking back past her. She involuntarily moved away. He tumbled his way back into his room and slid the door shut. Shabnam saw Parvathi move a little, turning to the other side of the bed from the door's crevice.

She found herself caught in a web of terrible thoughts.

This experience shook Shabnam, and she could hardly sleep the whole night. She then decided to vacate the house as soon as

---

65 Orgasmic moaning – equivalent to "yes", "yes"

convenient. She was ready to accept the offer of Parvathi of cook-cum-maid services she initially suggested.

Earlier, I had rejected the proposal because Abdul might not like me taking such a menial job. Abdul's house status had improved thanks considerably to his generosity in sending money home. Further, Asif got a job through campus placement in an Indo-German Company in Vadodara itself as he topped the class in electrical engineering. They are now a middle-class family with disposable incomes. My maid work would not agree with their newfound wealth. But I had no alternative. I cannot go back to Vadodara. I can't also live in Mumbai without the help of Parvathi. But her house was not safe anymore, as I noticed yesterday night. Yet, I decided to spend time in Mumbai and wait for Abdul to take me back to Vadodara.

Shabnam decided not to confront Parvathi during the previous night's event but requested her to help find a home where she could work as a cook-cum-maid with a full board and lodge. She apologized to Parvathi, rejecting the suggestion, having first mooted it.

Once Munni told me in big cities, migrant working couples would need a full-time maid to take care of their domestic chores and their children, the salary of which would be as good as that of any skilled mechanic, fitter, or driver. She further said, in UAE, such maids are in great demand, especially among expats.

Parvathi promised to find her some job with the contacts of her customers.

Shabnam realized Raju's action a few nights ago was a drama enacted by the couple as a signal to her to quit their home.

Parvathi's contacts helped Shabnam to end up in the house of Raj and Vaidehi as their house-help.

She called up Abdul to update him on her adventure, omitting the unsavoury episode of Raju and Parvathi.

"Are you sure the job you have opted is safe?"

"Most importantly, they are an elderly couple whose daughters are married and settled in foreign countries. The lady wanted some help in the kitchen as the husband always invited friends and office colleagues' home for parties. In addition, they have given me a separate room with an attached bath, which was earlier used by their second daughter, who recently left for Singapore after her marriage. The daughter negotiated with Parvathi about my salary and living conditions," said Shabnam.

"Did not they ask you about me and your background?" asked Abdul when Shabnam spoke from the phone kiosk nearby.

"They did. I told the couple about your job in Saudi, though not elaborately, nothing about the likely length of your employment condition in Saudi. If they learn that I may quit within a year, they might not employ me. I kept this part a secret. I will quit as soon as you land in Mumbai."

***

The delegation of executives from Jeddah and Riyadh kept Abdul busy. He set up meetings for them with other staff members, took them around the site, and explained the project's status. They marvelled at his efficiency. He was knowledgeable about every project phase, and they were impressed.

His days were full, and the work pressures kept his mind off Shabnam's problems. Regular telephone calls were the only means of professing love to each other. Shabnam was accommodative and never complained of his absence and preoccupation with work. She was optimistic Ganesha would take care of her. She was confident it would be a matter of months or so for Abdul to return, take her back to Vadodara, and they would lead a happy life.

Vaidehi

When not attending or hosting a party, the couple spent their weekend watching a movie or sitting on the entrance steps of a mall or in the park attached to a mall, watching people and commenting on them.

"That lady on the right could be his wife and another one his Saali[66]," said Raj.

Presently, they were watching two ladies and a man with shopping bags waiting at the entrance for their car pick-up.

"Sister-in-law? Why not his sister?" asked Vaidehi.

"Saali," reiterated Raj.

"Why not his sister?"

"His sister and wife? An improbable combination."

"What do you mean? When your sister was here for three months, we took her around wherever we went. What makes you think wives do not get along with husband's sisters?" said Vaidehi with an irritable tone.

"I am referring to a general family behaviour in Indian households. Nothing concerning our house."

"You men are all the same. However much we wives take care of your relatives, it is never appreciated," she said, disregarding Raj's explanation.

---

66   Wife's sister

"Listen, I am not talking about our situation here. Just a general comment," explained Raj.

"When your sister visited us and parked herself for three months, did I not take care of her?" retorted Vaidehi ignoring his reply.

"She came with a specific purpose of accompanying her son for his entrance exam in Narsee Monji. Not for any vacation or enjoying your hospitality," said Raj.

"I spent much time with her by accompanying her to visit her relatives in Dombivili and Nallasopara while her son was busy. I took extra care of her gastronomical needs too. So your comment that husband's sisters and wives do not get along is not right," announced Vaidehi.

Raj had to find a way to divert her from this outburst. Fortunately, he found a Kwality Wall's ice cream cart and bought her a bar of chocolate-coated Magnum stick, her favourite.

She was critical of almost everything that was not to her viewpoint while at the same time unerringly interpreting the most innocent general remarks of mine as being a criticism of herself. I was not required to give an opinion unless sought. An innocuous statement like "the dal has less salt" would have a different reaction when uttered unsolicited and replied when asked. It was impossible to please her often or for long, and I stopped trying. She had brainwashed her children towards her perceptions so much that their culinary tastes also reflected her biddings.

Over the years, Raj had been locked in a loveless marriage, its suffocating tedium only occasionally enlivened by periods of acute dislike.

In Jan that year, Raj retired after two extensions of his scheduled time. Post-retirement, Raj decided to shift to Hyderabad – the city of his growing years. Vaidehi was not interested in relocating from Mumbai as she had developed a fondness for the city. It had given her friendships, acquaintances, and pursuits that kept her busy one way or the other.

But she had no alternative.

Five years before Raj was to retire, Vaidehi insisted they start looking to own a house in Mumbai, as the present company provided accommodation would have to be surrendered. They mutually agreed and started searching. The couple had bitter arguments on the type (2 BHK/3BHK); location (Central Rly side, West Rly side, South Mumbai and North Mumbai); entry door position (facing east or north); ventilation; avoid west facing bedroom window and the like. It took two years of search after which an exasperated Raj gave in to Vaidehi and they decided on Ekta Apartment Complex in Sundernagar, Goregaon.

From the savings and pooled resources, Raj paid the initial advance of Fifty Lakhs as per the construction-stage requirement and waited for the anticipated occupation of the flat which was to be delivered within the next year. As Raj was at the edge of retirement, the Banks were initially not keen on funding him, but agreed to give loan with a repayment within 3 years of disbursement. To avoid heavy EMI deductions, Raj instead decided to pay up the balance from his gratuity after the retirement.

But fate had other designs.

Municipal Corporation found various illegalities committed in the course of construction of the building which included construction of additional floors without approval, increase in the height of the building and carrying of construction beyond the permissible limits of FSI. Construction was stopped and the members of the Society went to court for redress.

The Society appointed advocates pleaded that the buyers of the flats were not aware that the buildings had been constructed in violation of the sanctioned plan. They also filed applications for restraining the Corporation from demolishing the building. But the court ruled that there is no provision under that Act for condonation of illegal/unauthorized construction by the developers/builders and promoters or regularization of such construction.

Though the court directed the builders to return the advances paid, the members could not get their moneys back. The Promoters invoked various clauses of many acts on liquidation of the company and reneged on repayments. The case of contempt of court is still pending in Mumbai High Court, with the lawyers on all three sides squabbling on procedures and rules. Thus the dream of Vaidehi of owning a house in Mumbai was buried in the pending cases files of the various courts.

Fifty lakhs was a considerable amount. The couple blamed each other for the mess they were in. "You should not have listened to that dumbo Ravinder Kaur and her nincompoop husband"; "What happened to your corporate training? Could you not get the documents validated before paying?"; "But you hurried me lest we might lose the laboriously selected flat to other prospective customers." And the like.

When trust is missing in a marriage, any unfortunate event can widen the divide.

Fortunately, Raj had bought a flat in Hyderabad for ensuring rent income when they retire. Vaidehi's idea, it was. She did not want to depend on her children after Raj retires. It did not go well with his pride.

Vaidehi felt trapped now. No house in Mumbai. They had to move to Hyderabad. Finally, in April, they shifted to Hyderabad.

Vaidehi had requested Shabnam to accompany them as she said it would take another six months for her husband to come back to India from Saudi. Vaidehi had heard some scary stories of maid absenteeism in Hyderabad, which prompted her to request Shabnam go with them. She assured Shabnam as soon as her husband would be back in India, Raj would personally arrange to take her back to Vadodara or Mumbai as per her wish.

I should accept their suggestion, as finding another safe home in Mumbai would be difficult. Also, nowadays, a live-in maid is not convenient because of accommodation issues with grownup children. So working with home-stay is a boon for me. I have to inform Abdul tonight to take his approval too.

"Madam, I will have to talk to my husband on this matter. If he does not agree to this shift, please buy me a ticket to Vadodara," said Shabnam. She, however, was sure that in no way she would be willing to go to Vadodara to be with her in-laws. The very thought of living in the same house as Nusrat without Abdul terrified her. She convinced Abdul accordingly.

The shift to Hyderabad was a wrong move. Raj and Vaidehi had no friends or relatives to bond with. Vaidehi had a mausi who lived about 30 km from where they had moved. She soon connected with her. Raj had none. Both his sisters were settled in Delhi and Kolkata. Vaidehi's only brother immigrated to Germany. So they had to develop new relationships afresh. That annoyed Vaidehi. She was constantly cursing herself for the decision to relocate to Hyderabad, even though she knew the reason for the shift which was forced by circumstances, beyond their control. For Raj, he returned to a city that rekindled his childhood memories. However, people and the streets looked the same; the same boring faces; busy streets with vehicles honking; fruit vendors with skull-caps; police stopping vehicles for traffic violations and giving challans or taking bribes; people bargaining for the auto fare; youth staring at the group of jean-clad college girls. One city in India was like any other city. Hyderabad did not change but for some multi-storeyed structures. The same laid back style was still palpable. More so in the government offices. The government staff do not report to duty till eleven.

If Hyderabad had prospered, it was evident only off-outer ring road where the IT sector was entrenched, with covert help from the wakf board and past governments' largesse. Vaidehi could not adjust to Hyderabad, though her Mausi appeared happy to have her around. Mausi's children were in the US, and she welcomed Vaidehi as one would the hail storm after a scorching summer. Vaidehi never lost an opportunity to keep on raving about Mumbai.

"You know, in Mumbai, if a maid goes on leave, she would ensure a replacement. You are never without a maid. The same is the case with drivers who migrate from Bihar or UP. My husband tells me that even when the roads are flooded with rain with no proper transport, attendance in offices will always be over 90%. That is the work culture in Mumbai," said Vaidehi boasting to neighbours of her building complex about Mumbai life.

"What's the price of a movie ticket in Mumbai?" asked a plump lady with white hair knowing fully well that the cost of living in Mumbai was far higher than in Hyderabad. The remark was only to demean Vaidehi.

Vaidehi did not fall into the trap and ignored the question. She did not want to acknowledge that cost of living was one of the reasons for their shift to Hyderabad, as they now had to live only on savings with no regular income with their savings locked in courts. With mortality rates going northwards with better living conditions, retirees with no pension grants would have to be thriftier. Even Raj was finding Hyderabad uncomfortable. He could locate none of his school or college mates – the only ones he could, died prematurely by some rare affliction. He did manage to trace his friend's widow, visited her to comfort her and reminisce about their old associations. Vaidehi did not accompany him.

Prashant was his classmate in Degree College while Raj was pursuing his graduation in science. The house was located in a middle-class locality in Chikkadpally. It was a small house built on a 200sq yard plot. The house had a grilled veranda that opened into a small hall with a kitchen and a bedroom. Very compact and functional. Nothing opulent. He could notice a dining table in the hall topped with various containers filled with pickles, a salt and pepper stand and a ghee jar. The rest of the table was filled with books and a writing pad, and some loose sheets. Books of Telugu, Marathi and Hindi were prominent, apart from a Telugu to English Dictionary. Arpita, the widow of Prashant, recognized him and warmly welcomed him with a big beaming smile. Their earlier association was indeed a pleasant one. Arpita and Prashant were married when he and Raj were in the final year of their degree course. Raj spent considerable time with them in their younger days. They lost touch when Raj shifted to Mumbai and Prashant moved to Aurangabad.

Arpita was wearing a faded lemon coloured saree wrapped around clumsily, and her blouse could not cover the ample bosom, and one could see the exposed flesh. After initial introductions, Raj asked about her routine.

"When we were in Aurangabad, I learnt Marathi and became proficient in its literature. I am presently translating Marathi books into Telugu," explained Arpita.

"That's good. It keeps you engaged. How is your son, and where is he?" asked Raj.

"He is in Pune working with an engineering company. He has a daughter, who got married recently," informed Arpita.

"I don't see any computer or a typewriter? Are you writing in longhand?" observed Raj.

"I have no skill in typing or any modern gadgets. Fortunately, my eldest sister's son helps me transcribe my handwriting into soft copy," said Arpita, "How come we lost touch in all these years? How did you come to know my address now?"

"It was a chance meeting with Prashant's brother, Kishore, in a mall about fifteen days back. He gave me your whereabouts and updated me about Prashant too."

"It is good to see you after so many years", said Arpita "you should have brought your wife also."

Simplicity. Genuine happiness over memories rekindled—pure Love.

Raj discussed their early student life and the illuminating association with Prashant. Prashant was instrumental in educating Raj about films, film lyrics and Urdu poets.

"He introduced me to the works of Gurudutt, for which I am forever grateful. Though Gurudutt was a fine actor, Prashant regretted he did not get full credit for his artistic qualities. He said the actor was versatile. He referred to his portrayal of an unsophisticated rustic in Sahib Bibi Aur Ghulam, as the frustrated poet in Kagaz Ke Phool, and as a romantic hero of Mr and Mrs 55."

"Yes, he always sang that lilting song in Mr and Mrs 55: *Hum aap ke ankhon mein is dil ko basa de toh*?"

"Yes, he took pains to explain to me the meaning of the words of Urdu in Hindi film lyrics. He took considerable pains to teach me nuances of the Urdu language and the works of Sahir, who he was very fond of."

"During the last days of his life, he mentioned you many times and relived the time you guys have spent in each other's company and wondered where you were."

They continued their discussions for some more time, and Raj left with a promise to bring his wife the following week at a mutually convenient time. Under this promise, Raj convinced Vaidehi to accompany him to visit Arpita. After about a week on an appointed date, they called on her. Arpita cooked a sumptuous lunch with Raj's favourite brinjal. After lunch, they indulged in small talk, wherein Arpita explained to Vaidehi how Raj and Prashant's friendship grew and developed into a bond. Vaidehi's body language showed she did not want Raj to continue his association with Arpita. Vaidehi assumed that all single women have seductive designs on vulnerable men like Raj.

"I don't think you should meet Arpita again," announced Vaidehi in the car when they were driving back home. Women have extra sensory perceptions –some real and many imaginary. Vaidehi objected to his frequent visits to meet her, and she refused to accompany him. She saw something in Arpita that made her feel uncomfortable. So Raj, much to his annoyance, had to cut off his ties with Arpita. After Raj's retirement, Vaidehi had become a control freak. "Where are you going?", "Why are you going?" and "When are you back?"–such interrogation had become routine.

"You have become old now; if something happens on the road to you, how do I contact you? Also, at this age, you must have your meals on time and at home" was her undeniable reason for such controls.

Meanwhile, a chance encounter with his former colleague from Mumbai had changed Raj's life and the couple's relationship forever.

Raj Krishna

"*H*ello, sir," said a squeaky voice behind me.

I was in Inorbit mall shopping with Vaidehi and my youngest daughter Spandana. Spandana had arrived from Singapore the day before, and she was keen to buy Indian dresses for herself and her Indian friends. I saw a pretty young lady in her late twenties in jeans and a blue top fixing me with a friendly gaze as I turned around. She had her hair tied loosely with a colour band and carried a shopping bag. She was alone, apparently.

That voice belonged to Ritu Chawla.

"Oh, Ritu, how are you, and how come you are in Hyderabad?" I asked

"I am fine, sir. I joined Goud Pharmaceuticals as the sub-manager in their formulations department with Good Manufacturing Practices as my main focus," Ritu said.

I introduced her to Vaidehi and Spandana. After exchanging pleasantries, they left to continue their shopping and allowed us to have coffee and revive our old memories.

***

Two years before retirement, I was promoted to Product Manager in the department of parenteral drugs, specializing in intravenous infusion fluids. The clients were mainly corporate hospitals. Sales depended on contacts and credit. I needed a committed team of young *people willing to meet people and develop relationships essential for the department's success.*

On the second day of my initiation into my new assignment, our HR manager came to my room along with a young girl hardly out of college wearing white pants with a blue satin long top, obediently following the Manager.

"Good morning Raj. Let me introduce you to Ritu Chawla, who will be attached to your department. You insisted on the need for a pharma grad at your last meeting."

Pharma companies don't recruit many pharma graduates as they are expensive human resources and not loyal. So they prefer ordinary science graduates and persuade the managers to train them for the job. Training a commerce grad or even a science graduate on the nuances of pharma business with products that have tongue-twisting names require passionate and dedicated training. So I requested that it needed at least one pharma graduate help me run the department.

"Oh, thanks. Nice of you to accede to my request," I said.

He left, soon leaving Ritu in the room.

"Please sit down," I said.

She sat down while pulling her creased top down, revealing her firm, round and small breasts.

She was gorgeous. Punjabi girls have very fair skin. Ritu Chawla had her hair strung in a bun exposing her slender neck. Her hair looked like a cool breeze trapped inside, waiting to be unleashed.

I instantly liked her, though not in the sexual connotation.

"Tell me a little about yourself so I can put you in a job profile that is best suited to your liking," I said

A pleasant voice in low decibels spoke.

"Sir, I graduated in pharmacy from Delhi Institute of Pharmaceutical Science this academic year. The company recruited me in a campus interview. So I am here, assigned to your department."

"But Mumbai is far from Delhi; why did you opt for coming here all the way?" I asked.

"Sir, My papa was transferred here about a year before, so here I am," she answered.

I liked her confident appearance.

We decided what should be her job profile and introduced her to other team members. She instantly became a popular member of my team. She was computer literate. I was very relieved of that skill of hers, which was essential in this new managerial world of presentations, graphs and what-if analyses. It never occurred to me to use her pharma knowledge for which she was recruited. Our relationship was purely professional, and I enjoyed working with her. Also, she blended perfectly with other team members, even with the perennially complaining Srinivasan. We worked together through several crises in the office. In the increasingly competitive atmosphere in the office, I had taken her under my wings and offered protection from the boorish behaviour of corporate leeches. Our department broke many records in sales volumes and contributed handsomely to the company's growth, and all my staff members were well rewarded. When I retired last year, the team gave me a tearful farewell and thanked me profusely for being a good boss and a good mentor.

***

"Sir, what are you doing nowadays," Ritu said, disturbing my thought process.

"Nothing, much as you know, I am retired, and once in a way, I get an assignment for auditing Plant processes from pharma companies *which I take up. Even that has stopped now. Nobody invites me anymore now." I said, sounding rueful.*

"Are you married?" I asked.

"No sir, not yet," she responded.

"But, you must be around 26 now, dear?" I wondered

"26 going on 27," she replied.

"You could not find the right partner so far?"

"Well, no, sir, my parents are trying."

She did not elaborate. Meanwhile, my phone buzzed, reminding me to pick up my family. We exchanged phone numbers to be in touch. She said she was presently staying in a hostel-type accommodation in Ameerpet with two other girls.

That was my initiation to a relationship that would shatter my peace and expose my frailties. We became Facebook friends, and she started chatting with me regularly. Mostly about books and movies.

A few days later, Ritu called Raj on his mobile.

"Hi, good morning, sir," said Ritu.

"Good morning. We finally saw that movie you recommended," said Raj.

"You liked it, sir? That's nice. I called you for something else," said Ritu.

"Tell me."

"I want to introduce you to my Executive Director, Mr Ranga Rao. I spoke to him about you. The company wants to expand. Ranga Rao, sir, is a visionary but needs the guidance of an experienced man like you. Shall I fix an appointment for you, sir?" asked Ritu. Raj readily agreed. Any job that keeps him away from the control freak was welcome.

At the appointed time, Raj walked into GOUD PHARMACEUTICALS, where Ritu Chawla met him, and after some pleasantries, she requested the receptionist to announce his arrival. Raj noted Ritu has aged into a prettier woman since the time she worked with him in Mumbai. Raj stood behind Ritu at the reception area, while the receptionist punched a few numbers and spoke. Ritu's perfume stung him hard. Her energy radiated from her like electricity. He was reminded of Vaidehi during their younger days. Ritu requested Raj to relax on the sofa and wait for the call back, turned and walked out like a ballerina.

Raj was welcomed into Ranga Rao's cabin. Ranga Rao's office was a showpiece designed to make a statement. In this case, it was "I am the Boss."

Ranga Rao, while waving Raj to take the seat, punched a number on his table phone and spoke on speaker.

"Sir?"

"Could you please check whether my father-in-law has arrived?"

"He did, sir. He is already in his room."

"Please inform him Mr Raj Krishna Sastry has arrived, and we will have a meeting in the mini-conference room."

"Yes, sir."

Ranga Rao cradled the handset and looked at Raj Krishna.

"I am Ranga Rao. Ritu told me about you, sir. Thanks for coming with such short notice. We are happy that such an eminent person like you is from Hyderabad. We are proud of your Pharma Sector achievements, "said Ranga Rao.

"Thank you," said Raj.

"Shall we move to the conference room, sir?"

ED led Raj into a small room with a round table and five chairs. The room looked simple with just a small table calendar and a couple of notebooks with a pen stuck at the top. There was a bookshelf with many pharmacy-related books, some familiar to Raj.

***

GOUD PHARMA founder-chairman was Nageshwar Goud, the fourth child of the Goud family. They were mainly in the liquor business, with country liquor shacks in Baghlingampalli and Karmanghat, managed by the two elder sons. The third son had obtained a license for the IMFL store with the help of a local Politician for whose elections; the Goud family contributed with financial and workforce might. Unlike his siblings, Nageshwar, the fourth son, somehow managed education beyond the eighth grade and graduated in science. He, too, would have joined his brothers' business, but fate intervened in the form of a pretty Brahmin girl with whom he fell in love. The girl had insisted he should find a job and not join his family's liquor business.

Nageshwar had to agree and was employed as a chemist in a Central government-owned drug firm in Hyderabad. Like the teaser tag line of a Lee Van Cleef movie: "you cannot keep a good man down", Nageshwar found ways to make some side hustle. Many pharma graduates in the company assisted Nageshwar with his schemes. With their help and a go-getter attitude, he convinced private pharma companies to research their formulations in his workplace for a fee. He clandestinely used the infrastructure and chemicals of his employer to experiment to help his clientele on the sly. Because his department's work involved finding new formulations and process improvisations, he did not have to account for the raw material used up as in the research set-up; wastage was acceptable. Many pharma companies in Hyderabad owe their formulations, APIs, and documentation of such formulations' chemistry to this Government drug company staff's complicity, whose leader was Nageshwar.

After a few years of working and gaining knowledge of the drug industry in the country, Nageshwar quit the company and started GOUD PHARMACEUTICALS with the help of seed money he collected from his illegal activities in the job and with the generous support of his dad, friends and father-in-law. His wife did not object to this as the Pharmaceuticals unit was a respectable business compared to the liquor trade. However, Nageshwar did not have the insight to market new drugs or formulations as it required research and marketing set-up and talent, which he could not muster. His dream was to market a drug under the GOUD PHARMA brand remained unfulfilled.

However, GOUD PHARMA remained a contracting service provider as a secondary supplier for clinical materials for big pharma conglomerates, such as Zydus, IPCA, Glen Pharma, Alembic, Dr Reddy's etc.

These outsourcing companies in pharma industry parlance are labelled as CMOs (Contract Manufacturing Organizations). When a company has more orders for a product than it can fill, then it takes to what is known as contract manufacturing.

In a large organization with much higher overheads, it becomes attractive to have routine production of existing products manufactured by a contract manufacturing organization (CMO). Thus, the Principal concentrated on synthesizing APIs and clinical studies involving fieldwork, analytics and heavy paperwork for mandatory approvals.

GOUD PHARMA grew to be a reliable company for outsourcing contract manufacturing, including laboratory testing, qualification and validation as per regulatory norms and documentation, assessment and procuring raw materials, and the like. Within twenty years, GOUD PHARMA had reached the level of a corporation with three units across the State. Later his son-in-law Ranga Rao joined the firm as Executive Director. Nageshwar had relegated himself to public relations activities in the industry associations and left the day-to-day functioning to Ranga Rao, still nurturing his dream of developing a branded drug.

In Ranga Rao, he found an able ally. Ranga Rao was an ambitious management graduate; he started thinking big and decided to venture into product manufacturing and brand marketing of a formulation or a parenteral, as per the market survey. He had already shortlisted Metformin and Sildenafil Citrate as the possible two drugs he would want to explore further. He was more interested in the latter because of its multifunctional use for the treatment of erectile dysfunction – most common in diabetic patients, and its use against Pulmonary Arterial Hypertension.

Some CMOs tend to go for bulk drug manufacturing by circumventing the confidentiality of the proprietary knowledge they gained while performing the contracting services. Some major pharmaceutical companies would want to gradually shift from transactional outsourcing relationships to more strategic, relationship-based models by sharing their recipes. Ranga Rao wished to pursue the latter course, which was stable and legal.

***

"Sir, I had not met you before in person, but I heard your talk at the conferences of Pharma 2012 and 2014. You are a legend in the industry, sir. And you are from Hyderabad, as well," said Ranga Rao.

"Thank you," said Raj.

"Have you been briefed about GOUD PHARMA, its aims and objectives?" asked Ranga Rao.

"Yes, sir, Ritu briefed me," said Raj.

"She may not be fully privy to our long term plans. Let me be clear with what plans we have. As we presently work as a contract manufacturing unit, we manage mostly with science graduates though we have a few pharma grads at the entry-level. But we have high attrition of these pharma graduates as they are never loyal. Lately, we have changed our recruitment policy with managerial staff mostly with a chemistry background and few with quality assurance experience having worked as Quality managers in other firms. As we are not into R&D much, we never felt the need to employ more pharma grads," explained Ranga Rao.

"I want to change the perception in the industry that we are only into contract manufacturing. As we have now expertise in GMP and have the infrastructure for manufacturing with experienced staff, we need directions towards introducing new drugs with our brand in the market. It was my founder's wish too. We need to attract talent for such future," said Ranga Rao.

Meanwhile, Nageshwar walked in, and after formal introductions, he too welcomed Raj.

"Yes, where were we?" said Ranga Rao addressing Raj.

"Yeah, we were discussing the drug manufacture."

As you probably know, we are one of the contract outsourcing firms for Zydus and a few other companies," said Ranga Rao. Raj nodded.

"Sir, as you are well aware, Sildenafil Citrate has lately been found to be useful for the treatment of pulmonary arterial hypertension also, alongside its primary use for erectile dysfunction. At GOUD PHARMA, we want to get into the manufacturing of this drug ourselves independently and market it under the brand name, ERECTA," added Nageshwar.

"Well, that's interesting, but we need much more than a good marketing team. Also, we can only market the product with detailing to doctors by medical reps as a prescription drug. Apart from financial sustainability from R&D to market, it can be a costly proposition that may take years", opined Raj. He then gave a short glimpse of drug development to his audience, from R&D to patient delivery.

The journey of a molecule from lab to market has to go through many steps that may take years of hard labour with financial commitment, passion and perseverance, and a myriad of regulatory hurdles. Identification of hit molecules from a huge chemical library is a Herculean task which, in this case, is half the job done as the chemical is identified. One has only to check the IP rights to know where one stands as far as further work is concerned. In the case of Sildenafil Citrate, the patent is scheduled to expire sometime in 2020, which undoubtedly will give rise to several generic versions. It might take years before one can hit upon suitable crystalline salts, solvates, etc., which can improve the drugs' active ingredient properties to produce an optimal solid form based on stability, solubility, ease of use production, etc. Different from the citrate compound presently marketed.

The potential lead molecule's compound should exhibit good drug absorption, distribution, and metabolism profile. After that, we can take up pre-clinical studies. The lead molecules are subjected to pharma-kinetics, pharma-dynamics, toxicity profile, carcinogenicity profile and ADME tests by in-vitro and in-vivo assays using cultured cells and laboratory model animals to discern the potential pharmaceutical property of a drug molecule to process further for clinical trials on humans.

Afterwards, we have phase I, II and III studies on humans with humongous documentation and stringent regulatory rigor before it is approved to be released in the market. That's not all. The final phase of a drug on a large population ranging from 2000 - to 3000 patients with the targeted disease, which could reveal the effect of the drug on a more significant number of patients, its effectiveness on a large population, perform quality of life trials and gather all safety and additional adverse effect of the drug and will proceed further. The whole process usually takes 15- 20 years. You would have saved five years after the patent expiry as the molecule becomes generic, and many variants would flood the market.

"Thank you for the in-depth brief. I know most of what you have said, though the timeline is a bit of a dampener. As you have rightly said, creating a team solely depending on one product cannot be economically feasible. We also contract manufacture Metformin, another popular drug, because of the country's increase in Type 2 diabetes. We can attempt to study the same too simultaneously," said Ranga Rao.

"But this action of ours may result in the cancellation of contract manufacturing which is a risk since 60% of our turnover comes from two major companies. Also, we have entered into confidentiality agreements with both of these firms on the usage of their proprietary information. That's a huge risk we at GOUD PHARMA are willing to take," said Ranga Rao. "Sir, we want you to help us in this endeavour. We can work out the logistics of your association with us for our mutual benefit."

"I have to study the subject more closely as most of my work was not in manufacturing or R&D but GMP. During my last two years before retirement, I headed the Product Manager position looking after Parenteral drugs", said Raj.

"It is ok, sir; we are not in a hurry. You may study and come back within a week or so or at your convenient time. Ranga Rao shall be in touch with you," said Nageshwar.

After a week. Raj Krishna, Nageshwar and Ranga Rao met again. It occurred to Raj that Nageshwar was the brain behind his son-in-law's plans on drug manufacture, as he appeared enthused at the idea, though he did not say much. They spent close to one hour in the conference room discussing the future of GOUD PHARMA and how they want the firm to grow. Nageshwar and Ranga Rao were in sync, as per the discussions in which Raj participated. Nageshwar had not shown any dissent to what Ranga Rao had in mind on the subject matter of Erecta. He mainly talked in monosyllables. Ritu arranged to drop Raj back at his house in the company provided transport. During the journey, Ritu wanted to discuss the idea about Erecta.

Raj used sign language and told Ritu to be wary of the company employee's driver.

"Not to worry, sir, he is only three months old in the company and knows no other language other than Telugu. I have a tough time communicating with him whenever I needed to use him," said Ritu.

"Ok, go ahead," said Raj.

"Sir, you think this new molecule will be easy to develop and market? And does GOUD PHARMA have the technical, managerial and financial leverage to venture into this territory?" asked Ritu.

"As I have said in the meeting with the Directors today, the FDA and the regulatory authority of India would need at least fifteen years of data to approve any new formulation. I don't think GOUD PHARMA has the required financial backup to sustain the R&D, clinical trials of various phases etc. This Ranga Rao of yours is an incorrigible dreamer without a doubt but a foolish one at that," said Raj.

"Can you explain what Ranga Rao had in mind when he said Erecta would have a USP that present drugs do not have?" asked Ritu.

"It is embarrassing for me to explain this to you."

"It is ok, sir," said Ritu.

"One such drug, presently available in the market from a reputed Pharma company, is purported to work only after 2 hours of its intake, though their brochure says it starts its effect within half an hour to 2 hours. Independent researchers have doubted this claim. They say it needs a two-hour gap between intake and functionally effective and requires initiation by the opposite sex in cases of severe erectile dysfunction. Two hours is a huge gap, moods may change between partners because of extraneous conditions, and the drug cannot perform its designed action, not because of efficacy problems but because of circumstances and attitudinal issues between partners. So GOUD PHARMA wants to focus on the problems related to the relatively long time between drug administration and the onset of desired therapeutic action, which is a noble thought, no doubt," said Raj.

"It is difficult for me to explain the problems faced by ED patients, but take my word, we need the consumer to be ready for action within half an hour of its intake. That appears to be the idea of GOUD PHARMA, as explained by Ranga Rao to me. That is where they want my help to find a release substance that can enhance the effectiveness of Erecta, which can be an essential ingredient to the drug. Therefore disintegration tests have to be done with various substances that can quicken the release of the active ingredient."

"Another matter is I have limited knowledge of the chemistry of the drug. In fact, in my pharmacy course, I had to depend upon my colleagues to help me pass chemistry subject," added Raj.

"But you have over thirty-five years of experience in one company! Also, you are a popular speaker in the pharma circles, especially your lectures in conferences are never missed by anyone connected with the pharma industry," said Ritu.

"You see, that's a perception. I had spent all my life in the GMP area only. The firm where I worked had six units spread across the country; I had to ensure the processes and train the staff to follow the documentation protocols. For the last two years, I was in the Product Management field, which again did not require any chemistry knowledge – it was all management. As you very well know, you were with me during those last two years," said Raj.

"Even your emcee primer to the audience had never mentioned my work in molecule development, yet why GOUD PHARMA wants my involvement is a mystery," added Raj.

"I feel they want to use your association with GOUD PHARMA to entice experienced staff to join them. But that apart, this allows me to be working with you once again," said Ritu.

"But still, I feel something is fishy in the whole thing. Anyway, it does not matter to me as long as the firm pays what I had requested."

"If I am not being too personal, can I ask how much were you offered?"

"Originally, it was to be an annual package. But I insisted on monthly remuneration, as I am not sure I can survive here long.

I will soon be exposed. I do not know about drug development," said Raj candidly.

Her sudden interest in him was mildly intoxicating.

Meanwhile, the car reached Raj's apartment, and they parted company.

Hardly few months had passed since Raj joined GOUD PHARMA when suddenly his assignment profile of Raj had changed to his convenience.

He would be in the domain in which he was familiar and experienced. Also, he was feeling guilty about not being proficient enough to take forward the ideas of Ranga Rao and Nageshwar to their logical conclusion.

***

As a contracted organization, GOUD PHARMACEUTICALS had to replicate the processes it had put in practice and approved by the inspecting authorities at one plant to other locations, which entailed much expenditure. The systems and processes involved would have to be duplicated over all the sites, including mandating validation in all locations, which would be expensive. So, GOUD PHARMA had overcome the need to obtain approvals for all the manufacturing plants in various places but declared only those with acceptable GMPs as mandated by the principal licensee. It passed off the drug manufacture by the unapproved plant as from an approved and inspected plant to suit its volumes contracted which were beyond the capacity of its approved plant. It fudged data on the capacity of the approved plant to get a large volume of orders. It went unnoticed, as GOUD PHARMA ensured it followed all the required processes.

GOUD PHARMA was not alone in this dishonesty.

There are many ways the drug management intentionally puts public health at risk to profit. One Hyderabad based company was alleged to have tested drug batches in a laboratory the FDA was never told existed. Evidence collected by FDA inspectors showed that trained and appropriately skilled personnel were sorely lacking in overseas manufacturing facilities, especially in third world countries. Another instance could be data fabrication, which some firms had taken to a different level altogether. FDA has since changed its system of inspection of advance intimation as presently, the inspections are unannounced, making the new drug units alert all the time.

Lately, however, FDA has reverted to giving advance notice of its inspections to overseas pharmaceutical facilities – though not formally. All foreign visitors to India needed to get Visa from the Ministry of External Affairs, which involved detailed documentation, including a formal invitation letter from the business unit they were visiting. It was beneficial to some congenitally dubious managements.

But one can and does get caught when a duly diligent external inspector visits.

***

It was a Friday afternoon. Vaidehi carried the ringing mobile to Raj, who was having a nap.

"Boss wants you in office at 4:30," thundered the voice at the other end.

"Ritu, you know very well I don't come to the office on Fridays and also I have booked movie tickets for a 7 pm show," said Raj.

"I just conveyed what ED told me. He told me to arrange transport for you; I am sending the driver to your home now," said Ritu.

"Ok, this better be good," said Raj and stubbed the phone.

On arrival, he was promptly taken to the conference room where the Vishakhapatnam Unit Manager, Joseph, was present, along with Ranga Rao and his father-in-law.

"Thank you for coming on such short notice, Raj," said Nageshwar.

Ranga Rao briefed the problem to Raj.

GOUD PHARMA had three units registered with the certifying agencies as per drug authority mandate – one at Medchal (30 km from Hyderabad), Vishakhapatnam and Patencheruvu in Hyderabad. It had one other unit at Karimnagar, started by Ranga Rao after he married the Goud family member but not registered under GOUD PHARMA ownership. The firm had contracted to supply 5 million Ciprofloxacin 200 mg filled in 100 ml plastic containers to Schmidt & Cohen GMBH (S&C) in Germany through their Indian counterpart located on the outskirts of Delhi. The contract stipulated that GOUD PHARMA should outsource Ciprofloxacin from Bayer and prepare a sodium salt delivery system and supply these filled bottles within one month of the contract. They appointed a French Inspection Agency to inspect the product before shipping it to Germany. GOUD PHARMA had its own plastic bottle manufacturing unit at Karimnagar and supplied sterilized bottles to Vishakhapatnam, where the parenteral unit was situated.

The filling unit at Vishakhapatnam had some mechanical problems, and it was unable to manufacture the contracted quantity in the time stipulated. So Ranga Rao used their facility at Karimnagar, which was not approved by S & C, to fill the gap of about a million units.

This con could have gone undetected had there not been a cyclone at Vishakhapatnam, which delayed Karimnagar supplies. They arrived on the day the assessor had come for inspection. As the consignment from Karimnagar was being unloaded, the inspector noticed the containers did not belong to the permitted unit. He promptly noted the discrepancy after checking the details of quantity lying in the stores, which the store manager confirmed they had only 4 million units. He objected to one million's balance supply from an unapproved site. He informed his displeasure to the local Manager, Mr Joseph Varghese and left the premises without giving a Finished Product Release Note. The Regional Manager tried to convince the inspector to meet his boss in Hyderabad before leaving for headquarters. But the inspector said he had some urgent work during the weekend and regretted his inability to meet his MD. The local Manager promptly informed Ranga Rao about it and convinced the inspector to talk to his ED. The inspector and Ranga Rao spoke on the phone, and they mutually agreed to meet at the plant on the following Monday.

"We wondered how to come out of this," said Ranga Rao.

"If this gets reported as seen by the Inspector, we would be in deep trouble. It would be the end of this and future contracts with S & C, also the word would spread across the pharma circles, and we would be doomed."

"Can I see the inspection call letter from GOUD PHARMA to S&C?" asked Raj.

Raj was surprised to note the call letter did not contain the quantity offered for inspection but only the contract details, product description and specifications, proposed date of assessment, and other plant-related particulars with the contact mobile number of the Manager for further interaction. He internally felt dismayed that all the participants in the contract had compromised the call letter formats and inspection processes.

"What if we only offer 4 million units for inspection?" asked Raj.

"We would have to pay the penalty and ask for an extension of the Letter of Credit for one more week to supply the balance of the contracted quantity. They probably will ask for the inspection charges for re-inspection," said Ranga Rao.

"Isn't it cheaper than the other options you have?"

"Yes, of course," interjected Nageshwar.

"But how shall we explain the one million containers arrived from Karimnagar when the inspector was on the premises?" wondered Ranga Rao.

"Has the inspector seen the Transporters Note pasted on the packages of the containers that arrived from Karimnagar?" asked Raj addressing the question to Joseph.

"I don't think so. The inspector only saw the packages being unloaded and inquired about the same with the Stores Manager," informed Joseph.

"Can you please tell me what exact words the Store Manager said to the Inspector?" asked Raj.

Joseph phoned the Stores Manager and got the details.

"The Stores Manager purported to have said they have only 4 million to offer from this Vishakhapatnam unit, and those just arrived were the balance one million from another unit," said Joseph.

"I think we can salvage the situation because everyone in the chain had erred," said Raj.

"How?" asked Nageshwar.

"Do you have any buyers in Bhubaneshwar for these containers?"

"Yes, we are regular suppliers to CARE hospitals through their head office in Hyderabad."

"Please get a back-dated order from CARE to your Karimnagar unit to supply one million units to their Bhubaneshwar hospital," said Raj.

"Though it is difficult to convince CARE management on this, even if we do, how can it solve this matter," asked Nageshwar.

"We change the transporters label on the packages to show they were on their way from Karimnagar to Bhubaneshwar, and because of the cyclone, the transporter dumped the containers here in Vishakhapatnam for temporary storage to be picked up later when the weather improves," said Raj

"Sir, that is a brilliant idea," said Joseph.

"And?" wondered Nageshwar

"We say that we are offering only four million presently, as the call letter is absent on the quantity being offered."

The intervening weekend had come in handy for damage control. Nageshwar, with his old contacts, got an order printed which showed CARE contracted to buy one million Anti-infective Ciprofloxacin 200 mg filled in 100 ml plastic containers for its Bhubaneshwar multi-specialty 300-bed hospital. The store manager, conversant only in Telugu, was asked to go on leave and transferred a suave and young business management graduate working in another department. Joseph organized to print labels with the transporter's logo, with some random black vertical lines of various thicknesses for the authenticity of a bar code. They printed a loading slip that showed that the package was booked at Karimnagar for the onward journey to CARE, Bhubaneshwar.

The issue was resolved after Ranga Rao explained to the inspector with 'evidence' that the packages he had seen belonged to another client in Bhubaneshwar. And the Stores clerk erred in informing him. Ranga Rao convinced the inspector to check only 4 million units and release them for further dispatch. It did not occur either to the inspector or to the GOUD PHARMA Management to ponder why should a hospital order such a sizeable quantity of Ciprofloxacin, as though there was an endemic of bacterial infection in the entire State of Orissa. However, Raj's bluff paid off. Ranga Rao and Joseph together apologized to the Buyer. They asked for an extension to fulfil the contract balance. The S&C reluctantly agreed to a one-time financial penalty and a warning to be more transparent with their documentation and events at their plant that could affect their supplies. The Principal Company also could not penalize much as they had erred in not noticing the missing information of the quantity offered in the inspection call letter, which came in handy for Raj to wriggle out of the embarrassment.

Nageshwar and Ranga Rao were immensely thankful for the smart way; Raj had solved the tricky matter without damaging the reputation of GOUD PHARMACEUTICALS. Nageshwar finally realized if GOUD PHARMA does not immediately improve the staff quality & training and documentation along with the processes, it would be challenging to measure up to rigorous inspections of the Drug Control Authority and FDA. With reports of fraud committed by many pharma units in Western media, the inspectors had become more stringent with stricter surveillance systems. Nageshwar had to perforce keep his dream project aside and agreed with Ranga Rao to use Raj's services to improve their

GMP processes even if it meant paying a substantial price in the form of consultancy charges for a service Nageshwar was not convinced required the kind of expertise Raj was likely to bring.

But not being aware of this development, Raj had informed Ranga Rao about his inability to continue working for GOUD PHARMA on their drug development of Erecta because of his failing health, which was an excuse lest he is exposed to the lack of knowledge of molecular chemistry.

Both Ranga Rao and Nageshwar requested Raj to work for a few months more, audit their good manufacturing practices for all units, including documentation, and train the staff to interact with external inspectors. The result of the Vishakhapatnam fiasco.

Raj agreed to work in the domain area he was familiar with, albeit for a few months only.

"I think Ranga Rao took advantage of the fiasco", said Raj

Raj and Ritu were going to their Medchal plant for the first session of their scheduled GMP training program.

"Why do you think so," asked Ritu.

"Ranga Rao wanted some experienced hand to work on the Good Manufacturing Practices field, as he could have realized the latest practices in this GMP area had missed GOUD PHARMA, which could harm his future business. If he had proposed this to his father-in-law, it would not have found favour because Nageshwar being stingy and of the old school, would not be willing to pay the kind of consultancy charges for a person of my experience to teach them how to clean toilets, sterilize aprons, sending inspection call letters and the like".

"Thus, the incident at Vishakhapatnam came in handy for Ranga Rao."

"So, finally Ranga Rao achieved what he wanted, and it was advantageous to you too," said Ritu

"Unwittingly, yes."

As agreed with Ranga Rao, Raj quit Goud Pharma after six months of hard work to put GOUD PHARMA on an even keel in respect of GMP as per accepted norms of the Pharma Industry. Ritu helped in this process as a diligent colleague.

Their bond developed from more than just a Boss and Colleague to a more tempestuous association.

Ritu Chawla

It was difficult to pinpoint what stage 'Sir' became 'Raj' in their relationship. Her official association with Raj helped in the development of an intimate association. More so, as they often travelled between the two locations of Goud Pharma at Patencheruvu and Medchal. They even visited Vishakhapatnam together to do an audit. When the company could not provide the transport, Raj would take his personal car and drive himself, with Ritu occupying the front seat.

Later I realized Ritu planned this arrangement by giving false information about the non-availability of the company driver to ensure privacy in my self-driven car.

Raj picked up Ritu in his car at the appointed place to go to the Medchal unit. He opened the door of the vehicle for her to enter. While trying to adjust herself in the seat, her hair brushed lightly against his face; it brought with it a body odour he felt disconcerting. She looked like a brown Nicole Kidman with puffed up upper cheek but pitch-black hair and dark brown eyes. She cleverly covered her chest with loose tops, and he could not have imagined the size of her boobs until later when they popped out when she unhooked her bra.

She noticed that the inside of Raj's car was immaculate, clean and military.

She rolled down the glass window, breezed out the stowaway fly, and rolled it back.

"What prevents you from settling down in life with a husband?" Raj asked during the long drive just to start a conversation.

"Why are you obsessed with my marriage?"

"Just curious."

"The boys I met want to take me to bed as soon as possible. No one is interested in developing a relationship."

"All are not like that; you may have had some bad luck," said Raj. "I think you should take a cue from Pygmalion and sculpt a man of your choice."

"What or who is Pygmalion?" asked Ritu.

"It is a part of Greek mythology. Pygmalion, a sculptor, hated women until he carved a female form in stone and fell promptly in love. He then approached God to convert his creation into flesh and blood. Then, Aphrodite, the Greek God, felt pity for him and brought forth the stone to life. "

"Wasn't the Hollywood film My Fair Lady based on this story in which Rex Harrison played the part of the Sculptor?" asked Ritu.

"Partly."

"I am not a man-hater. Don't get me wrong. It takes longer to find an accomplished man who is a humorous conversationalist and nature lover and does not push me onto the bed as soon as he finds an opportunity. Also, my parents are trying too, and they keep sending me CVs and photos of some Punjabi hunks," said Ritu.

"Meanwhile, I want to enjoy life in whatever way I can before committing to a man."

Raj did not want to prolong the conversation and got immersed in his driving on the busy highway.

***

Raj opened his heart to Ritu in another of those long drives with his childhood and his marital woes.

He confided in her over the suffering he had with his dad and his wife. She looked at him with a knotted face, indicating sympathy. He had cheated on a college exam; ripped some pages from a library; had not returned a sweater borrowed from his friend. He also told about the good things he had done, which his wife would otherwise have misinterpreted had he confessed to her. His wife believed he was a ladies' man, and women would use him to their selfish ends, taking much of his time and financial assets. He told Ritu the circumstances that led him to go for a vasectomy - his wife's threat of abstinence till he got his vas tube tied up, as she did not want to conceive by accident.

These were many such things he told her. However, he did not disclose his clandestine affairs.

On Ritu's insistence, Raj met her often and went for long drives whenever Ritu took off from work. Slowly, the relationship developed into an intimate one without any initiation by Raj.

As Vaidehi knew Raj did not have any more contracting assignments, he had to find excuses to go on long drives with Ritu. Yet, the tipping point for the relationship to develop into a sensual one is difficult to fathom. Maybe unlike Vaidehi, Ritu acknowledged his wit, which he was once proud of. She said so many lovely things about him.

"I like the way you drive," she said once when they were in Raj's car to Medchal.

"You know you give a lot of respect to fellow road users. You let horn-blaring cars pass without cursing them. My dad always used choicest Punjabi abuses whenever he drives. My mom had a tough time bugging him to recognise my presence in the car."

"Thanks."

It was a Saturday morning. Raj and Ritu were driving on the outer ring road towards the airport. It was their regular long drive engagement. She was at her natural best – with a square neck white top sleeveless worn on pink leggings. She had her hair loose, and as soon she entered the car, she sat on the seat, took her purse and found a rubber band with which she tied her hair. Raj could see her chiselled face with no makeup.

Nice and Sexy.

"I suppose I should thank you," his gaze was on her while she shifted 45 degrees towards him.

"Then thank me," she said while laying her hand on Raj's thigh. A younger man would be jolted and lose control of his vehicle.

"Incidentally, what for?"

"I did not know what I was getting into once I retired and shifted to Hyderabad. When a man goes to a regular job, he need not account for his time. He can spend an evening or two with his friends at a pub or playing a game of badminton. The wife would think he was working at the office. No questions asked. But once you retire, you would have to account for every minute of your time, which is stifling. But once you have a revenue ensuring work, she does not ask questions. You have done a great favour by helping me sign a contract with Goud Pharma," said Raj.

"But you have resigned, now."

"Yes, that makes me worry about our future rendezvouses."

"Let us enjoy the present moment and worry about those things later."

She squeezed his thigh harder as a symbol of reassurance.

As if to say, 'I am with you.'

Quite suddenly, Ritu pulled his left hand and let him feel her 24-inch bare waist – open acreage between the top and the legging. She was driving him crazy. She turned her face towards him. "I love you," she said unexpectedly, and he lost control of the road, shocked. She was very different from the mature women he had affairs with, primarily sexual and none of them as sensuous. She swept her hair away from her back, exposing the naked neck. She demanded Raj lick her neck. He bent and moved his tongue around her neck with one hand on the steering. She moaned and squeezed his thigh in pleasure. He nibbled on her ear-catching the lobe gently. She pushed his left hand under her pants through the panty to the dripping vagina. Her moaning had reached a crescendo. It was becoming impossible to keep one hand on the steering while the other was trying to locate her clitoris. The car wobbled a little, and he immediately got it under control. Fortunately, the Outer Ring Road on which they were driving did not have much traffic that day. "Tell me how much you want to fuck me," she said aloud. Raj hardly could answer. He had his erection to control apart from the car. Suddenly, she decided to feel his crotch by thrusting her hand between his thighs. She felt the hard-on. He had to oblige by unzipping and pulling his penis out from his underclothing. The elastic of the undies was hurting, but the pleasure of a young woman feeling and rubbing the penis camouflaged all pain. He pulled the car to the side, entered the carriageway, and stopped the vehicle, ensuring no one was behind to notice the unusual activity. She was sucking him and biting him with her teeth; her hands were everywhere, pulling his hair to caressing his ear lobes. He was worried he might ejaculate inside her mouth. She did not stop moaning even while she was slurping him. He forcibly moved her head away to prevent semen from dripping into her mouth. She moved out and started kissing his chin and said, "Love me, fuck me, I want you now."

Ritu appeared determined she would somehow convince Raj to go all the way and give her the erotic pleasures she wanted. Raj was laid-back enough for her to indulge without the fear of pregnancy, and his timid nature with affable attitude would give her that extra cushion of secrecy. She finally found a man with whom she could have all the sexual fantasies she read in novels. She imagined herself as Ritu Steel[67], wanting to be caged by Raj Grey. These long drives happened many times and made Raj wonder whether he was lucky to spend sensuous time with a young woman twenty years younger girl or be afraid these meetings might prove embarrassing in the days to come. He found her most desirable amongst the women he had affairs with, barring Vaidehi. Ritu had forced Raj to find ways to go for long drives to have her moments of enjoyment. As soon as they were in the car, she would start kissing his fingers, licking them and putting her hand on his thighs to arouse him. She would force his hands through her top and feel her breasts, for which she would have already unhooked the strap. The moment Raj's hand started caressing her breasts and softly squeezing the nipples, she would begin to grunt, reminding him of Monica Seles.

Once Raj confided to Ritu, breasts were his weakness.

Even though they were his weakness, I found that he would never squeezed them hard. My friend in Chandigarh once confided in me that her husband hurt her a lot while playing with her breasts. Raj was different. He treated them – he called them cute containers - as

---

67   Steel and Grey are characters of a popular sensuous novel

though they had a life of their own. His caressing was very enjoyable. I would be wet in no time.

One winter evening, when the day darkened early, she forcibly made Raj stop the car at Himayatsagar bund, and she opened her top fully and let him have his fill of her breasts. While he was sucking her nipples gently, "I would have been a good wife to you if only you had borne later," she said coyly.

In another such meeting, Ritu said," Raj, let us go out of the station somewhere to Bengaluru or some such place and enjoy more privacy than this cramped car."

"I want to sleep with you," she said coyly, holding her head close to his shoulders; she felt his hands tighten against the steering. "Not yet," he said, "there is time and place for everything."

"You are talking like a dad," she complained.

"Have you gone crazy? We have had wonderful hugging and kissing moments that could be the envy of any passionate and committed lovers. But beyond that, I don't want to violate your chastity."

"But I want it. Why are you afraid when I am willing? Incidentally, my roommates are going out for a picnic this weekend. I dropped out on the pretext I had periods. Please come over to my place this Sunday," said Ritu.

"Sunday? It would be impossible; what excuse can I give my wife that I shall be out of the house on holiday. Lately, she has been checking my movements with precision. She controls me on the pretext of my well-being: You have to have lunch and dinners at the appointed time; otherwise, your health will be affected. I have no way of countering this without creating a scene," said Raj.

"Also, it could be dangerous if anyone knocks on the door. You said your maid has a key. How about the delivery boys of any e-commerce site, who may visit you? "wondered Raj.

"You need not worry on those fronts. My door has an extra bolt inside, so the maid cannot open it with her key. Secondly, I will inform the security not to disturb me as I am sick and resting. Is that Ok? Or any other doubts you have?"

"You seem to have covered everything."

"After all, it is your training, remember?"

With much persuasion by Ritu, they decided to meet on Saturday afternoon post-lunch at her shared apartment. It was left to Raj to find an excuse to inform his absence from home on a non-working day. At around 3 in the afternoon, Raj walked into her apartment with trepidation and guilt. As soon as he rang the bell, she just flung the door open and dragged Raj in by pulling at his collar and bolting the latch. The apartment Raj entered had a TV, a sofa in the common hall, a couple of chairs, a table with textbooks, and some notebooks spread chaotically. The couch was covered with clothes dumped, waiting to be folded. Two chairs had towels hung on them to dry. There was a used pizza box. There were two other rooms: one with an attached bath and one with a shared toilet. Before he could observe any further view of the environs, she said, "I had to rush the maid out before she could finish her job." An explanation for the disorder, he presumed. She offered Raj some water and guided him to her room which was neater compared to the main hall. The bed was single with a clean mogra printed light blue bedsheet and one pillow with a matching cover.

The room had a mid-sized wood-grained table with a slightly tilted mirror fixed at its far edge. At the front of the table, a laptop was open with MS Windows screen savers alternating. The table had cosmetic tubes and face cream bottles, a lipstick case with a couple of sticks without the cap, two combs – one large and one small - hair clips of all sizes and colours. Before Raj could look at the room and its surroundings, she kissed him; passionately putting her tongue in his mouth; moaning, signalling him to do the same. Standing in front of him, she confidently worked with her fingers on her shirt buttons, snapped at her bra strap and exposed her smooth, finely shaped breasts. No man can resist such a temptation. He could not have imagined what he was gifted in his most wild fantasies.

Meanwhile, Raj had unzipped his pant, opened his shirt, and presented her with a full naked view of his hairy chest. He felt her eyes crawling over him.

"Wow, beastly," she said.

She gently caressed his shoulders with her breasts. She was brushing the nipples back and forth to feel his rough skin. She pushed Raj back, so he fell on the bed on his back, and she climbed on him, licking him all over. She sat on him, putting legs on both sides of his thighs and letting her bare breast rub against his chest, moaning while enjoying the roughness of a man. She could feel his hard crotch and squeezed as though she was removing the last remnants of a toothpaste tube. He grimaced but showed no annoyance. Raj was scared some vendor, or a neighbour might ring the calling bell.

Meanwhile, she dropped her leggings and the panty and moved up to Raj's face. She sat on his face, her vagina touching his mouth. He had understood her need and started licking her vagina, which was dripping wet. She held her hands onto the cot's headrest and moved her vagina up and down his throat, egged him on to put his tongue right inside the opening, and he obliged even though he was not comfortable with the smell of the fluid. After her fill, she climbed out of him and fell flat on her stomach next to him, exhausted with pleasure. He could now see a naked young girl spread-eagled with her arms stretched with palms under her head. She was beautiful, even naked, with clean-shaven genitalia fully parted and inviting labia folds. From the breasts to the parting of her legs, her body was like a sine wave, with a belly button as the centre of the trough. He could not resist rubbing his palm on the nipples, which were now erect. She opened her eyes and gave a pleasant smile. And then she turned over and gave him a Full Monty hug.

"That was very nice, Raj," she said, "Please come over on top of me and deflower me. I cannot wait any longer." She fell on her back once again, parting her legs wide.

"You have such a sexy body; you could be better off with a younger man," said Raj.

"I am quite happy with what I am getting. What more can a young man give me?" asked Ritu

"For instance, harder penis, warmer semen, multiple orgasms," said Raj.

"I am not interested in added risks. And to avoid risks, I either have to ask my partner to use a condom or plan for suitable days or take pills. All have their attended problems." said Ritu.

"For an unmarried girl, you seem to be well aware of these issues," said Raj.

"I may not have direct experience, but I have friends who are married and a few bold friends with boyfriends. That apart, the young men want to jump directly into penetration without any foreplay, which I am enjoying with you," said Ritu.

"Now, don't waste time and get on top."

"Wait, let me clean my mouth; it is full of your vaginal fluid," said Raj and went into the bathroom.

While in the bathroom, he recollected his discussion on virginity with Ritu during a long drive on the outer ring road.

"Don't you think your obsession with masturbation may one day damage your hymen, which can jeopardise your marriage?" asked Raj.

"Raj, you think I shall be happy only with necking and fingering? I want to lose my virginity to you someday. Whether you call it love or passion, I am not bothered. Want to live in the present and enjoy," said Ritu.

"Isn't that a bit risky, considering you shall be married shortly?" asked Raj.

"You are partly right," agreed Ritu. "Punjabi men give considerable importance to a virgin bride. Even if they are not virgins themselves. The majority of them are not – except some nerds. But we have our ways to overcome that."

"Such phenomenon is not peculiar to Punjab only. All Indian men want a virgin bride, "said Raj.

"Probably. Punjabi men aren't aware that hymen may break even without penetration either by accident or during masturbation," Ritu said.

"Majority of them are dumb as sexual matters go, even if they show off their outward manliness. A lot of it is due to their upbringing of not knowing how to respect women."

"So we girls designed our tricks to beat them," added Ritu smilingly

"What is it? If I may ask," inquired Raj.

"It's not any secret. We keep a safety pin under the pillow on the first conjugal night of our marriage. As soon as the groom goes to the toilet after the intercourse, we puncture our thumb a little and let the blood drip onto the middle of the bed cover, giving a false sense of comfort to the groom he had indeed succeeded in marrying a virgin. That is how we girls fool our boyfriends and husbands," said Ritu.

Raj quickly washed his mouth and gargled with water, walked out into the room wiping, with Ritu still in the same naked position he had left, with eyes shut. Hearing the sound of the bath door, she looked at him with tired half-opened eyes. Raj admired the view of her naked body. Her hair was dark. His eyes travelled the length of her tired naked body, the curve of her cheek, the fullness of her breasts, the softness of the thigh. He imagined her hip to match the thigh in softness.

Meanwhile, Raj's mobile shook the table. It was on vibration mode. He picked it up involuntarily and found his wife at the other end.

Raj heard what Vaidehi said and replied," I am just fifteen minutes away. Please hold them." Ritu heard what was said made her sit up.

"I have to go home suddenly as my eldest daughter's parents-in-law have come visiting us," said Raj

"What a time to abandon me? Why can't these people come with an appointment?" Ritu shouted angrily.

"We are old people with traditional upbringing; we tend to knock on the door unannounced. These people came from Delhi to attend a marriage and also visit us. I can't educate them now on manners. I can't ignore them too, as they are my son-in-law's parents, whom I have to attend."

"Ok, Ok," said Ritu showing annoyance," I will let you go only if you assure me one thing."

"What is it?" said the Raj with towel unwrapped, displaying his hanging penis in a mourning position.

He reached for the towel to wipe his wet face, zipped up his jeans, pulled on his shirt, and combed his hair. He combed his hair and slipped back the finger-rings from the table, slipped and clipped his watch onto his wrist. He had removed these before climbing onto the bed so as not to hurt the lady during the process of lovemaking.

"You have to promise to take me out of Hyderabad for a couple of days so we can have undisturbed time with each other," said Ritu

That is impossible. However, I have to get out now, and it is not the time to go into arguments.

Any other man would give his right hand to grab at this opportunity. A 63-year-old given a chance to deflower a virgin 26-year-old pretty girl! Nevertheless, Raj had two reasons to be wary of this engagement. One was he did not want the young girl's life to be damaged psychologically with this avoidable interface, the repercussions of which she would not comprehend now. Secondly, it was difficult for him to find an appropriate excuse to get out of Hyderabad alone.

"Sure, let us plan it properly," said Raj.

Let me gain time.

She finally gave up and retreated to the bathroom, covering herself with clothes in her other hand. She came out having slipped into her panties and bra and started to fix her hair, half-naked.

Raj walked out of the house while Ritu was still examining herself in the upright mirror on the table.

Little did he know this could be a significant turning point in their relationship.

Had he just awakened a rogue tigress?

RAJ KRISHNA

"Who is this Ritu sending so many messages?"

Vaidehi and Raj were sitting on their sofa with Raj's mobile browsing an app of an online cloth store. Vaidehi wanted to buy a couple of duvets to be presented to a newly married couple who were due to call on them.

Shabnam was watching a Marathi soap intently on the telly in her room.

He didn't want to answer until he'd given the question a little more thought but decided otherwise and said what came to his mind at the instant.

"Oh! She was assisting me in GOUD PHARMA," said Raj.

I should have blocked the messenger notification checkbox; foolish of me. He mentally kicked himself for the oversight.

Another message pops up: *when are we meeting, dear?*

"If she is an assistant, why does she address you as dear?" asked Vaidehi

He gasped. His face went red as if it had caught fire. He pulled his handkerchief from his left pocket and closed his mouth and nose with it as though to prevent a contagious bacteria from entering his body.

"I think she must have overlooked to type Sir," explained Raj.

Fortunately for Raj, the conversation ended as they were busy deciding on the gift.

Later Raj changed the notification icon on his Facebook page settings. To be extra careful, he changed her phone contact name from Ritu to Navjyot. Sikh names are gender-neutral. A call coming from Navjyot could pass off as a male. Safe bet.

***

For years, Vaidehi and Raj had any intimate hugs or patting, let alone full-fledged intercourse. Raj tried to entice her a couple of times with a tight embrace. She pulled him away. In the beginning, he had thought it would pass, and they would have normal relations. However, they started blaming each other for the lack of intimacy. When Raj tried to entice her by caressing her breasts, first, she responded by letting him push his hands inside the top of her nightdress. It was a challenging exercise. One had to go over the shoulder and stretch the hand inside. He found erect nipples instantly. He wished to suck them. However, for that, she had to undress. Slowly he raised the bottom of her housecoat and let his hand caress her bare thigh.

"You show up only when you want sex, right?" she growled, pulling his hand off her thigh as one would a persistent housefly.

This affront had put off Raj.

A younger man would put up with your rudeness, appease you by saying some sweet nothings, and get you into the mood.

Not when you are over 60. I expected a positive and instant response, with so much history between us. How do I know when you are ready for sex unless you express or give some hint? More so, I am not a small-talk man. You know that very well.

Raj remembered those younger days when both would decide that they should have intercourse that night. Accordingly, the children would be made to sleep early and while watching a soap on TV then indulged in prelim-stroking. When enough mood had set in, they would move to their bedroom. That was how communicative they were in sex matters. Today, she blamed him for not coming to her when she wanted.

Women are like that. They expect their man to know their minds and act accordingly. "We have been married for so long; don't you know my wants and when I am in the mood for sex?"

Raj had then walked out of the sofa, collapsed limply on the bed, stared at the ceiling, and retired to bed. These moves by Raj had happened many times with the same result.

***

Raj was going bald. Domestic life ruined his boyish charm. Sex was no longer a distraction or an outlet for dull days. In western societies, loveless marriages would have broken up. In India, you have to keep up the pretence. Vaidehi had been fascinated by money and all it could buy. Nothing much for herself, though. To demonstrate her generosity to relatives, friends and neighbours to bask in the euphoric feeling of Giftors' high. Raj noticed she bought a gift for her neighbour's six-year old's birthday.

"Why did you buy that expensive gift for Sachin?" asked Raj.

"Today is his birthday." *Announcement.*

"Such presents are given only if our child of similar age is attending the birthday party. All our children are grown-ups settled abroad. This gift is a needless expense."

"I wanted to give, and I am giving." *Just a declaration.*

"Meaningless. I disapprove of such expenditure," said Raj.

"What is wrong with you? I have not bought anything for myself. Anyway, this expense is from the money sent by

Spandana. So I am not touching your monthly allowance; you need not worry," said Vaidehi.

Any other husband would show anger on such an impertinent answer and potentially enraging statement. But Raj wanted to avoid confrontation and looked for a peaceful resolution or complete withdrawal.

"It is not about where the money has come from. Is it required to give such an expensive gift to a neighbour's six-year-old child with whom we have no interaction? And that too when our child is not attending the party!" asked Raj.

"So what? We know the parents," said Vaidehi

Raj kept his dignity and did not condescend to answer for fear of being caught in a slanging match.

Such was her subconscious need to show her benevolence as though she was a princess with access to unlimited wealth.

Vaidehi failed to live in the present. Her childhood always caught up with her. She indulged in vanity. Raj had to pay a heavy price for it. Further, to her attitude to men bordering on misandry, she doubted her husband's fidelity. For most of the later years, she spent tending to her children and grandchildren, in whose company she found solace and a sense of accomplishment. Raj's presence in the house was only a necessary inconvenience.

When Raj retired, she could not freely indulge in liberality that gave her the feeling of one-upmanship. They had to live only by their savings with no regular revenue stream except some pittance of dividends and interest income and with the generosity of their children. And also the money struck in Mumbai Courts worried them. This kind of hand-to-mouth existence annoyed her and left no opportunity to lament their "poor" status, as she could not demonstrate her generosity freely. What all Raj had given her in his corporate life of over thirty years: expensive vacations in India and abroad; fancy restaurant visits; the big fat wedding of both of their daughters; decent living in Mumbai with a full-time maid and a chauffeur; classy four-wheeler; fancy accommodation [though, company paid] and finally a decent retired home to live peacefully. Vaidehi took all of these for granted till now. But post-retirement, she missed her gifting privilege. But once in a way, as in this case, she succumbed to her nature, much to Raj's chagrin.

It was late night; Raj and Vaidehi were watching ZEE's reality singing show. The phone buzzed, and Raj picked up and, seeing the caller's name, moved out of the room to the balcony. Vaidehi was busy watching the singing skills of young children in the program. Rain battered Hyderabad, and there was a frequent power outage. She noticed Raj talking animatedly on the phone on the balcony.

"Ritu?" worriedly asked Raj.

"I am flattered," Ritu said, "You could recognise my voice and did not cut off the line. You have been avoiding me for the past three months. You never answered any of my calls."

"This late-night call is not expected from you; you know it's embarrassing and risky."

"So let me get this straight. You want me for my body, not for giving me long-term companionship," complained Ritu.

"We went through this discussion many times," said Raj. "What we did was with mutual consent. I have never forced you. Not even for the blowjobs. In the same way, you have never forced me to come to your place, though there was some persuasion for which I succumbed."

"Do I look to you as a frustrated woman, out to grab any cock that is available? Or I have an unsatisfied obsession?"

"Don't put words in my mouth. Like a TV anchor."

"You sound like a puritan, and I am the one who ruined you," said Ritu

"No one has ruined anyone. We did not go beyond pecking. Though we could have; fortunately, I have resisted the attempts," said Raj.

"Inserting fingers into the cunt, licking the nipples and squeezing the breasts is not pecking!" shouted Ritu.

"You are crude."

"You are rude."

Raj cut the phone. She called again repeatedly, but Raj did not answer. He had to turn off the instrument to avoid the missed calls list. Raj wondered whether they were not a compatible match - just like his wife. A couple of days later, one night, Ritu called, and he took the phone to the balcony on the pretext of not disturbing his wife's sleep.

"I am sorry, Raj, I was ill-mannered the other day."

"It is ok, but what makes you call now? Again at night?" asked Raj annoyingly.

"I thought we should meet."

"I don't think that is a good idea. I don't want to jeopardise my family life," said Raj

"One last time, please. There is a Tom Hanks movie showing in Inox. Why don't we go together?" coyly asked Ritu.

"Film? Have you gone crazy? Anyone can see us, and I will be doomed. "

"We shall go inside the theatre after the lights are off and get out before the last scene. No one can spot us."

Ritu tried to reason. After many no's and pleases, Raj got trapped by her persuasion. Unconsciously, he wanted to take a fresh look at her boobs, feel them, squeeze them and suck the nipples—one last time. Intimacy with the opposite gender is a vice as alcohol, smoking, gambling, etc. More so if you are missing it for long periods.

***

"Who was on the phone last night," Vaidehi asked.

The following day Raj and Vaidehi were having breakfast.

"A friend from Mumbai who had come on an official visit to Hyderabad, we are going for lunch," Raj lied.

"Who is this friend? Don't I know?"

"He was my colleague in another department in the company I worked. You haven't met him."

"Then call him home. I shall serve lunch for both."

He did not answer. He took a slice of the bread, dipped it in Sambar and slurped it.

"You are not going to lunch, and neither do you have a friend visiting you. I can read you like a book, Raj. That was not a male voice on the phone."

"What makes you say that?" looking at her more closely.

. "Answer me."

"Why are you interrogating me?" he hollered, showing annoyance in his voice.

"I am your wife, and I have the right to know your whereabouts," she said.

He abruptly stood up irritably without looking at her and walked towards his bedroom to change.

"I will be back in a couple of hours or so. I have told you many times that where I go and what I do are no concern. If in case I don't come back home by 9 p.m. only then, you start worrying about me. I shall give an updated timeline at nine, if not home by then."

He tiptoed to the shoe rack, wore a slip-on, and walked out, banging the door on the way. That was the first time Raj had spoken to her in such a coarse and abrasive tone.

Vaidehi sat by the window, holding her tears back and began to wonder if her forthright questioning could provoke him to be more candid.

She found herself pacing the floor. It happens a lot these days. Vaidehi paced not because she could not keep still. Vaidehi doubted his fidelity, though no evidence was forthcoming. She would have liked to ask him directly about his inexplicable frequent visits outside their home but decided against it.

But one incident changed all that.

***

Raj and Ritu went for a drive after the movie as usual. The smooching continued as per routine. Ritu pleaded with him to spend one last night with her away from Hyderabad. He politely but firmly refused.

"We decided against these clandestine meetings during our last date. There is no change in my decision. Please do not call me again. I shall block you on WhatsApp, Facebook, and my contact list. Let us forget our association. You are very young; you do not understand the implications of these meetings in your future life. When you find a loving husband and settle down in life, you shall regret these misadventures. It will affect your psyche and relations with your husband. Guilt will trouble you," pleaded Raj.

"Also, my domestic life is in turmoil as I don't have any job or assignment. I have to account for all my out-of-home trips. It is becoming difficult for me to have such secret get-togethers. Please let us close this chapter once and for all. I am grateful to you for having given me immense pleasure and company. I enjoyed every bit of it, and no further, please."

"And my happiness?" demanded Ritu, her voice harsh with pain, "does mine not matter?"

"You are selfish, Raj. On the pretext of some imaginary situation, you are condescending. I hate you. You enjoyed my body, and now you seem to have fed up with me," accused Ritu raising her voice.

She undid her seatbelt, suddenly moved from her seat and forcibly pushed the steering dangerously to the left and got out, banging the door. Raj was shocked. He only hoped it was good riddance, as he was finding it difficult to find excuses to go out alone out of the house without Vaidehi.

Raj arrived home in the afternoon and went to bed for a siesta after watching the telly for some time; he later went for a walk and came late home for dinner after attending a resident committee meeting.

At the dinner table, there was pin-drop silence. When Vaidehi is under stress or angry, the whole house gets electrified. You touch anything; you get a shock. Even the voice or wind carries a charge. Raj felt the tense atmosphere. In the night post-dinner, Vaidehi cornered him again after watching the TV for some time. Her mind was not what was happening on the telly. She had to confront him for an explanation about what she heard.

I can't explain exactly how it started. How do these things ever begin? It was our average night dinner time, nothing special. She once again brought up this topic of my absence from home without intimation. Where I am going, what I am doing and when I am returning.

"Men never change. I should have known that. They are obsessed with women with heavy bosoms and those who laugh out aloud when a bawdy joke is whispered. But did you take it this far? Seriously? You have been bluffing me all these days. Sheila saw you in Inox today. She asked me whether I'm not fond of English movies. You told me you went to attend lunch with a friend. She might have seen you with a woman, but she did not tell me, probably not to embarrass me. But I felt insulted," shouted Vaidehi

She half expected and half hoped Raj would deny everything, feign surprise, maybe even outrage at what she implied. But Raj did not answer. He was dumbfounded. In any interrogation, denial is the tipping point. From the moment of denial, things would never be the same.

How could I have explained the association did not progress beyond some trivial sexual touches? I went to close the unsavoury association and got ensnared. It's like getting caught while shoving the dropped wallet back into the owner's pocket.

How could I have clarified that it was an attraction I succumbed to because of its lack at home?

The brawl continued. Each was accusing the other. Vaidehi equated his behaviour to his gene pool – referring to his dad's covert activities. That was the final nail. He protested for this reference, angrily threw the sofa bollard, and moved to the bedroom. She, too, moved towards the bedroom and sat on the bed. She turned towards him, staring and still did not speak. Her glare was penetrating, and Raj detected anger. She would not give up without an explanation that satisfied her. She was a strong woman and needed an answer.

"Come on, dear; this won't do," he exclaimed in a friendly, falsely cheerful tone. "I did not do anything to upset you."

Raj knew as soon as he spoke that was a ridiculous statement. She was disturbed about what Sheila told her, which alarmed and frightened him. Raj could not admit it was a one-off and would not repeat it. It might have calmed the situation. But then it would be admitting adultery. As was her norm, she continued her rant on various commissions, omissions and transgressions he had committed in their entire married life until late at night. Calm never returned. Raj could not sleep. His mind had been running over the events of the night. It was as if a video was playing in his mind, showing the same scenes of arguments with Vaidehi. If they weren't from the night just passed by, they were from previous nights- some of them years before, in different segments of their life. He surprisingly found Vaidehi asleep peacefully, with a slight snore.

Once the issues are off her chest, she sleeps like a child. Whereas I ruminate on what-if, I could have said this or countered that etc.

Raj finally slept, exhausted.

***

It was the morning of Friday, the 1st of July 2016. A date Raj would unlikely to forget in a hurry. Last night's rain had subsided, though pools of stagnant water remained all over the roads.

I came back from a walk at about 7 a.m. I pushed the front door open; it did not budge. It is not our practice to bolt the door when we are inside, awake. We are lazy to lift our bums often. I was about to ring the bell, and I saw Shabnam climbing the stairs. "Mummy is still asleep; I went out to get milk," Shabnam said, handing over the keys. Was she so tired to sleep this long? I did not let my mind think too much on the matter and went into the second toilet avoiding the one in our bedroom lest she is disturbed. Shabnam had not learnt to make coffee. Instead, she made tea for me and handed it over with the day's newspaper. She sat at the kitchen corner and had her tea in the saucer, pouring little by little from the ceramic cup, as she always does.

"Saab, shall I make breakfast?"

"Let her wake up; she will prepare."

"Mummy kept all the masala ready; I can make it," she tried to persuade me.

I succumbed.

It was almost 7:15 a.m. Raj was surprised Vaidehi did not wake up yet. He went inside the bedroom to shake her to get up. She did not budge. He called Shabnam and asked her to shake her up too. No movement. Raj panicked. He rushed to the nearby Prime Hospital and found the reception cubicle unmanned. He was distraught. They looked around to find a helpful soul that could guide him to the duty Doctor. Then he heard footsteps down the stairs opposite him and saw a ward boy approaching him.

"What can I do for you?" No salutation.

"I am looking for the duty Doctor."

"He is sleeping now as he was awake until 2 a.m. Other Doctors will come at 8 a.m."

"I am in an emergency. My wife is not waking up from her sleep. I need some Doctor to check her vitals immediately," Raj pleaded.

"Sure. I will inform the Doctor" He consented apologetically and ran up the stairs.

It took a few minutes for the Doctor to come down the stairs.

Raj was looking at the buzzing fan and was lost in thoughts when a voice behind him said," I understand from the ward boy you need my services to check your wife. Right?" He noted that the Doctor was wearing dark brown corduroy jeans and a blue linen shirt with a Chinese collar and a white apron. A cloth label shabbily stitched on his coat showed his name as Dr Partha T.

Dr Partha had completed his MBBS course a couple of years back, including the mandatory internship, and was waiting to enrol in a Post Grad course that required clearing the National Board Examination. He had not been successful in the last two attempts. He was preparing for the third trial, which had kept him awake till early morning as he was determined to be successful this time around. Nowadays, pursuing a specialised course finishing in Master's or Diploma has become mandatory because patients prefer to see a 'specialist' Doctor. A cardiologist. A gastroenterologist. A neurologist. And the like. Also, his market value in the marriage arena would depend on his take-home pay: present and estimated future income.

Raj introduced himself as the resident of Daffodils apartments nearby.

"Please accompany me; we are just four blocks away from your hospital."

"Let me get my stethoscope and the kit," said Dr Partha

Raj took Dr Partha in his car and proceeded to his house. He was not sure whether this was the procedure.

Shouldn't I have consulted the neighbours?

Dr Partha was led to the bedroom and wherein he found a lady flat on her back with hands above her head in a caret-bracket position. The lady appeared in a deep sleep. He did what was taught at his medical school. Measure the five vital signs of respiration, pulse, skin, pupils, and blood pressure. Partha ran his ball-point pen across her sole to check for reflexes. He found none; concluded the body on the bed was a dead body. Dr Partha asked a few more questions about the morning routine the household members had undergone that day. And he noted the same as trained in his forensic chemistry class.

"When does she wake up normally?"

"Around five, if she takes a Restyl[68] she might wake up later," said Raj.

"Did she take Restyl yesterday?"

"No. Not to my knowledge." Dr Partha wanted to examine the corresponding medicine strip in the medical kit box but ignored the impulse. He was about to leave the room when something got to his attention that needed more inspection.

"Could you please leave me alone in this room? I need to examine a little more thoroughly in private."

Raj left the room and closed the door as indicated by the Doctor. Besides the head of the body, he found a cotton pillow with a dip which he presumed to be the image of a face. The Doctor took his mobile and clicked and stored the picture. He noted the only entry door to the room from the hall was the one he had entered. Daylight came into the room through a 3' x 4' window thinly curtained – partially opaque. He did not want to touch anything, so he let the curtain remain as drawn. However, he peeped through the curtain. The window opened onto an adjoining street. Another door led to the toilet, a western

---

68   A Brand of sleeping pill

commode, washbasin, a shower and a geyser. The commode had its lid upright, suggesting that a man last used it.

He noticed the air conditioner was off. He switched on the air-conditioner; set the temperature to 16C; ensured the vents closed, including the toilet door, with his gloves. He was aware that warm atmospheric temperature would accelerate the post-mortem petrification of the body, which made determining the actual time of death difficult.

He came out of the room, shut the door, and said, "Please do not go into that room; I will be back shortly."

He walked out of the house. He left a bewildered look on Raj, who could not grasp what was happening. Raj called up Vaidehi's Mausi, who lived around twenty kilometres away and updated the situation. Mausi sounded very concerned and assured him she would come over right away with her husband. Vaidehi was her favourite daughter, as she had two sons. Raj did not want to inform his sisters or her brother until he gained more information. Vaidehi's brother lived in Germany, worked with Siemens and rarely visited India. The last time he visited India was for Spandana's wedding, which was five years back. Also, it was 2 a.m. in Germany. Dr Partha went back to his hospital, kicked his scooter to life and rushed to the police station in the area.

"Can I see the SHO[69]?" he asked the constable sitting at a table on the veranda.

"Who are you, and why do you want to see him," asked a person in mufti sitting next to the constable.

"I am a Doctor attached to Prime Hospitals, and I had been to a house on a call to verify the death of an old lady, about

---

69   Station House Officer – the chief of a police station

which I want to talk to the SHO," Dr Partha said in a staccato manner.

"Saab is sleeping as he was on bandobast[70] the whole night. He just came back at 5 in the morning," said the constable.

"This is urgent, and I need his help as I think the lady's death was not natural as I suspect some foul play."

The constable reluctantly left the room, peeped inside the SHO's room, and found him in a swivel chair with his eyes closed. The SHO, Adarsh Naik, opened his eyes to sense someone was peeping and rang the bell on the table.

***

Adarsh Naik was hand-picked by a benevolent Collector of Rajahmundry from the tribal areas of Rampa Chodavaram and admitted as a resident student in a nearby navodaya school. The collector personally took an interest in the tribal children of the agency area and ensured their education. Amongst them, Adarsh shone as a bright boy. With the help of generous scholarship programs designed for tribal children, Adarsh completed post-graduation in sociology from Andhra University. However, he was not interested in pursuing academics, though he was good at it. He appeared for police recruitment tests and, with ST reservation criterion, joined the Andhra Police, later shifted to Hyderabad after the state split. He served at many stations across both the states. He trained all the personnel under him towards rules of the laws, which they were ordained to observe. Whenever a new station was inaugurated, the Commissioner and the DGP called him to take charge for a few months to establish the processes. Such was his reputation in the Police circles.

---

70   Night patrol

He performed as per the norms of his bosses and never interfered in their not-so-over-the-board behaviour; at the same time avoided succumbing to the political pulls and pressures. He adopted a live-and-let-live kind of policy that helped him survive in an otherwise corrupt police department. With over 20 years of experience, you would expect him to rise in ranks, which his other colleagues who joined the force with him had: – to posts of SPs, Commissioners and the like. But Naik risen only to the rank of Dy. SP and remained as an SHO, presently posted to one of the prominent and prestigious police stations in Hyderabad.

***

"Yes," he said drowsily.

"Sir, a Dr Partha wants to see you urgently regarding a death within our station limits."

"Send him in."

After the initial introductions, Dr Partha explained in detail from the moment Raj entered the hospital till his visit to the police station.

"What makes you think the death was not natural and needs to be investigated by a government pathologist?"

"I had seen an extra pillow next to the head of the diseased, which had a dent of a faint image of a face. I had kept the pillow as evidence to be examined later; it could be death by smothering by a pillow."

He then explained why he needed a second opinion by a Government Doctor and police help in simple terms.

The death could be caused by Asphyxia caused by the blocking of the mouth and nose by smothering. Asphyxia occurs when the free flow of oxygenated air is cut-off, thus preventing it from reaching the brain or other body parts. It could be death by mental trauma that someone she believed could not harm her was actually strangulating her. Or she might have died naturally by myocardial infarction, also known as a heart attack. All three possibilities exist.

"Have you ensured the room is secured?"

"Yes, I have it bolted and told the inmates not to enter the room. However, it is unlikely to happen as I see the victim's husband is in a state of genuine shock."

The SHO rang the bell again. The same constable reappeared.

"Is the Inspector, Venugopal, in the station?" asked the SHO in his usual authoritarian tone.

Venugopal Rao rose to the rank of Inspector from the post of a sub-Inspector – his first direct entry into the precincts of the State Police. He was skilled in forensic aspects by training at the Central Forensic Lab. Noting the delays in forensic reports from Central Labs, the State Home Secretary had decided to train at least one Inspector per Zone on analytical and scientific techniques to examine evidence from crimes and prepare legal statements that summarise the results for court arguments. Thus Venugopal Rao had been selected by West Zone Deputy Commissioner to be so trained. Accordingly, as per the GO so issued, he is authorised by training to collect and document evidence, take photographs of the crime scene, interview witnesses, and document the crime scene observations. Thus, apart from his regular duties, he doubled as a forensic inspector and is often called by other police stations nearby when in need. He is known to be brash, a floater of all norms of decent behaviour and reputed to be corrupt. Soon he became the enfant terrible of the police force. He managed to survive various indiscretions because of his political connections. He could convert any situation to benefit his covert plans. He was capable of searching for gold in the same stream as many before him but would come back with chunks no one else spotted. Whenever politicians or their cohorts needed help to wriggle them out of precarious situations, Venugopal would be the man. No SHO in the city wanted him in his police station, as they could not control him. The SHO of this particular police station, Mr Adarsh Naik, is a no-nonsense man and is reputed to be a strict enforcer of discipline. The Commissioner of Police had personally requested the SHO to accommodate Venugopal Rao in his station.

"Yes, Sir."

"Send him in."

Venugopal Rao appeared dishevelled, having slept on a sofa in the staff room. He rushed into the room and saluted the boss.

SHO explained the situation and said, "Venu, please go along with Dr Partha, do a thorough investigation and if necessary, send the body to Gandhi Hospital morgue for further examination," said the SHO.

"Also, take a written report from Dr Partha on his observations and his signature and registration number."

"Yes, sir," the Inspector saluted again and walked out of the room with the Doctor.

He put a hand through his unkempt hair and arranged it to appear decent. He slipped on his expensive Adidas sneakers.

"Do I look presentable?" he asked.

"Yes," said Dr Partha.

They proceeded to the house on separate motorbikes. Before they entered the house, Venu asked a few more questions to Dr Partha to close some loose ends, including the number of persons in the household and the background information he had gathered while he was examining the dead body.

As they entered the house, Dr Partha found one other couple present. Vaidehi's Mausi and her husband. The maid and Raj briefed them about the events of the morning. As Raj and the Doctor instructed, Shabnam prevented them from entering the bedroom to check on Vaidehi.

"What is causing the delay? The body may decompose if you don't release the same for storing in a refrigerated casket," said the husband of Vaidehi's Mausi, addressing the Inspector in a tone that was not friendly.

"If you are not already aware of it, and I suspect you are – this is an investigation. I shall tolerate no triviality. A lady is dead, and I have to discover the why, when and how. After I have done, I shall report to my superiors and not to you. Do I make myself clear?" said the Inspector harshly.

It was one of those remarks that seem loaded with threat, though merely pointing out what must be obvious to all.

Venugopal Rao then went into the bedroom accompanied by Dr Partha. He noted the bed had three pillows instead of the standard two for a couple. Venugopal Rao surveyed the room once again. He looked at the bed, the window, the closets and the body on the bed. He noticed the lady was indeed a beautiful woman.

Dr Partha was pleased his instincts had been right on one count as the Inspector examined the pillow next to the head of the body more closely without touching the body. The dip with the image of a face on the pillow Dr Partha purported to have noticed was not evident now. Venu ignored the observation, left the scene bolting the door and entered the hall.

Hearing the commotion in the corridor, the neighbour Vinay Desai entered the flat and addressed Raj, "What happened?"

Raj explained to him the sequence of events surrounding the death of his wife.

"You should have called Dr Nilesh, who lives in this building. He is a surgeon attached to many hospitals," said Desai.

"I was not aware. I don't know all the residents. I panicked and rushed to Prime Hospital and asked the duty Doctor to examine my wife," said Raj.

"Shall we call him now?" asked Desai. The Inspector came out of the room and announced, firmly addressing no one in particular, "Not required. We have to shift the body to a Government hospital for post mortem before a death certificate is issued," said the Inspector.

With the help of Dr Partha, the Inspector checked each corner of the bedroom, carefully took inventory of all things lying around, and asked Shabnam a few questions. As a forensic inspector, he carried his paraphernalia to do his job – gloves, a digital camera, fingerprint equipment such as an electrostatic finger dust collector etc. Venugopal rarely used any help in doing these duties. He thought he had covered everything, but in this kind of situation, the simple fact was you could never account for everything. However, he planned to turn the situation to his advantage as his norm. Venugopal Rao had sent his head constable, Narsimha, to fetch a new garbage bag to collect and store for later analysis of the evidence collected. He also took away the cell phones of Raj, Vaidehi and the maid.

On Raj's protest, the Inspector said," you can get a new device and a new SIM; they will provide you with the same number. We require this device for forensic analysis."

He called for an Ambulance and instructed the head constable to send the body to Gandhi Hospital, and he would reach there in an hour or so. He left to report his findings to the SHO. He thanked Dr Partha and informed him Police did not require his services any longer, as the matter was with the Police, and their processes would follow. However, he instructed him to file an FIR with all the observed data. Dr Partha was elated to be a part of a crime scene; he only read in novels of Grisham and Cook. He did as told. When Venugopal Rao returned to the station, the SHO took the brief from him and asked him to note the same in his case diary and proceed further. He was given the additional charge of the Investigation Officer (IO) to lead the case to its logical conclusion. SHO instructed Venu not to make any conclusions based on the observations but only record the facts as he saw. He also informed him that even if his notes did not tally with the Doctor's, SHO told him to stick to the evidence he collected.

Venu had ignored the suggestion and went about writing his diary corroborating the observation of Dr Partha. However, there was no sign of a dip mirroring a face on the pillow. However, the cover appeared soiled. He instructed the constable to store the evidence gathered, including the pillow to be handled with care, duly marked with bold red ink in the Staffroom: Forensic Material – no hand touch. The constable placed all the material in a plastic bag, flexible enough to open and close quickly. Naik could in no way prevent Venugopal Rao, designated IO, from writing a diary report as he desired, whether the scene at the site validated it or not. If the evidence and the data collected were not recorded as per the actual scene at the site, one could challenge later in the court with due procedures. By the time the case went to court, much damage could have been done to the suspects, and none had any recourse to such blatant misuse of power.

A senior police officer may delegate any duty assigned by law or by a lawful order to any officer subordinate to him and may aid, supplement, supersede or prevent any action of the assistant by his action or that of any person lawfully acting under his command or authority, whenever the same shall appear necessary or expedient for giving full or convenient effect to the law or for avoiding any infringement thereof.

But these rules are never followed.

The Sub Inspectors and Inspectors are a law unto themselves, abetted by their political masters or pecuniary gains – mostly the latter. Their diary records are sacrosanct; no senior officer – even an SP rank Officer- can alter, edit or delete. In rare cases where there is significant contrary evidence, the senior officer could record the same but cannot altogether obliterate what is reported by his subordinate. Thus these inspectors would have a field day.

Mausi had informed Raj's daughters, sisters, and brother-in-law about the death without revealing all details. It was mutually decided to keep the body till at least one of the other family members arrived. This decision also helped keep the lid on the controversy surrounding the death.

***

Raj was not allowed inside the mortuary. He watched from outside through a not-so-clean glass window that gave him a fuzzy look into the happenings of the hall. The elderly Doctor came with a scalpel. With almost casual speed, he incised skin and muscle layers. The stubby fingers tenderly worked round the mass. The attendant saw Raj watching and quickly drew the curtains as though they were on to something sinister.

Surprisingly, the reception area was almost empty except for one man in his thirties. Raj's stomach churned as the hands on the clock opposite were making rounds. He heard footsteps in the hall and looked to see if it was Leela, the nurse-cum-typist, with the report. But to his surprise, Venugopal Rao, the Inspector, walked into the room, pushing the swivel door. Raj glanced through the door whenever it opened to let people in and out and noticed the two men lean towards each other in a huddle that indicated a conspiracy was being hatched. Being aware of the reputation of the Inspectors of the Indian Police Force, the sight unnerved him.

I had to wait for almost 40mins before the Inspector left the room. He might have seen me and ignored or did not notice my presence. I was not sure. I could not wait any longer, pushed the entry door, and went in. The Doctor pointed me to sit on the chair in the corner of the room opposite his work table. He appeared somewhat disturbed and did not talk for almost 5 mins leaving an embarrassing silence around the room, except for the rickety fan, which was making more noise than an old Canadian railway engine.

Meanwhile, Leela came with a print, and the Doctor scribbled in hand on it. She was asked to re-type what was corrected and given to him back. Leela did what was told, keeping the original also in the machine. He shoved the updated report in his bag that he carried from home.

"I have completed the report and mailed it to the Police station as per my instructions," he bluffed.

"Sir, you said you would give me a copy?" I pleaded.

"I never promised that. I allowed you to be present during the process, which normally I don't allow anyone. I made an exception for which the Inspector was upset," he said

"Anyway, I shall give a death certificate to allow you to take the body to complete the rituals," he added.

He called Leela to type out the death certificate and put it up for his signature. Which she did, based on the original PM report she had on her machine. The Doctor simply signed on the dotted line as per the norm, and the nurse handed over the death certificate to me. I walked out disappointed for not getting a copy of the PM report. As I had important things to attend to, I thought I would confront the Inspector later. It took a few more hours to complete the formalities to take the body out of the mortuary.

Raj did not have any remorse for the death of his wife, though publicly, he was grief personified. He believed it was GOD's recompense for the loathsome and despicable way he was treated. In different eras of his life, his dad and his wife had dealt with him as a child, making him cry at most times. The only redeeming feature of their existence was his dad supported him in his education. His wife gave him enviously satiated sex, two children and a place in the society as a respectable member, wherever they lived. He did take revenge on her with his clandestine affairs. Vaidehi was not going to fall back into his life, and he was conscious of that. Raj had spent the night ruminating over every possible scenario in his head, with the bucket list he had once thought over.

Things do not work out the way you want all the time. You have to move on.

He had to think about how to move on. Maybe it was time for him to enjoy the future; he did not know how it would pan out. Raj did not hear from Venugopal Rao since the surprise presence at the mortuary, though the Police agreed to hand over the body for cremation on the fourth day of the death. His grieving daughters arrived just on the day of the funeral. Raj was not in the mental frame of mind to do the cremation formalities, which his brother-in-law, who flew in from Germany, managed with the help of Goud Pharma office staff.

The daughters were surprised about the turn of events that required post mortem, as it was clearly a case of a sudden heart attack, as was reconfirmed in the death certificate. Raj did not disclose the details of the reasons the Police gave for the requirement of a post-mortem. When they asked their mama, he, too, was evasive. They did not press for more details as they were busy remotely managing their children's welfare. The elder daughter, Sagarika, had left after two days of the funeral, citing her children's school curriculum matters. She insisted Raj spend some time with them in the US to overcome his grief.

Raj would not be inclined to accept his elder daughter's invitation to visit them.

Sagarika was a party animal with all the attendant gossip and card games, boring her husband. Her husband had given up on her and immersed himself in his office work. He either went to play Golf with his American friends or cricket with the Indian Community on weekends. The town they were in did not have public transport. One had to have a personal vehicle to go around, even to buy day-to-day groceries. Thus Raj and Vaidehi, whenever they visited the US, were at the mercy of their daughter to take them around. He, therefore, loathed the idea of spending time in the US. In addition, Raj and his son-in-law were never great friends. They tolerated each other because of the relationship. Rare conversations ended in divergent views on Indian Cricket, England football and World Politics.

Raj's sisters were critical of Raj's children for having abandoned him in difficult times. They, however, helped in distributing the personal belongings of Vaidehi - those items they could find in the closets of Vaidehi's bedroom - amongst Raj's children as per their interests and needs, sent the balance to charity.

Except for Raj's youngest daughter, Spandana, all visitors left for their respective homes. Spandana stayed back to help Raj to set his house in order. She arranged the required documentation and Visa Process for Raj to visit Singapore to spend time with them. Spandana left after another week and promised to come back whenever he needed her. She loved her father as she witnessed the treatment her mother gave him when they were in Mumbai while she was pursuing her engineering graduation. Also, she was indebted to her father for facilitating her marriage to a Bihari, much to the annoyance of her mother. She felt sorry for him and always wanted to make amends by inviting them to Singapore whenever her children had vacation.

RAMACHANDRA REDDY

Few days later, the Police came back with their calling card.

A tall man with a salt-and-pepper stubble on his face and a burly lady at his side about a foot and a half shorter appeared at the door as Raj opened, hearing the bell. The man stepped forward, his hand outstretched. "Ramachandra Reddy," he said. As he reached out, Raj noticed he was much older than his rank would typically employ. "I am very sorry for your loss." The exact words Venugopal used the other day. The lady wore khaki pants, a blue-and-white wide-striped top and pale sandals. A large purse hung from her shoulder.

It was just 7 a.m., and he had not had his morning coffee yet. Shabnam had gone to pick up a fresh packet of milk as last night's milk got split.

"I am now in charge of this case. I have with me Rupashree, my assistant and sub-inspector."

"Venugopal Rao is now transferred to Adilabad," said the Inspector, who was dapper with an upright stance.

Venugopal Rao messed up the investigation of an accident in which one Riaz Khan died while travelling from his workplace at Ranigunj to his house in Anand Nagar. Riaz Khan's politically influential family complained to the authorities about the same. That night at about 10:30, Riaz was driving his bike at an average speed and overlooked a parked street light repairing ladder mounted-

truck without mandatory signage to divert traffic. Riaz hit the truck, and the death was instantaneous. Venugopal had let the truck leave the place of the accident without noting down the license plate number, the driver's name, and the vehicle ownership details in the first information report. It could not be established whether it was a genuine error or a deliberate oversight for monetary gains. However, Venugopal Rao's reputation always preceded him. Based on Riaz Khan's father-in-law's complaint to the DGP, who was waiting for an excuse to punish Venu, the DGP ensured the transfer as a punishment of sort.

The officers cannot do more than that, especially if you have political bosses to support you.

Raj offered coffee to the police officers. They both politely refused.

"When did this happen? I mean his transfer," asked Raj.

"Almost the day after the autopsy report from the hospital was received by us in the mail. He noted the same in his diary, including his observations of the event at your home," informed Reddy.

Adarsh Naik, who was about to proceed on leave because of a family emergency, found the Venugopal's investigative report and his diary noting were not complete enough to proceed further and had requested Reddy to probe further.

He was conscious of his image of a stickler for rules. He was proud that no Magistrate had ever passed strictures or comments on his staff's conduct of investigations, custody matters and record-keeping during his entire career. Naik wanted that record to be intact.

"We are asked to re-check for further investigation," he said.

"An investigation?' he questioned dumbly.

No answer.

The lady officer placed herself right in front of Raj with her notebook and a pen, which she was twirling. Reddy went out to call on the neighbours to understand the general conduct of Raj and Vaidehi in the society.

"Before you start the investigation, I have a request. My maid, Shabnam wants her phone to call her husband, which she was not in touch with for the past three weeks," asked Raj when Reddy returned.

"That is not possible, as it is required for forensic analysis. Surely, you can get her a new phone! Or she may use yours for calling her husband," wondered Reddy.

"Unfortunately, she does not remember the phone number of her husband. With the country code and nine numbers no one can remember. We want to note down the number from the contact list and give the phone back," said Raj with a disheartened tone.

Shabnam told Raj she could not use the phone for a couple of days before the day of madam's death, as she was waiting for Vaidehi to help her repair the phone's sound and volume button or help her buy a new one. Meanwhile, this unfortunate incident happened, and her handset was also seized. Later she wanted to use Spandana's phone to call her husband. But unfortunately, she did not remember his number; she tried various combinations with no luck. The same was the case with Asif's Vadodara number.

Factorial nine is a humongous number, indeed.

Raj was unsure whether the BSNL service provider would have record of her old calls. He decided to try. But later events had changed his priorities.

"As soon as we finish our work here, I will check the phone and pass on the number to you," said Rupashree

"She was inconsolable the whole night yesterday. I thought she was upset about the death. When I inquired, she informed me of her predicament of not being able to call her husband or her brother-in-law in Vadodara; that was when I decided to send her home to Vadodara in a couple of days," added Raj.

Reddy and Rupashree looked at each other. It was an exchanged glance that said, "This is worrisome."

Raj called Shabnam from the kitchen where she was busy making kanda-poha[71] breakfast for Raj, informed her of the developments, and assured her she would call her husband that day positively. She nodded with satisfaction writ on her face and returned to her work.

"We have a few questions that have arisen after we read the diary posting, and after we receive the answers from you, we shall take further action as per the law," said Reddy continuing the purpose of their visit.

The first question was about the pillows. The Inspector asked why there were three pillows for two persons.

Raj explained that her Doctor advised Vaidehi to keep a pillow under her feet to avoid night cramps that she often experienced.

Some people may have four pillows too! What is suspicious about it?

"Then the pillow should have been either under her foot or down at the ground near the foot. Why was it lying next to her head?"

"I don't know," said Raj

"When you left for your morning walk at 5 a.m., did you notice the pillow's position?"

---

71   A Popular Maharashtrian breakfast made of pounded rice

"I don't remember."

That was a surprise for me too. Now I am doubting my conduct. I remember the dream wherein I had strangulated Vaidehi with bare hands. However, that dream woke me up suddenly in the night, and when I visited the loo to urinate. Did I then use the pillow to suffocate her? Fear filled me, then anger. How could I have been such stupid to think of strangulating my wife, however much we had our differences? Of course, she accused me of adultery. No, I don't think I have done it. Strangulated her that is. However, if I were to do so as purportedly hinted by this Inspector, there could have been some struggle from her side; kicking of legs, arms, etc. There were no tell-tales of the same. I think I should not present myself with guilt in the presence of these officers. Cops having suspicious minds is like saying parrots can be trained to talk.

"Venugopal had reported that both of you generally wake up early by 4:30, and you alone go for a walk by five and return at about 7. Could you tell me why you had not awakened her when she did not?" asked Reddy.

"Sometimes, she does wake up late when she is agitated in the night and does not have a proper sleep. At that time, I would not want to disturb her. I make the coffee myself and keep the decoction ready for her."

"Was there any squabble the previous night that may have disturbed her?" asked Reddy.

"No, in fact, all the three of us were watching a dance program on the telly till about nine and we went into the bedroom to retire. Shabnam shifted to her room to watch the balance program on her TV."

Why should he know what happens between a wife and a husband?

"My colleague wants to question your maid. Could you please ask her to go to the other room for privacy?"

Raj had informed Shabnam to accompany the Inspector to the study room. They did and bolted the door.

Rupashree had noted the missing details of the maid's employment and her relationship with the couple, which Venugopal had not recorded. She asked a few more questions about Shabnam's own family, which Shabnam complied with respect.

Shabnam omitted to give her home address in Vadodara as she wanted no third party to break the news to Nazma about her stay in Hyderabad. She wanted her in-laws to believe she was in Parbhani tending to her Mausi.

She had narrated all her life moments from the day she married until that day, including why she changed her name to Shabnam from Saarika. Shabnam wanted her husband's phone number, which she thought would be best accomplished if she parted with all the information asked by the policewoman. That apart, she found Rupashree to be friendly and engrossingly interested in her eventful life story. Rupashree specially asked Shabnam about Vaidehi's behaviour towards her and whether she was subjected to harassment. She answered in the negative. Rupashree wanted to probe further but decided against it.

Rupashree found a large burn scar on the dorsal side of the left palm. She noticed the damage was severe enough to cause blistering of the skin, which was apparent. She asked Shabnam the reason for the same.

"While I was pouring boiling water into a hot water bag to help foment madam's back, the pakad[72] slipped, and the boiling water fell on my hand."

---

72   Tongs

"When did this happen, and why your madam did not take you to a doctor?"

"It occurred two days before her death, she applied Burnol and Borolin alternately, and she said it would heal in a few days."

"Does it pain now?"

"No. but I had the burning sensation for a few days. Madam applied the creams regularly," said Shabnam.

Rupashree noted the scar was still visible. She also recorded this in her notebook and proceeded to ask more leading questions, and noted the replies: birth dates, family members, the significant events in her life, the works. The interrogation sank into tedium. Shabnam did not disclose her Vadodara address, though. On which she proved sufficiently elusive, blaming herself for the lack of education for the memory loss. She choked up twice when talking about her beloved husband.

"Would you say the relationship between these couples was - good, bad, in between?" asked Rupashree

Shabnam did not hesitate. "Very good. He was good for her, and she was good for him. I truly believe that. Some domestic flights do happen. I am not fluent in their language, so I don't understand much. She made good pakwaan for him all the time. From that, you can say they loved each other. Beyond that, I don't know much," she added, "Most importantly, they looked after me well. I had no complaints about their behaviour with me. On a few occasions, they took me to theatres and restaurants also. However, I have confined myself to my room when there is no pending kitchen or domestic work and my small TV. "

"Anything else you want to share?" Typical cop interrogation technique.

"Any other burn injuries or scars you have had you want to show me. Please be frank with me," said Rupashree

"No, none," said Shabnam, "However, recently madam was openly critical of every action of Saab, and I thought it could be a part of a normal loving relationship," added Shabnam, "lately, I find madam is often going to her Mausi's house and spends the day with her. Once she took me too. They are a retired couple and treat madam with respect."

"Were you asked to do any work there too?"

"Only once, they had a function at home, and I helped maasi in cooking. That's all," replied Shabnam.

More questions and answers followed, and the officers were about to leave the premises when rain battered the city. They had to accept the breakfast offer of Raj to gain time for the rain to recede. It did not. They had to leave urgently, as information of an emergency at the Police Station came about via a text message sent by a constable. As SHO was on leave, which made Reddy the senior-most member of the Station.

While leaving the premises, Reddy asked for his passport of Raj to prevent him from going abroad till the investigations were completed.

"Sorry, my passport is with Singapore Consulate for visa stamping. What do you mean by not allowing me to go abroad? Can I see my sister at Kolkata as I want to spend some time with her to recover from the shock?"

"You can, but you have to formally apply for permission giving full details of the place you are going to and the relatives' mobile number etc. Also, our SHO has to permit you," said Reddy ignoring the passport matter.

I will return to this matter later after checking the procedures with my seniors on serving the notice to Singapore Consulate.

Raj did not like the tone of the Inspector. But he had no way but to comply.

The rain stiffened, and despite holding her handbag over her head, Rupashree was soaked. They ran towards their jeep.

"Please do not forget about the number Shabnam wanted from her phone contact list," hollered Raj.

"Please call me in the evening, and I shall inform," assured Reddy while climbing the jeep.

The heavy rain drummed on the jeep windshield as it roared towards the police station.

Police could not find Shabnam's phone in the pieces of evidence bag tagged by Venu. The item count confiscated from the house also did not list Shabnam's phone. It wouldn't be. When the head constable was alighting the jeep with the evidence bag, the phone fell off and rolled under the driver's seat, which the constable overlooked. It ended as a birthday gift for the driver's daughter with a new sim. Venu was not in a mood to do a physical recheck of the evidence and tally the list as he was under stress with the complaint on his last assignment.

Raj decided to visit personally the police station instead of phoning to note down the phone number of Shabnam's husband. Reddy was not available. Rupashree welcomed him to her seat in a room filled with computer terminals. She regretted that Shabnam's phone could not be found. He demanded to see the SHO to complain about their sloppiness. SHO had gone to the headquarters for some conference, he was told. However, better sense prevailed. He believed that nothing would come out of it, except he might make the staff hostile towards him, which might jeopardize the case in the closing stages.

Nevertheless, it disturbed Raj. He was apprehensive about facing the crying Shabnam. He was determined to send her back to Vadodara as soon as he got the reservation done for her. She deserved to be treated with due respect. She went about her job with dedication and skill. Raj asked Shabnam whether, at any time, she used Vaidehi's phone to call up her husband.

He thought this information would enable him to retrieve the telephone numbers from Vaidehi's phone in police custody.

"*Nahin*[73]. She ensured enough balance on my mobile so I could talk to my husband at any time. It was never necessary for me to use her phone. Madam always called me on the landline whenever she was out to instruct me to cut vegetables or put the cooker on the gas etc., before madam came back from wherever she went. She found it difficult to hear me on my mobile, so she always used the landline to talk to me," said Shabnam.

Raj felt sorry he was unable to help Shabnam to contact anyone. Raj booked the ticket for Shabnam to leave for Vadodara in Rajkot Express, for which he could get a reservation only after four days from that day and showed the ticket to her to assuage her she would be with her family shortly.

"Rajkot Express takes you to Vadodara directly from Hyderabad without the need to change trains at Mumbai, so I made the reservation on this train. But unfortunately, the reservation is available only four days later. Tomorrow I shall try for Tatkal through an Agent so that you can leave sooner," said Raj apologetically. Shabnam nodded and rushed to the kitchen to clean up.

It was night ten p.m. when Raj's phone buzzed. He picked up on the second ring. It was Reddy. He demanded Raj see him in

---

73   A firm NO

private the following day at a place he would text later. He hung up the handset with a shake of his head.

As per Reddy's message, Raj met him at a dilapidated-looking building with no sign of life. Raj found it challenging to locate, but for the Reddy's mobike parked in the corner of the joint with bold letter of "Police" written on it. He found the place dark; no signboards or door numbers; no activity whatsoever. He later learned it was a hookah bar, which had mushroomed in Hyderabad to circumvent the public smoking ban. Presently the bar was not open to the public as it was only ten a.m. The notice said it would be available to customers from 02:00 p.m. onwards. However, some privileged customers can walk into the place at any time. It was an unwritten understanding between the registered pre-validated customers to use the facilities in the morning hours for clandestine meetings: police personnel, extortionists, politician's planning their strategies, lovers trying to iron out their differences or making escape plans.

Reddy was sitting at a corner table with some papers and waved Raj to come to him. Raj walked in and placed himself in front of him. Reddy lit a cigarette, drew on it, and said, "Please listen carefully to what I will be telling you. You may have to make a decision soon on the matter. The post mortem report contains some damaging information that can put you in some inconvenience," said Reddy.

"Could you please elaborate?" worryingly asked Raj.

He then came out with a statement that defied rationality.

"The PM report, in conjunction with Dr Partha's observations and the diary noting of Venugopal, can force me to arrest you on the grounds of strangulating your wife to her death," said Reddy.

Raj leaned back into the chair and stared into oblivion. He had no words to express. Reddy continued.

"The post mortem report mentioned that the death could be due to asphyxiation that could have come about by strangulation. The report left some doubt enough requiring further forensic analysis and a warrant to search your house. Also, Dr Partha's FIR and subsequent jottings of Venu can force me to arrest you to prevent you from tampering with available evidence we may collect after a search warrant. And impound your passport. Of course, I have to produce you before the Magistrate within 24 hrs. And you may get bail, though our lawyer may ask for police custody for further interrogation. All this is a nuisance. Have you seen how our custody cell is? No respectable man, especially someone of your qualifications and experience, would want to spend even a minute there. Neither do I want you to," said Reddy in a tone that sounded sympathetic to his plight.

Raj was ablaze with fury. He was at his wit's end.

"I believe, with the help of the Pathology department of Gandhi Hospital, Venu had fabricated the PM report with an eye for extortion," said Reddy in a conciliatory tone to smoothen the shock he saw on Raj's expression.

"Surely you can expose them, right?" asked Raj.

"I have no contrary evidence as of now to expose. Also, the report is already in digital mode, accessible to all in the department and cannot be deleted or edited. However, a supplement can be added with sufficient evidence, which can only come by further forensic examination," said Reddy.

As though he would do it otherwise. The brotherhood amongst the police personnel is too strong to expose a minor issue of an unnecessary arrest, however irrational.

"Then what do you suggest? I don't want to be in police custody," said Raj, "Can you give me some time to consult a lawyer and revert?"

"I don't think such a scenario exists, as I have to go by the book now. You can surely consult your lawyer and apply for bail later. But I have to arrest you now based on the evidence presented."

"So, what do you suggest?' asked Raj, as it seemed Reddy was hinting at some possibility of an alternate scenario.

"From the report, the death occurred between 5:30 a.m. and 6:30 a.m. You have an alibi from 5 a.m. onwards as the security gatekeeper had seen you going out at your normal time of 5 a.m. for your routine morning walk. He had not seen you coming back, as, at five past 6, the guard received a call from his intercom that the overhead water tank was empty and he needed to pump water urgently. He went to attend the same. However, though he could have come back within 5mins or so as the pump operation required just pushing on the toggle switch of the starter, he could not do so as the starter did not respond. He got panicky and went to the fourth floor to meet the Secretary for further advice. The entire matter of water problem took over an hour and a half. The security man returned to his post at the gate at around 07:30 a.m. However, as per the building society rules, the security man's wife was supposed to operate the gate in his absence. But she could not replace him as she had to attend to her crying child in the security room, which doubled as the family accommodation for the security person. At 7 a.m., as per your statement to Venu, you had come back home from a walk. However, there is no witness to your re-entry into the building, as the security gate was not staffed. So, that leaves much scope for interpretation, which can damage your complicity. Venu diligently recorded all this in his diary, noting that you could be a suspect as reported in the made-up Autopsy report that the death could be an unnatural one requiring further forensic analysis," said Reddy.

"I never knew he was collecting this kind of data from my apartment," Raj expressed surprise.

He thanked his stars he did not discuss his dream with Venu. He would have nailed him further.

"Because you were busy accompanying the dead body to the mortuary as instructed by Venu, you were never in the loop of his investigation," said Reddy.

As anxious as the Police were to paste a case against him, the pieces of evidence were too scant. Or so he thought.

"I still don't understand how I got trapped in this. I did not kill my wife. She died of natural causes. I am a pharmacist by profession; I have exposure to medical issues, as I have interacted with Doctors of very high calibre daily for the past thirty years. I am sure the death was due to sudden heart failure; the medical term for that is myocardial infarction," explained Raj in a confident tone. In the confusion and anxiety, Raj forgot to say he had a death certificate which confirmed the death was natural.

"Maybe. I do not deny that. Presently, I have to act as per the information available with me: arrest you, lodge you in police custody, and within 24hrs present you in front of a Magistrate," informed Reddy.

"So, you are not allowing me to consult any lawyer, and you have come with a fait accompli?"

"You have to decide now, and there is no time to consult anyone," warned Reddy.

"What nonsense? Citizens don't have any mechanism to stop irrational behaviour of Police?" Raj yelled.

"Please lower your voice. You are a suspect, and I can arrest you right away and further, I can make your release from custody difficult by noting you are resisting arrest, which can be added to your offence," said Reddy.

"I am carried away. It's so confusing, and you leave no room for me to think," said Raj in a peace-making tone.

"Who said there is no room for negotiation?" said Reddy showing a glimpse of hope to Raj.

"What is that?" asked Raj with surprise.

"Even though the reports are already in the police files, I can stop you from arrest if you agree to a mutual understanding," said Reddy.

Whatever deal he could cut him, he would have to take. He didn't care anymore for anyone except his safety. He had to spend some time with his daughter to recover from the death and the aftermath. That was what he cared about most.

"Please explain more clearly," asked Raj.

"We can frame your maid in this and arrest her instead of you. We can create an alibi for you with witnesses. The only person that would be present at the time of the death in the flat would be your maid. The PM report in the Police server does not give me any room from preventing the arrest of a suspect" said Reddy.

"She is the logical person for someone to frame for this. She had access to the bedroom. And the sub-inspector had evidence of maltreatment by your wife. Rage could be a reason for the homicide. Which could clear you of any suspicion."

"That is unfair. Shabnam has served us for over a year, and she is a very good, diligent and simple girl. I will not agree to that at all." Raj appeared shocked at the suggestion.

"What motive she would have?" asked Raj.

"Why do people murder? Material gain or jealousy or rage?"

"But we have not lost anything. My wife treated her well, as though she is a member of our family."

"Leave it to us; we shall work out something," said Reddy.

Raj understood but was nonetheless doubtful.

"There is no alternative unless you want to be arrested. Also, the maid can get bail; I shall see the APP does not object, but she has to be in police custody for a few days till we search your house, collect more evidence; await the forensic report of the pillow and get the mobiles verified," said Reddy.

Reddy had already asked Rupashree to postpone her debriefing report of Shabnam till his negotiations with Raj were completed. He perfectly knew how to frame the maid. The Inspector had to show Raj was out of the house between 5 and 7 – the time mentioned in the autopsy report as the time of death. With the help of the security staff at the building, Reddy knew he could manage.

Rupashree had to write in her report that Vaidehi regularly mistreated Shabnam, and rage could be the reason for the alleged murder. Rupashree already had evidence of the scar on her hand.

Raj had seen the world, and thus he knew Reddy would not be doing this kind of favour without asking for any monetary return. He directly came to the point.

"OK, if I agree to your proposal, how much it will cost me?"

"Ten lakhs," said Reddy

"Ten?"

"Yes, I have to share the bounty with many people in the chain, including the operator in the server room at Police Headquarters," said Reddy.

They haggled on the price a little longer and settled for Seven Lakhs.

"But for that kind of money, why can't you delete the diary noting of Venu completely?" Raj asked.

"Firstly, I cannot completely delete the report. I can only edit some words/sentences that are damaging to you. Secondly, we have the PM report in the department's central server. The report cannot be altered. The only advantage is that the PM report is not entirely conclusive; it leaves room for further forensic analysis of the pillow and the Doctor's interrogation who performed the autopsy. We have to create an alibi for you coinciding with the time of the death, "said Reddy.

Raj had to redeem some of his mutual funds and get the cash ready. He asked for four days to arrange the money. Reddy reluctantly agreed and took leave for four days to disguise the delay in arrest. There could be a query from higher-ups in the department on the delay when the PM report and other evidence showed the death was not natural but homicidal.

In government offices, one officer's files are not transferred to another staff member while he is on temporary leave for a few days unless the matter has media exposure or political ramifications. An unwritten understanding protects each position: your case, your prerequisite. The system helped gain time for Reddy, with no eyebrows raised or explanations sought.

For the first time, Raj rued his decision to shift to Hyderabad. He had no contacts in this city. If it was Mumbai, Raj could have easily found someone from his network of friends and colleagues to advise him and get him out of this unsavoury episode. Since he relocated to Hyderabad, he was unable to develop such influential contacts, and also, his association with Goud Pharma and Ritu prevented him from pursuing any other leisure activity. Raj had to contact Vaidehi's mausa[74] to confide and ask him to recommend a lawyer.

Upon his suggestion, Raj met Lokesh Kumar, a practicing lawyer and a partner in Kumar and Natekar, Solicitors and Chartered Tax Consultants. Their office was located in the dwarakapuri colony, punjagutta—a commercial office in domestic environs.

It is normal in Hyderabad – probably in other cities too – that a commercial office, which does not require direct customer interactions, sets up its office in a domestic zone to save on electrical energy bills and property tax. The domestic electricity tariff is almost half of what would be for a commercial organization. The electrical department officials would be aware of such violations but ignore them for monetary gain. There would never be any 'site audit' by any external auditor, but only a paper trail, which would invariably show the apartment where the office is located is indeed a domestic household. Even the municipal records show the apartment belonged to a family. Whenever a new zonal officer gets posted, he would conduct a 'raid' and settle the matter with a higher 'tariff' for himself. It is interesting to note that an officer of integrity does not get posted to such zones, which means the pay-off link goes all the way to the top.

It took over two days for Raj to get an appointment. That, too, late in the evening. Finally, Raj met Lokesh in his office, which was buzzing with activity even at 8 p.m. The office seemed like a bank that opened after a long recess. The office entrance was through a non-descript staircase to the 4th floor of an old building

---

74   Mausi's husband

that belied what was inside. The reception room was decorated with the choicest paintings and photographs of legal luminaries like Chagla, Sorabjee, Jethmalani, and Palkhivala. Marigold flower petals were neatly arranged in a brass bowl of water in the centre of the room depicting a formation that was not very clear to Raj. Raj was called in after a wait of over half an hour. Raj could notice state-of-the-art décor with cubicles and computer screens with staff peering over them intently inside the office.

As soon as he was seated after mandatory formal introductions, Raj explained the entire sequence of events to Lokesh and showed him the PM report, a copy of which was given by Reddy to him. He also informed of his offer of Reddy to frame his maid instead. The lawyer quickly glanced through the papers presented to him.

"The evidence is flimsy and can easily be struck off by a court. It does not stand detailed scrutiny under cross-examination," informed Lokesh.

"The court matter comes afterwards, but the Inspector insists on arrest based on the documentary evidence he has with him. Can he be stopped before that happens?" inquired Raj.

"Unfortunately, no. These inspectors have vast powers, and they misuse them to gain monetary benefits for themselves and their political masters. Police officers making a wrongful arrest under section 41 of CrPC are seldom proceeded against – much less punished. The CrPC gives vast discretion to arrest a person even in the case of a bailable offence (not only where the bailable offence is cognizable but also where it is non-cognizable) and the further power to make preventive arrests under section 151 of the CrPC and other several police enactments, clothe the Police with extraordinary power which can easily be abused. There is no in-house mechanism in the police department to check such misuse or abuse, nor does the complaint of such misuse or abuse to higher police officers bears fruit except in some exceptional cases," said Lokesh with an air of authority.

"This is sad and depressing," said Raj

"I am sorry. However, we can surely help you or your maid to get bail. That could be managed with some costs. But preventing arrest is not possible," said Lokesh

"So do you want me to take the offer of Reddy?" asked Raj.

"If I were you, I would," said Lokesh," the government officers have vast powers, and we are simply pawns in their designs. Only judicial intervention can help us. Sadly, that is the state of affairs in our country. I have many instances of such misuse of powers not only by the Police but also by commercial tax officers, revenue authorities, income tax inspectors who harass the public, for monetary and personal gains."

"However, in other cases, you have mentioned, the public is not exactly doodh-ke-dhule[75]?"

"True. But from the government side, they are a disproportionately high percentage of people who are out there to pocket whatever benefits – monetary or otherwise – they can get, by harassment and misuse of their position."

"Is there no solution for this?' asked Raj diverting the subject of his fate.

"Unless the moral fabric of the country changes and we become patriotic with no greed, we have no solution," said Lokesh and stood up from his chair to suggest the meeting was now over.

He had other important matters to attend to than discuss ideal conditions for a perfect society.

---

75   True Translation: washed in milk – meaning they are not clean either

Seven lakhs in cash – exactly. Reddy counted it in the bedroom of his two-bedroom apartment, not currency by currency, which would have taken too long, and alerted his wife, who was in the kitchen feeding her son. He shuffled through various bundles and kept a tally in his pocket note as he progressed. He was relieved to see that the denominations were a mix of one thousand and five hundred with one-thousands in the majority.

"What are you doing so long in the bedroom? Dinner is getting cold," yelled his wife.

"Just coming. My pyjama string got loosened, and I am fixing it." Reddy said.

"Do you want any help?"

"No, I can manage."

"The safety pin is on the lowermost shelf in a box marked pins, threads, and needles," Rukmini added.

"OK, I found it. Coming in a few minutes," said Reddy.

Reddy's wife was not oblivious to his cash earnings. Nevertheless, Reddy was afraid if she were to see such abundant cash, she might insist on repaying the loan he took from his brother-in-law for his son's admission to an upmarket international school. Also, Reddy might have to share the bounty with Rupashree to rewrite her interrogation report in the manner required to arrest Shabnam, the staff member who handled the digital side of FIRs, the computer server operators in headquarters, to enable him to tamper with the records to frame Shabnam.

A couple of days later, Rupashree went to Daffodils and arrested Shabnam.

SHABNAM

I was getting ready to board the train, anxious to leave Hyderabad soon. It is still eleven a.m. I was restless. Saab told me the train leaves at 03:00 p.m., and he said he would drop me off and make me sit in the reserved compartment to have an easy and safe journey. I was packing my clothes in the bag madam bought for me in the last sale at a Mall in Mumbai. Just then, the doorbell rang. I unbolted the door to find the same two police personnel who visited us four days back standing before me. While I was telling them Saab was not at home, they walked past me into the room inside and parked themselves on the sofa. The lady officer asked me to sit on the opposite plastic chair.

"We now have a doubt the death of your madam is not a straightforward normal death. We find there could be some foul play. Our senior officers asked us to investigate further," said the lady in Hindi.

What good is this information to me, I was wondering.

"The death as per the Doctor's report, occurred between 5:30 to 6:30 a.m. During that time, your Saab went out walking. The Security person had seen him and noted in the book," said the man in broken Hindi.

"You were the only person at home when the death occurred," added the lady.

This jugalbandi[76] was confusing to me. I did not utter a word, not knowing what they are hinting.

"Our senior officers asked us to take you to the police station for more questioning on your relationship with your madam," said the lady again.

"But Saab told me the death certificate said she died of dil-ka-daura[77]!" I said.

"He is not hundred per cent correct. There is a doubt. And we have to act as per police rules, otherwise, our jobs would be at stake," said the man.

"But I have to catch the train at three p.m., and Saab told me he would come to pick me up at two," I protested.

"You have to postpone your travel arrangements for another week. We have to take you to the police station," said the lady, "We have already informed your Raj Krishna Saab about it, and he was okay with it."

They did not utter the dreaded word "arrest." So I thought maybe they would have to do their job and another couple of days delay would not be much trouble though I was deeply disappointed. I was unable to contact either Abdul or Asif or Kaamini because of the irresponsibility of the staff. But I have no alternative. And as luck would have it, Saab was not at home. I locked the house and accompanied them. They insisted I bring the bag that I was packing, so they would arrange to drop me at the station after a few days.

I never knew I was being taken for a ride at that time! I signed the paper given to me, which was written in Telugu.

It surprised Shabnam that Raj did not accompany her to the police station. Raj assured her through Rupashree's mobile that

---

76   Two musical instruments playing together
77   Heart failure

she would be free and she could go to Vadodara in two days. The cell Shabnam shared with one other woman was dark. The toilets were small-sized, and the cement floor cracked. A small hole with two bricks on both sides passed off as a latrine. It was full of faeces and smelt awful. Flies buzzed around the hole. The cell opened into a corridor, which led to the office that was at least fifty meters away, so the condition of the cell was not visible to the visitors. Rupashree gave her a small parcel in a second-hand amazon cardboard box containing toiletries, a small hand mirror, and a packet of bindis, an antiseptic cream and a sanitary pad pack.

"You must thank your stars that you are in this police station managed by a good SHO who ensures the women in custody are treated with respect. The welcome pack I gave you is unique to this station. No other police station has this kind of care," said Rupashree, "today, the safaiwaali did not report to duty. Otherwise, the lavatory would be not this bad. If SHO comes to know the condition of this cell, he will reprimand us."

Rupashree had to follow police procedures for the arrest.

The police officer carrying out the arrest of the arrestee shall prepare a memo of arrest at the time of arrest, and such memo shall be attested by at least one witness, who may be either a member of the family of the arrestee or a respectable person of the locality from where the arrest is made. It shall also be countersigned by the arrestee and contain the time and date of arrest.

Shabnam gave the name of Asif, her brother-in-law in Vadodara, but she did not remember the telephone number. Shabnam once again declined to provide her home address in Vadodara: she feigned memory loss.

There is no law against silence, thought Rupashree.

I did not want any police personnel visiting my home in Vadodara. I can visualize the aftermath of a policeman visiting our home in Vadodara.

"Aa Shabnamnu ghar che?[78]," asks the police.

Nusrat comes to the porch.

"This is Altaf's house. Shabnam used to stay here. Not anymore. She is now in Parbhani."

Hearing the doorbell, Nazma shouts from her kitchen. "Who is that?"

"Police," says Nusrat

On hearing 'police', Nazma and Munaaf come to the door. "Why do you want to know about Shabnam?"

"We have got a message from Hyderabad police to locate her address and inform her relatives of her arrest."

"Arrest?" Munaaf shocked.

"I know this Shabnam is not fit for our house. She brought disgrace. We should not have accepted her into our house at all. She is a curse on our family," says Nusrat.

"But why did she go to Hyderabad?" wonders Munaaf.

"Let us call Abdul right away and inform him," says Nazma.

"Ammijaan, this is working time in Saudi. It is not wise to disturb him now. We shall inform in the evening," says Munaaf.

The more I think of this scenario, the more I am scared of what they will tell Abdul about me.

So, I decided to not to disclose my house address in Vadodara to anyone in the police department.

---

78   Is this Shabnam's house?

Rupashree was at her wit's end. She was wary of her boss, who would rebuke her if she did not follow the procedures.

Rupashree contacted Reddy to take further guidance from him. Reddy suggested that Raj's neighbour's signature be taken and Shabnam's thumb impression.

Shabnam spent the first twenty-four hours of her custody in total isolation. She sat at one corner and copiously cried and prayed to Ganesha.

Memory was experienced events reflected in a broken mirror. Some you can visualize; many are hazy. Though Abdul's features are clear enough in her memory, she could never see his face in its entirety. She could feel the beard, the hair on his chest, soft lips, and smell the cool touch of his breath. But she couldn't see him. She remembered the nonchalant way he brushed away anything not to his liking. His eyes showed remorse that he was leaving her in a hostile environment. Shabnam yearned for him to return.

She trusted Abdul and her Ganesha that they would protect her.

The next day, Rupashree presented the folder containing all the case-related documents to the Government Pleader, Narayana Swamy, in the Magistrate's office corridor. She explained the case to him. Narayana Swamy was the grandson of the past CM of erstwhile Andhra Pradesh, born to his fifth daughter who married a boy out of her caste and lower social status, much against her family's wishes. The family duly excommunicated her.

Narayana Swamy managed to complete his Law degree; subsequently, thanks to his father's contacts and the government's reservation policy, he was appointed a government pleader. He earned the dubious reputation of a sloppy and careless advocate.

Magistrates across the Metropolitan region had passed strictures against him for his unpreparedness before taking up cases. He often fumbled when asked to repeat an argument that was not convincing to the presiding officer. Thus he exposed his lack of knowledge of the law and reluctance to rectify his image time and again. He knew one rule: you cannot be sacked in government jobs, however incompetent you were. Therefore, he never bothered to learn from the rebukes and improve.

The court summoned Shabnam as its first case for the day. The Magistrate always insisted on finishing matters of women prisoners, suspects, detainees, remanded persons, defenders and plaintiffs first in the morning. Accordingly, he instructed the clerk of the court to ensure the same.

Narayana Swami opened the argument and said, "Sir, this lady appears to pose an immediate threat to herself if left alone. She does not answer any of our queries about her background. Our investigation has not been able to gather any information on her background. The husband of the diseased does not also know much about her as the victim employed her in Mumbai. We had checked the house with the permission of the husband to know tell-tales of information of her family written somewhere in the house, but no luck. Her phone is also lost."

"Her phone is lost?" said the Judge in complete bewilderment.

"The previous Inspector, Venugopal Rao, collected all the items required for investigation and forensic analysis as per the procedure. That included the suspect's phone, as reported by the head constable accompanied by the Inspector. But it was not on the list of the items recorded by the HC. When asked, he said he had specifically put all three phones in the bag, and he is at a loss to know how and where that particular phone went missing," said the Pleader

"You are incorrigible," said the Judge frustratingly.

"Have you checked the phone number from the house owner? You can easily find the address from her last call records," asked the Judge.

"Sir, the house owner does not know her phone number. The suspect said her number was registered in her husband's name in Vadodara, and she did give her number. We are trying to find the calls she made from that phone to contact her relatives in Vadodara. We have given the request to the cyber cell to investigate. They are yet to respond," said the Pleader

"How long do you think this investigation will take? And what are you aiming at? Are you expecting a confession? You very well know the confessions in the police station are not admissible," said the Judge.

"Sir, the evidence we have collected from discussions, interrogation sessions and the reports made by the first IO[79] indicates sufficient motive for the suspect's involvement in the crime. These details are in the docket presented to you," said Swamy, "When the death occurred, she was the only person in the house. As per the PM report, the death could be by strangulation. The house owner had not reported any monetary or other losses. We expect the murder could be because of rage built in the suspect caused by the maltreatment by the lady of the house, as proven in the report of the SI submitted. We need a week more to complete our interrogation."

"It is well settled that the post-mortem report or an injury report is not substantive evidence unless it is to be proved by its maker. And it has to stand the cross. I cannot, therefore, allow the PM report to be admitted as evidence now," said the Magistrate.

---

79   Investigating Officer

He perused the diary note of the SI. He glared over his reading glasses.

"Let me talk to the Suspect."

The Judge had, after the perfunctory swearing-in, turned towards the suspect and addressed her;

"Madam, are you comfortable in Telugu or Hindi."

"Hindi"

The conversation proceeded in Hindi

"What is your name?' the Magistrate asked

"Shabnam."

"Have you been treated properly at the police station?"

"Yes, sir."

"Which is your home town, and please give the complete address of your home?"

"Vadodara"

"Don't you remember your house address?"

"No"

"Do you have your husband's phone number or any of your relatives so we can contact them?"

"All my phone numbers are on the mobile, which is with the police, and they are not giving me."

"The police said they lost your mobile. Have you written the number in any book or paper in the house so we can search and find"

"No"

Then the Magistrate turned towards the Advocate and said, "Seven days? Out of the question. I shall give you four days to find her address, inform her relatives, and ensure a counsel to represent her, or the court shall appoint one. Also, from the cyber cell, find out the last few numbers dialled from the telephone, whose number you already have. One more thing. Not a scratch on her body. Do not force a confession to collect more evidence of the so-called maltreatment you have referred to in the report. That is the only motive that can establish the case as you sought to imply."

"We are on the job, sir," said the PP, "Sir, we are afraid if she is left alone, she might commit suicide as she is already showing aggressive tendencies. The housekeeper also is not interested in keeping her. Therefore, we request the custody for seven more days," he bluffed.

Shabnam was, in fact, very cooperative and friendly with all the staff and her inmate. Except she refused to share her Vadodara address.

"We have also sent her photo to Vadodara Police to check her address," added the Pleader," Sir, this lady has no place to go. Her homeowner now refuses to take her in. It would be better to keep her in police custody till the charge sheet is filed."

"A person is not liable to arrest merely on suspicion of complicity in an offence. There must be some reasonable justification in the opinion of the officer effecting the arrest that such arrest is necessary and justified. But the evidence presented is not enough for you to arrest her in the first place. Anyway, find the motive you have referred within four days," said the Magistrate, "You need not worry about where she should be accommodated after the release. The court can find her a shelter home. I cannot give more than four days of custody to you. That is it. Arrange to submit the PM report and request the Duty Doctor who wrote it to be present on the next date of hearing. Also, the

Forensic report of the object which as per the FIR was used for strangulation."

"Not to forget the cyber cell report of the phone details."

The annoyance in his tone was unmissable.

"One more thing. Please send your constable to the ISKCON[80] centre and request Swami Gunasekhara Das to contact me at his convenient time. Who is your SHO?"

The Magistrate was aware of the condition of shelter homes in the State. He did not want Shabnam, whose involvement in the case was still to be established, to be sent to such homes with a debauched reputation.

"Adarsh Naik, sir."

"Ask him to contact me at night at my home. Say that it is an order," said the Judge, "Next, please."

***

Reddy and Rupashree could not provide any further evidence to link the death to Shabnam, as they found no tell tales of maltreatment by the victim. And also, on repeated interrogations, the suspect denied any such abuse. As per the directive of the Magistrate, they presented the suspect after four days of mandatory custody with an affidavit on the lack of evidence to buttress their theory of maltreatment as the reason for her involvement in the crime. On the advice of the Government Pleader, the police presented the suspect in the court of the Magistrate, but forensic report of the pillow and the cyber cell investigation of the phone data could not be presented as the reports have not been received.

The Magistrate then observed:

---

80   International Society for Krishna Consciousness

"The court, with its vast experience, should be quick to notice mischief if there is any. Incompetent prosecuting agencies or those driven by extraneous considerations should not be allowed to take the court for a ride. Particularly in offences relating to women and children, which are on the rise, the courts will have to adopt a pragmatic approach. No scope must be given to absurd and fanciful submissions. Therefore I am releasing Shabnam from police custody. I am sending her under the care of ISKCON until you find her contact details. Please submit the forensic report of the object, which was purported to have been used for strangulation, within the next four days. That's an order. The autopsy report, which hints at death by strangulation, shall be examined in greater detail during the trial. You may continue your investigations towards a charge sheet as per procedures. The suspect would be in a safe environment of ISKCON and can be called in for further trials along with her lawyer and as per the consent of her husband or other relatives. You have to locate her Vadodara address, through her phone records and report to the court quickly."

Consequently, Shabnam was released sent to ISKCON under the care of Swami Gunasekhara das, who had employed her in the kitchen and gave her accommodation as per the directive of the Magistrate.

On the instructions of the Magistrate, Adarsh Naik had contacted Swami Gunasekhara Das of ISKCON and, ensured the necessary affidavits; arranged the transfer of Shabnam from Police Custody to the premises of ISKCON. The HC, Narsimha, was given the task of verifying the presence and well-being of Shabnam at ISKCON daily and recording the same. He dutifully did the same.

Narsimha noted that Shabnam was given the task of helping in preparing the Mid-Day Meal program of The Akshaya Patra Foundation, an organ of ISKCON.

ABDUL

Eighteen months passed since Abdul came to Saudi to gain experience and, most importantly, prosperity to uplift his family life and have a pleasant time with Shabnam in their new home at Alkapuri. He was happy he was successful in the goal he set for himself. But on some nights in the loneliness of his room, Abdul did sometimes feel burdened and degraded. He felt sorry for Shabnam and longed to rush to her to hug and profess his love. He felt her soft hands caressing his hair, which only could comfort him. He would drop off to sleep, fatigued by his work and thoughts of her. Abdul was concerned there had been no call from Shabnam for a couple of weeks now, and his calls also went blank with no sound from the other side.

"The number you have dialled does not exist."

He called Asif, "When did you last speak to your Bhabhi?"

"About three weeks back, bhaijaan. Bhabhi called and informed me she might be changing her phone handset, as per the request of her house owner. She did not call back later. I told her not to forget to inform me as soon as she got the new piece. I was busy with my work, so I did not notice the absence of her call. Sorry, bhaijaan," said Asif," did she not call you too?"

"No, I am now worried," said Abdul.

He wanted Asif to go to Hyderabad and help find her. But he had no information about whereabouts of her. All the time when the lovers were talking on the phone, it never occurred to either of them they should exchange the address of Shabnam in Hyderabad. For four days, Abdul did not go to the site on the pretext of sickness. He was ill mentally – not physically. In those four days, Abdul lived through an entire hell. They were moments when he would start thinking about quitting and rushing home. His imagination would even run particularly free on those occasions. He pictured the worst for Shabnam. He feared something had happened to her. He took a bus to Riyadh to talk to his agency and Ameer to discuss the matter and the suggested course of action. The bus journey to Riyadh took him four hours. He went straight to the agency office, met the chief, and explained his predicament.

"As per the contract, you have at least five more months to go. Please somehow manage these five months, and then you can go," suggested the Manager.

"I cannot work with the stress I have. I must go now. I need at least two weeks to leave; if necessary, they can extend the contract by two weeks with the same pay and terms," said Abdul

"We have no control over your employer once you sign the contract. You have to negotiate with them directly," said the manager

"I understand; I had come to you because you are the initiator of this assignment, and I would not want to do anything without informing you; hence I came here. Of course, I will take permission from the employer before leaving," said Abdul.

"Thank you for your decency. Rarely do we find such responsible clients—Good Luck to you. If they contact us, we shall guarantee your return to work as soon as the sanctioned leave is completed. That much we can promise. They would surely contact us as they have invested much in your training. They would want an assurance from a third party guaranteeing your return," said the Manager.

Later, Abdul contacted Ameer, who also said Abdul should go in search of Shabnam with due permission from his employer. Edward Jenkins was very cooperative and assured him of help. He recommended to the HG group head that he be given leave. As anticipated, they wanted assurance from Shafique Travels and Tours, which they did. There was no mention of the ticket fare, even though he did not take the mandatory leave after the contract's first year as per the terms, because of the pressure of timelines, He thought it was not the right time to discuss these matters and bought his ticket at his own cost and left for Vadodara via Mumbai and onwards to Hyderabad.

***

Abdul could receive the attention of Mohd. Ghouse only by the afternoon when he re-appeared from his house. Abdul briefed Ghouse about his reason for coming to Hyderabad and the lack of the address where his wife was living, before he lost contact.

"I am sorry, Abdul, I had not given enough attention to you so far; I was not aware you were in such distress."

"It is all right. Now you have to tell me how to go about finding my wife. I have just two weeks' leave, of which I have already spent three days travelling. Travel back will take two days more. In short, I have just ten days to find my wife. You have to help me. I am new to this city," said Abdul despondently.

"I can take you to an Inspector cousin of mine, Dilkhush Hussain. We shall take his opinion and proceed".

Ghouse handed over the reins of the shop to his senior assistant, called his eldest son on his mobile phone, and asked him to skip his college and look after the shop for that day. He then took Abdul to meet Hussain.

They were now sitting in Hussain's office, a narrow room that could have once been a storeroom. There were remnants of old files with cobwebs in one corner. The table was surprisingly impressively neat, with a computer monitor at one corner of the table. A file cabinet of the ordinary design was to the left of the chair where he was sitting. Two mobile phones were lying on the table – one appeared to be the latest Android model. A framed photo was facing him. Somehow Abdul expected the old files could have been removed to make the room more pleasant.

"This is my temporary room. My original room is being refurbished on the first floor," the Officer clarified, sensing Abdul's body language.

For the second time of the day, Abdul explained the purpose of the meeting.

I wonder how many times I will have to repeat this narration in the next few days!

Hussain listened with great attention and said," Firstly, please give a missing person advertisement in a couple of newspapers. I am not sure any police station would take the missing complaint as there could be jurisdictional issues. Every PS inspector would ask you the last address from where she went missing, the information of which you don't have. So the best method is to meet the Commissioner of Police, Rahul Kanwal and request him to circulate your wife's photo to every police station."

"Newspaper advertisement is fine. We shall do it right away. But it is a long shot. Will the Commissioner meet us without a formal appointment?" asked Ghouse.

"Normally, no. The Commissioner is a busy man. But sometimes, at 3 p.m., he meets the members of the public. That is, if his boss or some minister does not call him. You have to take that chance. If not today, try tomorrow or the day after. You have to keep trying. One other thing I want to suggest. Please calmly recollect the telephone conversations you were having with your wife. She could have mentioned the name of the building she was staying in, a nearby shop she frequented, the name of a lane, Or some other hint to know her last address. That will go a long way in locating her"

"I cannot remember off-hand. Tonight I will deeply think and get back to you tomorrow," said Abdul.

They thanked Hussain and proceeded to book *lapata*[81] advertisements in English, Telugu and Urdu newspapers. Fortunately, they could find one agency from google search, which accepted the ad for all newspapers.

After thanking him for his help, Abdul took permission from Ghouse and shifted to a hotel to have a more pleasant atmosphere to think calmly. He raked his memory of her telephone conversations. But Abdul could only think of her as a lover with a calm personality. He felt sad he had subjected her so much grief and decided to make it up when they meet. He was confident no harm had come to her, and she was safe and waiting to fall into his arms.

It seemed only last night she made love frantically like quenching some terrible thirst. After he was satisfied, she rolled onto him and carried on, kissing him hungrily, pinching his beard, until she was exhausted with pleasure. Those days were gone. He did not keep his side of the bargain.

---

81   Missing

He watched television. There was nothing that interested him. He shifted to BBC World news. Some more distressing news of riots, bombings etc. He shut off and tried to sleep. There was nothing left for him to do to quell his anxiety, so he dozed off.

Then suddenly, some old conversations with her started ringing in his mind.

"My building name is....D.... it is a six storied apartment, Very nice and we are staying on the fourth floor. They gave me a room all for myself with a small TV. The same facility they had extended when we were in Mumbai too. They treat me as though I am one of their family members. Especially madam's youngest daughter. She sometimes calls me on the land line, if madam was not home to inquire about me and through me about madam's health."

"I could not lift your phone because I had to go to Golden Bakery to buy some bread. Normally madam does not send me, but some urgency had come up as the grocery delivery boy had not given the garlic bread ordered".

Abdul suddenly woke up and noticed the time to be 4 a.m. He thanked Allah, the merciful, for giving him some tips. However, the name of the building she stayed in was unclear to him. It started with D, as he recollected faintly. And Golden Bakery was near this apartment building. He was sure. Abdul cursed himself for not paying attention to his wife when she was speaking on the phone with some mundane gossip that women often indulge.

They just want to pour out, whatever thoughts come to their minds. At that time the dialogues appear inconsequential, so we don't pay much attention.

His wait for daylight was torturous. He quickly washed, dressed and ran downstairs for breakfast. But the breakfast room was not open yet. The board on the door showed the breakfast time was from 7:30 to ten a.m. One more hour to kill. Anyway, he could not go to see Hussain and discuss the future course with the information he recollected until he came to the office, which could be ten or even eleven a.m. as Baroodwala informed him about the laidback nature of Hyderabadis.

He read all the newspapers lying in the reception waiting room until the breakfast room opened. He decided to do his investigation meanwhile. He peered through the Google Maps on the networked computer placed in the reception area to note the location of Golden Bakery in Hyderabad. The search showed three locations: one in Ramgopal Pet, the second at Tappachabutra and another at Tilak Nagar. He requested the concierge to arrange a taxi to these three places and later to Hussain's office. The receptionist was cooperative, but he could only organize the cab at 09:00 a.m., not immediately.

"If you had booked yesterday, we could have arranged by seven. All taxis get booked the previous day itself. But we could find one available at around nine," said the receptionist apologetically.

While in the taxi, he called up Ghouse and informed him of his proposed investigation on his own, based on his hunch of recollection of his dialogues with Shabnam.

"Can you name some apartment complex names starting with D?" asked Abdul

"Well, it could be Deccan, Delight, Diamond, and Dollar Apartments – if NRIs fund them - Dukes... and so on."

"Okay, thanks. I shall try my luck and call you back. Thanks," said

The visits to the bakery at Ramgopal pet and the one at Tappachabutra did not yield any results. Abdul inquired whether nearby buildings have names starting with D. He received blank stares from the store owners and some random customers he interviewed. What was now balance was the one at Tilak Nagar.

The taxi driver could not locate the Tilak Nagar, as there was more than one Tilak Nagar in Hyderabad. He looked again at the Maps and found three Tilak Nagars he would want to visit. He followed the same pattern of asking questions wherever he found a Golden Stores and Sweets, which was in Tilak Nagar near Uppal. No luck with other attempts too.

Exasperated, he met Hussain at his PS and explained his failed attempts.

Abdul's dependence on google maps to help him locate Golden Bakery and the subsequent apartment name starting with D was not fruitful. Google is not a Mr Know All, as it is given credit for. Google collects its information about where a given place is by using different methods like the IP address of the network to which the area is connected, its GPS, Satellite imagery, and the proximity of other Android devices around it. It takes it out of its search if it finds only one source but cannot verify it.

Also, apart from satellite imaging, some of its efforts depend on customer interaction to place their requests on its maps. Many establishments, especially small traders, are missed out on. Google does have a facility to take your request for placing your name and street address on its map sites at no charge. However, for that, the establishment has to take the lead. The bakery stores cater to local customers within a 5 Km radius max. They would not gain much in taking the trouble of requesting Google to place their address on the maps unless some owner wants to brag to his friends and relatives that his shop is now visible on Google. Hence, it is likely Abdul may have missed out on a few Golden Bakeries, which Google could not locate for him.

"Only way is to request all the Police Stations to find Golden Bakery within their precincts. But for that, I cannot help as the request has to come from the top. I am simply an Inspector; I cannot demand other SHOs," said Hussain.

"There must be some Police stations where you would have your friends or erstwhile colleagues working. Let us first close these contacts before I go to the Commissioner's office," pleaded Abdul.

"Okay, let me rake my brain on that. It is 3 p.m. past lunchtime; I was busy so far and could not take lunch. Let us have lunch," said Hussain, taking him to a nearby Biryani establishment Hyderabad is famous for.

Hussain chose to call up his contacts in four police stations and requested the information that Abdul needed. The head constable at SR Nagar PS informed a small but popular bakery that sold delicious cakes in a lane next to its station. And its name was Golden Bakery and Sweets. Abdul was anxious to run to the place. Hussain calmed him and said it was better his constable accompanied him to the bakery to get the desired response. Hussain buzzed, and a trim young person in a crisp uniform responded immediately with a salute.

Abdul could not read the label on the name plaque in the local dialect.

"Shiva, accompany this gentleman to SR Nagar," ordered Hussain and explained to the constable the details of his assignment.

"Yes, sir," and he waited outside the room for Abdul to come out.

We were driving to SR Nagar through heavy and disgusting traffic. But my mind was disturbed, and I could not concentrate on the surroundings that apart, the driver had a nasty habit of blowing his horn often. I was sure what happened to Shabnam was all my fault. I shouldn't have left her alone in the house at Vadodara, knowing fully well Nusrat's antagonism towards her and ammijaan's reluctance and inability to control her.

Shiva was giving directions to the driver as per the details provided to him by Hussain. They saw the signboard in a lane. Golden Bakery and Sweets. The scent of the baking bread filled the street. It was a clean, slightly sweet, yeasty aroma that was inviting. Upon entering the eatery, they were greeted by the warm and polite staff manning the counters, eager to serve. This bakery also showcased its expertise in the skilful art of designing toppings on cakes from basic and simple cakes. The bakery was busy with clientele buying loaves of bread, birthday cakes with and without toppings, plum cakes, pastries, muffins, puffs and the like. The business seemed to be booming. Abdul interacted with customers who came to buy the merchandise to pass the time while the constable was looking for the owner. The taste was on point, the spices were well balanced, and the presentation was satisfactory. Some said that the garlic bread and pizza were a bit overpriced. The kheema and mutton puffs seemed to be a rage.

The constable took charge and asked for the owner. An older man appeared from a door at the back of the shop. He probably was once a short handsome man with a pleasant manner. In his career, with all the indulgences that the shop perquisites provided, he would have bloated to his present figure with a tummy that stressed the thread that held his shirt button.

"Do you know any apartment complex here with D as the first letter?" asked Shiva.

"There are a couple: one Deccan Heights and other Daffodils. Deccan is at the end of this street. Daffodils in the opposite lane, just four building away from the opposite shop," said the man.

Abdul thanked him and decided to visit Daffodils first. They walked past a barbershop and a welding shop and entered the lane. The lane had apartments lined on both sides. The only commercial entity was an ironing cart operated by a couple filled with bundles of colourful clothes – a few ironed, folded, ready to be delivered. They soon found the apartment they were looking. It was a six storied building built with an attractive façade. The search party approached the security person sitting on a stool, cleaning what appeared to be a motor part. He looked up at the intruders.

"Could you tell us whether any maid named Shabnam worked here?" asked Shiva.

She is not a maid, you fool. She is the housekeeper.

Constables in uniform continue to be respected or feared in India. The man quickly stood up and said, "Yes, in 402."

Abdul was elated.

It reminded me of a scene telecast on the BBC news last night. A Palestinian woman was looking for her son in the rubble of a multi-storeyed structure damaged by the Israeli Defence bombing. Airstrikes had caused a tunnel to collapse, bringing houses down with it.

"We saw nothing but smoke," the mom told the news reporter. "I couldn't see my son next to me, and I was hugging him, but suddenly I could see nothing." The mother was inconsolable. As she, other onlookers and authorities were rummaging through the pile, they heard a feeble voice coming from the debris. She got anxious and requested to peek deep into the crevice from where the voice had come. With the cooperation of the people around and the firefighting

personnel, they dug the rubble carefully and found the 5yr old boy perfectly healthy but was crying out of fear. The scene showed the mom hugging her child and hollering as much as the child.

I felt the same as soon as I heard Shabnam lived here. I wanted to cry. Thanked Allah for his mercy and miracles. Alhamdulillah.

"Can we go up to the flat?" Abdul asked

"The flat is locked as the owner has gone out of Hyderabad."

"At least can we speak to the neighbours?" asked Shiva.

"Please write your name and details in the registry, and you may take the lift."

They found four houses on the floor, with 402 and 401 locked. They rang the bell of 403. After what seemed to be eons, an elderly lady opened the door with a bizarre face of astonishment. She found the uniformed person disturbing.

"Is Vinay Desai in the house?" asked the cop in Telugu. They read the nameplate on the wall.

"No, he has gone to the office," she said and banged the door shut before they could react.

Shiva rang the bell again. The same lady appeared, showing irritation. He had a feeling that the only thing that could satisfy her would be to roll him off the stairs.

"Can we speak to anybody else in the house? Maybe his wife," said Shiva in a more appeasing tone to avoid the door from banging in their face again.

She ran back into the house as fast her feet could take her- slippers slapping on the floor. They heard her yell.

"Madamji, *aapke liye koi aaye hain*"[82].

---

82   Someone has come to see you

After a few minutes, a middle-aged lady in her late forties presented herself.

"What is it, Officer?"

Abdul did not want Shiva to answer; instead, he spoke.

"Madam, we are looking for the person working as a caretaker in flat 402. Do you have any idea where we can find her?"

"You don't know?" she addressed at the constable, ignoring Abdul.

"No, madam."

"You are the police, aren't you? You guys only took her to the police station."

This information shocked Abdul. He composed himself.

"Madam, he is from another police station. He would not know. Could you please give me some more information?" said pleadingly.

"Please come in". The lady led them to the sitting room, gesturing them to sit on the sofa. It was a tastefully furnished room with a clock ticking somewhere. She chose a chair opposite and sat down on it, her back upright and legs crossed.

"Can you tell me who you are and why are you interested in the maid if you are not from the local jurisdictional police station?"

Abdul introduced himself to be the husband of Shabnam, who worked for the family of flat 402 and explained the circumstances that made him come in search of her.

"I have no idea where she is. My husband knows. There was a death in the flat. The housewife, Vaidehi, died almost twenty days back, I think. Maybe more. The exact date I cannot recollect. I know that the local SR Nagar police personnel had come to the flat several times. Once, they interviewed my husband also. Finally, they took the maid with them about a week back; I have not seen her since then. My husband told me that Mr Raj Krishna left for Kolkata the day before to be with his sister.

Abdul wanted to ask for more details of the family and other information. But, Shiva nudged him to leave the place and visit the police station nearby to get more information. They left the premises, thanked for the information, extended courtesy, and left.

Adarsh Naik

A darsh Naik came to the police station after almost twenty days of absence. He went to see his ailing mother in Raipur, and as soon as he reported back to duty, he was asked to attend a one-week training program on Cyber Security at the National Police Academy. Presently, he was taking briefs from his Inspector and other staff.

Adarsh Naik had come to know of the arrest of Shabnam when he spoke to the Magistrate on the 18th evening as per the Magistrate's direction. It was the first day of his training, and he had to find an excuse to use his phone, which otherwise was not allowed as per the training rules of the Academy. Adarsh Naik was disturbed and was upset during his entire training period because of the overbearing attitude of his staff. He was determined to make amends for their oppressive behaviour. Naik knew that he had to proceed with caution because he was not aware of Reddy's backup power support. Naik directed his staff on what was to be done per the Magistrate's instructions.

As soon as Adarsh Naik had resumed duty on the 25th of July, he requested the files related to the death at Daffodils. He wanted to get to the bottom of the matter before reporting the high-handed and arrogant actions of the Inspector and the Sub Inspector; their culpability of any act of omission or commission in the exercise of their powers of remanding a person to custody.

"I want to review the day-wise actions concerning the FIR 236/2016," said Adarsh Naik," Please get me prints of all diary reports and the PM Report filed by the Hospital."

Rupashree got them neatly filed chronologically. Naik made his Station a replica of a corporate office, amalgamating it with the Police procedures, laws, rules and hierarchical reporting norms, which were unique to Police governance, right from the days of Crown Rule.

"Reddy, please explain to me the events that had made you arrest this lady."

"On Friday the 1st of July, Dr Partha had come to the station early in the morning and met you as he feared the death he was asked to certify did not appear normal."

"Yes, I recollect that. I had then requested Venugopal Rao to accompany Dr Partha and take further action as per rules."

"Subsequently, Venu endorsed the report of Dr Partha that the death did not appear natural but could be by smothering apparently by a pillow found near the body," said Reddy. "On your direction, they shifted the body to Gandhi hospital for examination by a Government Doctor and Post Mortem, if required. The PM report prepared by Dr S Gulati was uploaded into the server by the Doctor's secretary, Leela, on Tuesday, the 5th of July. The copy is now in the files."

"On the complaint of Dr Partha, FIR no 236 was registered," added Rupashree.

Naik opened the file and read the FIR.

12. Contents of the Complaint

On the 1st of July, at around 8 a.m., Dr Partha came to the police station and reported death at Daffodils apartments flat no 402, which in his opinion, was not natural. Dr Partha was the duty doctor at Prime hospital, road no 9 SR Nagar, a Mr Raj Krishna Sastry s/o Raghunath Sastry, aged 62 years, resident of Daffodils, approached him to certify the death of his wife, Vaidehi. Dr Partha opined that the death could be by strangulation as per evidence he had seen and reported. On the directions of SHO, the body was shifted to the mortuary of Gandhi Hospital for Post Mortem at noon on the same day.

Signed – IO Venugopal Rao

The SHO was aware of Section 154, 155 and 156(1) CrPC. The police officer is bound to register a case when he receives information about a cognizable offence. At the stage of receiving the news of a cognizable offence, the police officer is not supposed to inquire about the correctness or otherwise of such information. That stage would only come after the case is registered.

"The Hospital took three days to release the body for the cremation? Have you seen the death certificate" asked Naik

"Yes, Sir, in between, there was a Sunday. No, Sir, we don't have the copy of the death certificate issued by the Doctor."

"Can I see the report of Dr Partha and the diary of Venu?"

After reading the reports, Naik commented, "I notice that Venu's diary does not endorse the pillow dent as reported by Dr Partha. Also, his inquest is incomplete." The Inspector's diary had the following entry:

Under Section 174 of CrPC, and as empowered by the State Government, I conducted the inquest in the presence of Dr Partha, HC Mr Narsimha and the neighbour Mr Vinay Desai. I noted the same in this diary, to be forwarded to the Magistrate. The purpose of preparing the inquest report is merely to make a note of the body's physical condition and the marks of injury thereof noticed at that point of time, and a witness' signature is not required as per various judgements of the courts. Hence the signature of Mr Desai was not insisted upon as he was unwilling to sign.

"Can I see the PM report? Also, send someone to get a copy of the death certificate."

Rupashree sent a constable to get the Death certificate copy from the crematorium.

Meanwhile showed the SHO the flagged PM report in the file.

Fibres recovered from the victim's nose and face indicated that the victim could have been smothered by an object such as a pillow. Asphyxia occurs when the free flow of oxygenated air is cut off, thus preventing it from reaching the brain or other parts of the body. The number of fibres help distinguish between criminal and legitimate actions (such as sleeping on a pillow). Hand and finger marks left on the smothering object provide information about how the object was handled, which requires forensic examination. Thus, death by strangulation, by smothering with a pillow, cannot be ruled out. Further confirmation can be had after the pillow is sent for forensic analysis.

Adarsh Naik smelt a rat. He asked Rupashree to check the date and time of uploading the Report from the server. She reported that the same was uploaded on the 5th of July at 4 p.m. Naik noted the body was handed back to the relatives on Monday the 4th afternoon itself. And Venugopal Rao was transferred on the 5th of July, after the disciplinary action was initiated following the errors committed concerning FIR 232 of 2016.

"When did you report to duty in place of Venu," asked Naik, addressing Reddy.

"I reported to duty on Monday the 11th of July, sir."

"Your diary entry shows you have gone to the victim's house on the 14th of July," observed Naik.

"I could only contact the previous IO, Venugopal, on the 12th of July to take brief on all the cases under his jurisdiction."

Adarsh Naik asked Narsimha, the head constable manning the computer terminal, to bring the diary report of Venugopal with the date of uploading his information.

Naik was surprised to note that though the original Report was uploaded on the 5th of July itself, it was edited again on the 16th of July when Inspector Venugopal was not in the PS as he had been transferred. He called Narsimha for an explanation.

"Sir, on the 16th-morning, Inspector Reddy had requested me to check with Venugopal about the missing entries in his diary regarding the experience and academic particulars of Dr Partha, which Venugopal Sir, did not record. So I contacted Venu Sir, and asked his permission for the correction, to which he agreed. Accordingly, I made the corrections on the 16th of July," said Narsimha

"Were you aware of this?" asked Naik addressing Reddy.

"Sir, I had a function at home on the 17th of July for which I took leave from the 16th afternoon to the 19th of July. So I was not privy to what Narsimha had done, but I was aware of the missing information I had pointed out to him to check with Venugopal," said Reddy.

One can open one file at multiple locations for editing. An intelligent operator can mask his location and yet edit the document without the knowledge of the other person working on the doc at the same time. When Narasimha was editing the doc for entering the details of Dr Partha in the diary noting of Venu, Reddy arranged for the server in-charge at the headquarters also open the document at the precise moment and make the corrections in the record to show Raj Krishna had a pucca alibi, as corroborated by the security staff. Also, he added the manufactured details of the interrogation of Shabnam, to prove that she mas maltreated by the house-lady. With the result, the date, location and time of the last editing were shown as that of Narsimha's id at the Police station, camouflaging the entries of the Server Operator who opened the file at the precise time as that of Narsimha. Thus the other statements exonerating Raj Krishna, based on the alibis corroborated by the security staff and other shopkeepers in the vicinity, were shown as written by Venu on the 5th of July itself.

Reddy took advantage of the dubious reputation of Venugopal Rao and cleverly camouflaged his complicity.

Rupashree had then informed Adarsh Naik of the arrest, as directed by the Inspector and the subsequent court observations and the suspect's release and arranged for her stay at ISKCON.

"I am aware of the further developments as the Magistrate talked to me," said Adarsh Naik.

"By now, you must have received the forensic report of the pillow," said Naik addressing no one in particular.

"Yes, Sir. It is in the file at the end," replied Rupashree.

The forensic Report of the pillow read as under:

No saliva or frothy fluid was found on the pillow; however, some tissue cells were found. By examination, it was noted that these are the dead skin cells that flaked from the foot of the victim, indicating that the indentation mark noticed by the house doctor could be because the victim may have been using the pillow for resting her leg.

Adarsh Naik was distressed by the way the case was handled. He instructed Reddy to call Dr Gulati to his Station.

"Sir, Dr Gulati has since retired," said Reddy. Reddy was trying to evade the possibility of Dr Gulati spilling the beans.

"So what! Ask him politely to come and discuss with us. Otherwise, you apply to the court and ask for a summons," thundered Naik. "Also, who is the computer operator in Doctor Gulati's office? And he must be still in service and could through more light on the PM report, which I want to examine with the help of a medical professional."

"Also, I would like to see the COD[83] written by the Doctor while handing over the body for the last rites.

"We shall find out, sir," said Rupashree and dialled the PBX number of the Hospital. After several minutes of transferring the phone from one desk to another, the call finally arrived on the desk of Leela Madanna.

***

When Dr Gulati arrived at his desk on the last day of his retirement, he found Leela haggard and seemed to vibrate with tension. Leela was a woman in her late thirties and had been with Dr Gulati for over six years through her stint at the Hospital was longer. She was initially recruited as an LDC clerk in the Secretariat of the ministry of health. On insistence by the Gandhi Hospital Superintendent, who needed clerical staff, she was transferred to the Hospital. Leela got posted as a common pool steno-typist to pathology, forensic and mortuary departments to help digitize records. She reported mainly to Dr Gulati, though she worked for many other sections. Leela was a model of diligence and efficiency and devoted to Dr Gulati, whom she admired. He also held Leela in considerable affection, as she was almost 20 years younger than him.

---

83   Cause of death

"What is wrong with you? Did you have a fight with your husband?" jokingly asked Gulati.

"Nothing. Just tired, that is all," Leela said.

On the last day of Gulati's retirement, Leela wanted to clarify the issue that had troubled her since the previous week. Yet she did not find it appropriate to bring the matter up. Gulati sensed something was bothering her but decided to wait for her to confide and be immersed in his day's work. The day passed, yet he found no change in the conduct of Leela, who became increasingly disturbed and started making silly errors in typing while posting the reports to various departments.

"Why don't you confide in me? You are not in your mood today," reiterated Gulati. He wanted to leave his office with pleasant memories on the last day of his work.

"The PM report of the lady Vaidehi we sent to the Police last week, you have re-edited the conclusion, which was different than what you originally made. That worries me. I do not know how the change would affect and whom it will affect. But I feel you have done wrong," said Leela in a calm but disquieting voice. Their relationship was such that she could be forthright with him.

"Oh, that one. I altered the inference because I had second thoughts about my conclusions. You need not worry," Dr Gulati said, brushing aside her concern.

I hope no one noticed Venugopal's visit to my home on the night of the 4th of July.

But his reply did not satisfy her.

Leela immediately knew something was amiss; after all, she knew him so well by now. She left the matter there and got immersed in her work, though the incident troubled her. A sixth sense told her to be on her guard.

Dr Gulati never did that: made more than one Report on the same matter. He would typically write one account of his conclusions, and after a thorough check and text validation by Leela, he would ask her to re-type it on the desktop, where it would be stored and mailed to whichever department requested it. In this case, Gulati called for the hard copy report after having typed, taken it home, altered the same the next day and asked her to send the altered one to the Police. However, Leela ensured the original draft report was also saved as "original draft" when it was first made in the same folder as the final one. Leela was experienced enough to understand her hospital working system. The final one was mailed to the police headquarters' central server and the corresponding Inspector's email id, as directed by Gulati.

***

Leela Madanna had never been to a police station as an adult. Her father was once jailed when she was in her teens. Her father accompanied Dalit families of his ancestral village who were violently protesting against the Zamindar, having learnt of the sexual exploitation of one a Dalit employee's daughter. She had accompanied her mother to request the authorities to release him. Leela did not have much remembrance of the incident but only a hazy recollection.

But she was told of the atrocities of the Police by her parents, which scarred her spirit.

When the constable came to pick her up, she had approached the Superintendent of the Hospital for advice. The Superintendent had already been briefed on the telephone by Adarsh Naik about the need to interrogate Leela and promised her that she would not be kept in the Station for more than an hour. The Superintendent had assured Leela that it was safe for her to go to the Station and give accurate information on whatever was being asked. Rupashree welcomed her at the Station and noted the particulars of her name and other identification details along with her professional work particulars. She then led Leela to SHO's room.

Adarsh Naik rose from his seat and made her comfortable.

"Madam, sorry to trouble you, we have a few questions. Would you mind answering us? We cannot force you, and you may refuse to answer. Please be free. No harm shall come to you," said Naik

Leela was pleasantly surprised by the reception she received. She was not aware of the reason for her presence at the Station.

"Yes, Sir, thank you. I shall do by best," said Leela

"Many PM cases come to your laboratory, and you may not remember the details of all. I want you to recollect one particular case involving the case of a lady named Vaidehi who presumably died by strangulation, as reported by Dr Gulati. Can you shed any light on the same?"

"I remember the case well, Sir. What would you like to know on the matter?"

"Did you type the report and post it to the main server of the police department?"

"Yes, Sir. I work for three departments as a pool computer assistant, but mostly I am stationed in the office of Dr Gulati in his lab."

"Did you find anything amiss in the report or the behaviour of Dr Gulati?"

Leela was on guard immediately, and she could not see Adarsh Naik eye to eye and just looked around the room, trying to avoid the SHO gaze. The experienced Naik noticed the same and said, "You need not be afraid. No harm shall come to you. You have to tell the truth. Dr Gulati has retired now, and he also cannot do any damage to you. My staff and I will defend you and protect you. Truth shall always triumph," said Naik.

"Sir, I am not sure what I am telling you is useful to you or not. That day I remember very well, Sir. He was not his usual self. He made a handwritten report as he normally does, and I typed it and gave a print to him for the final check, as he asked. But instead of asking me retype it and mail it, he asked me to wait for the next day and took the copy to his home, which I felt was unusual. He never takes such reports to his home." said Leela

"What happened the next day?" asked Rupashree. She knew very well what had happened. But Rupashree had to act dumb.

"The next day, he corrected the observation and the conclusion and asked me to re-type and requested me to send the corrected report to the authorities as per the norm."

"Do you by any chance have the copy of the original report?" asked Naik

"Yes. I have the copy in my file as I saved it as "Original draft with the corresponding FIR number," said Leela.

Rupashree's face reddened. She immediately got up and left the room on the pretext of visiting the toilet.

"Is this the death certificate you have given to the victim's husband duly signed by Doctor Gulati?" showing her the copy of the certificate his office had obtained from the crematorium.

"Yes," she said after examining the certificate.

"Thank you, Leela. I will send my constable with you. Please send me a copy of the Original draft with your signature and confirmation that it was later altered. My Head Constable Narsimha shall tell you what authentication would be required for you to sign. I hope you have no objection." said Naik.

"Sir, you have to take permission from the Superintendent for that. I am not authorised to give the reports to any person without his authorization except posting it to the Police Server as per the rules of the department," said Leela

Adarsh Naik had sent an official letter addressed to the Superintendent as requested by Leela and sent Narsimha to accompany her to the Hospital and obtain a printed version of the original draft, duly authenticated by Leela and the Superintendent. Adarsh Naik was now ready to confront Dr Gulati. He sent Reddy to bring Dr Gulati to the Station either by persuasion or intimidation as convenient. "Gulati should be present in the PS soon," ordered Naik.

***

Dr Durgaprasad Gulati retired a week after the autopsy of Vaidehi. He spent ten days on a post-retirement holiday at Mahabaleshwar near Mumbai with his wife. He needed some serious time in the hills after such hard work of over thirty years of dealing with cadavers. The couple indulged themselves by hiring a private car with a driver and went around the hills. He could spend money like water, as the Inspector promised him a bounty for the alterations he made in the Report. He hoped to collect the money as soon as he returned after the holiday. Little did he know Venu would be transferred; his calls would not be returned; after many such attempts later, Venu would even have the audacity of changing his phone number: *the number you dialled does not exist.*

After he arrived from his holiday, he was surprised to receive a call from the SHO, PS SR Nagar, to present himself at the Station. The SHO introduced himself and said he wanted his help understanding the recently posted PM report. "My Inspector Reddy would bring you to the station at a convenient time."

As per the instructions of the SHO, Reddy ensured that only after Leela left the SHO's room would the Doctor be made to arrive at the Station. For records, Reddy requested Dr Gulati to state his particulars, identity details, academic qualifications and experience details. He made him wait to meet the SHO, as per the instructions. The SHO wanted to see the "Original Draft" before talking to Dr Gulati.

After three-quarters of an hour, Dr Gulati entered the SHO's room, where he found one more person sitting opposite the SHO, who introduced himself as Inspector Reddy. Gulati glanced around and relaxed in the chair offered next to Rupashree. He noted the nameplate on the table: Adarsh Naik. A constable served him tea in a yellow-stained ceramic cup. The office was not big but was neat with a framed photocopy of the Preamble of the Constitution. There were no other photos of leaders or politicians that he would typically find in police stations. One phone was off the hook and a mobile telephone guarding some papers from flying off by the fan's breeze that was swirling in a motion reminding him of the fans one finds in Railway retiring rooms.

After reading the Original Draft arrived from the Hospital sent by Leela, SHO decided to confront the Doctor.

"Dr Gulati, let me inform you, you are not here on any warrant by the court. You are at liberty not to answer and walk away free from my PS. In the latter case, I have to go to court and obtain a warrant for interrogation. But if you cooperate now, much inconvenience to both of us will be avoided," calmly explained Naik.

"I have never done any wrong in my career. Court warrants are not new to me. I had deposed and defended many of my autopsy and post mortem reports under intense scrutiny and cross-examination. However, I would have liked your Inspector to be more polite with me when he came to me. He acted as though I was a criminal," protested Dr Gulati.

"It was never our intention. My Inspector is acting under my instructions. If he had exceeded his brief, I am sorry. I will handle the same separately," said Naik assuring.

"We need some explanation on the PM report of one Ms. Vaidehi you had signed recently before you retired."

As far as he was concerned, there was no way he could be asked to confess to the alteration of observation and the autopsy report's conclusion. SHO might not be in the know unless Venu compromised. Did he? He had no way of knowing it. But of course, he would stick to his guns. I wrote what I observed. Period.

"I have discussed with your assistant Leela Madanna who had given me the first Report you made of the autopsy of Ms. Vaidehi on the 4th of July. This Report has now been authenticated by the Superintendent of the Hospital as that stored in the secure folder of your other reports marked "Original Draft – FIR 236/2016. We learnt from Leela this Report was modified the next day, and she was asked to post the altered Report to all the concerned authorities. The altered Report was dated the 5th of July. Could you please enlighten us why you changed this first Report after the body was handed over to the victim's relatives?"

Adarsh Naik noticed that Dr Gulati was unstable in his chair, and his hand movements showed some anxiety: A nervous reaction. A lifetime's experience dealing with people of all shades had augmented Naik's natural ability to assess his visitor's handicaps and fears. He knew Dr Gulati was uncomfortable facing him at once, though his tone and words were masking his weakness.

Gulati moved by shifting his weight from one side to the other as if he had a backache. He leaned forward and announced that he had a nature's call to answer and left the room. He unzipped his pant at the cubicle and began to urinate. A slight burning sensation occurred. He gasped and held the wall tight with his palms. He did not know what was happening to him. He was surprised at the turn of the events. He never anticipated Leela would do what she had done. Of course, she hinted once, but he took it lightly and brushed away her objection. The SHO was not harsh. But he was afraid the cop could implement the threat of a court warrant.

He came back and sat on the chair he had occupied originally. He found one other person in the room, who was not present when he went to the toilet. Doctor Jambu Lingeshwar, Adarsh Naik's neighbour and a renowned general physician of the locality where Adarsh Naik lived, was next with an extra chair ordered. Naik had requested the Doctor for help in deciphering the autopsy reports. He requested Jambu Lingeshwar be a mute witness while Dr Gulati was questioned. Later he would seek his advice on the matter.

"I am at liberty to change my conclusions based on further research on the subject as is the practice with every doctor." Gulati was defiant.

"Surely. But let me read the original conclusion you had written. Then you can explain what more observations and research have you done to reverse the original decision, especially after the body was already handed over to the relatives for funeral arrangements on the 4th itself. You changed the observation and the conclusion on the 5th. Rupashree, please read out the Report the Superintendent sent in."

Rupashree got a printout of the mail sent in by Leela and read the relevant portions of the Report loudly.

"The patient had no evidence of trauma, surgery, cancer, or past ailment records (see Dr Partha's Report); therefore, these are unlikely. In summary, this patient died of a pulmonary embolism, the underlying cause of which is currently undetermined. The suggestion given by Dr Partha in his prelim examination at the scene of the event that death could have occurred because of asphyxiation caused by smothering of the pillow does not stand reason as there are no fibres recovered from the victim's mouth, nose or face. Some traces of fibres found on the nose could be because of sleep posture on the pillow, which could have misled Dr Partha. The distribution of hand and finger marks is well-distinguishably different on pillowcases around pillows used for smothering compared to pillowcases only touched when changing the pillowcase. Dr Partha was tricked into thinking that the hand and finger marks were caused by pressure exerted on the pillow by an external force. But the victim used the pillow to rest her leg, on her Doctor's suggestion for free blood flow, as she often complained of leg pain. Inspector Venugopal recorded this during the discussions with the patient's husband. The markings on the pillow could be because of this. Also, there was no indication of any of the following characteristics which are to be found in the case of such asphyxia death or death by strangulation or smothering:" (a) Right lung is full of blood, and left is empty. (b) Lividity of faces, fingers and nails. (c) Congestion of the brain. These characteristics were not observed. Reference is made to Modi's Medical Jurisprudence and Toxicology, 23rd Edition (for short, "Modi") to support the absence of symptoms related to death caused by asphyxia.

I surmise that the death is caused by pulmonary embolism. "

Rupashree concluded by closing the file.

Before Gulati could react, Naik said," I also have the copy of the death certificate you have given to the deceased husband, which had a different COD. Is this the original Report you made on the 4th of July?" asked Naik, presenting him the copy of the Original Report given by the Hospital authorities and the death certificate obtained from the crematorium.

What an error I made? I should have checked the contents of the Death Certificate before signing it. I usually don't because Leela is trained to issue the certificate based on the PM report copy. I sign as I have complete faith in her ability. She copied the original conclusion of the 4th of July in the death certificate given to the relatives of the deceased. At the same time, I had to alter the Report on the 5th of July, succumbing to the persuasion of Inspector Venugopal. I had not accounted for the damage this death certificate would cause me. This death certificate has no relevance to Police but only to the Crematorium authorities and, later, the municipal authorities, based on which they will issue an official death certificate to the relatives of the dead. This SHO is more intelligent than all of us. I better keep quiet till I am forced to talk.

Dr Gulati did not reply. Stared at the ceiling.

"You have changed the observation in the final report to: 'Fibres recovered from the victim's mouth, nose and face indicated that the victim could have been smothered by an object such as a pillow'. You altered the observation to suit your new conclusion, which was different from the one you wrote on the 4th, as shown in the Original Draft saved by Leela Madanna, your computer assistant. We have recorded her statement also. But how could you change the observation on the 5th morning, as you had already handed over the body for the last rites on the 4th afternoon itself?? That is the fabrication of evidence. It is an offence u/s 194 of IPC. Also, the final observation and the conclusion posted on the server are much different from the COD given to the woman's relatives."

Dr Gulati did not reply. He looked straight at the SHO without batting an eye-lid, upon which the SHO said," If you do not wish to answer, you may have to answer the same during the cross. If proved correct, you could be prosecuted."

"What do you want me to say?" asked Gulati with a worried look.

Gulati was ashamed of this nonsense. The shame flared up in his soul, burning and exacerbating everything. He shuddered, imagining his incarceration.

What would his daughters think of him, what would they say about him, how would he enter his home, what whispering amongst the neighbours would pursue him for the whole of his balance life? What a strange thing to find out one day that you had built your retirement life gift on impulsive greed.

"If you want me to help you, you have to confess you have changed the observation and the conclusion for some pecuniary gain promised by someone you have to name."

"You have left me no option!" said Gulati," but how do you plan to absolve me of the crime if I confess. As you have said, my confession would surely be my path to jail."

"I have a good equation with the Commissioner. With his help, we can maintain that the wrong Report has been posted on the Main Server by a clerical error. We can replace the same with the Original Report based on which your assistant had given the COD as pulmonary embolism in the death certificate. Also, incidentally, your Original Report was more elaborate and had valid scientific explanations, whereas the altered Report is vague. That should clinch our issue. You have cleverly put the onus on the forensic evidence of the pillow to confirm that the death was not natural but homicidal. The forensic report of the object does confirm your original observation too."

"Once he approves, we can proceed further. Fortunately, the Magistrate had not accepted the PM report as evidence, and hence the same is not in court records, though it is in police records. We can manage to reverse the situation. Please leave it to me. I need only a signed statement from you and your assistant that a false report was sent by error. That is all is needed."

Adarsh Naik did not insist on Dr Gulati's confession of monetary gain for changing the Report, nor did he insist on naming the person on whose advice or force or persuasion Dr Gulati indulged in the fabrication.

***

The constable staffing the front table went into the room, saluted the SHO and informed him someone from Saudi had come wanting to see him urgently. Abdul insisted on seeing the SHO immediately. He explained to the constable briefly why he wanted to see him. Shiva also added about their visit to the nearby apartment and the information they received from there.

Abdul was called in and seated. Shiva waited outside.

Naik asked him to sit and leaned forward with hands crossed on the table. His pose asked the question, what can I do for you? Abdul noted the flat hostile stare of a government official he was so used to all these days was missing. He was the opposite of the average cop you encounter on roads and police stations, who rarely appear and act as people-friendly, as though it was blasphemy. And he was trim! No pot belly.

He looked dapper and carefully groomed with a large head over his shoulders. His light brown eyes made him look polite, confirmed in his later interactions. When Abdul introduced himself as Shabnam's husband. Reddy and Rupashree, who were present in the room, exchanged glances. Naik asked Reddy to explain the situation to Abdul while he got himself engrossed in the diary reports of the last few days. Reddy and Rupashree, in turn, described the events that led to the arrest of Shabnam.

"We have tried to elicit information from her whether the deceased lady ill-treated her. She replied in the negative. The neighbours were also questioned. The house search had also not yielded any evidence. So the Magistrate refused to allow us to keep her in police custody any further. The Judge requested the SHO to send her to ISKCON, where she would help the kitchen staff and also be safe and available for further trials, if so required. The Magistrate could not release her until the final charge sheet was filed or FIR was withdrawn. We are in the process of withdrawing the FIR, as we found some foul play in the entire episode, which we are investigating further. But your wife would be released, but it would take a week to ten days more as some more formalities are to be attended to, as the court has to release her. We have no jurisdiction in the matter."

At that moment, Adarsh Naik intervened, "Mr Abdul, I am sorry your wife had to go through this turmoil for no fault of hers. But let me assure you I shall try to quickly resolve the issue by talking to my superiors and arranging for her release."

"Can I see her now?" asked Abdul.

"Surely, I will send my Head Constable with you to ISKCON and will also inform the head at ISKCON to permit you to see her."

ABDUL

HC Narsimha had briefed the personal assistant of Swami Gunasekhara Das on the purpose of their visit, and he also confirmed that the SHO had already had a talk with Swamiji regarding the visit of Abdul to meet his wife. PA took Abdul to meet up with Shabnam.

The room into which the disciple of Swami Gunasekhara Das took Abdul and Narsimha appeared to be an ante-room of the kitchen of the temple. It had two long tables flush to the room's sidewalls. A variety of vegetables in various stages of preparation were placed: eggplants, cabbage, green chillies, okra, and different types of gourds. The upper portion of the tables was adorned with laminated cabinets labelled with assorted condiments. There were no chairs but only stools on which a few ladies and a man were furiously slicing, chopping and marinating the vegetables. Abdul noticed Shabnam's profile at the rearmost seat and quickly moved towards her. He lightly tapped on her shoulder.

Shabnam stood up and stared at the person, shocked. She was immobile for a moment, slowly coming to terms with what was in front of her. She couldn't look at Abdul. She couldn't meet his eyes. Her head bent down with eyes riveted on her bare feet. When she lifted her head on the call of Abdul, she was shedding copious tears. Through the blur of her tears, she saw his face, that face she loved, that face she trusted. On a cue from the disciple, Narsimha and the other staff vacated the room to allow the couple some privacy.

Eventually, the heaving sobs subsided, and she looked up to him, a trembling smile on her face. He wiped her tears from her face with his sleeve, stared at her and said," I never want to see you unhappy again as long as I live." These simple words, uttered with firmness and conviction, finally penetrated her aching brain, her battered heart. She began to sob again, her whole body heaved as the choked and pent-up emotions were released. Shabnam stood up abruptly and offered him a glass of water, which he refused and asked her to sit quietly. They sat there on their respective stools, watching each other without speaking. Then he broke the silence and explained what had happened in the intervening period of her communication muteness, his forced leave, his search for her, his meeting with the very cooperative, gentlemanly Police Officer. She, from her side, narrated the entire episode of her shifting from Mumbai to getting arrested with as much detail as she could muster with a choked voice, interspersed with tears and emotion.

Patting her, he said," Let me talk to the Chief to take his permission to take you along with me. I will be back shortly." Abdul left the room and met the disciple, patiently waiting for Abdul to come out. At Abdul's request, he took him to meet his guru – Swami Gunasekhara Das.

***

Abdul found the Guru in a meeting with more disciples around him. Abdul's accompanying person asked him to wait in the adjoining room. The place was reverberating with chants of Hare Rama and Hare Krishna from the temple downstairs. After about an hour, he could meet the Swami Gunasekhara Das. He found Swamiji to be a man who radiated warmth and humility. He greeted Abdul with a smile and with folded hands. The room he was led to, reminded him of a large corporate office he had once been to in Gujarat when he had to pick up an Executive client to take him to the Registration Office. A centre table behind which Swami placed himself in a swivel chair was full of books on one side and a notebook with a pencil as a marker. Swamiji offered Abdul almond milk as a welcome drink, which Abdul politely refused.

"I hope your wife had no complaint about our hospitality," inquired the Swamiji.

"Of course not, sir. I am thankful to your Organization and the judicial system that cared for my innocent wife, who was not exposed to the cruel world of treachery and deceit."

"I am told you have come from Saudi Arabia to see your wife. I pray that Lord Krishna shall clear your path of thorns."

"Can I take my wife along with me, sir?" asked Abdul, ignoring the information given by Adarsh Naik on the suspect release formalities.

"She is here under the Orders of the Magistrate, and I have no authority to move her from here," said the Swamiji. "Firstly, the court has to relieve her of the accusation she is under and formally release her with a Court Order. Until then, I cannot help you, young man."

"Sir, how do I go about getting the Court Order?" asked Abdul

"I am no authority on the subject. You have to approach the Police and the Judiciary for that. Sorry."

"Oh! I am back to square one?" said Abdul

"You know, everything comes at its appointed time. Lord Krishna always helps the innocent," said the Swamiji

"Thank you, sir. I will contact the Police and take their advice. Can I again see my wife before I leave because I told her I shall pick her up now?"

Swami Gunasekhara das directed the disciple who accompanied Abdul to take him back to Abdul's wife. Abdul met Shabnam again and told her he would come again the next day with the necessary paperwork, without which she could not be released.

***

With Narsimha in tow, Abdul had approached Adarsh Naik at the Police Station about the procedure for the release of Shabnam.

"Sir, My employment contract in Saudi needs another six months before I am permitted to leave Saudi for good. I have come here with a bond and a written guarantee that I would be back in fifteen days. Otherwise, I may be put to loss and also possible prosecution. I cannot stay any longer. You have to help me in this," pleaded Abdul.

"You know, there are procedures to follow once the case is in a court of law. We have to present the evidence to withdraw the FIR and release the suspect. We have no authority to act on our own. Also, she is not in our custody. The Magistrate had already bailed her. As she did not give her home address, we had to put her up in ISCKON to access her for further interrogation if need be. Technically speaking as she is on bail, so she can go home in Vadodara. But, when and if the court needs her, we have to summon her. It is a huge pain for us, as you know we would have jurisdictional issues. Hence it is better for both of us she continue to stay in ISKCON, Hyderabad, which is very safe place as you may have noticed. We shall do our best to present the facts of the case to the Magistrate and seek permission to withdraw the FIR. All this will take time as the courts have many pending cases", said Adarsh Naik.

Upon the assurance given by Adarsh Naik and his staff that they shall personally supervise to close the case and help release Shabnam from all encumbrances, Abdul bid a tearful goodbye to Shabnam after explaining to her the future process. He left for Riyadh to complete his contractual obligation.

Upon the application of the withdrawal of the FIR, the Magistrate noted: "I have perused the records including the crime file brought by the IO Inspector Reddy in the court. The IO could gather no incriminating evidence against the accused person during the investigation of the case. The evidence submitted by the Police and the Hospital records show that the victim died of natural causes. Therefore, the present report filed by the IO regarding the closure of the case is accepted."

Epilogue

On the last day of Abdul's tenure as per the contract, while completing the formalities of handing over the responsibilities to his deputy, he received a message from Jenkins to meet ASAP. Abdul must have done something right to deserve this last-minute message from his Boss. The stars decided to shine right and shower bright on him, finally. He had already spent considerable time with the Department and Jenkins to wind up the assigned tasks during the last few days.

"Ah! There you are. Did you wind up your final rites here?" Edward Jenkins never lost his penchant for a quip or two, whatsoever might be the occasion.

"Yes, sir."

"I have a proposal from my headquarters for you. Our company has received another contract from Saudi Government in Al-Khobar, and we were hoping you could stay back and work for us as the Project Coordinator. We can surely discuss pay and other perks if you are interested. Surely, the position they are offering will include family accommodation as well."

A last-minute effort to entice Abdul to stay back.

"Thank you for your unceasing faith in my ability, sir. But you know that I cannot take up this offer," he reasoned. "Sir, Even ABB and Siemens had offered me similar positions, which I declined."

Abdul was aware that women in KSA have little to no freedom to step out from the thresholds of their homes unless accompanied by their male counterparts. The country remains incredibly prohibitive on what women should and shouldn't do. Being a Hindu, Shabnam is neither comfortable with naqaab, veil, or hijab nor any such restrictions on a woman's attire and movement.

Abdul couldn't even imagine causing distress to Shabnam anymore, either knowingly or unknowingly. She had already gone through enough for many lifetimes to come. He had to return to India and start finding his moorings again. Venkateshwar Rao had reaffirmed his commitment to accept Abdul back in the same position. He is pretty confident of being able to find another job if PPC's offer is not to his liking because of his skills gained over these two years in Saudi.

"Ok, then, young man. As you wish. But if you change your mind, you know whom to contact. I will have to start looking for another Abdul here", said Jenkins. They bid their farewells and parted for good.

***

After ensuring the quashing of the FIR, Adarsh Naik arranged for his constable to escort Shabnam back to her house in Vadodara. He saw this as an atonement for the way his staff treated her.

Shabnam believed in trust. Trust in her Love. Trust in her GOD. She firmly believed that love would always triumph in the long run, which it did. Her husband and her GOD stood testimony to her faith which she bequeathed to her children. Life with Abdul was like a soothing balm that comforted Shabnam to forget all the terrible nightmares and horrors of her scary past. Shabnam eased into her domestic life, employing the tips and tricks of managing a kitchen she learnt from ISKCON in her daily chores for which was forever indebted to them.

Her mom told her repeatedly that ultimately GOOD will triumph because Ganesha takes care of his devotees.

Abdul returned to India, rejoined his last employer and lived happily with Shabnam at their Alkapuri house. They had twin daughters, Nazneen and Namrata, who were taught to appreciate both religions' tenets and allowed them to pursue their spiritual path in whichever faith they chose. Abdul's brother, Asif, took the responsibility of running the ancestral house and family at Navrang Park Society while winning accolades in the multinational company where he worked as an engineer. He married selecting his bride from amongst Nazma's extended family, making his mother happy.

***

The cause of the death of his wife remained a mystery to Raj Krishna. He was consumed with presumed guilt that he might have somehow contributed, however unintentionally, to her death. His dream of strangulation of his wife continued to haunt him. It troubled him to such an extent that he neither followed up on the case nor showed any concern for Shabnam. He felt awful about letting the inspector frame Shabnam because the Police were cornering him to extract money. He was trapped, which was the reason he did not check on the fate of Shabnam, deserting her to her future.

. Raj was unaware of a kind soul helping Shabnam from being unjustly convicted. He fled to his daughter's house in Singapore, away from the idiosyncrasies of the Police governance. After spending as much time as his visa allowed, Raj returned to India. Even after returning to India, he did not have enough courage to go anywhere near the police station to check on Shabnam's whereabouts. He sold his Hyderabad apartment and lived as an ascetic in a retirement community in Pune. He visited his daughters and grandchildren during their vacations, his health and resources permitting.

Raj Krishna could not acknowledge that love exists as described in novels, stories, and movies. For him, it was a myth perpetuated by writers to sell their books. His life saga was filled with scepticism. He believed all human beings are self-centred. His wife's love also seemed like a ruse to live up to her womanhood and prove her motherhood. If they both got some pleasure out of it, it was just an unintended consequence. Ritu's apparent love was for her carnal desires that a sterilised and sexagenarian man could safely fulfil without the unintended side effects.

***

Venugopal could not compensate Dr Gulati for his 'help'. He could not use the engineered Autopsy report to his advantage because of his unexpected sudden transfer. He wanted to negotiate with Raj Krishna for eventual extortion. Ramachandra Reddy took advantage of it, though.

Reddy could not enjoy the kickback payment received from the gullible Raj. On a fine day in November 2016, the government of India announced demonetisation, invalidating five hundred and thousand rupee notes as legal tender. After apportioning the spoils amongst his co-conspirators from the inducement received from Raj, Reddy could hardly convert fifty thousand rupees. The rest of the notes were consigned to flames, perforce.

Venugopal managed his transfer back to a PS of his choice in Hyderabad with his political contacts.

Ramachandra Reddy and Rupashree's complicity in the case got subsumed within the system. Though Adarsh Naik doubted their roles in the matter, he had no evidence to nail them. Dr Gulati was not prosecuted as was promised by Adarsh Naik and the Commissioner, Rahul Kanwal.

Ritu Kohli married, divorced within a year, and remained a childless spinster. She achieved success as an accomplished pharmacist with many publications to her name.

REFERENCES[84]

https://bit.ly/3Ei2W3u → Islamic Quotations.

https://bit.ly/3tCCYCS → hadith writings

https://bit.ly/2VDe7Ca → On Sufism

https://bit.ly/3nwfKx9 → Indian Kanoon.org

https://bit.ly/3Ae5EEw → case law from Indiankanoon.org

https://bit.ly/396CRGc → Case law from Indiankanoon.org

https://bit.ly/3AcCPIC → case law from Indiankanoon.org

https://bit.ly/3lrAdkd → case law from Indiankanoon.org

https://bit.ly/3zdAwDQ → District Courts of India

https://bit.ly/3CdCbuW → Hookah Bars

https://bit.ly/3tGrGxx → Islamic Religious Police

https://bit.ly/2XaCmbn → Death Scene Investigation

https://bit.ly/3lkgT8s → Asphyxia

https://bit.ly/3k9tJXK → smothering by pillow

https://bit.ly/3nx6Hfy → Employment Contract in Saudi Arabia

https://bit.ly/3htXKzA → Podcast of Gazala Wahab on Indian Muslims

https://bit.ly/3nBAyU9 → Foreign Workers in Saudi Arabia

https://bit.ly/3nvU44n → Challenges Builders in India face

---

84   Copy the link in your browser and press enter to know more

https://bit.ly/3Cc0nOo → Corruption in Registration Departments

https://bit.ly/2XjtiAT → Contracting in Pharma Industry

https://bit.ly/3nKqokb → Pharma Company problems as reported by India Times

https://bit.ly/3nvUJ5R → An Article by the Whistle Blower in Ranbaxy case

https://bit.ly/2VEvEtM → Divorce by a Muslim woman – case law

https://bit.ly/3z9oFXz → Pharma Industry in India

https://bit.ly/3AbyWUs → Bloomberg Investigation on Indian Drug Quality issues

https://bit.ly/3lkkfby → About Drug Discovery and development

https://bit.ly/39eFoxT → An overview of Post Mortem Examination

https://bit.ly/3C7QEbU → On Communalism – an article in The Wire